JASON CRANE BOOK ONE

SLEEPY HOLLOW: RISE HEADLESS AND RIDE

RICHARD GLEAVES

Published in the United States by
Turtlebug Publishing

The places in this book are real, though.
Go find them, explore them, and celebrate them.

Edited by David Gatewood

Cover Art:
"The Headless Horseman Pursuing Ichabod Crane" (1858) by John Quidor

Design by Richard Gleaves

ISBN-10: 0615883753
ISBN-13: 978-0615883755

DEDICATION

To all grandmothers and grandsons
&
To my own Leah Kendrick, who took me grave-hunting

CONTENTS

ACKNOWLEDGMENTS

Thanks to Washington Irving, who made this book possible.

Thanks to Danny Smolenski, who made this book better.

Thanks to David Gatewood, who made this book legible.

And Special Thanks to my Mom, Pat Gleaves, who made this book's author.
In every sense.

Thanks to Jim Logan of Sleepy Hollow Cemetery, for teaching me about exhumation rules and old tombs, and for letting me wander his cemetery at night, so the ghosts and I could get better acquainted.

Thanks to Lance Hallowell, creative director of Historic Hudson Valley's *Horseman's Hollow* event, for his time and inspiration.

Thanks to Sal Durante, Dianne Durante, Will George, Jason Lockwood, and all my other first readers. You kept me cocky and you kept me spooked.

1 GRAVE-RUBBINGS

Jason Crane knelt before the grave of his great-great-great-grandmother with onionskin paper in his left hand and a stick of charcoal in his right. The paper rippled in the wind, threatening to twist and tear over the cemetery wall like an escaping ghost. He frowned and pressed it flush against the stone, pinning it at top with his palm and at bottom with his knee.

He was a thin boy, bony as a grasshopper kneeling in a field. He wore his auburn hair short on the sides and tangled on top. He pushed it out of his eyes now, smudging his forehead, and went to work. He fanned the charcoal back and forth, bearing down to capture the design above the name: scales of justice, proclaiming the Judgment of the Dead. His grandmother had taught him to read such symbols. The sunflower of adoration, the cedar of consecration, the crown, the cypress, a frog for worldly pleasures, and a butterfly for the freeing of the spirit—he'd seen them all in the past two weeks. The headstone to his left bore an image of the raven, guardian of the cemetery.

A horn blew. Eliza hunted him. A startled squirrel blurred through fallen leaves and was gone.

Letters shone through, finally, white against black:

ANNABEL CRANE
BELOVED WIFE OF ABSALOM
MOTHER OF JESSE
B. AUG 15, 1822
CALLED TO GOD AUG 1, 1856

Jason stood, rolled the paper, and tucked it into a cardboard tube, careful not to smear the imprint. His grandmother preferred to supervise his rubbings, but the path had proven too steep for her knees. She waited below, impatient to judge his work. He lingered, though, leaning against the battered walnut tree, brushing at his blue jeans, enjoying a brief escape from his grandmother's lecturing and the barking of her small black poodle (named Charley, though it was female).

The tiny cemetery perched on a hill overlooking Bridgeport, Connecticut. Once, it must have been a beautiful place to be buried, but Bridgeport had sprawled and suburbs had engulfed the area. Bulldozers had burgled away half the hill so that the former crest was now a cliff, leaving the cemetery situated precariously near an eight-foot plunge down to Chopsey Hill Drive. That's where the RV sat—on the shoulder of the road below, two tires off the asphalt, the cab tilting toward the drainage ditch.

Above Jason's head, the walnut tree raised thin arms in sad, leafless benediction. Seventeen graves huddled in rows, herded by a faithful border fence. The weeds grew lushly, overtaking the headstones. No groundskeeper had visited this place in a long time, but a stained mattress lay in the mud and someone had gang-tagged the marble of the single vault—someone named Naldi, apparently, who smoked Marlboro Lights and mistook the broken birdbath for an ashtray.

Jason wanted to stay, to pull the weeds from Annabel's grave, but the shadows were lengthening. Eliza didn't like to drive at night and he didn't want to be among the graves after sunset, oh no... even if they *were* family.

His imagination slipped its leash.

He saw himself clearing the earth, shoveling, finding the coffin, opening it, looking down at the browning skeleton and empty eye sockets of a woman he had never known but who had made him possible. And what? Thanking her? Weeping for her? No. Just... meeting her.

Hello, Annabel. Guess who I am.

Eliza honked again.

Jason pushed his hair out of his eyes and scrambled down the hill.

Reaching the bottom, he realized that very little shoveling would be required to reach that coffin. Thanks to the bulldozers, the dead were no longer six feet under but only two feet inward. If he were to stand on the road and dig into the soft embankment, his ancestors would be right there, within arm's reach, waiting.

"That's awful," he said as he climbed into the driver's seat. "A good rain and half the coffins could be exposed." He shuddered, imagining Annabel's coffin peeking through mud—first a corner, then a brass handle, and then the whole thing tumbling wetly onto the road below.

"Won't ever happen," said his grandmother. "A coffin from the eighteen-fifties is wood. It's all rotted through now. She'll stay put. The dead always stay put." She flattened the rubbing against the dashboard, admiring it. "Good one. Try to press a little harder next time."

Eliza Merrick was not a sentimental genealogist. She played at genealogy the way other old ladies play at solitaire or Sudoku: for the sake of solving the puzzle. To Eliza, Annabel Crane, wife of Absalom and mother of Jesse, wasn't a real person but merely an item in a scavenger hunt—to be checked off the list before driving on to the next.

But to Jason, the graves were scattered pieces of his family, impossible ever to gather again. And that seemed unspeakably sad.

He hated genealogy.

They drove on. The cemetery on the hill dwindled in his side mirror.

She'll stay put. The dead always stay put.

The thought did not make him feel better. He suspected it might not be true.

A dozen yards farther on, they pulled into a parking lot and ordered sandwiches from a strip mall Subway.

#

This is how they spent the last weeks of September—Jason, Eliza, and Charley of the unreliable bladder—touring the country in an ancient RV that had belonged to Eliza's fourth husband, searching out the graves of Jason's ancestors.

The trip began unexpectedly. In early August, Eliza had left Jason with credit cards and keys, explaining that she was flying to Southampton, New York, for an event honoring her ancestors' role in the founding of that town. She would be back in a few days. No worries. After all, Jason could take care of himself. But Jason worried whether *she* could take care of *her*self. Eliza was eighty, with swollen arthritic hands and cataracts that stole colors and dimmed sunlight. She'd relied on him more and more that year—for steak-cutting, for dressing, for necklace clasps and pickle jars.

"I have friends meeting me. New friends. It's fine. You've got school coming up. Take the MasterCard. Buy what you need. Within reason. And don't wreck the Mercedes."

On August tenth she gave him a kiss, wailed laments over her separation from the poodle, and climbed into a taxi.

Her leaving wasn't that unusual. Eliza's many divorces had left her with a comfortable standard of living, even a fortune, and she loved her research trips. Sometimes on a Monday she'd leave Jason the car keys, a few hundred dollars, a full refrigerator and pantry, and a hamper of clean clothes, then she'd disappear until the following Saturday, trusting him in the meantime to attend school, do his homework, and pick up after himself. It was a good system. Jason was responsible and self-sufficient. Child Protective Services hadn't whisked him away. There'd never been a single problem, except once when she'd come home to find the porch burned off the front of the house.

She'd never disappeared for this long, though. She extended the Southampton trip indefinitely. She'd call every other day, making sure Jason didn't become a delinquent and that he was pampering Charley appropriately, but she evaded his questions of when, if ever, she was coming home.

A few days stretched into a month.

Jason left the Mercedes in the garage. Mostly. He took it out for his driver's test only because he had no other.

Oh, doesn't a man sweat when parallel parking a sixty-thousand-dollar car.

Fall semester commenced and Jason had just completed his first week of classes when Eliza finally returned. Her face sparkled with excitement. She announced that they would be leaving together the following Friday, and he was not to ask why. She had a surprise. She signed him out of school only ten days after the term began. If the state of Maine had a problem, they could just answer to her and see who would come out the worse for it.

Jason supposed she needed him to chauffeur one of her genealogy trips. She couldn't hold a steering wheel anymore. Not easily. But he didn't mind missing a few weeks of school. He always read far ahead of his classes.

And he had few friends.

For two weeks they trundled down the coast of New England, maps and genealogies in hand. They slept in the camper, which had a small kitchen and leatherette couch, a toilet inside the shower stall, and two small sleeping alcoves one above the other. Eliza pointed, and Jason drove.

Driving the big RV unnerved him. His license didn't even have his picture on it yet, and before this trip he'd never driven more than twenty miles at a stretch. This was no Mercedes, either. The RV was a temperamental, gear-grinding machine that hadn't been serviced since the Carter administration. Eliza would snap at him not to ride the brake on the vertigo-inducing cliff roads of Maine, but he couldn't help himself. He felt the large camper looming behind him, like something big chasing him down the road. Charley barked and climbed across Jason's lap as he drove, licking his face, making him even antsier. He imagined careening through guardrails, crashing down onto rocks below, and drowning them all under a heap of metal, engulfed by salt water.

He pushed the hair out of his eyes and concentrated on the white and yellow lines, on keeping the RV "between the mustard and the mayonnaise," as his driving instructor put it. He was vaguely aware that a riot of fall colors streaked past his window: russet and burgundy and green edged with yellow, everything just barely turning towards exhaustion and rot and beauty, but he didn't dare turn his head.

They clopped over wooden bridges, down through the land of the Penobscot Indians, past markers of Colonial Heritage. Pumpkins pimpled a hill. The landmarks didn't have the good sense to agree with Eliza's memory, and her cataracts made the map a pastel blur. They lost the roads, found them again. She'd cry out and her stiff hand would flap in a gesture to turn. Charley would yip, and Jason would steer the camper down a snaking trail of graveled wheel ruts. They would park on the side of some road, the cab threatening to tumble into the weeds, and Jason would scramble to the passenger side and help Eliza to the ground. She would pause, sniffing the air, and then shamble across a field of pokeweed and nettles. Charley would leap in the cold air, happy to be out in the open.

Then Jason could stop and look at the countryside, at the ancient trees blazingly solemn, with leaves mottled like Indian corn. But Eliza would cut his sightseeing short. "Found the sucker!" she would cackle. They would push some rusted gate aside, clearing vines, and she would stride into the cemetery to pour bottled water over faded inscriptions, looking for the name **Crane**.

They found Jason's great-grandfather Jack Crane in a cemetery named Calvary outside Skowhegan, a brown hill surmounted by white obelisks. Jack had been buried alongside three brothers and one sister who'd all died in infancy, unnamed: Baby Boy Crane, Baby Girl Crane. Doubling back, they found Jack's wife Bethel Crane buried in a neatly manicured plot a hundred miles away, near Windham. Her headstone sported a cone of green copper. They slipped in a few orange daisies from the gift shop.

As they drove through Massachusetts, the graves became harder to find, the headstones more weathered, and nature more encroaching.

They drove into Connecticut, stopping at the Bridgeport cemetery above Chopsey Hill Drive. Jason began to suspect that the final destination of their trip would be Valhalla cemetery in Westchester County, New York. There in Valhalla, he knew, alongside the graves of Rachmaninoff, Ayn Rand and Danny Kaye, stood a joint marker for the man and woman who occupied two rectangular boxes just above his own on the family tree:

Andrew Crane   Dianne Crane

His parents.

He was ashamed to admit that he'd never been to their graves. They'd died when he was seven and, considering what he went through, no one had wanted to risk a relapse.

When they started this trip, Eliza had promised a surprise, but her idea of a nice surprise and Jason's idea didn't always agree. Maybe she'd decided that the time had come for Jason to pay his respects? If so, he dreaded the painful duty ahead of him.

The RV passed into New York State on the first of October. They'd stopped at six cemeteries, taken fourteen rubbings, and had been locked in a library when they'd lingered past closing. Two weeks into the trip, they were feeling ripe and exhausted. Fast-food wrappers cluttered the cab. Splashed sodas made the dash sticky, and black poodle hair stuck to everything.

They found a scenic route down the Hudson. The road became straight and level, and the dog stayed curled in Eliza's lap, for once. Jason felt confident enough to admire the sights. The wide blue of the river met the wide blue of the sky; stripes of green hedge raced them down the Albany post road and fell behind; houses drifted past, a few already bedecked with the orange and black crepe that announced Halloween.

"Our exit's coming up," Eliza said. "You'll see Saint Mary's Episcopal on the left. Turn right after."

"But Highway 9A takes us to Valhalla," Jason said, reaching for the map. "I'm pretty sure we missed it."

"We're not going to Valhalla."

With a flap of her hand she pointed the way. Jason passed the church and turned onto Sleepy Hollow Road.

Between them, Charley whimpered.

#

Welcome to Historic
Sleepy Hollow
Settled in 1640.

Jason had looped around the town and had come up Broadway from the south. Behind the retaining wall next to the sign, a yard worker turned on his leaf blower, sending a tidal wave of yellow and red up and over the stones to splash off the windshield of the RV. They passed antique shops, a Shell station, and a Food King grocery.

"This is the same Broadway, you know," said Eliza. "It goes all the way down to Times Square. Used to be an Indian trail— Manhattan to Fort Orange. For the fur trapping business." She kissed the dog. "Don't worry, baby. Nobody's gonna skin you. And you know what the town's most famous for."

"Well, duh," Jason said. Every kid named "Crane," especially one as tall and skinny as Jason, had heard a lifetime of Ichabod jokes. He hoped never to hear another.

"Did you know it was a real place?"

"Of course," he said, though he hadn't.

"Don't be so smart," said Eliza. "Turn here."

The streets sloped towards the Hudson, the hillside trying to shake the village off its back. Jason slipped in behind a UPS truck and drove upwards. They turned onto Gory Brook Road. He stuck his head out the window, trying to pass. The UPS truck turned aside to the right. And he saw The House.

"Here, here, here," said Eliza.

She pointed at the driveway of 417 Gory Brook. Jason brought the RV to a smoke-belching halt.

The house stood on a knoll, above a steep yard that angled downwards toward the Hudson. An ancient sycamore on the front lawn leaned precariously. The roof was an irregular A-frame, with a long slope on the left and a short one on the right, like a rotated check mark. The upper floors were trimmed with bands of chocolate-brown wood in a rectangular pattern. They made the house look as if it were trapped behind the bars of a jail cell. A tidy triangular portico extended over the front door, which was rough-hewn, rounded on top, held together by two vertical metal bands, and dotted with nail heads, a gothic novel in braille. The grey-blue curtains at the ground-floor bay window gave the place a veiled-eye aspect, like his grandmother's cataracts.

The house seemed to be inspecting Jason with that eye. *What are you doing here, boy? I'm watching you...*

Eliza put a hand on his shoulder. He jumped.

"This is it," she said. She slapped the dashboard.

"This is what?"

"Our new home."

"But..." Jason turned to her, baffled.

Her face sparkled with delight.

"Surprise!"

2 GORY BROOK

"Let me out so Charley can tinkle."

The poodle turned circles in Eliza's lap.

Jason's head swam. He could feel the edge of anger beginning to slice through his confusion, but he didn't want to start an argument. Eliza could be stubborn. He walked around the cab and helped her out of the RV. Charley sniffed the grass and sneezed.

"So… you rented us a place?"

"I bought it! Here. Does this one have a triangle on it?" She held up a key.

"No. What do you mean you bought it? For like a vacation house?"

"Find the one with the triangle."

She turned her palm and dropped a tangle of keys in his. The tags read: Garage. Mailbox. Basement. The basement key was heavy, ancient.

"I don't see a triangle. And none of them say Front Door."

"Back Door?"

"No."

"Never mind," she said, "they're probably in the box then."

She hobbled onto the porch. On the doorknob hung a realtor's lockbox with a numbered dial. Jason tugged at it.

"What's the combination?" he said.

"Hell if I know. Charley, get out of the road. Grab her."

The dog always yipped at nothing, at shadows, specks of dust, some blade of grass against which she bore a grudge. This time she yipped at a Hispanic teenager jogging past. The kid made for the trail.

It began near the house, wound into the woods and disappeared. Jason noticed the letters O.C.A. on a wrought-iron gate.

He tried to corral the dog. She growled at him, padded up to Eliza and looked down at Jason from the porch. Jason stood in the middle of the yard, his hands spread helplessly, and the anger poked through.

"Where the hell are we?"

"You'll get used to it. You might even like it."

"So we live here now? For how long?"

"For good. There's a moving van coming tomorrow. We can stay in the camper tonight. They're bringing all our stuff down from Augusta."

"Were you going to tell me?"

"I *am* telling you." Her voice had an edge to it, an undertow, some quality that suggested if you stood in its way it would drag you along against your will. "You'll start school next week. You're smart. You'll catch up quick." She paused, maybe daring him to correct her adverb. He didn't. "I thought the boxing and moving could get done for us while we were sightseeing. Who wants to deal with that bullshit?" She cupped her hands around her eyes and peered through a side window. "It's a good house."

"I kind of liked our old one," he said. And he did. It was a tall New England manse of whitewashed boards and balustrades. He'd lived in it since he was seven.

"This will have to do."

The *have to* was heavy with authority.

"Okay, but for the record—" Jason said, pointing to the welcome mat, "I agree with Charley."

Eliza glanced down. "Bad dog," she said.

The poodle had dropped off a housewarming gift.

#

Jason dialed, and Eliza left a voicemail asking the realtor to either call back with the combination or bring the key the next morning. The RV stood too tall for the detached garage, so they parked it behind the house. Eliza climbed up in the back and settled in. Jason decided to try the keys.

The foundation of the house was an immense block of grey stone, not a knoll as he had first thought. This stone box kept the house level as the land sloped west from the road. On one block he saw lettering. This cornerstone read **1837**. From the rear, the back door of the house hung above the lawn. A flight of thirteen steps led up to it.

He thought of Eliza.

This is a dangerous stair.

He climbed up, but found the door securely locked. None of his keys fit. He tried to peer in through the small window but sunlight reflected off the glass.

He found the basement door, set in the exact middle of the foundation, tucked beneath the stairs. He ran his hand across it, brushing flakes of rusted iron. He took out the heavy old key and put it in the lock. It wouldn't turn. He wrapped the end of his sweatshirt around his hand, twisted again. This time the door popped outwards, and a plume of dusty air whipped around its corners. The hinges sang like an old woman's laughter.

The sun dipped low in the western sky, setting over New Jersey. Jason's shadow lurched down into the box of stone, stretching out from his feet and falling into a void. He took four steps down into the space, which was cavernous and appeared to extend not just to the front of the house, but beyond, all the way under the front yard and maybe to the road. The air smelled humid, mildewed. He saw rusted pipes and a few rings set into the wall, suggesting a stable, and a small round drain in the floor. He felt for a light switch, reaching into the dark. The stones were cold and moist. Something delicate and many-legged skittered across the back of his hand.

No way in hell, he thought.

He pivoted, bounded up, closed the door again, locked it, and returned to the RV—just a little too quickly, laughing at himself.

Eliza had boiled brown rice for herself and nuked Jason a hot dog. They ate, and afterwards he helped her undress, undoing the buttons of her sweater, removing her shoes, averting his eyes as she traded elastic-waist sweatpants for light shorts. At last she slipped her bones into a nightdress and, holding his forearm, folded herself down onto the thin mattress. He tucked her in. Charley waited by the bed, whining to be picked up.

"Stay here tonight?" Eliza said. "Don't go wandering."

"It's early. I'd like to see the town."

"Not yet. Not by yourself."

"It's eight o'clock." Jason sounded as whiny as the poodle. He'd grown tired of the camper and wanted to stretch his legs.

"Here," she said. She slipped a hand around her pillow and slid aside a small panel in the wall of her alcove. She drew out a book. The cover was of old leather, tanned a caramel color, like coffee ice cream.

"Know what this is?"

"No." He reached for it.

"Careful with it. It's almost two hundred years old."

She put the volume in his hand. The spine cracked and threads of the binding were visible. A handwritten label on the spine read "The Sketch-Book by W. Irving."

"What is it?"

"Open it up."

The cover felt slightly loose. Opening it, he found a sheaf of yellowed paper. The title page read:

THE

SKETCH-BOOK

Of

GEOFFREY CRAYON, Gent.

No. I.

"I have no wife nor children, good or bad, to provide for. A mere spectator of other men's fortunes and adventures, and how they play their parts; which me-thinks are diversely presented unto me, as from a common theater or scene." Burton.

NEW-YORK
Printed by C. S. Van Winkle
101 Greenwich Street.
. . . .
1819.

He turned the pages. They were thin, almost transparent, with small spots of fungus, as if exposed to attic humidity.

"Looks fascinating," he lied.

The book consisted of some twenty or thirty short stories. He saw *Rip Van Winkle* about twenty-five pages in.

"Flip towards the end."

He did, and a familiar name popped out of the text:

Crane.

"Recognize it?" she said.

He skipped back a few pages.

The Legend of Sleepy Hollow

Jason frowned, remembering an incident in fourth grade. Squealing children. *Look, it's Icky-bod, Ugly Old Icky-Bod Craaaane!*

"Thanks, but I know the story," he said. "I think I'll just log onto Facebook. Tell people where I am."

He extended it back to her, but she ignored the gesture and tugged at the blanket.

"Read it. It's yours. I bought it for you. That's the first edition—eighteen-twenty. The original pamphlets all bound together. I bought it from a museum. Take good care of it. It cost ten grand, for God's sake." She looked hurt. Jason felt guilty. She bought him a book that cost ten thousand dollars? He turned it in his hand. Could this be a gesture of apology for uprooting his life?

"Thank you," he said, and kissed her cheek. Charley growled. Jason was poaching. Eliza gathered the poodle up onto the bed. Jason climbed the small stepladder to the bunk above her. He turned off the camper lights but for one pin-spot of his own.

"I hope you like it," she whispered. "Read it close. Pay attention. By the way, before the museum had it, that copy was your great-great-grandfather Jesse's. It's his handwriting on the spine. And it was his father's before that."

Jason lay on the top bunk, propped on his elbows, and turned again to the front page. Inside the cover he read a faint inscription: *Absalom Crane. September 17th, 1834.* He knew the name. Absalom, married to the woman in the lonely Bridgeport grave: Annabel Crane, Mother of Jesse.

The one who would stay put.

"Goodnight, my darling," Eliza said, and Jason hazarded a kissing noise in return. He hadn't been sure if she was speaking to him or to the dog.

3 THE RED MOON

Across town, Franklin Octavius Darley decided to get high.

He'd come out of the Tarrytown Music Hall around eleven with his date, but Susan had made a lame excuse involving out-of-town company and left him on the sidewalk. He didn't believe her. He wondered if he had b.o. He sniffed his armpit as he walked down the sidewalk. No stench so far as he could tell. He cupped a palm over his mouth and checked his breath. No problem. What the hell happened? He didn't want to drive home to New York tonight. Besides, he'd booked a hotel room over on Saw Mill River Parkway. It was a fleabag, but it would have been nice enough for a dog like Miss Susan Birmingham.

Fleabag. Dog. Get it? Ha ha ha.

None of the bars he passed looked inviting. Too many kids.

So he decided to get high.

Around midnight, he realized his mistake. He sat in Patriots Park, cupping his left palm around a lighter as he sparked his second joint, when he noticed something glittering on his finger. His wedding ring. He'd left the damn thing on. No wonder Susan had turned so cold. She'd probably been staring at it the whole night.

Oh, well. Her own stupidity.

He hoped the girl wasn't mad enough to google him. What if she found out where he lived? She didn't seem like the *Fatal Attraction* type. Eh. Stop it. The pot was making him paranoid. He was fine. None of the others made a scene in all his years of marriage. He sat back on the stone bench and looked up at the sky. He rested under an enormous tulip tree, ancient, bearing some historic marker he didn't bother to read.

"You look like a man who needs a beer."

Franklin Octavius Darley stubbed the joint. But this was no policeman. He could make out the shape of a woman in a long leather coat, standing a few feet away by the pond. He blinked a few times, forcing himself to focus and be suave.

"Hey," he said.

"Hey," she said. He heard an invitation in it. This was promising. She sat next to him, put a gloved hand on his knee. More promising, practically an IOU. It was too dark to see her face, but passing headlights lit up her cleavage. She smelled good. She was blonde. He was glad he'd worn a suit tonight, and his red-striped power tie. They gave him confidence.

"You're up late," she said. "Me too. I've got a cooler in my car... if you're sharing the smoke?"

"Absolutely," he said, and sloughed his wedding ring into his pocket.

They fetched the cooler, climbed into his car and searched for a hidden spot.

"Turn in here," the girl said.

The sign read Philipsburg Manor. They parked in the most secluded corner of the parking lot, which overlooked a lake or pond. The pond reflected just enough light to show him where to put his hands. They made out for a while. She popped the cooler. They had several beers and talked about real estate, of all things. His bladder filled up.

He was relieving himself in the water when he heard the car door slam. He turned and saw that the girl had left the car.

"You're not going already?" he said.

She twisted the radio antennae off the hood of the car.

She poked his eye out with it.

#

Franklin Octavius Darley opened his one eye and saw a red moon.

Why is the moon red?

He opened his mouth and bubbles came out. He floated underwater. He thrashed. Something held him under.

The moon is red because the water is bloody.

His wrists ached. The moon became redder.

The moon is red because it rose. It rose. Get it? Ha ha ha.

He was still stoned.

The air left his lungs and he sank. The red moon dimmed. It slipped away from him. It split into shards, rippling. The end of his red-striped power tie floated upwards, reaching. Then the weeds took him and his back thudded onto the bottom of the millpond. Clouds of silt billowed all around.

God, am I wasted.

Wasted. Get it?

Get it?

Get...

Then the moon was gone.

Ha ha ha.

4 THE BRIDGE

Jason whipped his horse, damning the animal and wishing it would find some speed. Something loomed behind him. A swarm of shadows, a tidal wave, a murderer with a knife. Something large and oppressive was *in pursuit*, and Jason's blood coursed through his body, urging him to flee, flee, flee! The hairs on his neck had risen. His fingers clenched the reins.

They tore through a Disney forest of long-armed beseeching trees. They leapt over rotted logs. Hooves beat against a cobbled road and sparks flew from horseshoes.

If only I can make the bridge...

If only I can make the bridge...

But where was it? The road forked. Forked again.

The evil was on him.

Where was it?

Then, there! Beyond a clearing, he saw the old covered bridge. Something tore at him as he turned. A branch? A hand? He yanked the reins, gave a kick, and the road flew past.

Joy leapt in his heart as they reached the bridge.

But the thing behind him laughed.

The bridge was out.

The planks had rotted.

Jason and his horse fell through space, toward a rippling red moon...

...and that's what you get for reading *The Legend* before bed.

He rubbed his eyes and cursed Washington Irving.

Jason had forgotten the dream by the time Debbie Flight arrived with the keys. The realtor was a sunny blonde in her thirties. She kept apologizing for leaving them camped in the driveway, to the point that Jason wondered whether her commission check had cleared. He decided it hadn't. She opened the lockbox and produced four keys. Front door and back. Two copies. The front door key bore a triangle pattern.

The inside of 417 Gory Brook was far more modern than the façade suggested. Debbie drew aside the grey-blue curtains so the bay window could see again. The living room was generous and inviting, the hardwood floors bright in the morning sun. At the rear of the house was the kitchen, and adjacent to that was a small guest bedroom. Eliza announced that this room would be hers. She did not want to take the stairs every night. This meant the master bedroom was Jason's if he wanted it.

Jason made his way up steep, narrow steps and found his room. It faced west, and the view was spectacular. To his right, the forest stretched off into the distance, a sea of orange. Below, the rooftops of Sleepy Hollow spread at Jason's feet. To his left, the Tappan Zee Bridge leapt the blue party-dress ribbon of the Hudson River.

"What do you think?"

Debbie Flight leaned on the doorframe.

"It's amazing."

"It's better at sunset. If you dangle out on a clear night you can see New York City. And look down there?"

She pointed at a building by the near edge of the Hudson, a whitewashed box on the edge of a round pond. He could see a mill wheel and a narrow bridge.

"What is it?" he said.

"Philipsburg Manor."

She saw no recognition in his face.

"It's a very historical building," she said. "It's three hundred years old." Her smile teetered somewhere between civic pride and condescension.

"Sounds cool."

"It is cool. They have tours in period costume and they show you how the Dutch settlers lived…" Jason's face must have betrayed him. "…and the Haunted House! They do the best Haunted House: 'Horseman's Hollow.' It starts in a couple of weeks. You'll see. Too scary for me, but you'll love it."

He raised the windowpane to gaze south. He thought he could see New York, barely. And to the north…

"Is that a cemetery? Past those trees?"

"*The* cemetery. Sleepy Hollow Cemetery. And the Old Dutch Church burial grounds. Haven't you seen them?"

Jason shook his head.

"They're in *The Legend*," she said, eyes rolling.

This, Jason would learn, was the way of the village. For over a hundred years this patch of Westchester County had been "North Tarrytown." Nothing special. But the residents took a vote in 1996 to change the name to "Sleepy Hollow" in honor of Washington Irving's story (and as a bid for tourist dollars). Once they made that decision, the entire machine of civic life turned toward *Legend* booster-ism; the Horseman galloped endlessly, and the former North Tarrytown-ers were keen to show him off.

"You need a tour guide," Debbie bubbled, "and I am happy to volunteer."

Charley barreled into the room, snuffling and scrambling. She spun, her nails clicking on the hardwood and her back legs overshooting the turn. Her tongue lolled out in chaotic joy. Then she stopped, swallowed, her face went blank, and she howled. She cocked her head toward the ceiling and let out a long low keening moan.

Jason looked up, and saw on the ceiling a four-foot-wide ring of darker color. It looked like the house had once been upside down and a small puddle had settled there, tea-staining the plaster.

"What's that?" he said.

"Your grandmother knows about that. It's just a water stain. We can fix that. A storm came through about six weeks ago. Branch fell off the big sycamore out front and put a hole in the roof so the rain got in. Roof is fine but the plaster needs a little paint."

"Charley, stop that noise," Eliza said from the foot of the stairs.

In a flash, the poodle lit up again and ran downstairs.

"Cute dog," said Debbie.

Jason shook his head. "It hates me," he whispered.

#

The Debbie Flight Guided Tour of Sleepy Hollow and Environs

is very informative, particularly if you have a keen interest in property listings, which houses are on the market, which are bank-owned, which she sold to whom and how cleverly she marketed them. Her phone rang and she kept stopping at intersections to answer it. Jason tuned her out.

Eliza had chosen to stay behind, in case the movers showed up.

"Wait for me before you go to the Old Dutch Church, okay?" she had said. "Stay on this side of the bridge."

What bridge? Jason didn't remember a bridge.

The bridge?

As Debbie drove and bubbled, he remembered his dream from the night before, and the details of *The Legend* came back to him.

He imagined the pharmacy, the auto-supply, the dry cleaners, the kosher deli all becoming transparent and vanishing. Grass grew where they stood. He pictured a small Dutch farming village circa 1790. He pictured it in detail. He saw fields of cabbages and corn, houses tucked into little coves carved from the woods, husband behind the ox, wife spinning.

This was a talent Jason had possessed since he was a boy, his favorite trick of imagination. He saw *beneath*. He could look at a city and imagine dinosaurs tramping through it. He could look at old women and imagine them as little girls. He could stare at his own driveway and see, with perfect clarity, his father's Chrysler pulling in and his parents emerging with armfuls of Christmas presents.

Today he imagined himself to be Ichabod, the new schoolteacher, riding into Tarrytown. Tipping his hat to all the ruddy-cheeked blonde farm girls. *Good day, ladies.* He smiled. His schoolhouse would have been… there, where the big brick high school stood. It would be a little cabin of logs, where he would lord over the local children as their schoolmaster. He'd have to strip a birch branch at his first opportunity. Spare the rod, you know. Anything less would make him derelict in his duty to their parents. And the manor house of Old Van Tassell? Down thataway. Bulldoze those condos and put it there: a big old farmhouse, the larder brimming from the harvest. He would ride up, tie off his horse, straighten his wig, and knock. *Is Miss Van Tassell at home?* And there would be a giggle from inside, from blooming Katrina, a country coquette with vast expectations.

"Are you getting out?"

He pushed his hair from his eyes.

The car was stopped. Debbie Flight held the passenger door open and was staring down at him. How long had she been standing there?

"Sorry," he said.

They left the Suburban and walked. Debbie's phone rang. Another realty emergency. Her ring tone was "We Are the Champions."

Jason lost the thread of his thoughts and the past slipped away again. He took his own phone out and began taking pictures. For Eliza. They stood on the corner of Broadway and Beekman Avenue. Beekman sloped steeply toward the river. Sleepy Hollow was tricked out for tourist season. Next to the pedestal clock in the center of town, a pumpkin-headed scarecrow menaced traffic; a green witch smiled from the window of a Sushi restaurant; over the street hung a banner announcing in orange and black:

The Village of Sleepy Hollow Presents
HAUNTED HAYRIDE & BLOCK PARTY
October 26-28th, 5:00 – 11:00

Hidden behind clouds, the sun could have been mistaken for the moon. Jason took a photo of it, with the banner in the foreground.

"You folks looking for the Horseman?"

A man in a red fleece and jeans was walking up the sidewalk. He was blond-headed, affable-looking. "Oh. Hi, Debbie," he said. Debbie Flight ended her call in the middle of someone's sentence.

"Hello, hot stuff! Where's the fire?"

The man blushed easily. He practically burst all his capillaries. He extended a hand to Jason.

"Mike Parson."

"*Fireman* Mike Parson. He keeps us from burning up around here." Debbie was more bubbly than usual.

He shook the man's hand.

"Jason."

"Jason *Crane*," Debbie added, and he wished she hadn't. "He's one of mine. And with a name like Crane he'll feel at home in no time, huh?"

"I saw you taking pictures and I thought you might be looking for Horseman stuff? Yeah?"

"Sure. Great." Jason nodded. This was the Sleepy Hollow pride again. The *Legend*-boosting.

"We'd love it. I'm giving Ichabod here the grand tour."

"Come on, then."

They jaywalked across the street. A car squealed to a stop, the driver shouting something unintelligible behind glass.

"You just yield to pedestrians, mister!" Mike said with authority, pointing a finger.

Mike disappeared into the small firehouse. Debbie tugged at Jason's sleeve.

"Do I have lipstick on my teeth?"

She didn't. Her phone rang again and she switched it to vibrate.

Steel doors rolled up with a clatter. Jason got his camera out. Mike was behind the wheel of the fire engine. It rumbled and rolled into the street, blocking traffic.

"Great, huh? The other one's out on a call. It's even better."

On the rear of the engine was a cartoon of Ichabod, terrified, clinging to his equally terrified plow horse. Under the ladders, a hurled pumpkin flew down a forest path toward them, eyes and jagged mouth trailing flame. And on the cab reared the Headless Horseman. He was all in black—his steed pawing the air, its hooves heavy as hammers. He brandished a sword in one hand, the other outstretched, having just thrown the pumpkin. Between the two wings of his collar lurked a small wedge of purple: the hollow where his head should be.

Inside the cab, the radio began squawking.

Mike held the pickup to his mouth. "Parson here."

A distorted paragraph. Jason made out "water" and "extra pair." Mike's face turned redder.

"What's the matter?" said Debbie.

"I've got to cut it short, guys. Did you get your picture?"

"Yeah. Thanks for showing me the truck."

"Welcome to town, Ichabod. Don't let the Horseman getcha."

Ugh. Adults.

The fire truck rolled into the street, Mike waved, turned onto Broadway, and disappeared.

Debbie took Jason by the sleeve.

"Come on," she said.

#

"Oh, God," Debbie gasped. "That's Philipsburg. You think it's on fire?"

"What's Philipsburg?"

Jason was trying to keep up. Debbie was power-walking down the hill.

"The Manor. The old farm on the millpond. You saw it out your window. Please let it be okay. Oh, please, please." She was crying. This wasn't just about property values. She was frantic.

"I don't see any smoke," Jason said.

Under the trees of the parking lot, the fire truck and a couple of police cars sat by a building that might have been a gift shop. A patrolman blocked the parking entrance and waved them on. Debbie clopped past, toward a low stone balustrade where Broadway spanned the stream that fed the millpond.

"Do you see anything?" Jason said.

"It looks okay," she said, calming down.

He caught up.

Philipsburg Manor was a nondescript square box with four dark windows on each side, like one half of a giant pair of dice. A peaked grey-shingled roof and two bright white chimneystacks bore down upon it. An ancient brown gristmill nestled by the water, the wheel dipping into the murk. The setting made the building beautiful. The millpond yawned, wide and sinister, choked with leaves, yet peaceful somehow. A narrow walkway spanned it at the far end. Trees loomed on all sides, gathering the site in. The only gap in the canopy occurred where they stood, on the bridge.

A spot of bright red caught Jason's eye and he tugged on Debbie's sleeve. Mike Parson had joined a few other men on the far shore near the millwheel.

Jason put his camera to his eye and zoomed in on the group. The lens struggled to focus. The sun had come out, and it distorted the image. He saw the bald patch at the top of someone's head. A blond man in a red fleece and jeans. Mike. A policeman in dark blue. And a third, between them. Dead.

His finger must have pressed the shutter by reflex. A still image of that face was frozen on the screen. He turned, his back to Debbie, and looked at it. He'd caught the image of the corpse in the moment when its head rolled over Mike's arm, a pallid white fishy color against the red fleece. One eye was open. No—it was gone. Missing. A void.

"What's wrong?" said Debbie.

"I think... I think they found somebody dead in the pond."

"What?" She whirled toward the water.

"I saw a body." He was about to show her the picture when he thought better of it. What if it was someone she knew? "It was a man. He was wearing a suit."

"A suit? What color suit? What did he look like?"

She was straining to see. He left her, and walked up the sidewalk. Beyond the bridge, to the north, Jason could see a church building on a hill.

He fought the urge to look at the picture again. He was thinking of his parents. They had also been pulled dead from water.

He reached the other side of the stream. At the end of the balustrade he found a historic marker.

THE HEADLESS
HORSEMAN BRIDGE
DESCRIBED BY IRVING IN THE
LEGEND OF SLEEPY HOLLOW
FORMERLY SPANNED THIS
STREAM AT THIS SPOT

Jason turned, and looked behind. Debbie Flight stood on the Horseman Bridge, talking on her phone.

He had crossed over to the other side.

5   THE RUNAWAY

Jason didn't tell Eliza what they'd seen.

He and Debbie returned to the house and found the movers unloading. A dresser and nightstand came off the truck, along with boxes of books, some filing cabinets, and clothes on racks. Debbie didn't come in. Some women smile when they're frightened, and Debbie's smile had grown broad and bright. She shook Jason's hand.

"Don't give it another thought," she said. "I wouldn't want you to get the idea that… Hell. These things don't happen every day."

"I know," he said. "I promise not to hold it against the town."

"Is that your bike?"

A mover had lowered it off the truck. Jason nodded.

"Okay, then. See there?" She pointed to the trail that led into the woods. "You've got some of the most beautiful country right at your front door. That's the Old Croton Aqueduct trail."

Jason remembered the gate with the letters O.C.A.

"That goes to the Rockefeller land. Acres and acres of old forest. You can bike, or hike. Or horses. There's a stable just over… well, it's a good town for young people. All right. Enjoy the house. Call my office if you need anything." She reached into the back seat of the Suburban.

"Don't you need to talk to my grandmother?"

"Oh no. No. She has my number. Take care now."

Debbie Flight pulled on a long leather coat and, with a wave as quick as the flash of a hummingbird's wing, she jumped behind the wheel and drove down the hill.

#

26

That night Jason slept in his own bed.

The movers had done little more than carry the larger pieces to their places. They'd stacked most boxes in the downstairs living room, eyeing the house warily as they worked, and hadn't even waited for a tip. Jason spent the rest of the day unpacking under Eliza's direction, putting dishes in cupboards, hanging clothes, setting up beds, and carrying the unneeded things to the garage. He had no intention of descending into the basement again. It was too wet for storage anyway.

As he worked, he thought about The Picture. He didn't want to look at it again. He didn't have to. He could still see the hollow eye socket, the grey skin, the mud caked as if the man had been riding motocross in a pigsty. He pushed the image out of his mind.

Why did they come here? Why wouldn't Eliza tell him? He posed questions from time to time, but she'd change the subject. She spent the evening leafing through her archive, locking the filing cabinets when she was satisfied.

Eliza would want to know about the millpond death, Jason knew. He could imagine her morbid imagination chewing the material. He didn't want to discuss it, though, so he didn't tell her. He helped her to bed, put food out for Charley, and staggered upstairs.

He'd exhausted himself. His arms were sore from lifting. But he couldn't sleep. He lay on his back staring at the stain on his ceiling. He hadn't hung curtains yet, and a full moon filled his window. A tiny reflection of it glinted off the distant millpond at Philipsburg Manor.

He rolled over.

On his dresser, alongside his keys and a few wadded dollar bills, sat the camera phone. *Oh, God.* He thought of the face again. The face as white as the moon. The head dangling over the red fleece, a pumpkin slipping from a red wagon, a hollow for an eye.

He flipped onto his stomach.

He thought of what that man's body would look like on an autopsy table. The mortician sawing off the top of the skull, slipping a candle inside. He saw a human jack-o'-lantern grinning on the mortician's front porch, a nasty surprise for Spongebob and the Little Mermaid.

He put his pillow over his head.

He saw the mortician again, bounding onto the porch a few days after Halloween, scooping the softening head into a bag, dumping it for the trash men. *Holiday's over. Time to start thinking about Thanksgiving. Gobble gobble!*

He rolled onto his back and stared at the ceiling again.

He heard a cough downstairs. The door of Eliza's bathroom opened, closed again. Silence.

The stain on the ceiling had spread. In the blue light, it was darker than it had been that morning. *(Really? Just that morning? Not a thousand years ago?)* It loomed above his bed, a tunnel inviting him to rise up and pass through it, the way people claim to rise when they lie dead on an operating table.

He pressed his palms to his eyes. Stop thinking about death. *Stop it. Stop it. Stop it...just stop it...*

He was just seven when his parents died.

On October twenty-ninth, almost exactly ten years ago, Andrew and Dianne Crane motored down to New York City for an anniversary trip. Dianne wanted to see *The Phantom of the Opera*, so they took a couple of nights at the W Hotel in Times Square.

Jason hoped they had a great time. He hoped they got drunk after the show, ran up a tab at a nice restaurant. He hoped they had amazing sex. He hoped the maid came in the next morning to find a wrecked room and an empty minibar. He hoped they had the time of their lives.

Because their time, and their lives, ended the following night.

The police concluded that Andrew lost control of the car while crossing Kensico Dam. The car tumbled over the retaining wall and into the deep black far below. When the bodies were found, after days in the water, the coroner had ordered a toxicology report. It came back negative. No drugs or alcohol. The police were satisfied that the event had been an accident.

When he grew up and read the report, Jason doubted that conclusion. The retaining walls were four-foot-high, foot-thick masonry walls, hemming two lanes of traffic across the dam. Sightseers had complained that the walls were too high for drivers or passengers to see the Kensico Reservoir. The police had found no sign of a second vehicle, no one who had witnessed the event, and nothing the car might have struck that could have flipped it. They found no marks on the stone. Had the car been lifted, end over end, and thrown over that wall? And why had his parents driven there, anyway? It wasn't on their way home to him. But the case had been closed. About a year after the event, the road had been closed as well. The mayor of New York closed it, citing concerns about a terrorist attack on the city water supply.

His parents had left him with his grandmother, just for the weekend. Eliza received the news of their death on Halloween morning, but she kept it from Jason for two more days. She sent him out trick-or-treating. He was a vampire. His step-grandfather John Dawes (Eliza's fifth husband) made a contraption for him to wear. The string went around his neck, suspending a little square of wood over his heart. Grandpa John sawed the handle off a hammer and nailed the pieces together. When Jason put on his shirt, the handle poked out of a little hole. A dollop of fake blood, and Jason the Impaler was convincingly staked through the heart. They finished him off with a widow's peak of eyebrow pencil, some dime-store fangs, and a black and orange polyester cape that Eliza had sewn upon for weeks. He spun around in the living room, eyes wild, shouting "I am the living dead!" and wondering why they didn't laugh.

He bat-winged into the night, in search of Kit Kats and Milk Duds and chocolate kisses. An hour later, he mummy-shuffled home with tears that had eroded the greasepaint from his cheeks. A werewolf had scoffed at his costume. He'd ripped the stake from Jason's chest and howled with laughter. Jason hadn't been able to reattach the hammer handle, so Halloween was ruined.

The next day, November first, was his seventh birthday. Two local kids, strangers, came over for ice cream and cake. They all watched *Return of the Jedi*, and the kids ate candy out of a plastic pumpkin.

On November second, after school, Eliza told him.

His parents were dead. He wouldn't be going back to his school in Connecticut, and would be living with her and Grandpa John in Maine.

Jason had never experienced death. He'd never lost a pet, and wouldn't until years later when Pokey, his little white terrier, broke her back falling off the porch. Eliza had brought Charley the poodle home afterward, but Charley was instantly *her* puppy. Jason didn't want a replacement.

Andrew Crane's parents had died long before Jason was born. So had Arthur Pyncheon, the love of Eliza's life and Dianne's father.

Eliza's later husbands, the ones Jason knew, were temporary grandfathers that lasted a few years and then scrammed, never to be spoken of afterward. Grandpa John achieved the longest run. She threw him out after four years, for drinking.

Jason didn't attend his parents' funeral. He didn't want to, and the adults felt he was too young. Eliza flew down to New York and made arrangements at a local funeral home, and his parents were buried in Westchester at Valhalla, just a mile from the dam where their lives had ended. They never came home.

It was a bleak time. Jason felt that little piece of wood still covering his heart. He grew numb and shuffled around the house, not listening when he was spoken to. He would walk into a room and switch the television off. He wanted silence. He wanted darkness. He wanted to be hungry. Sometimes that little piece of wood transformed itself into a stake again, and he would scream and rant and throw shoes at Eliza's face. He would beat his fists against Grandpa John's chest. He refused to go to school. He cried great rolling tears.

In early spring he ran away from home—which means he stole five dollars, put a box of Cheez-Its in a pillowcase and walked seven blocks. He stayed out all night. He slept in a field, glad to be miserable. He wanted to freeze to death, to be with his mom and dad, to not feel anything.

His grandmother found him at a playground near the river, fallen in the dust with his shoulder against the slope of a teeter-totter, the other end riderless, suspended. He saw her trudging up the hill. She looked twice her usual size in her winter coat, and frightening.

"Let's go home, Jason," she said.

He shook his head. He knew he was in trouble. He knew what "home" meant. It meant a paddling or worse. Eliza never spanked him, but this time he thought he deserved it, and he was afraid that they hated him.

"Jason?" she said, not raising her voice.

She might have seen the tears on his cheeks. Maybe not. The light was dim. The sun was just peeking out between some low hills in the distance. His teeth were chattering. Eliza opened her big winter coat and, straining, slipped down into the dust next to him. She drew him in to her warm body, wrapping him in the coat. She flipped the collar up, rubbed her hands together, and cupped them over his ears.

"Brr," she said. "You're an ice cube. But it feels good, kinda. It's good to get really cold sometimes. Wakes you up."

They were cheek to cheek, against the teeter-totter, bundled together, as the sky turned from grey to orange. The ground stung, but they sat a long time.

"Why?"

The word was just a tiny puff of vapor that slipped from his lips and into the wind. But it was also big. Big and heavy.

She didn't ask "why what." She didn't evade his question. She knew what his little-boy heart had asked. She understood the universe of longing and confusion and hurt in that one whispered word.

"We all die, baby." She said it oh-so-gently, just a puff of vapor herself. "In all the long, long, history of the world, there's not been one of us who didn't."

"I'll die," he said. It wasn't a question. But it was.

"Yes. And I'll die. A lot sooner. And the *why* is just… it's just *there*. It just *is*. We're not around to see what was before us, and we're not here to see what happens after."

The trees on the edge of the playground shivered with dawn.

"But we're here now," she said, and pulled him tighter, until his cheekbone felt sore from pressing against hers. "And it has to be enough. It *has to be*. Look at all we have now. Really look."

He really looked.

It was just a small playground off the main road of an unimportant New England town. But in the distance he could see the wide Kennebec River, and the sky was pink above it. He saw small ships moored, trimmed in red and baby blue, rocking against the current. He saw a robin on the railing of a dock, toes pointed inward, making occasional hops that were also flight. The town was waking up. There was a light in the bakery and one in the grocery. There was an empty can of beer on a picnic table and wildflowers by the road. There was wind, and trees swaying gently. There was his own breath in his own lungs. There was a car passing on the road, going somewhere.

There was his grandmother, her body, her heartbeat against his back as he leaned against her chest. There was his own life, and hers, and a world to live them in.

And it was enough.

He went back to school the next day.

Jason and Eliza shared a bond after, born of that sunrise on the playground. He knew a secret about her: for all her morbidity, for all her obsession with genealogies, with cemeteries, with graves and mysteries, Eliza Merrick harbored a passionate and reverent love of this earth and of living on it. She appreciated every one of her long years.

And that was the treasure she passed on to a boy of seven who had, for a short perilous time, given up on life.

Jason heard a flush. The bathroom door downstairs opened and closed again. Eliza must have stubbed her toe. He heard muttered curses and Charley yipped.

He smiled.

His thoughts came back to earth, down from the tunnel on his bedroom ceiling. He sat up in bed. Outside his window, the lights of Philipsburg Manor had gone dark.

That was good.

He stepped to his dresser, picked up his phone and, without reviewing his pictures, deleted all files.

6   THE LAST OF THE BONES

The Tarrytown Caller reported the death as a suicide.

Franklin Octavius Darley, age 47, senior risk officer for a Manhattan brokerage firm, had been in town for a jazz performance at the Tarrytown Music Hall. His body was found by Annie Baxter, a local resident. His wrists had been cut. His wife could not be reached for comment.

The eye wasn't mentioned.

The fish took it, Jason thought.

He put the paper down and that was that.

By the end of his first week in Sleepy Hollow, Jason had forgotten about the body in the millpond. He'd stored the white face somewhere alongside the zombies of George A. Romero films. Unreal, toe-tagged in the mental morgue with everything else Jason had seen of death, from Bambi's mother to Darth Vader and Boromir.

Jason focused on organizing the house.

He stacked dishes. He had the cable installed. He hung the blinds. He arranged Eliza's pictures in places of pride—pictures of himself, of his parents, of his grandmother on trips around the world (only two of these had the husbands cut out). Daguerreotypes of well-loved ancestors went up in the downstairs hall, along with Eliza's framed pilot license from 1964, token of a long and interesting life.

Eliza couldn't help much. She gave "opinions," and Jason carried them out. She busied herself with the organization of her genealogy materials. Boxes and boxes hid the threadbare Persian carpet. Filing cabinets stood in an arc around the sofa like an incomplete

Stonehenge.

She spread genealogical charts the size of architect's blueprints. She spent long hours at these, a professor preparing herself for a lecture or presentation. She made notes to herself on a little laptop. Tap-tap she went, two knobby pointer fingers hunting and pecking happily into the night.

Jason did some painting in his room, and the wall with the windows became a shade of sky blue that made a continuation of the Hudson. He played music while he worked, and the house rang with everything from Beethoven's "Eroica" Symphony to Fountains of Wayne to a geek band called Ookla the Mok. He danced around with his paintbrush in a way that, if filmed and put on YouTube, would ensure his virginity for the next thousand years.

And so they settled in.

On Sunday morning—their fifth day in the house—a buzzing noise stirred Jason out of bed. The buzz was almost human, but it sounded like a radio caught between dials, a mix of static and speech—a low, unnerving growling sound, yet somehow singsong. It came from downstairs, and Jason wondered if the TV was on. But tuned to what? A lumberjack competition? He plucked some shorts from the floor and grabbed a T-shirt.

On the stairs it was louder.

"Eliza? What's that sound?" he said. "I'm hearing some crazy weird buzz."

It stopped. "What the hell *was* that?" he said. He reached the living room.

His grandmother roosted on the blue davenport, a porcelain teacup raised to lips pursed so tightly she might have been drinking pure lemon juice. In an armchair, her back to Jason, a woman with short-cropped black hair raised a palm.

"It's okay. He didn't—know."

The voice was inhuman: deep as a man's voice, but labored and breathy as if spoken through scuba gear. The woman turned. She had a tracheostomy valve in the front of her neck.

"You must—be Jason," the woman buzzed.

Her features were dark, Lebanese or Iranian maybe, with laugh lines and crow's-feet. She wore pearl earrings, a white jacket, white skirt, and white Mary Janes (her ankles demurely crossed). She wore a rigid tube around her neck, inhaling through a small valve in front which, when closed, directed exhaled air to her vocal cords. This apparatus was also white and somehow flattering, like a Bakelite necklace from the twenties.

"I'm so sorry. I— I—" Jason stammered, scrambling.

"Please. I'm—" (breath) "—used to it." (breath) "—Join us." (valve pop).

He considered sitting by Eliza, saw her face, and chose a straight-backed chair.

"Jason, I'd like you to meet my very good friend Valerie Maule."

"Ma'am," he said.

"Please. Valerie." Her eyes were bright, her smile contagious. Her voice was a penny stuck in a vacuum cleaner. "Eliza has told—me so—many good—things about you."

She hasn't mentioned you once, Jason wanted to say, but opted for a nod.

"My friends were courteous enough—" (Eliza put particular emphasis on the word *courteous*) "—to bring our car down from Augusta."

Jason glanced out the bay window. The silver Mercedes sat parked in the drive.

"Our pleasure," said a low, smooth male voice.

A man leaned in the dining room archway, hands in pockets. He wore a stylish black Armani suit with a red tie that looked like the incision on a heart patient.

"It drives like a dream," he said. "Beautiful car. You're lucky I gave it back."

"I made him," Valerie buzzed.

"If you can afford the gas," said Eliza.

The man walked over, bent down and gave Eliza a peck on the cheek. His hair was blond, his eyebrows thin and almost nonexistent. He was handsome, his smile toothpaste-commercial bright. He put an arm around her thin shoulders and brought his lips to her ear, his voice husky.

"Maybe you and I can go parking later."

Eliza swatted at the man and covered her face, reddening.

"Oh, you."

His eyes met Jason's.

The boy stood and extended a hand. He felt an urgent impulse to separate this man from his grandmother.

"I'm sorry, but we haven't met?" Jason said.

"No, we haven't. Pleasure to meet you, Mister Crane."

He gave a slight emphasis to the last two words. The hand that clasped Jason's was small, but strong.

"Hadewych Van Brunt."

Jason must have blinked.

"It's the Dutch form of Hedwig, which unfortunately is a woman's name. Blame my mother. Don't worry. I won't quiz you on spelling. Though 'Liza here tells us you're a clever boy. Top of your class?"

"Somewhere in there."

"Good. Though not too smart I hope. Trust me. The girls don't like it." He closed on Jason, invasively. "You do like girls, right?" He slapped the boy's shoulder. "Just kidding you." It was a game-show host's voice: ingratiating, twinkling, inviting his audience to play along from home.

Eliza lifted her purse from the floor. "Don't let me forget to write you a check. How much did you spend coming down?"

"Not that much."

Eliza turned to Jason. "Thank Hadewych. He took care of our move for us."

"Oh?"

"He packed our things. He and Valerie did. They made it very easy on an old lady."

Hadewych spread his palms, opening a hymnal to sing his own praises. "I had fun doing it."

Eliza caught Jason's eye and tilted her head toward Hadewych.

"Thank you. Um—we appreciate it," said Jason.

But he did not appreciate it. He didn't appreciate it one bit. He didn't like the idea of this man going through their possessions unsupervised. What if some bauble of his grandmother's now glittered in Valerie Maule's jewelry box?

"He found us the house too," Eliza gushed. She put her hand on Hadewych's arm.

Hadewych slipped next to her on the davenport, and Jason wished he had taken that seat.

"How do you like it?" said Hadewych.

Eliza's hand went to his shoulder. "It's just the right size. My old house was too large. And this one has so much history." She turned to Jason. "It belonged to Hadewych's family once."

Hadewych looked up at the beams. "A long time ago," he said.

"Before the—Civil War," added Valerie.

"Eighteen... fifty?" Eliza said.

"Eighteen thirty-seven," said Jason. Eliza's jaw dropped a little. "There's a cornerstone out back."

Hadewych smiled, solemnly. "Eighteen thirty-seven. Yes. He built it for his mother..."

"Who did?" said Jason.

Hadewych appraised the boy from behind his teacup, an antique dealer deciding what to bid on a chest of drawers.

"Let me think." Eliza counted off on one hand. "He was your... your great-great-great-great-great-grandfather? You'll never guess who Hadewych is descended from, Jason."

"Let's not—say too much—just yet." Valerie looked pointedly at the others.

But Jason knew. The name thundered in his head. He was descended from—

"Brom!"

He blurted the name, without thinking.

"Very good." Hadewych said, without smiling. "How did you guess it?"

"Have you been through my papers?" said Eliza.

"No. I just..." But he couldn't explain how the name had come to him. It had simply come. *Brom Brom Brom.* It was a drumbeat. *Brom! Brom Brom Brom!* The whole house shouted it at him. How had he not heard it before?

"He's read *The Legend*, hasn't he? It's right there, if you pay attention." Hadewych stood, patting Eliza's knee. He bounded to the fireplace, turned, and put his foot upon the hearth. The women brightened, knowing what would come next. Then Hadewych Van Brunt began reciting Irving's tale from memory.

"Among these the most formidable was a burly, roaring, roystering blade, of the name of Abraham, or, according to the Dutch abbreviation..." here he paused for effect, *"...Brom Van Brunt, the hero of the country round, which rang with his feats of strength and hardihood."*

He made it a Shakespearian oration, posing. Eliza was delighted. The man gesticulated, a ham actor loving every minute.

"*He was broad-shouldered and double-jointed, with short curly black hair, and a bluff, but not unpleasant countenance…*"

He admired himself in the mirror. Valerie blew kisses.

"*…having a mingled air of fun and arrogance.*"

Next came a series of ridiculous bodybuilder poses. Eliza laughed. Valerie rolled her eyes. Even Jason had to chuckle, just a little.

"*From his Herculean frame and great powers of limb, he had received the nickname of BROM BONES, by which he was universally known.*"

Hadewych turned, his hands outstretched, and bowed deeply. Valerie and Eliza applauded. He bowed again.

"And that's who I am. Or who I was. My people at least. The Van Brunts haven't lived in Sleepy Hollow in ages. But neither have the Cranes, eh?"

"What do you mean?" said Jason. "My family never lived here."

Hadewych put a hand on the back of Jason's chair and knelt, looking him in the eye. He took a breath, but—

"Not yet, Hadewych," said Eliza. "Tonight. When we can discuss it properly."

He stood. Some silent agreement passed between the adults.

"Fine," said Hadewych. "Tonight. When you come to dinner."

"Hold on. Discuss what? Tell me now."

"Later, Jason." Eliza's voice had that undertow again.

"We were—just doing—a reading," said Valerie, changing the subject.

On the coffee table lay an arrangement of tarot cards.

"You interrupted us," said Eliza. "It was just getting interesting."

"Would you—like me—to do a—reading—for you?" Valerie gathered the cards into her hand.

"No," said Hadewych, "not yet." It came out as a command. Valerie jumped, then continued reshuffling. "Jason doesn't look like the tarot card sort," he added.

"I'm not. I don't believe in that stuff."

"Good for you," said Hadewych. "It's too early for all that anyway."

Disappointment crinkled Valerie's face. "Early is—when you do it. I don't—read for people—at night."

"The energies," nodded Eliza with enthusiasm, "are much better in the day. Besides, I'm The Sun. That's my significator." She beamed like the sun, too.

"Most people—are court cards. Eliza is—special. Powerful."

"The sun is one of the Major Arcana," said Eliza.

Jason had heard enough.

"What's going on?" He was yelling. He couldn't help himself. Eliza's face told him he had crossed a line. Charley, hearing the noise, yipped somewhere in the house. "Can someone tell me one thing I can understand?"

Eliza began to speak, but Hadewych held up a hand.

"How much do you know, Jason?" he said. "What has Eliza told you?"

"She's told me nothing."

"Nothing?" He turned to the old lady, shaking his head.

"He might have said no," said Eliza. She pouted.

"No to what?" Jason felt his face reddening.

"Jason…" Eliza's voice was measured out in teaspoons. "I couldn't explain before. I had to wait for Hadewych and Valerie to arrive. Now that they're here, I think we're ready to put some things to you."

"Okay. Let's hear it."

She surveyed him and sighed. "Go put some clothes on."

Jason glanced down at himself, realizing that while their guests were sleek and stylish, he stood barefoot, un-showered, wearing knockabout shorts with holes in them. His T-shirt bore an image of a piñata and the words "I'd Hit That!"

He cringed.

Eliza wore a navy cardigan sweater over a blouse. She wore makeup, and her hair was neatly brushed. A fine silver necklace glittered, but who had done the clasp? Who had helped with the buttons? These people, probably Valerie, had *dressed her*.

"Jason? Go get dressed. You look like an urchin."

He sighed and turned to go.

Just as his foot hit the first stair, Hadewych said "We'll still be here."

And in the pit of his stomach he knew they would be.

#

Brom. Brom. Brom.

The name drummed in his head, diminishing, leaving a dull ache. He showered and shaved, changed into a button-down shirt, a pair of slacks, and shoes that bit his feet. He overdid it a little, dressing to armor himself.

"How did you guess?" Hadewych was standing in the door.

"Excuse me? This is my room. Could you knock?"

"Apologies." Hadewych closed the door, rapped twice. "May I come in?"

Jason wanted to say no.

"Fine."

Hadewych re-entered.

"How did you guess my ancestor?"

"Like you said. I read *The Legend*. Just a few nights ago. I recognized your last name." He glanced at the *Sketch-Book*, which lay on his dresser.

"Oh, how wonderful. She bought it after all. May I?" Jason nodded. Hadewych flipped the pages. "I've never held an original *Sketch-Book*. Could never afford one. And here it is. Absalom Crane's own copy, too." He set it down, reluctantly.

"What do you want?"

"To apologize. I know this must all seem odd to you. Do you miss your friends back in Augusta?"

"Sure."

"And here you're moved into a new house, with no explanation of why. I am sorry for that. I didn't mean for Eliza to tell you *nothing*. I asked her to wait and allow me to make an appeal on behalf of the group."

"What group?"

"Valerie, Eliza and myself. And, I suppose, all our families, living and dead. Yours and mine. And Valerie's in a way. We have a proposal for you, and I hope you will find it as exciting as we do."

"Let's hear it."

"Not yet." He studied Jason. "You're thinking, 'Who the hell is this guy?'"

"Yup."

"'How does he know my grandmother?'"

"How do you?"

Hadewych took Jason's coat from its hook behind the door, handed it to him.

"Let's go for coffee. My treat."

Jason hesitated, but Hadewych seemed different, somehow. More relaxed. More sincere. Almost like... a friend.

"All right. But I want some answers."

"No problem. Come on. The ladies are doing their reading, and I'd hate to interfere with Valerie's energies."

He rolled his eyes and laughed because, of course, the supernatural is the most ridiculous thing in the world.

#

Leaves hit their backs as they walked. A wind whipped from the north. They walked down the hill toward Broadway.

"Do you like the town?" said Hadewych.

"It's nice enough. But you're supposed to be answering my questions."

"Try me."

"How do you know my grandmother?"

"We're family."

"We are?"

"Distantly. Through my ex-wife. She was the daughter of Martha Pyncheon Bridge. Martha's uncle was your great-grandfather. That makes you my son's... something something cousin. We'll have to look that one up."

"I trust you," said Jason, though he didn't.

"Just a happy coincidence. Eliza puts great stock in such things."

"She shouldn't. If you go back far enough..."

"Everybody's related to everybody. I know. And I'd be a monkey's uncle." Hadewych chortled.

They reached Broadway. Jason turned left, away from Philipsburg Manor. Hadewych steered him back to the right.

"I know a place," he said.

He led Jason to a small bistro. The door set tiny bells to chime as they entered. The place shivered with smells: coffee, hot chocolate and croissants.

"This," he said, extending his arm towards a woman in an apron, "is Jennifer. She makes the best scones and is, tragically, spoken for." He kissed the woman's hand. She was plump, in her fifties. She had left one curler to dangle at the back of her head this morning.

"If it's a tragedy to you, this is the first I've heard of it." She swatted at him with a menu. "Why didn't you speak up twenty years ago? Lady-killer."

Jason sat. Jennifer put a glass of water in front of him.

"And who is this fine gentleman?"

"This," said Hadewych, joining, "is my son's great-grandfather's great-great nephew."

"That's a lot of greats," she said.

"I'll try to live up to it," Jason murmured.

"Any great great great whatever of Hadewych is great by me."

She giggled at her own wit.

"I'll be back for your orders."

Hadewych swatted her rear end with a menu as she left.

He made small talk, about the bistro, the specials, what was good (the Benedict) or not-so (the hanger steak). When their orders came (coffee for both, eggs for Jason, a scone for himself), he got down to business.

"I met your grandmother about, oh, a year ago. Valerie and I have a mutual interest in old families, particularly old families related to *The Legend*, for obvious reasons. Valerie's lived in Tarrytown for years, though her family's up near Boston. Now, don't worry, I don't believe all that nonsense about a Headless Horseman. Valerie's the superstitious one. But the Van Brunts are definitely the family in Irving's story. Hermanus Van Brunt and his wife Agathe were farmers in the village, back in… seventeen-eighty or so. This was during the revolution. Hermanus grabbed title to lands left by a Tory family who'd been tarred and feathered and shipped back to Britain. Do you know your history?"

"Sure. Tory. Loyal to the king. Benjamin Franklin broke with his own son who was a Tory."

"Smart boy. Traitors to the cause. And that was serious business. The British marched straight through here during the war. Chased George Washington off Manhattan and out to New Jersey. And after they were kicked out again a lot of Tories were kicked out with them.

Anyway, the Van Brunts took over some farmland north of Tarrytown. They had a son Abraham…

Brom Brom. Brom.

"…and, of course, their son Abraham married a wealthy heiress."

"Katrina Van Tassel."

"Yes. All that is true. It's public record, just like *The Legend* says. I have papers from my mother written in Brom's hand. He was powerful around here. With Katrina's money he became the biggest stone merchant in the state. He died in… eighteen-fifty. After him it's Dylan Van Brunt his son, Joseph the grandson, then Cornelius, then…"

"Sorry. Genealogy is… not my thing."

"No? It wasn't mine once either. But when your parents die… and you're young… it's practically the only way I could be close to my family."

"I guess I understand that," said Jason. He stared at his eggs.

"I wish I'd known them. My mother left behind quite a few documents written by Abraham Van Brunt. Brom. In Dutch, mostly."

"Why was Eliza doing research on the Van Brunts?"

"She wasn't. She was looking into the Cranes. That's what made us such fast friends."

"I don't get it."

"We do go back a ways. Your family and mine."

"More coffee?" Jennifer appeared at Jason's elbow. Hadewych nodded and she poured.

"Still not getting it," said Jason.

But he did. With a flash of certainty, just as he had known that this man was the descendant of *Brom Brom Brom.*

Hadewych turned to the waitress, and Jason knew what he would say.

"My lady, may I present…"

He raised his coffee cup, proclaiming:

"… the last descendant of Ichabod Crane."

7 THE HOUSE THAT SHOUTED

Of course. Here it is, Jason thought. *They think they've made some big genealogy discovery. This is the surprise.*

"Didn't you hear me?" said Hadewych.

"Sure."

Don't encourage him.

Jason picked at his scrambled eggs. He reached for the pepper. He kept his face blank.

"Aren't you going to say anything?"

Next came the salt. Jason decided the eggs were a little runny and bland. The coffee was good, though. Jennifer was making a fresh pot. She'd rolled her eyes at Hadewych's pronouncement. She thought he was joking. He wasn't.

"Jason. This is important." Hadewych's face flushed a little pink. "We can prove the lineage. We have every document, going back two centuries. There's no mistake."

"Got it. That's cool, I guess."

"You guess? I'm telling you Ichabod Crane was a real person, and you are his descendant."

"So what?" Jason said.

Hadewych's mouth fell open a little.

"So what if I am?" Jason said. "I mean, so? I don't see how it affects my life."

"Oh, you don't?"

"No. Not in the slightest. As far as I'm concerned my ancestor could have been Scrooge McDuck. I don't have tail feathers, so what does it matter?"

"What does it matter?"

"What does it matter? Is this why you had me dragged here?"

"Partly."

"And what's the other part?"

Hadewych hesitated. "There's a letter I want you to read," he said.

"What letter?"

"I'll show you tonight."

"What letter? What? Has the Sleepy Hollow Brigade invited me to open a shopping mall? What?"

Hadewych frowned.

"Oh, hell," Jason huffed, standing. "You people have got her convinced this is some mystical voodoo thing." He whipped his coat on. Hadewych remained seated, unconcerned, crumbling his scone. "I'm going home," Jason said. "No. *We're* going home. We're moving back to Maine where we belong."

"No. You're not."

"Watch us. No. Stay the hell away from us."

"She won't do it," said Hadewych. "Eliza is committed to the project."

Project?

Jason leaned in, his nose less than an inch from Hadewych's face.

"Okay. Listen. I love my grandmother, sir. She loves me. And I'm not about to see her get played by a couple of con artists from the psychic hotline. So whatever you've told her, whatever you've got her believing in, it's over. Goodbye."

Jason stuck a fist in his jeans pocket and threw a five-dollar bill on the table.

"That's for Jennifer. You're buying the eggs," he said, and walked to the door.

"You won't be able to go." Hadewych said. "You won't ever leave."

Jason turned. He'd pulled the door wide. The little bells danced as he did.

"And why not?"

Hadewych pushed his chair back from the table. He straightened his tie, turning to face Jason. He spread his arms, palms up in a gesture that encompassed the bistro, the street, the entire town. His voice possessed the confidence of a party boss who knows the fix is in, and his eyes brimmed with laughter.

"Because Sleepy Hollow owns you."

#

The Mercedes wasn't in the drive of 417 Gory Brook, and a baby blue post-it fluttered on the door.

Jason—
Will pick you up at seven. Look nice.
Eliza and Co.

The "Co." was Valerie. The note was not in Eliza's handwriting, which was a cramped scrawl. Valerie's penmanship was as feminine and intelligible as her voice was not.

Look nice. Hmph. He wadded it.

Jason spun on his heels and marched back down the hill. But where would he go? He wouldn't find Hadewych at the bistro, he knew. He probably called Valerie's cell the moment Jason stormed out; the silver Mercedes might be in front of the bistro right now. Jason hadn't seen it pass on the way back. Maybe they left down a side street...

He was wandering, wishing he'd dressed more warmly.

He passed a colonial-style house, decorated for Halloween, the cemetery of plastic tombstones in the yard flatly banal in the early afternoon sun. Plastic zombie hands clawed up through the Kentucky bluegrass. A skeleton stretched its bones on a garden bench. It held a cigar, and wore glasses with black cardboard moustache and eyebrows attached. The bleached bones of Groucho Marx, Jason guessed.

He sat on the ground and pulled off a dress shoe, rubbing his leather-bitten foot.

The last descendant of Ichabod Crane.

He pushed his hair out of his eyes.

The idea didn't bother him. It was kind of cool, actually. He remembered picturing himself as Ichabod only a few days before, riding a horse into Tarrytown. If people found out they might make fun of him, true, but it would be gentle joshing, like Debbie Flight and Fireman Mike calling him Ichabod. Nothing malicious. The locals might love to put a modern Ichabod on their tourist brochures. Jason had been on the cover of the *Kennebec Journal* once, two years before. He'd posed with his copy of *Giant-Size X-Men #1* for an article about comic collecting. This even won him some approval at school, mostly from other nerds, but still.

Descending from Ichabod was fine, though weirdly, inescapably *odd*.

What bothered him was that Hadewych and Valerie might be taking advantage of Eliza. She was a tough old lady, blunt as a hammer, but like so many honest people she expected everyone *else* to be honest. She had a tendency to be taken in. She was... what's the word? Credulous. Two of her husbands were fortune hunters, eager to plunder her checking accounts. One skulked away in September of '74, never to return; the other one Eliza beat to tears with a frozen lasagna in August of '82.

She bought priceless emeralds off cable channels, indignant when she received green glass; her stockbroker ran up twenty thousand in commissions because Eliza "didn't want to be nosy." She believed in ancient aliens, nodded when politicians spoke, played the lottery and invited Mormons in for coffee. Jason, to his shame, could fib her into anything. He tried not to, but he was sixteen; and she was so cussedly gullible sometimes. Still, you never wanted to get caught in a lie. Oh, no. Not by Eliza Merrick.

What had these people told her? Hadewych had said, "Eliza is committed to the project." That didn't sound good. That sounded involved, vaguely epic. He mentioned a letter, too. What letter? Who sent a letter?

Jason sighed. Groucho leered down at him. *Say the secret word and win a hundred dollars, Bucko.*

He regretted shouting at Hadewych. He didn't know the facts. Maybe he'd overreacted. Ugh. He'd called Eliza's friends "a couple of con artists from the psychic hotline." *Oh, she will love hearing that.* Hadewych was probably repeating the conversation word for word from the back seat of the Mercedes. *(Back seat? Nah. Hadewych always drives.)* Jason would get a talking-to. Eliza rolled out the welcome mat, and Jason stepped in a pile of poodle shit.

He wanted to leave Sleepy Hollow. *(What did he mean "it owns me"?)* How would he convince Eliza? She'd bought a house. That was a serious expenditure of time and money; that was long hours listening to Debbie Flight gush, wire transfers of half a million dollars or more, titles, deeds, a hundred things to do and sign. She wouldn't jump in the RV and head home just because he whined at her. No, Eliza was definitely "committed to the project."

And eighty years old. She must intend to leave that house to Jason someday, and she never would have bought it if she didn't think he would be grateful to have it from her. But the house gave him shivers.

That's why he was sitting with Groucho when he could have been warm in the house. He didn't want to be alone there. The rooms, somehow, were never what you expected, never how you remembered them from the day before, one square foot too many or too few, a little extra space behind the door or around a corner, just enough for something to be crouching there, watching you.

And it had shouted at him earlier.

Brom Brom Brom.

Shouted at him? Or for him? Or for someone else? *Oh, come on.* That's stupid. He'd been honest when he'd said he didn't believe in tarot cards and stuff. He did, once. After his parents died he became obsessed with the supernatural. But as he grew up he decided he preferred science. History, too. On the mirror of his bedroom he'd placed two pictures: one of Howard Carter and one of Carl Sagan. The first discovered King Tut's tomb, and the second challenged Jason to question everything.

That morning Jason had experienced something strange. So he questioned it.

He'd imagined the shout, of course. Houses can't shout. Maybe he *had* recognized the Van Brunt name from *The Legend*, even if on a subconscious level. Maybe he'd seen something in Eliza's papers. Maybe it was a blind guess. He refused to believe he'd had a "paranormal experience."

Except it had happened before.

Jason's stomach flipped over. Someone pulled a stopper and sent his eggs and toast down down to goblin town.

He didn't want to remember his friend Owen.

Owen with the brown paper bag.

In his last year of middle school, Jason had sprouted like climbing kudzu, growing almost nine inches and four shoe sizes. Already a lanky kid, he was verging on giraffe. This made him a target, and he was cut down mercilessly. He felt like a freak: awkward, inelegant, hands dangling, buying his size-seventeen sneaks off the internet. So he gravitated to his fellow freaks, and found Owen. Owen was as horizontal as Jason was vertical. He wore suspenders that no bully could resist snapping, and he lugged his books as if protecting his navel from somebody's fist. He was mild mannered, but enthusiastic as a puppy when you met him on his home turf of sci-fi and comics. He could quote almost every joke from old *Mork and Mindy* episodes, and was prone to mutter "shazbot" when he tripped on his shoelaces.

The two cleaved to each other, one short and fat, one tall and thin, as if they wanted to average out to one normally proportioned person. The lard and the scarecrow. Laurel and Hardy. Yes. A comedy team, full of quotes and quirks and pimply mirth. They took the show on the road as freshmen at Cony High School. But their great friendship ended abruptly just after Thanksgiving.

Eliza invited Owen over for the Thanksgiving meal. Owen nibbled some turkey, that's all. He never ate much that Jason saw, which was surprising for his size. Maybe he binged late at night when no one was looking. Jason gorged on an enormous mound of stuffing and giblet gravy, potatoes and warm rolls. If old Ichabod possessed "the dilating power of an anaconda," Jason had inherited it.

Afterwards, upstairs, they reverently slipped Jason's *Giant-Size X-Men #1* from its Mylar protector, drinking in the sweet aroma of browning paper and three-color process that signals only the best and rarest and most wonderful of collectibles. On one page, Professor X raised his fingers to his temples and rallied his X-Men, his psychic commands radiating from his bald head like waves off hot asphalt.

"I have psychic powers," Owen blurted.

"I want Wolverine's claws." Jason was turning a page. "Snikt! Or—hey, get this! Get this! Lightsabers poking out the backs of my hands. Or even—"

"No, no! I'm totally serious. I have psychic powers."

"No you don't."

"I do."

Jason laid the comic on the bedspread. He sighed. Owen could be such a spaz sometimes. "Okay," he said, indulgently, "what number am I thinking of?" Jason closed his eyes, put his index fingers to his temples, and whistled like a flying saucer on a roller coaster.

"Stop. It doesn't work that way." Owen pulled Jason's elbow

down. He was grave-faced, earnest. "What I can do is called a psychic reading. Off an object. Like getting impressions. When the doorbell rings, if I put my hand on the knob, as soon as I do I know who's there."

"It's called looking through the peephole, moron."

"Shut up! And when I touch the phone I know who's calling."

"I'm sure, Mister Bullshit from Bullshit Mountain."

"Like my sister or my grandmother. I just know it's them."

Jason stretched and flopped back onto the floor, his arms splayed above his head. "Then prove it."

"Okay. Give me something to do a reading on."

"Here." Jason rolled over and plucked a roll of socks from the closet floor. He lobbed it at Owen. The sock bounced off Owen's head and under the desk.

"Gotcha!" Jason said.

"Something better than that."

Jason sat up, annoyed.

"Fine," he said, rummaging. He produced a single ancient cowboy boot, a man's boot, snakeskin, its toes scuffed, mudded with long use. He set it down between them. "Read this."

Owen scooted over to the boot. He closed his eyes, gathering himself, slowing his breathing. He made a low shamanic "Om" sound. Jason snickered and was shushed. Owen hovered his palms above the boot, warming them before a psychic campfire He laid hands on it, leaning into the thing.

Ten seconds passed. Jason realized he was holding his breath.

"Well?"

"I see a farm… and a man… and he's wearing…"

"Boots. Duh."

"Shh. He's got a long pipe and a green jacket. And his name is… Hans."

"Han Solo."

"No. Hans with an S. He's got a wagon and…"

Owen stopped, frowning. Jason made the ragged sound of a game show buzzer.

"Nope! You lose! This isn't a farm boot, you idiot. It's snakeskin! This was my dad's. Andrew! Not Hans. Face it, you can't do shit!" Jason tossed the boot onto the bed. He bolted upright, panicky, but it had missed the comic book. He fished for the Mylar wrapper and put The Precious away.

"You think you can do better?" said Owen.

"A blind man could."

"Okay. You try."

"Don't be stupid."

"Are you chicken?"

"Fine," Jason snapped. Why did that old taunt always work? He slid the comic into a long white box, securing the lid on his collection.

"Okay," said Owen, looking around. He snatched up a brown paper bag, spotted with grease, and dumped a few stale French fries into the trashcan. "I'll put an object in this bag, and you try to guess what it is. Turn your back."

Jason did, and heard a rustling behind his head.

"Okay, you can look now."

Owen produced the bag. It was rounded with some object now. Jason reached for it.

"No, don't touch yet. Just think. Try to imagine what's inside."

"Your lunch?" Jason sneered. But he closed his eyes and tried to imagine. He could hear Owen's breathing. His friend always breathed through his mouth. Allergies. Jason's nose itched. His brain grew bored with nothing to look at, and fragments of images swam in and out of his imagination.

"Strawberry," he blurted.

Owen reached into the bag, producing a white bowl. Jason had eaten Frosted Flakes from it, about three days ago. A few stuck to it like little beige fish scales.

"See?" Jason said. "I lose. There's no such thing as psychics."

"No. Look here."

Owen pointed. A design went around the sides of the bowl, a long string of vines and painted fruit. With strawberries.

"That's…" Jason began, but didn't know how to end the sentence.

"It's cool. See? What did I tell you? Do it again."

Jason closed his eyes. An image like daisies and sun and…

"Yellow." He blurted after three seconds.

"Oh my god. Open your eyes."

Owen held a bright yellow highlighter pen.

"I hadn't even put it in the bag," he said.

And so they went, for thirty minutes or more. A staple remover, a toy soldier, a sweat sock, a pencil. Jason never said precisely what was in the bag, but it was always close or related. He'd imagine a cockpit, and Owen would produce a game controller. He'd say "plate" and the object would be a CD. He made right angles with his pointer fingers, shrugging, only to have Owen pull out Eliza's knitting needles. His friend became more and more enthusiastic, but Jason became a little scared.

"You have a real gift," Owen said. "You're, like, brilliant."

Owen babbled for a long time, about astral projection and ESP, how Jason was picking up signals from Owen's own psychic powers, which had obviously been doing the broadcasting. Owen left that night full of plans and experiments, vindicated in his beliefs.

Jason sat on the bed after Owen left, thinking hard. He had no explanation for what he'd done but he knew he hadn't faked it. He couldn't believe, but he couldn't deny either.

The boot lay on the bed. His father's boot. He set it in his lap and closed his eyes.

Nothing. Empty darkness. He put his hands on the thing, on the slick snakeskin, feeling the cool of it, the roughness of the heel, the weight...

He wasn't breathing. He couldn't breathe. He couldn't open his eyes, and he was suffocating. He was glued to the bed, his hands on the boot. Then he broke the surface of the water *(the water?)* and took a great gasping breath. His hand pounded at the window of the sinking car. He felt water up his nose. Then he coughed and gagged and...

His eyes flew open and he hurled the boot at the wall. Downstairs, Charley yipped. Eliza called out a question and he answered automatically.

"I'm fine."

But he wasn't. The next day at school he avoided Owen. He ditched the one class they shared. Owen came up to him in the hall, tugging his elbow. Jason turned and snapped the boy's suspender, hard. He regretted it immediately. Owen wept, from wide hurt eyes. They didn't speak to each other for a week, but then Jason gave Owen his only copy of *Spider-Man #298* (the first appearance of

Venom), and all was forgiven.

But it was never the same. The act was breaking up. Over Christmas, Owen went with his family to Indiana, and the time apart sealed the deal.

Jason never spoke of the brown paper bag to anyone. He never admitted to himself that he'd seen his father's death. He never tried to repeat the experiment, to grab something, feel it under his hands, *read* it. Whatever that meant. No. Never again.

He wore his gloves far into the following spring.

As he pulled his dress shoe back on and tied it, the whole episode came roaring back to memory, like the tug of conscience, or a past regret. Groucho was grinning, but Jason didn't return the smile. He didn't know the secret word, and he didn't want to know it. He stood, and shuffled back to the house.

The House that Shouted.

8 THE PROPOSAL

Eliza returned around six thirty to find Jason in his room, reading comics. She told him that he'd made a wonderful impression, that Hadewych had gushed about what a bright boy he was, how clever, how polite. The incident at the bistro had, apparently, gone unreported. Jason couldn't help but feel grateful.

She inspected him, deciding that he looked nice, but she licked a napkin and was working on his ears when the high note of a car horn announced that Mr. Van Brunt was waiting.

#

Hadewych rented an apartment by Patriots Park, the top floor of a multifamily building. Valerie was his landlord. But, he said with a twinkle, he "doesn't pay her in cash." Valerie blushed at that. She lived downstairs.

Hadewych shared his place with one other person, his son Zef.

Another weird Dutch name. Ugh.

"He's about your age. He's out with his girlfriend tonight. You'll meet him at school on Monday."

"Monday?" Jason pushed his hair out of his eyes.

Yes, of course. Hadn't he guessed where they'd run off to? They'd driven Eliza down to Sleepy Hollow High so she could enroll Jason. *That's why she made herself up,* Jason realized. *Not to make an impression on her guests, but because she was going to see the administrators.* He felt better.

They didn't go upstairs when they arrived. They went into Valerie's apartment on the ground floor.

Jason stopped at the entrance, wondering.

The place was a fortress. Valerie twisted and fastened a half dozen bolts, chains and locks behind them. The walls of the cavernous space were brick, though they had looked like wood from the outside. The downstairs windows bore metal shutters that could be shut tight. There was a gun safe against one wall containing four rifles. Along another wall stretched a long shelving unit stocked with freeze-dried food and camping supplies.

Yet the place was lovely. A fringed lamp hung from a tall stem-like support, casting a crème-colored glow. Beneath it, a chenille blanket draped the arm of a pale green chaise lounge. Delicate antique furniture gathered around a low round table. He saw crystals, fashion magazines, and a stem vase with a single rose. In an octagonal side room Jason saw a grand piano scattered with sheet music. The place was a mixture of the elegant and the industrial, like Valerie herself.

She served dinner in a dining room patterned after a Chinese box. Not freeze-dried survival food, either. She had cooked for a special occasion, presenting the group with goose in onion sauce, a juicy ham, fresh-baked bread with honey, apple tart and pumpkin pie. Afterward she produced an antique silver coffee pot and tray with sugar, amaretto and cream, and invited her guests into the parlor.

As his eyes adjusted to the darkness, Jason saw what looked to be a clothesline or length of twine encircling the room; on it, the onionskin-paper rubbings that he and Eliza had made on their cemetery adventure hung like carnival banners.

The four nestled into high-backed armchairs around a fine New England fireplace trimmed with panels of slate. The fire quivered and shadows danced. Hadewych raised a glass.

"To Jason," he said.

"To Jason," the ladies repeated.

"He has been an extraordinarily good sport through what must have been a trying time. We are all sorry that you've been 'out-of-the-loop' and let us begin by apologizing to you."

"Okay," Jason said, embarrassed.

"The three of us," said Hadewych, "have been working on this project for so long, it was easy to forget how strange and sudden it would seem to you. I hope we can help you understand."

He produced a leather satchel from beside the hearth, opened it, and took out a piece of paper encased in a plastic sleeve like one of Jason's comic books.

"This letter was left to me by my parents. Mother's name was Christina Greyfield. My father was Jonus Van Brunt. You can see his tombstone here." He indicated one of the rubbings. Jason could barely see the date of 1972. Jonus had died when Hadewych was just a boy.

"Jonus Van Brunt received this letter from Tonnis Van Brunt, short for Anthony. He was my grandfather."

The next rubbing was confidently made, the dates clear. 1898 to 1950.

"Before him, it came from his father Nicholas, who received it from his father Cornelius, who received it from his father Dylan."

These three rubbings grew rougher. The stones had weathered unevenly. On the last, the name **DYLAN VAN BRUNT** was arrogant and angry-looking; a hollow-eyed face scowled above the lettering.

"We don't have a rubbing for Dylan's father, Abraham—the author of this letter. Yes, Brom again. Born August 31st, 1780. Died November 22nd, 1850. He's buried in the Van Brunt tomb in Sleepy Hollow Cemetery, alongside his father, Hermanus. It's not marked anymore, thank heavens, or else *Legend* fanciers would have chipped it down to nothing for souvenirs. But I could show it to you, if you wanted. The tomb is impressive, though a shadow of what it was once, when the Van Brunts were rich and the cemetery was young."

Get to the point, Jason thought.

"A little more amaretto, Val, and warm it up." He handed Valerie his cup. "Why don't you read the letter for us now?"

He presented the paper to Jason. Eliza adjusted the dimmer on a lamp at his elbow, providing light. Her knobby old hand patted his arm. The letter had been written on parchment, the words in rusty ink across the vellum, spidery, difficult to make out.

"I can't read this."

"Of course not. Hardly anyone can. The Van Brunts have always written to each other in Old Dutch. Sorry. The translation is behind."

Jason turned the page over and found a piece of white cardstock taped to the outside.

"November 10th, 1850."

"Twelve days before he died," said Hadewych.

"My dear Dylan," Jason continued.

"His son," Hadewych said, pointing at the angry headstone.

Jason frowned. He would never get through it if Hadewych kept interrupting.

"My dear Dylan, I have buried what you seek. You will not recover it. She is gone, our Agathe, and her prize rests in my hands at last. Looking upon this thing, I know I shall not keep it or use it myself. I cannot, though this be, ay, the foundation stone upon which our fortunes rest. I leave you with ample stone, my son, stone enough. You have no need of the Horseman's treasure."

Jason glanced up. Hadewych prodded him onward.

"I have built within the new graveyard a tomb where I shall lie with my sire, when God calls and when it shall be his mercy and pleasure to accept this poor sinner. I would take the boon into my own grave, were it not for your demanding want of the thing, which I would not satisfy. Therefore in our tomb I have buried, in service to his widow whom we [cannot] find, the body of the unfortunate Absolom [sic] Crane. I think it meet that this son of old Ichabod and I shall lie side to side for eternity. As I share Irving's Legend with the father, I shall share a tomb with the son. It is with Absalom that the thing is buried. You shall not look upon it again, for without consent of the man's widow he may not be raised.

"Do not long for that of which I have deprived you. My quarry you shall have, and my gold, and whatever you—"

Jason turned the page over, frowned, and looked up from the letter.

"It cuts off. Is there more?" he said.

"That's all we—have," said Valerie.

"It's two-hundred years old, Honey," said Eliza. "We're lucky to have that much."

"Do you see?" whispered Hadewych.

"What's the Horseman's treasure?" said Jason.

"We don't—know," said Valerie.

Eliza bent forward. "We have some guesses. Hadewych laughs at me, but I say it's his head."

"I don't think so, my dear. Irving made the Horseman up. More likely it's a jewel, or some other item. 'Horseman' could be a coded reference to something we don't know about. Who can say, two hundred years later? My family has argued this for generations. What did the letter mean, what is the Treasure, how did Crane die, what did Dylan want so badly, and why did old Brom hide it away? The bickering has gone on for two centuries. If Dylan knew, he never told anyone. He died in the Civil War, when his own son was a baby."

Jason glanced at Dylan's rubbing, then to Cornelius the son. Dylan's read "died 1864." Cornelius's said "born 1862."

Poor kid.

"So," said Jason, "Brom buried this thing, whatever it is, in the Van Brunt family tomb." He was curious despite himself.

"Yes, here in Sleepy Hollow Cemetery."

"Then why don't you just dig it up?"

"Ah, well…" Hadewych beamed, and looked around. The ladies leaned forward, turning to Jason. "That's where you come in."

"Me? Why me?"

"Think about it. Brom's son wanted the Treasure very badly, so what does the old scoundrel do? Plays a trick. What a trick. It's very clever. He buried the Treasure with the body of Absalom Crane. We don't know how Absalom died, or why he was even in Sleepy Hollow. His wife was somewhere in… uh…"

"Bridgeport," said Jason. "Her name was Annabel."

"Good. So old Brom buried Absalom, where? In the Van Brunt tomb. Do you see what he did? How he kept the Treasure from his son? Why we have never been able to dig it up?"

"No. I'm not following."

Hadewych turned to Eliza, ceding the stage to her.

Eliza touched Jason's arm. "Pour me a coffee, dear." As Jason did so, she said, "The rule that all cemeteries follow is strict. If you want permission to open a tomb, you have to be a descendant. Hadewych can prove his descent from Brom. He could go to the cemetery right now and authorize them to dig the old boy up and put him on display for Halloween. Sorry, Hadewych. I want Jason to understand. But he can't open *Absalom's* grave. Absalom's not a Van Brunt. And you can't do it either, because the tomb doesn't belong to your family."

"Brom's last trick." Hadewych lit a cigarette. "In order to open the tomb, and to find this thing, whatever it is, *two* people have to request the disinterment. The descendant of the tomb's occupant, and the descendant of the tomb's owner. They have to collaborate."

He blew smoke.

"And that means *you*… and *me*."

9 THE CRUSH

"Forget it!"

Jason gaped at the others.

"I'm not digging up anybody," he said.

"You don't have to," said Eliza.

"All you have to do is sign a few papers," said Hadewych.

"I'm sorry, but no."

"Honey," said Eliza, "we've worked on this so long."

"We need you," said Valerie.

"Without your signature it won't happen," said Hadewych. "You and I have to go in together. Believe me, I've tried. I met with the head of the cemetery. I showed him the tomb, I explained who I am. But he told me flat out that if the name on the slab says Crane, a Crane has to request it."

"We went looking—for you," said Valerie.

"Valerie said we should try. I didn't think it was possible," said Hadewych. "I mean, it was silly to even hope. A direct descendant of Ichabod? If such a person existed, I thought they'd have made themselves known. *The Legend* is big business. As short as it is, only a few dozen pages, it's spawned a huge industry. Movies, books, adaptations on television every Halloween. This whole town bubbles with *Legend* events. They recite it aloud in the Old Dutch Church, the annual Haunted House is called Horseman's Hollow. The football team is the Horsemen. Did you see the name of the place where we ate this morning?"

Jason shook his head.

"The Horseman restaurant! This town has an Ichabod Street, a

Van Tassel street. Crane Avenue, Irving Lane. The only character that doesn't have at least one stretch of asphalt named after him is my ancestor. He's the villain, you see. There's no Van Brunt Avenue. No Bones Boulevard. They'll name a shopping center after Gunpowder the plough horse before they name one after Brom. Anyway, with all this, what are the chances that Ichabod's descendant is still around? Wouldn't he make himself known? The Van Brunts have never put themselves forward, but surely someone descended from Ichabod would. But, no. The line vanished. Far as we could tell. We thought your branch of the Cranes died out or, if we found you, we wouldn't be able to prove your descent. But then we met Eliza."

"And I put the pieces together. I'd done half the research already."

Hadewych spun to the opposite side of the room, pointing at the other banner of rubbings.

"William Crane. Soldier. Died 1792. Ichabod Crane, 1775 to 1849."

"I found him on Staten Island," Eliza said.

Ichabod's epitaph was drawn in small square letters:

Sacred to the memory of Hon. Ichabod Crane.

"Absalom, Ichabod's son, is here in Sleepy Hollow. Then we have Absalom's son Jesse, Jesse's son Jack, Jack's son Adam, then Andrew Crane." The rubbings fluttered as Hadewych gestured to each. Finally, he put his hand on the arm of Jason's armchair. "And Andrew's son, Jason. What do you say?"

The adults waited for his answer. He tried to think, but he was looking at the last rubbing in the sequence. He had never seen his father's grave. He felt guilty for that, and he couldn't drag his eyes from the letters.

ANDREW CRANE
Beloved Husband and Father.

"Jason," whispered Eliza. "Say something."

He pushed his hair out of his eyes.

"Can I think about it?"

"How long—do you need?" said Valerie.

"I don't know. It's a lot to… take in."

"That's fine. We're not going anywhere," said Hadewych, looking disappointed. "But we can't put this off too long. If we decide to request the disinterment, *if*, it should be before winter whips in."

"I'm not saying I'll do anything. I just think Eliza and I should talk first. Alone."

"Of course."

#

Hadewych drove them home in the silver Mercedes. At the door, he kissed Eliza on the cheek and handed her the car keys.

"I'll walk home. I shouldn't get used to driving it," he said. "Goodnight, young Mister Crane. I hope you say yes. I think we could have some fun. Whatever you decide is fine."

Charley yipped and scratched the door. Eliza went in.

"Shush, you little monster," she cackled.

Hadewych and Jason shook hands.

"I'll give you a call," said Jason.

Hadewych nodded. He turned and ambled down the hill, his head down, hands in pockets. A waning gibbous moon hung over the Hudson.

#

Jason helped Eliza undress, draping the blue cardigan over a chair as she slipped under the covers. He shucked his dress shoes (was he getting a blister?) and climbed onto the pink bedspread. He sat cross-legged, his back against the wall. He hugged a pillow across his chest and sighed.

"So you brought me on a treasure hunt."

"Tell the truth. You're excited, aren't you?"

Jason broke a smile, immediately suppressed it.

"You can't fool me, Jason Crane. I know you too well." She patted his hand. "I know you too, too well…" She looked sad. She squeezed his fingers. "What happens to you when I'm gone, Jason? You're so young. Too young to be out on your own. I… I want you to have… oh, a purpose. A path. Every one of us has a path, Honey. And we need somebody else, sometimes, to put our feet on it. To

61

drag us there, kicking and screaming, and… anyway. What do you want to be, my love?"

Jason ran his thumb across the back of her hand. It was spotted, thin, but strong. He wanted to weep, for no damn good reason.

"I don't know," he said.

"Yes, you do. You just won't admit it. What do you think I want to hear? Hmm? Doctor, lawyer, Indian chief? No, not for my Jason." Her hand left his and pushed the hair out of his eyes. It laid back, smooth, for once. "My Jason is better. He's a hero, this one. I want you to have a heroic life. Like me." She grinned. "Oh, I may not look it. Old lady. Can't see, can't walk, can't dress herself. But I was a hero. Heroine, whatever you call it, once. I flew airplanes when I was twenty, and girls just didn't back then. When I was hungry, I made nets out of window screens and fished in Reed Creek. I've had seven husbands, seven honeymoons, six divorces, one true love… I raised your mother. I made money and traveled, and did things. And I want that for you. All that life, without the heartbreak of course, though that's part of it."

Charley whined from the floor next to the bed. Eliza glanced down.

"Help her up?"

Jason laid his belly across the old woman's legs and hoisted the dog. It scrambled over him, nails scratching his shoulder. It turned a circle next to Eliza before settling in.

"But what will Jason be? I've wondered. What would be big enough for my boy? Where will he belong?" She scratched the poodle's black head.

Jason sighed. "I guess I'll go off to college and study… history."

"And then? Be a teacher?"

"No. I'm not the schoolmaster type. That's Ichabod." He grinned. So did Eliza.

"True. Then, what?"

He hugged the pillow again, shrugged.

"When you were a little boy, I used to take you to Pennywhistle Park, remember? You loved the rides, my word. Those danged bumper cars. You'd go back and forth and round and round and barf your insides out and go again. I'd buy you ice cream and you'd point and say 'Grandma, who's that there on the horse?' You'd point at some general, some statue there. 'Oh, Grandma, I think that is an adventurer.' You said it so cute. 'What did he do?' 'Why is he here?' 'Why, why, why?'"

Jason remembered Eliza bringing out the Encyclopedia Britannica. How he lay on the floor with her, looking at pictures.

"And when you were, oh, eleven-twelve. You wanted to buy that book of magic. Out of the back of a comic book? 'Cast a spell on your enemies!' All that rubbish. I put an end to that. Twenty-four-ninety-nine plus shipping? Lord. Oh, you may like your science books now, but you loved your spooky stuff once. The things I'd catch you reading. *Varney the Vampire and the Feast of Blood.*"

Jason smiled, remembered the cover, a pen and ink drawing of the bloodthirsty fiend rising from his grave.

"Old horror comics," Eliza scoffed. "But I never could get you to read *Sleepy Hollow.* I loved that story. And, when I was a little girl… oh, maybe this is just an old woman being silly."

"What?"

"I had a crush. Such a crush. Mister Walt Disney made a movie out of my favorite. This was 1949. *Ichabod and Mister Toad.* The 'Toad' part was dreadful. I used to duck out when it started. But I went back and back again to see the Headless Horseman."

"You had a crush on the Headless Horseman?"

"No," she said, giggling and covering her face with her hands. "On Brom."

"Oh, God."

"Brom Bones, the cartoon Brom. Black-haired and lantern-jawed and all muscled up. Woo, baby!"

"I don't need to hear this."

They laughed, easily, for the first time since they'd moved to the Hollow.

"I hated that Katrina. So fickle and la-de-da. I thought oh, you little bitch. If I had a man like that I'd show him a time."

"Not listening," Jason put the pillow over his head.

"That was my first big crush. Brom Bones standing in front of that fireplace singing about the Headless Horseman. In that deep, bass voice that just made my little girl toes curl up. I love a man's voice. I can't listen to the women singers. None of my husbands had a voice like Brom, I'll tell you that. Except for Arthur. All the rest of them, there wasn't a man I couldn't have snapped into little pieces and picked my teeth with. Maybe there aren't any real Broms anymore. Maybe I never settled for less…"

Jason listened intently now. She so rarely talked about such things. Eliza was never big on self-analysis.

"And so, I meet the great-great-great-great-grandson of the *real* Brom and, oh sue me. I got carried away. I know the real one was nothing like the cartoon. And I'm not angling for husband number eight, if that's what you're thinking. Hadewych is half my age. But… I do like his voice. I can't say I care for *Valerie's*—"

They laughed.

"What happened to her?" Jason said, his hand straying to his throat.

"Oh, that's a sad story. Her *mother* attacked her. Don't ask her about it. That's why she's got all those locks and guns. Poor thing is a bit paranoid. Hadewych is such a good man to love a woman as disadvantaged as that. So I kept an open mind and… they've got me believing."

"In what?"

"Magic."

"Oh, come on. You know that's a pile of… bunk."

"Maybe. But what if? What if we find something… magical? What if?"

Charley whined a little, concerned.

"I have a lot of friends, old people like me. They're all finding religion. They go to church, they pray, they make life hell for us poor sinners. I hardly recognize them anymore. They're all getting ready for their judgment. 'Cramming for the final,' I call it. But I'm not like that. What I want is one last gasp of… life. Magic. Don't look so sad. This is good. Look at us. In Sleepy Hollow, just like when I was a little girl in a movie theater. It's real. We're part of it. It's fate. My daughter married a descendant of old Ichabod. And I never knew. What a trick or treat. But I don't have many adventures left, Jason. I thought we could have this one, together. It may be our last, you know."

"Are you okay?"

She hesitated, and put a hand on his knee. "Honey, I am way past my expiration date. I've got my pills, and my hands are better. But I can't do stairs like I used to. I can't see good. And, you know, bits of me are gonna start falling off any day. But that's fine. It's human. I've had my time. And it was a damn good time. Don't look so puny. It's a fact of life. So we got to face it. Why do you think I've been leaving you on your own so much? Because I don't love you? I miss you every minute I'm gone. But you'll have to be an adult sooner than other young people. So you've got to learn. And start early. This will be your house when I go. And Charley'll be your puppy dog. You take care of her."

Jason nodded and scratched the poodle behind her ears. Charley growled.

"You'll have plenty of money, I'm not worried about that," she said.

"Let's talk about something else…"

"Shush. But I am worried that you don't have people, Honey. I'm worried about you being all alone. Now, Hadewych's son is your third cousin. His great-grandfather and yours were brothers."

Jason made a face. "That's nothing. That's—"

"He's all you've got, Honey. The only family I could find you in this whole world. Try to make friends here. Put down roots. Let me go to my grave—"

He took her right hand in both of his. She patted them with her left.

"Let me go to my grave knowing you've got a home."

Her eyes had grown fierce. His throat had tightened. He nodded, and she looked satisfied.

"So you want to spend your last… however long… digging up a body?" said Jason.

"Solving a mystery. My last adventure. And your first. Don't say no. I think you're made to be an explorer, like the King Tut fellow on your mirror."

"Howard Carter."

"That's the one. That's what you *want* to be. I know it. I've always known it. My little explorer. I want you to have a heroic life, like me. I won't let you turn into a bore, young man. I'm going to drag you to where your path begins, kicking and screaming if I have to."

"Why didn't you tell me all this back in Augusta?"

"I wanted you to feel the place, first. And I wanted to live here. In an old house on a hill, with the millpond and the Old Dutch Church and the bridge where it all happened. Or would have, if it were true…"

She patted his knee and put her hand to her head as if suffering a headache.

"I'm sorry if I did wrong by you, Jason. I was… taken up."

"Will you promise me something?"

"The moon and the stars," she said.

"Just this. Remember that cemetery in Bridgeport? On the hill?" She nodded. "If we're going to dig up Absalom Crane, let's not rebury him here. Let's move him to be with his wife. And let's fix up that Bridgeport cemetery. Or at least find him a plot of his own here that people can visit. Okay? He deserves better than somebody else's old tomb."

"You're such a good boy."

"And promise me. Promise me you'll stay away from tarot cards and always tell me what's going on."

"Aye-aye, sir." She saluted smartly. "This is going to be fun."

We're digging up a dead body and she thinks it's fun. But it kind of is.

He took out his cell phone.

"Give me Hadewych's number."

As he dialed, as the phone rang, his stomach was a beehive, his whole body impatient to reach tomorrow. *I know what this is,* he thought. *This is the feeling little monkeys get before they leap off their first branch, or that baby sparrows get before their mother noses them off the edge of the nest. This is the sensation of knowing you are about to be tested, that you're about to fall into something.*

Someone answered.

"Hello?" Hadewych sounded half-asleep.

We always jump, you know. People can't help it. They yell Geronimo, they kiss the girl on the stoop. They step onstage, into the ring, onto the dance floor, into battle. They chip away stone to find the treasure in the tomb. They risk curses and dark magic and failure and fraud. They risk life, and jump.

We just can't, can't, help it.

"I'm in," said Jason, and hung up.

10 SLEEPY HOLLOW CEMETERY

Hadewych stood by the gate of the Old Dutch Church.

"You ready?"

Jason nodded. He'd worn his only suit and had tried to tame his hair, unsuccessfully.

Locust and elm trees bristled in the distance. The last shimmer of September sun had bled away. They skirted a gate of wrought iron. Beyond it, Jason caught glimpses of headstones, grouped within plots partitioned by low iron railings, one family separated from the next. Above ground, at least.

"We're going to the offices, on the other side of the cemetery. I thought we should walk a bit and agree on what we'll say."

"I'm not going to lie," said Jason.

"Of course not. But you don't need to mention the Treasure or the letter. Understood?"

They trudged uphill. The church looked like a bullet of fieldstones, flat end to the street, rounded cone of the nose pointing east toward the river. His eyes roamed from the spire and weathervane to the high arched windows. He could see the outline of pews inside and an embroidered cloth slung over the pulpit railing. Two harvest wreaths made russet circles against the whitewash of the door. He paused to read the plaque:

Old Dutch Church of Sleepy Hollow
Church of the Manor of Philipsburgh
Erected by Frederick Philipse
1697

They rounded the corner and Jason saw the graveyard. Row by row they stood, like fins on the back of a beast: grey headstones, red headstones, baby headstones, broken headstones, tilted headstones, fallen headstones, headstones and headstones and headstones all marching up the hill.

"Do we have to go this way?" Jason said.

"Scared?"

"No."

"There's no sidewalk north of the bridge. Come on."

They trudged along.

Jason wasn't scared, but walking over graves isn't like strolling through a meadow; it's like creeping through a barracks at midnight, stepping over cots and trying not to wake the sleepers.

"Look here," Hadewych said, stopping. The stone to his right had eroded away but Jason could still read "Catriena Ecker Van Tessel" beneath a wide-eyed face with wings, effigy of a rising soul.

"Is that…"

"Katrina? The locals think so. See how they put the little pumpkins on graves that are *Legend* related? But they have it wrong. Her married name was Van Brunt." Hadewych poked the pumpkin with a finger. It fell, bouncing down the row and into a shallow depression strangely empty of markers.

"Leave it," said Hadewych.

They reached the end of the Old Dutch Burial Ground and entered Sleepy Hollow Cemetery. They strolled on shady pathways, slipped between mausoleums, beneath weeping statuary, down paths dotted with urns and wreaths and flowerpots, past Martin and Vale and Adams and Delovan and Stringer and Johnson and Smith and the tomb of the unknowns, onto a driveway playful with somersaulting leaves.

A man waited at the administrative center. "It's about time. The appointment's at eleven." He was about fifty, balding, with the feeblest attempt at a comb-over. His accent was southern. Texas, maybe. "You must be the boy," he said. He shifted his cigarette into his left hand and stuck out his right. "Vernon McCaffrey, Junior."

"Jason." He shook the man's hand.

"Vernon is *our* funeral director," said Hadewych. "He works for the two of us and us only. Once we get everything signed, he'll be overseeing the actual exhumation."

Jason fought the urge to wipe his palm on his jeans. He was thinking about formaldehyde.

"Let's not keep them," said McCaffrey. He tamped his cigarette on someone's marker and entered the building.

Hadewych stopped at the door. "One more thing, Jason. How old are you?"

"Sixteen."

"No. Eighteen. Here." He handed Jason a small card of plastic. It was a photo ID from the state of New York, a driver's license with Jason's picture, but his birth date had been pushed back two years.

"This is phony."

"They won't check."

"I'm not giving them this."

"Yes. Well. Unfortunately, a minor can't sign for a disinterment."

"Then we call it off."

"It's just a technical point."

"Does Eliza know you're...?"

"Of course. Look, you can use it this once and then throw it away. Who is it hurting?"

"I told you I wouldn't lie."

"They'll just glance at it. They'll be looking at the ancestry documents mostly."

"And did you change my age on those, too?"

"You said you were in."

Jason would have turned back and walked home but he thought of Eliza saying "I don't have many adventures left."

McCaffrey's sweaty face appeared at the door.

"Are you comin'?"

"Are we?" said Hadewych.

Jason nodded, and pocketed the ID.

#

James Osorio, superintendent of Sleepy Hollow Cemetery, leaned forward across his desk. "All right. What are you *really* up to?" His voice was knowing, winking. His eyes flicked back and forth from Hadewych to Jason. Jason looked away. Hadewych did not. "Your name is Crane, yes?" Osorio said, putting on glasses and scrutinizing the paperwork.

"That's right," said Jason.

"But this has nothing to do with *The Legend*?"

"No," said Hadewych.

"Oh, come on. I wasn't born yesterday." He leaned back in his chair, chuckling to himself. "Van Brunt. Crane. Those two names together, digging up a grave in my cemetery, three weeks before Halloween? What sort of show are you planning?"

"There's no show," said Hadewych. "In fact, I'd like your assurance that the whole matter will be kept between us."

"You're not after publicity?"

"Furthest thing from our minds."

Osorio bent forward and his glasses reflected Hadewych's oh-so-winning smile.

"I don't believe that," he said, returning to the papers.

Osorio's office was a little crypt itself. The narrow windows were Gothic, peaked on top, suitable either for a church building or for pouring oil down on barbarian invaders. The walls were checkered with photographs of the grounds. No fewer than seven featured the Headless Horseman, an actor on horseback clopping among the graves—backlit, raising a sword.

"Let Mister Crane talk."

Jason pushed the hair out of his eyes. He saw his own reflection in the man's eyeglasses now.

"What's this about, son?" Osorio said.

"Does it matter?" said Hadewych, his voice tight. "We're not asking. The paperwork is in order and it's our right to request a disinterment. Our reasons are not your business."

"Everything that happens here is my business. My job is to protect the dignity of the cemetery." Osorio pointed a finger. "You've been after me for years to open this grave, Van Brunt. I think I have a right to know why."

Hadewych's smile remained, but the face around it whitened and hardened, transforming him into a marble cherub.

"Because *I* want it," whispered Jason. Hadewych and Osorio turned to face him. "I don't want my ancestor to be part of all this *Legend* stuff. I'm sorry. This is a beautiful cemetery," Jason gestured to the framed photographs, "but is *that* dignified, sir? A fake Headless Horseman riding across people's graves? Anybody named Crane is going to end up as a tourist attraction if they stay here. Not a person, just a tourist attraction. And *that's* why I want him dug up and moved. He deserves better. Don't you agree?"

Osorio frowned. Jason waited for him to bluster and become indignant. But the man's face softened. He leaned back, took the glasses off, and rubbed his eyes.

"You're right," Osorio said, "You're absolutely right." He pushed the papers across the desk. Hadewych signed and passed them to Jason. Jason hesitated, but wrote his name on the dotted line, dating it October eleventh. Osorio stood. "I'll just… photocopy this, and we'll go check out the tomb. Good deal?" He held Jason's fake ID.

Jason cringed, but nodded.

Osorio hesitated at the door, near a photo of the Horseman menacing a headstone. He took the photo down, tucked it under his arm and exited. The door clicked behind him.

Hadewych was staring at Jason, stunned. Vernon McCaffrey began to clap slowly.

"The boy's got balls," he said.

"Excellent," whispered Hadewych. "Excellent job. So much for not lying."

Jason stood, collected his jacket, and looked down at Hadewych.

"I didn't."

#

The Van Brunt Family tomb gripped the side of a hill with grey stone fingers. Retaining walls parted the earth, creating a narrow pathway down into the heart of the hill. An ancient stump, four feet in diameter, protruded from the right shoulder like a guard tower. A former branch had grown from the side of the stump to become a new tree; it twisted diagonally over the tomb and thrust upward in surrender or terror, trailing needle-thin twigs and brown garlands. Beneath it lay jumbled stones that had been the stairs to the tomb itself, a hollow cavity mortared and re-mortared over centuries.

Jason put a hand on the rust-brown bars of the gate and turned on the flashlight. A thrill ran through him. He half-expected to see an Egyptian mummy lying in a sarcophagus, wrapped in linen, riding its stone lifeboat into eternity upon a river of gold and alabaster.

The flashlight revealed a white marble floor and rows of bone boxes carved from sandstone or limestone. The corners of these were chipped, the lids cracked. Dirt and leaves had blown in, obscuring the inscriptions. He saw fragments of a bird's nest, a few feathers. His light caught two yellow eyes, feral, staring back at him. His breath stopped. Some small animal chittered and ran into a crevice.

"The Horseman's Treasure," whispered Hadewych, and Jason thought he could hear the word "Horseman" echo back at them from the tomb.

In a niche above the boxes perched the crude bust of a woman. Her features were leonine, severe, her hair short. A chip of stone had broken from one eye. A dark horizontal line sliced through the neck. The bust had not been carved in one piece.

"Who's that?" Jason said.

"Agathe."

The flashlight cast Agathe's silhouette on the wall behind. It rose and fell with the motion of Jason's hand.

"Brom built our house for her, you said."

"Oh, yes," said Hadewych. "She was the great matriarch of our family. Amazing woman."

"So, where is her box?"

"There isn't one. She disappeared. Her body was never found. She was ninety years old." Hadewych sighed. "Another Van Brunt mystery."

Someone cleared his throat. They turned to find Osorio waiting, hands in pockets.

"If you're done here, I need to get back to the office," Osorio said.

Jason rattled the chain on the gate.

"How do we get in?" he said.

"It's not that easy, son. It'll take about a week to file things. We'll call you then."

"McCaffrey will take care of it," said Hadewych.

He clasped Jason's shoulder and walked away. McCaffrey waited down the hill, smoking. Hadewych and Osorio joined the funeral director and the three men ambled down the path, back toward the administration building.

Jason stayed behind. He played his flashlight over the boxes again. *Hello, Absalom,* he thought. *Guess who I am. Annabel sends her love.*

"'Ey! What you up to?"

Jason spun, but saw no one.

"Up 'ere, mate. You barmy?"

A dark-haired boy sat perched on the stump above. His work clothes were brown with dirt and he carried a weed-eater. He wore safety glasses and enormous noise-canceling earmuffs that made him look like Princess Leia's yardman.

"I'm just looking," said Jason. "I've got... family inside." He turned the flashlight off.

"Family in there? In that old 'ole? Blimey! Not bloomin' likely. You're mental you are!"

Jason rolled his eyes. It was the worst fake Cockney accent he had ever heard.

"Do you always talk like that?" he said.

"Like wot, guv'nor?"

"Like an extra from Harry Potter?"

The boy frowned.

"Not buying it, huh?" The accent was gone. "Fine. It's a work in progress." He jumped down, extended a hand. "Joey Osorio. Future Academy Award winner."

The hand was dark brown with dirt. Jason shook it anyway. It was good to see somebody his own age.

"Jason."

Joey wiped a hand on his overalls, cocked a thumb over his shoulder. "You know that guy?"

"Which? The superintendent?"

"No. That's my dad. The other one. Van Brunt. The blond guy."

"Yeah." Jason grimaced.

"Not your best friend?"

"Definitely not."

"Mine neither. He's bad news, brother. I caught him trying to break in there once." Joey pointed at the tomb. "I swear he had a chain cutter, like for stealing bikes?"

"That wouldn't surprise me."

"He shoved it in a bag pronto, so I couldn't prove anything. But, oh, did he put on a show. He said 'don't you know who I am' and I should watch myself. The guy's a bully."

"I know."

"He bullies his son, too."

"Zef, you mean?"

"Uh-huh. You know him?"

"I haven't met him yet," said Jason.

"Zef's a good guy," said Joey. He sat at the end of the retaining wall, hugging the weed-eater. Jason recognized him now. He was the boy who had jogged past the house on Jason's first day at Gory Brook.

"So why the British accent?" Jason said.

"I have an acting job."

"Congratulations."

"Thank you. I am a Redcoat zombie at this year's Horseman's Hollow."

"The haunted house? I am impressed."

"You should be. I'm the youngest zombie they've ever hired. Two callbacks. I had to skip school. That's between us, by the way."

"What's the school here like?" Jason said, sitting.

"It's a school." Joey shrugged. "Not much of a drama program. Plenty of jocks."

"How about history? I start on Monday."

"Then you're just in time for Halloween. Halloween's big here."

"I noticed."

Joey waved an arm. Beneath them, down the slope, Sleepy Hollow Cemetery spread in curved roads and platoons of headstones.

"The Halloween capital of the world, my friend, and I'm the gravedigger."

"Alas, poor Yorick." said Jason.

Joey beamed. "'I knew him, Horatio. A fellow of infinite jest, of most excellent fancy.' I'll make a great Hamlet, don't you think?"

"You need a skull," said Jason.

"Yes I do. Get me one."

Jason cocked a thumb back towards the tomb. "Get me some chain cutters."

They laughed together. Down the slope, a car stopped and James Osorio honked the horn.

"Joey," Osorio said, "You're on the clock!"

Joey jumped up. "Sorry, Dad. I, uh—" He held up the weed-eater. "Jason here was walking past and I didn't want to hit him with rocks and stuff."

"Yeah," Jason said, "it was my fault, sir."

"Then Mister Crane should keep walking, shouldn't he?" said Osorio.

"I was just going," said Jason.

"He was just going," said Joey.

Joey's father shook his head and drove away.

"*What's* your name?" said Joey.

"Jason…." He hesitated and then plunged ahead. "Jason Crane."

"Crane?"

"Yup."

"*Crane?* And you're starting classes Monday? At Sleepy Hollow?"

Jason nodded.

"Ouch," said Joey.

"Will they rag on me, do you think?"

"Oh, my dear Ichabod." Joey donned the earmuffs and gassed the weed-eater. "Run for your life."

#

Jason met Zef Van Brunt on Saturday night.

The Horsemen, Sleepy Hollow's football team, had an away game scheduled, followed by the midseason Spirit Dance. Hadewych volunteered his son to pick Jason up and introduce him around the event.

Jason didn't want to leave Eliza. She'd had a bad spell Friday night—her chest had started hurting and she'd been shaking and sweating. But Eliza insisted that he go. She wanted him to make new friends and settle in, and she fretted that he'd missed too much of the semester and would find himself shut out socially. "Half their little groups start clumping together in the first week," she said.

No, thought Jason, *half their little groups start clumping together in the third grade.*

That morning she took him to Revel's Menswear in Tarrytown and bought him a new blazer and tie. Zef showed up around seven-thirty wearing a maroon hoodie and jeans. He was blond, like his father, but had thick dark eyebrows; he was almost as tall as Jason but broader and square-jawed, a sullen teenaged Viking. He mumbled greetings to Eliza and directed Jason out to the car. He never took his hands out of his pockets or looked up from his shoes.

Zef's car was a dented blue cruiser with one green door on the driver's side. It was a piece of junk parked next to Eliza's Mercedes. Jason came round the passenger side.

"Back seat," said Zef.

They climbed in and Zef cranked the stereo so he wouldn't have to talk to his passenger. The speakers were powerful, and right behind Jason's head. It sounded like the drummer was beating a herd of cats to death.

They drove down Gory Brook but turned right on Broadway, away from the school.

"So I hear we're cousins," Jason shouted, trying to be heard over a guitar solo.

Zef snapped the music off.

"You don't go for that bullshit, do you?" he said.

"No. Guess not." Jason loosened his tie. So this was his only family in the world. Great. "Where are we going?"

"I have to pick up Kate."

"Kate?"

"My girlfriend," he said. He sounded morose and edgy. They drove in silence the rest of the way. The silence was louder than the noise had been.

That kid Joey had called Zef "a good guy," but Jason didn't see it. He wasn't too surprised, though. If he had lived under Hadewych's thumb his whole life, he'd be angry too. He stared at the back of Zef's head for a while, trying to guess his story, but then he caught Zef looking back at him in the rear view mirror so he turned away and watched the road.

They drove past the Old Dutch Church and cemetery, turned onto a winding street, drifted past a large reservoir ringed with red and gold trees. The sun dipped behind these, and you couldn't tell where the leaves and sunset met, the two were so alike.

Jason didn't look forward to the dance. He'd be a third wheel, an unwanted guest, tagging behind Zef and his date all night, surrounded by strangers. How had this become his life? So much had changed. When would something change for the better?

"Wait," said Zef.

He parked in front of a colonial-style house on a hill. Zef left the car at the curb and walked up the driveway. A small jack-o'-lantern flickered on the porch, the first smile Jason had seen all night. A middle-aged man greeted Zef at the door before he had even knocked, throwing arms wide and hugging him. He was tall, fit, with wavy brown hair, pinstripe shirt and suspenders. The girl's father, Jason guessed, and a big fan of Zef. The man gestured inside, but Zef shook his head and pointed at the car. The man nodded and disappeared. Zef stood on the doorstep for a long time, hands in pockets. He walked to the porch railing and looked up. So did Jason. The first few stars were appearing.

Then so did she.

She was tomboyish, this girl. He could tell by the way she swung the door closed, the way she jumped down all three stairs at once, the way she walked straight across the lawn, ignoring the path, leaving Zef in her wake. But she wore her femininity as a party dress tonight, something for a special occasion, her dark blonde hair pinned in back except for a few wisps that curled in front of her ears and brushed her cheeks. She had dimples and a mouth made for laughing. She wore a light fuzzy jacket over a black top of thin silk, and as she slipped into the car, Jason's eyes trailed to a tiny sliver of exposed skin above the waist of her jeans.

"Hey," Kate said. "Eyes up here, mister."

She'd seen him looking. He blushed and turned away, though she'd sounded amused, not angry. He glanced back at the girl but she was watching Zef slip behind the wheel, her expression one of pure adoration.

Oh, well, Jason thought.

She threw her arms around Zef and kissed him.

For a long time.

11 HOME OF THE HORSEMEN

The headlights of Zef's cruiser swept across the sign: **Sleepy Hollow High: Home of the Horsemen**. Dozens of cars climbed the hill to the school, windows rolled down, every radio tuned to a different song. Jason saw a girl with a carnation in her hair, swinging a handbag on a gold strap, pretty, a freshman probably, sparkling with just enough childish delight that Jason guessed she would be skipping to the dance if others weren't watching. Jason saw low necklines, short skirts, ruffles, pleats, and bright earrings. Three girls paraded through traffic, arm in arm down the middle of the street. Above the entire scene, two baby-faced boys with scraggly chins sat on a huge paint-splattered boulder, laughing at the show and smoking cloves. One had a megaphone in his lap.

The parking lot snarled with student drivers and brake lights. Zef swore and drummed the steering wheel. He honked and waved to a group of boys. These bounded over, battering the hood with their palms, bowing to Kate, hands to their hearts. They wore matching maroon jackets and gap-toothed grins. The tallest ran in front of the cruiser and directed traffic, making a gap for Zef's car. Kate leaned out the window and hugged the boy's neck. This gave Jason a view of rounded denim, rivets and long curving seams. Zef gassed the car playfully, the hug broke, and Kate slipped back inside. Someone behind them wailed, "I love you, Kate!" with exaggerated despair. Boys laughed and pounded on the trunk. Zef stuck an arm out the window and raised his middle finger in farewell. The wheels punched off a speed bump and Jason's teeth clacked together.

They pulled in alongside the football field, perched on the hill above the school. Four lights blazed down from a stainless steel cross arm. The shadow of a goalpost stabbed across the field, a broken pitchfork. A painted Headless Horseman threw his blazing football across the scoreboard.

Kate made tracks towards a distant line of yellow buses. Jason was out of the car next. The cold air bit his cheeks and he missed the car heater. He stood on a strip of grass, pulling on his jacket, watching Kate go. Zef had introduced her to Jason on the way over, but after a few minutes of polite back-and-forth she'd turned her attention back to Zef, talking about mutual friends, their parents, the dance. Jason sat, staring at the passing streetlamps. Or at Zef's hand on Kate's knee.

"Grab this, dude?"

Zef popped the trunk and lifted out a canvas garment bag. He heaved it into Jason's arms. Jason fumbled with it, trying to find a grip.

"What's in here?"

Zef shouldered a duffel.

"Oh nothing," he said, grinning. "Dead body."

Zef slammed the trunk and walked off. Jason wrestled with the garment bag, got it to fold over his shoulder, and followed after, muttering to himself.

Rounding the last bus in line, they saw a parked truck with a horse trailer. A black-haired man of about fifty stood alongside, talking to Kate. She'd climbed onto the trailer hitch, leaning in to scratch the snout of a sleek rose-gray horse.

"You're my beautiful boy," she cooed in its ear, her left hand twining in the bridle. "My best fella."

"Look at that," said Zef, "I've been replaced. Hey, Carlos."

The man wiped his hand on his windbreaker and shook Zef's.

"You never had a chance, mister," said Kate. "Gunsmoke is my true love. Aren't you, baby?"

The horse nodded twice and snorted at Zef.

"I watered him before we left," Carlos said.

"Good," said Kate. "How's his leg?"

"Oh, fine. It's just a little stretched tendon. He limped for a few days, that's all."

"Poor thing," she said, and scratched the horse's cheek.

"But I can still ride him?" said Zef, his voice a little sharp.

"Oh sure."

"Good deal," Zef said. He reached up and wrapped an arm around Kate's waist. She came down like a tree felled by a lumberjack, her body against his, kissing him before her feet touched the asphalt.

"How'd he hurt his leg?" said Jason, looking away.

"My fault," said Kate, breaking from Zef. "I rode him in mud."

"And you go too fast, Miss Usher. Too fast," said Carlos.

"No such thing. Gunsmoke loves it when I ride him fast, don't you baby?"

"Who wouldn't?" said Zef with a mischievous leer, and Kate bit her lip and punched him in the shoulder.

"So we slipped a little and he threw me," she said. "I didn't mind it. It was fun. Like being shot from a cannon. Look at this, though." She sloughed the jacket and pulled her blouse away to reveal a dark bruise on her shoulder.

"Ouch," said Zef. Kate pouted a little, and he kissed the spot.

Carlos turned to Jason.

"This girl is crazy, you know?" he said, rolling his eyes.

"I'm just sorry my big boy hurt himself." She pulled her jacket back on and stroked the animal again. It shook its head and snorted vapor against her palm.

A band began to play in the distance. Jason turned and saw that the sea of headlights had thinned. A few lonely stragglers hunted for parking spaces.

"That's our cue," said Kate. "Will you be okay?"

"Oh, no problem," said Carlos. "I got *Slaughterhouse Five* on tape. Just come up when you're ready. I'll have his saddle on."

Kate hugged the man, kissed his cheek. Carlos flapped his arms in embarrassment, tucking his chin into his chest bashfully. He pulled open the door of the truck, waggled a palm towards Zef and Jason, and climbed into the cab. Kate noticed Jason struggling with the heavy garment bag. She shook her head, took the thing by the hangers and tossed it to Zef, frowning. Then she did the impossible. She flung an arm across Jason's shoulders and walked him across the lot, leaving Zef to trail behind.

When they reached the stairs she stopped. They half-stood in a pool of light from an overhead bulb. Kate glowed, bridal white, Jason in shadow beside her.

"So. This is our school," she said.

From where they stood together, the Hollow was a glittering layer cake of sky and palisades and the Hudson River, of lit windows and the jousting red and white car lights on Broadway. The school itself took massive square bites from the sky and the river and the village below. A few floodlights made vertical puddles of red brick down the sides, revealing stone columns, a few rectangles of yellow and blue that were bulletin boards, and a pumpkin propped cheerily by the doors to the gym, which were thrown wide and spilled caramel light. Something warm and sweet played inside.

"What do you think?" she said.

Kate's arm lay draped across his shoulder. His own hand had slipped around her waist, somehow. And she didn't seem to mind.

"Feels like home already," he said.

Zef cleared his throat. "What's the holdup?" he said.

Kate broke the moment. She danced down the stairs, alone, her arms out, spinning, enjoying the cold air and the romantic music, leaving the two boys in her wake.

#

A round plug of dancers filled the square hole of dance floor, answering the band's backbeat with a throb of dress shoes on wood; answering with shouts, with laughter, with hands clapping, fingers snapping, with palms raised to testify, with hands on shoulders, hands on breasts, hands around neckties, thighs and Dixie cups.

Zef stripped down to his black tank top, Kate to her black silk. She grabbed his belt loops and launched him into the center, where they orbited each other, radiating heat. At their table, Jason made silent conversation with the maroon hoodie and the fuzzy jacket, which had remained behind to keep him company.

Come on, Jason. Dance with me, said the fuzzy jacket.

I want to, he replied.

Touch her and I'll break your neck, said the hoodie.

The senior class held court from the bleachers, laughing at the groundlings below, spitting ice, giving thumbs up or thumbs down, dispensing favor or social death. Juniors and sophomores sat at purple-draped tables, holding hands around disco-ball centerpieces as if competing in a séance tournament. Freshmen milled near the stage where a rock band played beneath the scoreboard and American flag.

The band was named *Hollow Praise*. They were a dismal bunch, but the lead singer was fantastic. He wore a white jacket and black jeans. He was young, dark-haired and animated, riffing on lyrics, improvising over the din with a powerful tenor voice. He pulled the band along, lifting them up, making them better. In a gap between songs, the kid waved to Jason amiably. It was Joey Osorio, the cemetery worker, the boy who planned to win an Academy Award.

Or a Grammy, thought Jason, impressed.

He chewed a pretzel. The crowd roared. He wanted to dance tonight. Yes, dance with her. Why didn't he? He could. He would! He stood.

He sat.

Come to me, Jason, whispered the fuzzy jacket.

He stood again.

He began to dance. Not really, but he started bobbing his head in a vague way and pivoted his hips a little, trying to find a groove. He moved his feet, his elbows, bit his lower lip. He made tentative steps forward on each second and fourth beat, and he entered the crowd, sideways, feeling like a lame virus infecting a cell. He reached the nucleus, where a group of dancing football players had carved a place for Kate. He saw her before she saw him. She laughed as she danced, her arms up. He could see her navel. *Eyes up here, mister,* he thought. She'd seen him. She reached out a hand. *Beautiful.* He moved towards her.

The song ended.

"That's our break, guys. Back in ten," Joey said.

The kids applauded. Couples broke, milled about, and dispersed.

"Where have you been?" said Kate, breathing hard, her hair dark, her face wet and full of reflected light.

"Around," he said.

She smiled.

"With who? Did you meet somebody?" She fixed his tie. "Be good."

The football players moved in. Kate pulled away. One boy threw his arm around Jason's neck and pressed a Dixie cup to his chest. Jason smelled beer.

"You the newbie?" the kid said, his palm on Jason's chest. He wore a black knit cap and chewed a swizzle stick.

"Never mind, Jimmy," said Kate.

"I said, are you?" Jimmy persisted, with a drunken good cheer. The swizzle stick threatened to put Jason's eye out.

"I start on Monday," Jason said.

"Crane, right?"

Ugh.

"Yeah, but—"

"HEY!" Jimmy pulled the swizzle stick from his mouth and bellowed across the dance floor. He twisted Jason to face the bleachers. "CRAAAANE!" Someone waved back, rose, and came to meet them.

"Leave it, Jimmy," said Kate.

Jimmy whipped back around, still gripping Jason, who felt like he was at the chiropractor's.

"But it's Craaaane!" he said, as if that explained everything.

"No kidding. Shut the hell up, Puleo," someone growled.

A broad-shouldered boy strode onto the dance floor. The players parted, as instantly and obediently as a puddle would for Moses. He wore a tight white muscle shirt and a tiny crucifix on a silver chain. Jason thought that if this kid flexed his neck the crucifix might put someone's eye out. Goliath reached forward as if to grab Jason's ear. Instead, he took the Dixie cup out of Jimmy's hand and took a drink.

"So. Crane. No shit," he said, smiling. He stuck out a hand. "E. Martinez," he said. "Number twenty-five." He crushed Jason's hand bones into a small bundle. "So you're the new kid."

Jason nodded.

"Say hi to Jason, guys," said Martinez.

They passed him around, slapping his shoulder.

"Hi, Jason," they said as one.

"Excellent. Welcome," said Martinez. "You play?"

"Play? Play what?" said Jason.

"Be nice," said Kate.

"I'm nice. I'm always nice," said Martinez. "Do you play a sport?"

"Yeah, do you play a sport?" repeated Puleo.

"I—" Jason began, trying to decide whether to tell the truth. The boys stared at him. "No," he said. "I don't play."

"No? Nothing? He plays nothing. What a tragedy."

"It's a real a loss to the school," said one.

"There goes State," giggled Puleo.

"Not even basketball? Tall kid like you?" Martinez grabbed Jason by the bicep, testing it, finding it skinny, breakable, a little hilarious. "No? Too bad. Hm. Have you considered... tetherball?" he said. Laughs all around. "Maybe you could be the pole."

Puleo and the others found this hilarious.

Kate intervened, slipping her right arm through Jason's left.

"Let him be, Eddie. He's mine."

"He's yours? Zef would love to hear that." Martinez touched a wisp of hair that had fallen forward onto Kate's cheek. His thumb fanned against her skin. "No need to trade down, baby," he said, in the tone of a john propositioning a whore.

Jason batted Martinez's hand away. Heads turned to stare at him, mouths open. Jason's opened too. He flexed his fingers as his arm dropped back to his side. What just happened? Was his hand suicidal? Was it ready to end it all, and determined to take the rest of him with it?

"Sorry," he said, and his voice was surprisingly firm. "You're being rude."

E. Martinez drew himself to his full height.

"And you're being stupid," he said.

"Oh, stop it," shouted Kate. Despite the noise all around, a dozen heads popped up as if a twig had broken in a still forest. "Jason just moved here. He's new. He doesn't know anybody, and he doesn't know the rules. So ease off. It's Spirit Week, right? Let's show some spirit. This isn't how we welcome new people to Sleepy Hollow."

Martinez put both hands to his chest in mock apology. "Then we got to welcome him, don't we? Let's welcome him, guys."

"Yeah, we got to."

"Definitely."

"You know it."

Martinez, Puleo, and the others pushed into the crowd and were gone.

"Jesus," muttered Jason.

"Zef's friends, not mine," said Kate. She took a pull off a water bottle, sighed. "The Sleepy Hollow Boys." She pushed the wisp of hair back behind her ear. Jason watched her do it. He had been about to do it himself, and now he wished he had.

"Attention, please."

A man had taken the stage: about forty-five, gaunt, with too much nose, too much chin, and too little hair.

"Owner of the silver Volvo, your lights are on," he said.

A fat kid disengaged from the buffet table and ran out the door, holding his pants up by the belt. A few boys laughed.

"Congratulations, everybody, on the game tonight."

A cheer went up.

"34-31 is not too bad. We made Croton work for it."

A general grumble, determined applause.

No wonder those guys were drinking, thought Jason.

"On behalf of the English department, I want to thank the teams competing for this year's Spirit Awards, and congratulate Amy Louis's group for keeping SHHS bully-free."

An enthusiastic brunette raised an arm and pivoted like a gymnast sticking a landing. No one clapped.

"Now, Halloween's in a few weeks, and you know what that means."

"Stupid tourists," said someone from the back, to general agreement.

"No. It means it's time for…" he said, his voice becoming exaggeratedly spooky, *"…the Horseman's Hollow.* Now, we want to keep Philipsburg Manor nice, so I'm looking for volunteers to clear the trash after."

"Hey hey, Mister Wollenberg."

"What, Martinez?"

Martinez climbed up to the stage, to laughter, some applause, and a few female catcalls.

"I'm'a let you finish your speech, but—"

More laughter.

"Get off the stage," said Wollenberg.

"No, no. You got to hear this, sir. You're into history and everything. It's a Halloween surprise. Come on. Please? Just for a second."

Wollenberg rolled his eyes, relinquished the microphone. Martinez waved to the crowd.

"Hey, ya," he said. "We got a new student."

Jason turned to walk away, but Jimmy and Nathan lay in wait. They hooked him under the arms and pulled him toward the stage. Kate followed, her face full of exasperation and weariness. She disappeared in a flash when someone turned on the spotlight.

"This is Jason. Say hi to Jason, everybody."

"Hi, Jason," said the crowd.

"Where'd you move from, Jason?" said Martinez.

"Maine." Jason said.

"Maine? Damn. What's in the water up there? Growth hormone?" The crowd chuckled.

"Is there a point to this, Martinez?" said Wollenberg.

"I'm getting to it, sir." He turned back to the crowd. "Now there's something you might not know about Jason. Our boy Jason is descended from somebody very special."

What? Jason thought, panicking. *How does he know that?* Then he realized. *Zef. Of course Zef knows.*

"Bring him up here. Don't be shy."

Jason felt hands under his armpits. His feet left the floor. He was onstage now, light in his eyes, looking down at the school. Martinez put a hand on the back of his neck.

"Jason's descended from…"

Behind them, someone started a drum roll.

"You guess it?" shouted Martinez. "He's skinny. He's a scarecrow. Say hi to my boy Jason CRANE!"

A crash of cymbals.

"Bullshit!" someone shouted, to laughter.

"Nah, get this. Jason is descended from Ichabod. Aren't you?"

Jason stared into the microphone. Martinez's hand, on the back of his neck, threatened to make a fist and pop his head off. He gave in.

"Yeah. I am," he whispered.

There was a moment of silence, then crowd erupted into applause.

"Ich-a-bod," Martinez prompted.

"ICH-A-BOD! ICH-A-BOD!" shouted the crowd, clapping in rhythm.

Jason shaded his eyes. He didn't see derision, or contempt, just a general Halloween-y good cheer. Okay. This might not turn out too bad. Then he saw Kate's face. She looked worried and apologetic.

She had guessed what was in store for him.

"Now, my buddy Ichabod," Martinez continued, raising his voice over the din. "I got somebody you need to meet. See, we spared no expense. Just to make you feel at home." Martinez leaned off the stage, shouting at someone. "Do it!"

Jason looked about, remembering the climactic scene of Stephen King's *Carrie*, half-expecting pig's blood to pour down on his head from above.

What happened was worse.

The drummer crossed to the sound system, hit "play," and the big speakers stabbed out three famous organ notes, a Bach toccata, that organ music from a thousand werewolf movies. The gym doors flew outward, revealing a dark blue night beyond, admitting an icy gust of wind and leaves.

A figure stood outside in the moonlight. A black figure on a horse.

"Say hi, Ichabod," said Martinez, fiercely.

The spotlight swung like the beam of a lighthouse, framing the doors.

And in rode the Headless Horseman.

The crowd broke into cheers. Jason's jaw dropped.

But then he saw that this Horseman rode Gunsmoke, Kate's grey horse, and suddenly the horse, the trailer and the garment bag made sense. This was Zef. Zef crouched under there, under the heavy black cape, under the padded shoulders, the buckles, the black gloves. Zef nudged the reins and urged the horse towards the stage. Zef was in there, somewhere, beyond the hollow space, down the neck, somewhere in the darkness between the flared collars.

But it didn't feel like Zef. It felt like a predator, like a childhood fear. It felt like death coming. Death with an old grudge.

The kids screamed now, clapped, parted. Jason looked for the stairs, but his eyes couldn't adjust. He saw only a border of fat pumpkins along the edge of the stage. Martinez gripped one arm. Wollenberg was shouted something. This had gone too far. Jason couldn't hear the words. Maybe the teacher meant to protect Jason from the Horseman, or maybe just the basketball court from horseshoe damage. Either way, no teacher could be heard over the relentless, thundering organ music.

The Horseman rode to the edge of the stage, so that Jason would have been face to face with it, if it had a face. A gloved hand left the reins, went to the waist sharply and, with a slicing sound, drew a wicked-looking sword, brandishing it overhead. Jason tore himself from Martinez, startled, backing away. His foot caught an electrical cable and he began to fall. He saw himself falling, in slow motion, hands rotating, grasping. He tumbled into the drum set, wrapped an arm around the high hat, and fell off the back of the stage, drums and pumpkins crashing around him.

A moment of awed silence. A roar of laughter.

The figure of E. Martinez appeared above, looking down from the stage, blotting out the lights.

"Welcome to Sleepy Hollow," he said, and disappeared.

Jason disentangled himself. He peered over the edge of the stage and spotted Kate across the room. She saw him too. Her face darkened and her brows knit. The Horseman extended a hand to her. Eddie and Nathan appeared, stirruped her foot, and lifted her into the saddle. Zef brought Gunsmoke into a turn.

Jason thought of *The Legend*: how the Horseman may have been Brom Bones in disguise, how Brom defeated his rival and won the hand of the fair, fair Katrina. *The Legend isn't a ghost story,* Jason thought. *It's a love story. Where the nerd loses and the bully wins. As always.*

The last descendant of Ichabod Crane sighed. He picked pumpkin seeds out of his hair. He watched dejectedly as the last descendant of Brom Bones dug sneakers into Gunsmoke's flanks and, with a flourish of his cape and to loud applause, rode into the night with the fair, fair... Kate.

12   THE ONE

"You okay, Jase?"

Joey Osorio leaned down from the stage, offering a hand.

"Not really," said Jason in a small voice.

"Come on out, then."

Jason shook his head. He was happy just sitting against the cinderblock wall, staring into the black plywood abyss beneath the stage.

"You've got to," said Joey.

"Why should I?"

"Because. You're on my mike cable."

Jason grinned, but it was frost on a hotplate, disappearing as soon as it came. He took Joey's hand and stood.

"Sorry," he said.

"Just let Dave get in there and fix his drums."

Dave the Drummer stood behind Joey, murderous.

Jason picked his way around the stage. Something Top 40 was playing from the speaker tower. The crowd had forgotten him, had returned to swilling and bouncing. Nearby, a girl in gold gyrated her butt and arms in opposition, either dancing or working out on an invisible elliptical machine.

"Let's get you some air," said Joey. He stiff-armed a door. When it closed after, the sound of the dance cut dead, just a few muffled bass notes remaining. They walked in silence down white halls as empty and gloomy as a hospital ward after visiting hours.

"Don't you need to be back in there?" said Jason.

"No. We'll be on break until Dave sets up. And I need a soda."

They walked on. Jason felt better, little by little, as the gym fell farther behind.

"You've got a great voice," said Jason.

"Thanks. It's a great band."

"No. It's a lousy band."

"Maybe."

"But you've got a great voice."

"I've been working on them. You should have heard them before."

"Bad?"

"Oh yeah. Christian rock. It took a month just to convince them they should ditch the choir robes."

They stopped by the trophy case. A number twenty-five jersey hung boastfully there, on permanent display. Jason frowned and rapped knuckles on the glass.

"Of course," he said. "He *would* be the quarterback."

"Martinez is a jerk," said Joey. "He got held back. Last year. Got arrested for possession and missed a semester."

"Drugs?"

"Steroids."

"But they still let him play? Is he that good?"

"Oh, yeah. They call him the Monster. Not to his face, though."

Jason pointed down at a framed photo at the bottom of the case, tilted against the trophies. The Headless Horseman, again, galloping across a football field.

"Is that Zef?" he said.

"I think so," said Joey. "He's been school mascot since he started here. He shows up at halftime, chases a player dressed up as the other side, runs him down, that sort of stuff. The crowd loves it. He's the most popular kid in Sleepy Hollow. Kate's dad is probably going to make him a congressman someday."

"Who?"

"Paul Usher," said Joey.

"Not following."

"Kate's dad is a state senator, didn't you know that? He *loves* Zef. Promises to do things for him, get him into a good school, pull strings, you know. And Zef slobbers all over the man, calls him "sir," laughs at his jokes, lets him win at tennis. But he has to. His dad would kill him if he didn't."

"I can see that. Hadewych's a backslapper. So Zef is a climber too? Just using Kate?"

"I didn't say that. He's always been real good to her, far as I know."

"Far as you know."

"I'm sure. He's a good guy. And maybe he does love her. Zef's not a jerk. He's not."

Jason made a face and cocked a thumb over his shoulder.

"Did you see what he just did to me?" he said.

"He's not like that. I know. Okay, maybe he is a little. But—it was a joke. I'm sure he didn't mean it. Look, I'm not defending him. Okay, I am. But—"

Joey was stammering.

"What?" Jason said.

"I shouldn't," Joey said, obviously torn. "It's private. And Zef would murder me. But… I saw you looking at Kate. Go after her if you want, Jase. You do have a chance. I promise."

Joey turned away before Jason could question him further. He thumbed some quarters into a soda machine. Above the recycling bins, a hand-lettered sign proclaimed optimistically: THIS IS A BULLY-FREE ZONE.

Jason walked into the central atrium. He found another Horseman there, painted on the floor like a huge Rorschach blot. He scuffed his shoe at it. "I shouldn't even be here," he said. "If anybody should be at a different school, it's me."

"It'll get better," Joey said, joining him.

"Sure," said Jason, unconvinced.

"It will. Just wait. I promise."

Jason pushed his hair out of his eyes. "It can't get any worse," he said.

Joey popped the top of his Mountain Dew. It spat liquid, spraying them both.

They stood in the middle of the atrium, blinking, soda running down their faces. If there had been a label at their feet it would have read: *"Never Say It Can't Get Any Worse," an Ironic Study in Bronze*. Jason was the first to break the pose. He broke into a grin, and then laughter. Joey joined in, doubling the noise, which made

Jason even more raucous and loud, which made Joey snort and slip and shout and Jason laugh and slip and fall and soon the empty atrium and long dark corridors of Sleepy Hollow High were bubbling with the caffeinated, carbonated, high-fructose sound of two silly kids becoming friends.

#

Joey returned to the stage, grabbing the microphone and jumping into a rockabilly song. Jason sat at the table again, grinning, dipping a napkin in a glass of water, wiping his face. Zef walked up and pulled the hoodie on.

"That was all Martinez, you know," said Zef. "I was just supposed to make an appearance."

"You went along."

"Everybody was looking."

"And you went along."

Zef's face darkened.

"You just don't get it," he said.

He sat down, fished the duffel bag from under the table. Jason saw the sword inside. Zef produced a flask of something, took a hit off it, coughed. Whatever was in the flask, it was strong. He offered it to Jason, who shook his head.

"Right. Good idea," Zef said, nodding. "Yeah. You should be." He stood, pocketed the flask, clapped Jason on the shoulder, walking away.

"Should be what?" Jason called after, confused.

"Designated driver."

Kate walked up ten minutes later.

"Have you seen Zef?"

Jason pointed. Zef was with Martinez and Jimmy and Nathan, on the bleachers. They were huddled together, passing the flask.

"Great," said Kate. She crossed her arms and turned to Jason. "You okay?"

"Never better. I love looking like an idiot." He gestured; all the chairs around him were empty. "Look how popular it's made me."

"Do you care about being popular? I don't."

"Only because you *are* popular."

She glanced toward the bleachers.

"I don't feel very popular right now. Come on." She extended a hand, palm up, as if offering him a gift. "Dance with me."

"No thanks," said Jason.

She cocked her head. Her eyes shouted *What?*

"I don't feel like it," he said.

"Okay, no problem," she murmured, barely audible over the band. She sank into the chair next to him.

Jason was amazed that he'd refused. He'd been longing to dance with Kate all night. He'd wanted to touch her, to hold her, he'd wanted her to put her arms around his neck and see her gaze up at him. And now the chance was here and... he didn't want to.

"Why not?" said Kate, trying to hide some emotion that Jason couldn't identify. Hurt? Amazement? Irritation? Disappointment? All of these and none of them.

He shrugged. He didn't know. Maybe it was the way she'd asked him. No, she hadn't asked. She'd ordered him to dance, assumed that his interest was a foregone conclusion. Jason Crane must say yes because every boy says yes. Maybe it was the way she had been looking at Zef, annoyed by his inattention and wanting to get back at him. Jason didn't know. He just didn't feel like dancing.

"Hey," said Kate, "I told Zef to apologize for what he did, you know."

"I don't blame Zef. I blame Martinez. And my own clumsy feet." He gave the little disco ball centerpiece a spin.

"Eddie didn't like you challenging him in front of his boys."

"I know."

"Thanks, by the way," she said.

"For what?"

"Defending me. I know that's what you were doing." She looked sad now, lost in thought, the bright red cup halfway to her lips, suspended. The disco ball wound down. Sequins of light drifted lazily across her cheek. "Everybody thinks they own me," she said. "Martinez treats me like the town slut. But I'm not, you know."

"I never thought you were," said Jason.

"Not you. But some people think that, because the boys are just... because they're always..."

"Always..."

"I don't chase after them. They just..."

"Chase after you."

"Right."

"And you don't like it."

"No, I don't," she said and put the cup down firmly. She stared off again, toward the bleachers where Zef stood telling a joke, and Martinez howled with laughter.

"But," said Jason, "you don't like them ignoring you, either."

Kate grinned. "I like you," she said. "You're smart." She put a hand on the back of his chair. "Are you really related to Ichabod?"

"Does it matter?"

She leaned in, her eyes scanning his face, noticing the details, his green eyes, his eyebrows, his shaggy auburn hair.

"I don't see a resemblance. No, no Ichabod here. Ichabod was never this cute."

She smiled, stood, and reached for her jacket.

"Yes," he blurted, stopping her.

"Yes, what?" she said, turning.

"That's my answer. Yes."

"Yes to what? That you're related?"

He shook his head. He stood. He pushed the hair out of his eyes.

"Yes, I would love to dance."

"Oh?" she said, with elaborate skepticism. "I thought you didn't feel like it."

Jason offered his hand to her, palm up. "A guy's got to play hard to get."

She grabbed his wrist and pulled him into the crowd. A new song had started.

"Are you a good dancer?" she said.

"We'll find out."

She threw her arms over her head and laughed.

"The trick is not to care if anybody's watching," she said.

And she was right. The music was loud and fun and they forgot themselves in it. Jason found his groove at last. He stopped thinking about it. He stopped worrying. He swung her, spun her, bumped hips with her.

They danced for a long time. Up on stage, Joey grew hoarse, his voice raw. The band tired, but that only made them push harder, bring more of themselves to the music. The dancers pushed themselves harder, rolling up their sleeves, tossing jackets on chairs and losing ties, keeping the night going, refusing to let it end, until midnight came and faculty members tapped their watches.

"Last song, everybody," said Joey, "last song."

Joey leaned into the mike to croon something soft and slow. Couples slipped into each other's arms. Bodies pressed close, swayed and clung together. Kate and Jason stood awkwardly apart, out of place among the rest.

"If it's the last song…" muttered Jason.

"Yeah. I should…"

"…find Zef. I know."

"This was fun," said Kate. She walked away. But she glanced back over her shoulder. Twice.

Jason drifted over to the stage. Joey saw him standing alone. He put his hand over the mike while the guitar took over. "Hey. I'm only playing this for you two," he whispered. "Dance with her."

"I'm not her date," replied Jason.

"Let her decide that."

"Decide what?" said Kate. She had returned, and stood at Jason's elbow. He looked up to Joey for assistance, but Joey was singing again. And smiling, just a little.

"Did you find Zef?" Jason said.

She shrugged, looking a little helpless. She reached for him, drew him into the dance. His arms closed around her, but he hesitated.

"What if he sees us?"

"I told you," she said. "The trick is to not care who's watching."

Her arms came around his neck and her fingers played in his hair. She melted into him. Jason smiled. He had not wanted to come to this dance, but now there was nowhere he would rather be. His arms circled her, his palm pressed flat against the small of her back. They swayed together. She tightened against him, and the sheer black silk of her blouse rode up, slipping from beneath his fingers, until his palm lay pressed against the naked skin of her body.

Then there was no music. No breath. No life. Nothing. There was no time, no memory, no sensation. He felt the touch of his hand on her, nothing else. He wasn't dancing with a girl anymore. He was holding a column of energy, a warm golden energy that raced into him through the palm of his hand, pouring out from her, into him, up his arm, across his chest, along the artery, flushing his cheeks, blocking out his sight. But what sensation was this? It felt strange. Wrong, even. Where was the beat? He couldn't find the music. He couldn't... He...

Oh, no, he thought, *oh no no No!*

He recognized this immobilizing, muffling sensation. He wasn't just getting caught up in the girl. He was *reading* her. This was *psychic*. This was Owen and the Brown Paper Bag. This was... *oh no no no... not now not now not now!*

He fell into it, helplessly.

He rode with Kate, on the back of Gunsmoke, down a long trail framed with ravishing autumn leaves. She held the reins, leaning back against his chest for warmth. Blue sky twisted on the periphery of his vision, rippling. He was a pebble dropped through the surface of things, a splash in the substance of the world.

"I'll show it to you," she said. *"It's beautiful. People say Spook Rock is the place where the Indians bewitched the Hollow."*

He inhaled her scent. A twig snapped under Gunsmoke's hoof.

So vividly real, but it can't be. It can't be...

He broke through another surface. He still held Kate, but now they rode fast through a fearful windy night. Did something chase them? Gunsmoke galloped, they burst from the trail, past the house and down Gory Brook Road, plunging toward Broadway. A car pulled out in front of them, terrifying the horse. Gunsmoke started, reared, Jason began to fall, pulling Kate down with him, but he lost his grip on her and, when he fell, he fell backwards and through another surface. The night sky rippled, became blue again.

He lay on his back in a drifting boat. Kate leaned over him and kissed him on the nose.

"Stop being lazy. It's your turn to row."

He sat up. They skippered a rowboat, on the sea, off a ragged coast. The air wrapped them with summer heat, but the spray cooled their faces. He whirled to stare at her. *So real so real.* She wore shorts and a blue checked shirt tied off in front. Her arms had reddened. She should have worn sunscreen...

"What's the matter?" she said. *"Bad dream?"*

He tried to speak, but his breath blew a bubble that engulfed her and carried her away. Or perhaps she had remained still and he had fallen back? No time to wonder.

Because Kate screamed. Vines reached for them both, mist coiled in a sickening green light. Something lived in the mud. It had her. Jason ran, reached for her. She grabbed his wrist, his grip twisted and her slick hand rotated around his forearm. He couldn't hold her. He was about to lose her in the swamp. He fought for purchase, reached for an immense chunk of mortared brick that lay tipped over in the mire. His fingertips caught the edge, scrabbling to find a crevice. *So real so real so terribly real.* But the broken structure lurched beneath him when he pulled. *No.*

He couldn't feel her now. Had Kate fallen through the surface of the swampy marsh or had he fallen away again himself? He didn't know. He couldn't tell anymore. His heart beat in his ears and he screamed for her, but heard bubbles escaping his lungs… bubbles, and then a rising music. The music of an organ, a wave of sound that lifted him up.

Light broke again, and Kate walked toward him, slowly, up the aisle of a tiny church built of fieldstones. The Old Dutch Church. A white veil dimmed her face, but he could see that she smiled happily. She wore a white dress, and carried a bouquet of white roses and baby's breath. As she drew nearer, his eye traced a path from a tiny pearl earring, to the tiny crystals sewn into the fabric, to the skin of her shoulder barely visible behind the floral lace. She joined him at the altar, turned to him. The veil rose… and everything broke again… irreparably.

Something struck Jason and he flew backwards, falling. He was in the gym, lying on the dance floor. Kate stood over him, her face twisted, her eyes wide and terrified. She'd struck him, pushed him away, and he had fallen hard.

"What the hell was that?" she said.

Jason raised his hand, turned it, looked at the palm. He half-expected it to glow. It didn't. He reached for her.

"Don't touch me," she snapped. "Don't *ever* touch me again!"

Kate spun and ran.

A crowd stared down at him now. Joey still sang, halfheartedly, as if he couldn't decide whether to help Jason or to give him cover.

Jason stood. The details of the vision evaporated. His eyes went wide with wonder…

She saw it too.

"What did you do to her?" said a girl, suspiciously.

"I—I don't know," said Jason.

A pimply freshman raised his hand. He had the obvious answer. Everyone turned to him. The boy frowned at Jason and wagged a finger, sternly.

"Did you touch her boob?"

#

Jason moved to follow Kate, but one of the Sleepy Hollow Boys stopped him with a palm.

"Easy now, Ichabod, she said to leave her alone."

Jason considered. The boy wasn't quite as tall as he was, but he was broader and stronger.

"Fine," Jason spat.

Jason found a dark corner halfway between the double doors and the risers. He crossed his arms. What had happened? What had he seen? A psychic vision? That was absurd. But... it had happened before, of course.

He exhaled slowly.

Back in his last year of middle school, when Owen had come to Thanksgiving dinner, when he'd challenged Jason to read objects and Jason had had his strange experience with the boot, had it been like this? No. Then he had seen a vision of the past, of the night when his parents' car went off the dam and into the Kensico Reservoir. Though the memory of that vision still disturbed him, no matter how he tried to put it out of his mind, he could at least lie to himself. *Well, Jason, that was just your overactive imagination working. You've thought about that event so many times, it's no wonder you could picture it clearly.*

He hadn't seen the past this time, though, had he? He'd seen scenes of himself and Kate, scenes of the two of them in the future.

No. Get over yourself. You don't have any powers. You had an intense daydream. You were just worked up. Both times. Worked up over your parents, worked up over this girl. And something went cuckoo in your brain both times.

He looked down at his hands. Tiny disco lights revolved across them. What if he'd caught something? What if the flashing lights had set off a seizure, and his brain had experienced a rush of... daydreams? But they'd been so specific. Riding with Kate on the horse. He had seen that twice, once in daylight and once at night.

Then they'd been in a boat together. Then had come the terrible swamp, and then…

The last part of the vision, daydream, whatever, scared him the most.

After all, he was only sixteen.

I've kissed three girls in my life.

He listed them now. He had kissed Lily Clark, his Homecoming date, before she dumped him to dance with Mitch Everett. He had kissed Chelsea O'Hara several times one heady afternoon, when Eliza had been away grave-hopping and the precocious redhead had come over to watch DVDs. The third kiss? When was that? Way back in the fourth grade, when little Anna Beck puckered up on the playground and dared him to risk contagion.

He had a long dating career ahead. Of course he had. A long journey before he met The One. A journey full of fumbling and mistakes and fights and breakups. He would fill his youth with girlfriends and ex-girlfriends and stalker girlfriends and unrequited love. He had decades, maybe, before he would have to get his act together, decide who he wanted, and find someone who could, possibly, maybe, by some wild stretch of the imagination, be able to stand him long enough to marry him.

It couldn't be *Kate*. He'd just met her. He felt cheated out of that whole long adventure. He looked forward to dating and playing the field and being young. *No. I refuse to believe it.* Knowing something like that is like… reading the last page of a book first. No. Worse… like… like *spoilers before a Star Wars film.*

Me and Kate?

"Jason?"

Joey Osorio poked him in the shoulder.

"What's the matter with you? Why are you grinning like that?" said Joey.

"Was I grinning?"

"Like a pumpkin. What happened in there? One minute you and Kate were steaming up the place and the next I thought you were going to lose teeth. Hey? Hey? Are you listening?"

Jason pushed the hair out of his eyes. He'd remembered something from the vision. Something that Kate had said to him, as they rode her horse through the woods. Something specific and testable... *I'll show it to you...* she had said. *It's beautiful...*

"Joey, this is important. Think hard. Is there someplace near here where people say the Indians bewitched the Hollow?"

"Sure," said Joey, "Spook Rock. Why?"

A chill ran through Jason. This was confirmation. This was... true.

"Spook Rock..." he whispered. *That's what she said. In the vision. Spook Rock. And I know for a fact that I have never heard of that place before today. So it's real. What I saw was real... And that means...*

"What's going on with you?" said Joey.

"I think... I'm going to marry Kate."

13 ELIZA

Eliza fussed with a foil packet of Alka-Seltzer. Her insides felt uncomfortable and sour. She'd managed to fetch a long-stemmed wine glass from the lowest shelf and fill it with water, but she couldn't open the foil packet. Her fingers were stiff, unresponsive. She'd forgotten to take her arthritis medicine again, and her knuckles had grown as big as gumdrops.

You're getting old, she thought to herself, then chuckled. Getting? She'd gotten and gotten good. She wasn't just old, not anymore. She'd sailed right past old and into the port called Decrepitude.

She dangled the packet between two fingers. Charley sniffed at it, hoping for a treat.

"Open this for me, sweetheart?"

The dog spun in a circle and barked.

"Shh. You're no help."

She brought the packet to her mouth, palms together as if in prayer. She tilted her head and tried to tear the thing open with her teeth, but her dentures would give before the foil would.

Damn.

The blue packet slipped and fell to the floor. It lay there, a square fruit hanging in the leaf-pattern of her linoleum.

She cursed, real sailor cursing like her stepfather used to do when Laura burned the dinner. Eliza kicked the cabinet door with one slippered foot. She would have brought a fist down on the counter if she could make one. She leaned forward about three inches, air filling the front of her housedress. She couldn't bend far enough and the effort made her hips wretched and angry. Forget about kneeling.

She'd have to get steroid shots in both knees and a gallon of morphine before she even attempted it. She brought her heel down on the packet and felt the contents grind into powder. That, at least, made her feel better.

She found milk in the refrigerator. That would do. She slipped a thumb through the plastic handle, grateful that Jason had bought a half-gallon, not a quart. She never would have been able to open one of those paper containers. She pushed the white cap with the heel of her palm. It popped off and fell to the floor. It could just stay down there too. She didn't feel up to setting the jug on the counter, fetching the wine glass, emptying the water into the sink on the other side of the kitchen, returning, pouring the milk. Even thinking about it exhausted her. So she lifted the jug to her mouth and took a swig straight from the bottle. What Jason didn't know wouldn't hurt him.

She spit it back out. It had gone bad. Oh, that boy! She could really thump him sometimes. Rivulets of white ran down the front of the green refrigerator. She reached out impulsively to wipe them away. The milk jug went tumbling from her thumb. It hit the floor, bounced an inch, and tumbled over, spraying her slippers with sour milk.

She stood like that for a long time as a puddle formed. Charley licked at it, made a face, and ran into the living room.

No use crying, right? That's what her mother used to say. *No use crying over spilled milk.* Eliza hated that cliché. She hated all clichés. They irked her. She'd grown up a cliché, her life a bowl of cherries, duck soup, easy as pie, child's play behind a white picket fence.

Her mother had been the perfect little woman, with the emphasis on *little*, only four foot four, with a little head of brown hair, a little mouth suited to church gossip and thin soup, a little house, a little pension, and a very little imagination. Everybody liked Laura Merrick, but nobody admired her. Mother had been the Wyatt Earp of clichés, firing them off quick-draw: *"a rotten apple spoils the barrel," "smile and the world smiles with you," "every dog has his day," "children should be seen and not heard."* She believed them all, particularly this last. Eliza obliged, preferring to wander the streets of Wytheville, Virginia on her own lonesome terms. Anything to get away from mother's nagging twitter—high and tinny, full of hiss and scratch.

Father had a booming bass voice. His Liza-dumpling had adored the plummy, solid sound of it. She would climb on his stomach and press her ear to his chest while he sang "Old Man River," kicking her feet and closing her eyes. But the war had widowed Laura Merrick when Eliza was four. Widowed. What's the word for a child without a father? Eliza wasn't an orphan, no, though she felt like one. Waif, maybe, or wretch, or lost soul. Tired of living and scared of dying. Her father had been the joy and iron of her life, always would be, and she would look for him again through all her years of honeymoons and third-string husbands.

Her mother wore black crepe dresses, right up until V-J Day. She remarried: a nasal baritone who slurred words on Friday nights. Charlie Wright doted on them at first, hit Laura after six months, whored after nine, and filed for divorce by their paper anniversary. Laura took her lumps meekly, patiently, with a prayer to Jesus and a steak on her eye. Eliza drew murderous cartoons in her room. Charlie died in an auto accident that February, wrapping his pick-em-up truck around a statue of Robert E. Lee.

The divorce left Laura a spinster librarian, and one false step on icy stairs left her an invalid as well. The accident happened on New Year's Eve, nineteen-fifty. Laura had just locked the doors of Wytheville Public Library, a forbidding civic mausoleum on Jefferson Avenue. She always liked to organize the card catalogues at the end of the year, and she'd spent that particular New Year's Eve sorting out a thorny Dewey Decimal classification. She had to scurry home by nine, of course, to make sure her boy-crazy daughter didn't sneak out. Eliza had kissed more beaus at seventeen than most women had at thirty.

We must make black-eyed peas tomorrow, Laura had been thinking, *with turnip greens.* That ensured a lucky New Year and, if you swept some money over your threshold, a prosperous one too. She loved those old southern traditions.

She looked both ways, checking for negroes, but turned a heel on the icy marble of the stairs and fell into the bushes below, breaking the long bones in both legs. Due to the holiday, nobody passed the library that whole evening. One couple canoodled past at around one a.m., but they were too caught up in each other to catch Laura's feeble cries or her foot poking through the brambles. She lay numb in the snow, drifting in and out of consciousness, until 1951 dawned bright and sunny.

Eliza had taken advantage of her mother's absence. She'd lost her virginity that same night. She'd swept Ron Partridge over her threshold, initiating her own beloved tradition. She was nursing a hangover, giddily reliving the event, but around eight-thirty she realized that her mother had not come down to breakfast, had not criticized her eye makeup, had not made oatmeal or black coffee or tsked over the coupon section of the *Wytheville Enterprise*. She checked her mother's bedroom, found it empty, took the bus down to the library, climbed the high stairs, knocked hard on the library doors, and heard a groan below.

Laura lay under the William Penn barberry bushes—below the yellow-trimmed windows of the non-fiction section. She'd torn her skirt. Her white stockings ran Jezebel-red with blood. Sweat and melted snow had soaked her blouse, and her grey forehead blazed. Eliza doffed her coat, laid it across her mother's body, and ran to find help. She flagged a ride by stepping into the middle of Jefferson Avenue and slamming her palm on the hood of the first car that passed. The housewife driver shrieked. So did her little girls. Those two porcelain children screamed all the way to the hospital, until Eliza wanted to break their little legs too.

The broken bones didn't kill Laura Merrick. She lay in the hospital, wheezing, her legs mortared up in casts. She had few visitors after the first week. Her church group was glad to fret over a poor thing for a day or two, but they trickled away when Laura had the bad manners to linger. On Valentine's Day, as her mother slept, Eliza drew big sloppy hearts on her casts. Laura harrumphed when she woke and insisted on keeping her legs hidden beneath blankets afterwards.

But in late March, something miraculous happened. Laura's self-control dropped, her passions erupted. She ranted at nurses, spit at doctors, swore like a navy pilot dropping F-bombs on Hiroshima. She had dementia, the doctors said, brought on by the leg fractures, perhaps, by fats or proteins released into the blood. Or perhaps she had hit her head on the steps. Maybe the persistent fever had changed her from Doctor Jekyll to Mister Hyde.

Eliza decided that her mother had just stopped believing her own bullshit.

The spells continued over the next two weeks, and Eliza enjoyed her mother's company for the first time. They swapped bawdy jokes, ogled the handsome interns, and chattered like best girlfriends late into the evening.

The exasperated hospital shipped Laura home, and mother and daughter became a happy family at last: carrying on, watching TV, eating pork ribs and cornbread on Laura's bed, Eliza cross-legged with a paper plate and Laura holding court from a throne of pillows. They had long conversations, and Laura spoke her *own* mind in her *own* words about things that *mattered* too her.

It broke Eliza's heart when the prim, condescending librarian returned. Laura hardly acknowledged anything that had passed between them. She sat in bed, reading the Bible, her legs propped in their heart-painted casts and smelling of dead skin.

The clichés returned next. *You can't have your cake and eat it too. A leopard doesn't change its spots. Water, water everywhere, and not a drop to drink. Nothing is certain, except death and taxes.*

This last proved true. On April fifteenth, Laura Merrick marked her Bible with a tongue depressor, set it on her nightstand, leaned back against the headboard, and coughed blood down the front of her nightdress. Eliza found her that way, dead as the proverbial doornail, and, yes, the blood was thicker than water. Just as her mother had always said. Much thicker than water, in fact. Perhaps as thick as molasses in January.

So easy. She died quiet like a little titmouse. No, she didn't even squeak. And she left such a mess. Not just on her nightdress, either.

The little pension stopped. The bank foreclosed. Eliza wandered from relative to relative and couch to couch and bed to bed, just to keep a roof overhead. She'd found herself hungry, abandoned, poor, and ignorant about responsibility or money. Unprepared for life— because life is *not* a cliché. It's messy and it's complicated and it's scary. If she'd relied on Laura's clichés she might have ended up a statistic. Thank heavens that Andrew Pyncheon had loved her and rescued her, and crooned into her ear with that deep voice of his.

The white puddle of milk had spread. Eliza didn't know why she'd thought of her mother tonight. The room smelled sour, like her mother's sick. Maybe that was it. Eliza kicked off her slippers. Jason would have to clean up her mess. That's what the young always did. Clean up the messes the old leave behind. She dropped a few towels on the spill, tamped it with her foot.

But I won't *leave him a mess like she did me. Not when I go. He's going to be ready.*

She tossed a package of popcorn into the microwave, pushed a few buttons, and padded into her bathroom. She checked her face, brushed her thin hair as best she could, and grabbed a bottle of fingernail polish. *Fire-Engine Red. No. Jungle Red.*

Ow! Oh!

The bedroom swayed.

What the hell?

The chest pain intensified.

Oh, no you don't. No you don't.

She fished for her pills. For the prescriptions Jason didn't know about.

I'm not going without a fight.

She squeezed the nail-polish bottle in her left hand.

Not me. Not easy. No, ma'am. Not like her.

Jungle red. The polish was jungle red.

Not without one hell *of a goddamned fight.*

14   THE LIGHTHOUSE

"I am not going up if *Valerie's* there," said Zef, scowling.

"Come on," said Jason. "It's late."

"She's a witch. I hate her. I hate her voice, I hate her face. Just drive, man."

"No."

Zef stood and leaned his torso out the open passenger window.

"I hate you!" he cried to the dark house. He dropped back into his seat.

"No, you don't, Zef."

"Yes I do," he whispered. "I hate both of them."

They had double-parked on Washington Street, by Patriots Park, looking up at the yellow clapboards of Valerie's building. Zef was drunk. He'd been drinking bottles of warm beer from the cooler, and something stronger from a flask in his duffel bag. Jason wanted to get home. Eliza might be waiting up. Why hadn't he just accepted Joey's offer of a lift, instead of consenting to be Zef's designated driver? It had been a stupid decision.

He'd wanted to stay around Kate, to drive her home. But that just meant he'd had to play chauffeur while she made out with Zef in the back seat—and again on the front porch of her house. He felt invisible. She hadn't even waved goodbye to him when she went inside.

Zef peeled a pack of Marlboro Reds. He'd been irritated that Hadewych's fake driver's license couldn't score them some colder beer. While it bumped Jason's age up to eighteen, the drinking age was still twenty-one. Zef had settled for cajoling three packs of cigarettes. Jason reluctantly bought them at a corner deli. The old man behind the counter hadn't batted an eye. Jason was so tall.

Why hadn't Jason refused?

Ordinarily he would have the spine to say no and walk away. But the Van Brunts were smooth talkers, charmers. They made you feel like your objections were unreasonable and unfair. They both had that salesman's gift for getting you to drop your guard, relax, and give them what they wanted.

He started the engine.

"I'm going, Zef. Show me where I can park your car, then I'm walking home."

Zef stared out the window. "Don't make me go up there."

The motor idled. The car heater pumped warm air at their feet. The hazard lights clicked, like a metronome conducting the silence. A car honked, circled around them, the driver flipping the bird at Jason as he passed.

"Zef? Are you okay?"

"Just drive. Please."

"Are you crying?"

"Hell, no," Zef said. "I wouldn't give them the satisfaction." But he sniffed like he had a cold coming on.

Jason turned off the hazard lights, put the car in gear.

This is the last time. I swear.

"Where am I going?"

"Just go. Turn left on Beekman," said Zef. He wiped his face with his sleeve when he thought Jason wasn't looking. They'd driven about three blocks when he blurted, "Your parents are dead, right?"

"Right."

"Ever wonder if you were lucky?"

"No," said Jason, immediately.

"Your grandmother seems cool. That's all I meant. How long ago?"

"Ten years. End of this month."

"Yeah. My mom's gone twelve years. He tells people she's dead but she walked out on him. I know. She's in Philly. I don't blame her. He deserved it. I hate him."

"Come on, he's your dad."

"My dad?" Zef's voice burned, bitterly, and collapsed into ashes again. "He's no dad."

Zef made a fist and thumped the dashboard.

Jason wasn't going to defend Hadewych. He turned left on Beekman, and they rode in silence down the hill. Everything had closed. The tattoo parlor, the pizzeria, the gourmet coffee shop, all shut tight behind steel shutters. A playground stood empty. The swings dipped back and forth, blown by the wind. The cruiser rattled over railway tracks and, just as Jason felt they were going to hit the end of the road and tumble into the Hudson, Zef raised a hand and pointed.

"Here, here," he said.

He directed Jason to pull through a large chain link gate and into… *what is this?*

Jason saw nothing but immense concrete slabs in all directions, like a silo for nuclear missiles, blasted-out empty foundations as far as he could see, at least a dozen blocks of desolation. They lurched over random potholes and broken asphalt, past trucks, soda cans, plastic bags caught in the chain links. Stubs of girders protruded from the slabs, like a clear-cut forest of steel stumps. The car rolled through a hole in a second fence, into a parking lot beside the river.

"What is this place?"

"This," said Zef, handing Jason a bottle, "is the pit of Hell, my friend. This is where the General Motors plant was, you know? That, over there," he gestured, "was the factory floor. That was the admin building. That's where the lunch wagon pulled up." He was pointing at empty space, at black slabs bristling with the unshaven stubble of bolts and stubs.

"Where'd it go?"

"China. They knocked it all over and carted it away. Why do you think we do all this Headless Horseman stuff? Renamed the town? This place was dying, man. We'd have gone broke without the tourists. My dad couldn't find squat after he was canned. He didn't try, though, and Mom bailed. Forget the Old Dutch Church. This is the biggest graveyard in New York."

Zef threw an empty beer bottle. It arced over the chain fence and exploded like a light bulb across the concrete.

"Here lies North Tarrytown. Long live Sleepy Hollow," said Zef.

"It's hard to picture your dad as a… a factory worker. He's so…"

"Slick?"

"Exactly."

Zef grunted. "My dad's a 'keeping up appearances' kind of guy. He'll buy clothes even when there's no milk or toilet paper—"I have to look good for interviews, young man"—but he doesn't go to any damn interviews. Not one."

"So what does he do for money?"

Zef chuckled. He blew smoke out the window. "Valerie," he said.

Jason didn't know how to respond to that.

Zef noticed Jason's beer was still capped.

"You going to drink that?" he said. He took it before Jason could answer. "Let me show you something."

He left the car and started walking, raising his hood and tightening it against the wind. Jason followed, rubbing his hands together.

"Where are we going?" he said.

"You'll see."

Zef slipped under a chain and squeezed through a link gate. Jason followed behind.

They found a thread of sidewalk between a graffiti-covered construction fence and the foaming rocks below. The wind beat at them, bent by the strong fence, hurrying them along their way until the sidewalk jackknifed towards the water and became a tiny metal bridge.

About fifty feet from shore stood a short tower like the castle on a chessboard, white with a red base and black windows, dark and abandoned. A little island of rock protruded from the water alongside it. The bridge leapt over the water to this lump of rock and the concrete slab of a landing. From there, a narrow catwalk led up to the tower itself.

"What is it?" said Jason.

"My lighthouse," said Zef, crossing the bridge.

"Yours?" said Jason.

"We used to fish here. On his lunch breaks."

Waves splashed beneath Jason's feet, spraying droplets through the steel mesh. Zef stopped on the landing, waiting for him to catch up.

Someone had left a metal folding chair by the railing; an angler, probably. Jason leaned over the rail, looking down. Water churned against the jumble of boulders below. Zef finished his beer and tossed the empty bottle over the rail and into the river.

He climbed the gangplank to the lighthouse itself, waving for Jason to follow.

A covered walkway encircled the base of the tower. The one door looked rusted shut.

"Are we allowed up here?" said Jason.

"No," said Zef. "Isn't it great?"

A wave struck the base of the lighthouse, sending a wall of mist straight up the side of the building. Zef whooped and threw his arms out.

"Yeah, great," said Jason, wiping his face.

"This is about as far away from everything as you can get. I HATE SLEEPY HOLLOW!" Zef screamed the words, but they were buffeted away by the wind.

"Let's go back," said Jason.

"No," said Zef.

He grabbed Jason by the sleeve and pulled him to the landward side of the tower. The wind still whipped around them, but it was less strong, less cold.

"You've got to go home," said Jason.

"No. You don't know what it's like. You don't know what *he's* like. You'll find out. Listen. You know I'm straight A's? Yeah? I am. Top of the class. Is that enough for him? No. I've got to be school mascot, too, student government, intern. I don't have any life left. I hate him!"

"He's your dad. He's supposed to push you."

"Not like this." Zef grabbed fistfuls of Jason's jacket. They huddled together, now, just to be audible. "I'm going to crack. I will. I can't be everything he wants."

Zef broke away. He paced around the tower, talking to himself. He tried to light a cigarette, but his lighter kept sparking in the wind. Jason felt sorry for him. He just looked so damn helpless all of a sudden. He pulled Zef back around to the landward side again. He blocked the wind with his body so Zef could light up. With three hands cupped around it, the lighter caught. Zef inhaled, blew smoke, and nodded with eyes shut, immensely grateful for the tiny assistance.

"I've got nothing," he said. Jason had to lean in to hear. "I don't own my life. I've got my own dreams. Things I want to say and be and do and I can't." His voice broke.

Jason felt sorry for the guy. He was also freezing and wanted to go home. But he stood and listened.

"I have so much inside. I am a vast person." Zef was crying now, smoking constantly. "How did I end up with such a small life?"

"What about Kate?" Jason said. "How can you say you don't have anything?"

Zef fell silent, his brows knit together, staring at the river.

Jason looked away too. He was embarrassed. He wanted to give Zef his privacy. The Hudson slipped by, inexorably, fresh water on its way to rendezvous with the salty ocean. When he turned back, Zef was staring at him.

"I know what you're going through," said Jason.

"No. You don't."

Zef sounded desolate and miserable, and Jason forgot that this boy was his rival for Kate; he forgot that not two hours ago Zef had humiliated him in front of the entire school. He let all that go. The kid was in real pain. He needed a friend.

He put his arm across Zef's shoulder. Zef said something but Jason couldn't make it out.

"It's okay, man. It's okay," Jason said.

Zef looked up, two trails of tears bright down his cheeks. He slowly exhaled cigarette smoke. He looked like a guy summoning all his courage.

Alarm bells began ringing in Jason's head, but he didn't know why.

Zef glanced down at Jason's lips. And then moved in, eyes closing.

Oh, crap.

Jason pulled away, floundering backwards. His elbow hit the railing, sending a jolt of pain down the bone. Zef looked up, frozen, shocked, hurt, embarrassed. He looked scared too. He had revealed the wrong thing to the wrong person and his world had crashed in.

Oh, God. He's mortified.

Jason felt bad, too. He had pulled away too violently. He hadn't dodged the unwelcome kiss with anything like grace. He had made a horrified face and wrenched away.

"I'm sorry," he said, then repeated it louder to cut through the wind. "I'm sorry. It's not that… you're great, Zef. But I'm not… you know."

The shock on Zef's face evaporated, replaced by sadness. The moonlight drained his color and he looked like a corpse. He turned away, leaned against the railing, tightened the hood around his ears. He swept his face with one sleeve.

Jason felt like an idiot.

God, he's probably imagining I'm going to run off and out him to his father.

"It's fine," said Jason. "I won't say anything. We're cool."

"I don't know what you're talking about," said Zef, flatly, without looking at him.

"Zef, it's okay. It's okay if you're gay."

Zef whirled, his face harsh, his eyes fierce.

"What did you call me?" he said.

"It wasn't an insult," Jason stammered.

Zef pushed Jason, hard, knocking him back against the guardrail and almost over it.

"What did you call me? Huh?"

He gave Jason a condescending little slap.

"Zef, come on."

"Come on? Come on? You came on to me, punk."

Another little slap.

"You know I didn't," said Jason.

Zef regarded him calmly, then swung his fist and connected with the left side of Jason's face.

Jason twisted. Needles of pain shot up through his fillings and into his eye socket. He stumbled, caught himself. He tried to run, but Zef blocked the path. Jason scrambled around the other side of the lighthouse. Zef pursued him, doubled back, grabbed Jason's sleeve just as he reached the gangplank. Jason swung at Zef, connected with his left fist, but lost his footing and fell, barely catching himself before his face could slam into the metal mesh of the pathway. His right hand took the worst of it. The metal bit his palm and drew blood. He balled it into a fist, wincing. A hand grabbed him by the collar. He flipped over and kicked Zef in the knee, then crabbed backward down the catwalk to the small landing.

Waves hit the rocks below, launching a spray of drops. They were salty. They stung his eyes and the cut on his hand. Zef grabbed his leg, pulling him back up toward the lighthouse. The mesh scraped Jason's back. He wriggled loose, pulled himself into a crouch, lost his footing again on the wet landing, and fell hard on the concrete.

He raised himself. He had to get back to land, back over the bridge. He had to cross the bridge. Cross the bridge.

For once you cross the bridge his power ends.

But Zef stood over him now. He had the folding chair raised above his head, holding it by the backrest to bring it down legs-first and spike Jason through the face.

"Repeat that. To anybody. *Anybody,*" he said, his voice inhuman and cold, "and I will open your veins."

"Go to hell, *cuz,*" Jason said, fury welling up inside him.

"Do you hear me?"

"Yes. Fine." Jason said. "Nothing happened!"

Zef gripped the chair and Jason felt certain that he would now bring it down, scramble his brains, smash his vocal cords, and guarantee his silence forever. But Zef's face quieted and became still. He transformed into a boy of seventeen again, full of fear and guilt and embarrassment, full of shame and loneliness. His arms sagged, wilted. The chair came down. Then, with a new explosion of violence, Zef hurled it over the railing and into the river.

Jason looked out at the Hudson. His breathing slowed. A longboat drifted by, low in the water, indifferent to all this, going where it would, guided by computer and satellite and elaborate GPS controls, ignoring the useless, obsolete little lighthouse on its spur of rock, ignoring the boys frozen there, wordless in the wind.

Zef watched it too. He fumbled for his cigarettes.

Jason stood, his arms held away from his sides, his palms down, trying to find his balance even though the landing was motionless. He felt that he should say something, or that Zef should, but they had nothing to say.

Zef had broken his last cigarette in the fight. He twisted the filter off, wet the end, spit tobacco, and raised his lighter to the tip. The lighter sparked, but would not light. The wind caught Jason like a kite when he turned. It pushed him over the bridge and back to dry land.

Once there, he looked back one last time.

Zef had retreated to the lighthouse. He was a sentinel, silhouetted against a navy blue sky. He stood at military attention, immaculately straight, on the windward side farthest from shore, alone above the dark water. He had no friend now to help him shelter from the wind.

His cigarette lighter was a tiny torch, sparking endlessly, futilely, over and over, signaling to the world: do not dare approach.

15   THE FOURTH FALL

Jason's feet were killing him by the time he reached Gory Brook Road. He sighed, leaned into the wind, and kept going. It had been the longest night of his life, but soon he would crash into bed and fall into tomorrow.

Fall. Ugh. He'd fallen on his ass three times tonight. Three. At the dance, off the stage, he'd fallen on cymbals and pumpkins and made a fool of himself in front of the whole school. With Kate, on the dance floor, she'd knocked him off his feet; that had been the second time. And then, at the lighthouse, Zef had thrown him down the gangplank.

Jason nursed the side of his right hand where it had been cut on the metal mesh. It still stung, but it had stopped bleeding. His knee hurt too. Why did Eliza have to buy a house at the top of such a long hill? Okay, yeah, all of Sleepy Hollow sat on a hillside, on one near-ninety-degree slope from the Hudson to the high school, but she could have bought a place down by the river. He was wearing dress shoes again, too.

He'd walked from the lighthouse, through the concrete wasteland and back to the parking lot. He'd thrown Zef's keys into the front seat of the cruiser and trudged back over the railroad bridge, up the endless uphill stretch from Beekman Avenue to Broadway. He'd rested and now felt ready to try for the summit.

His jaw hurt. He swore never to be someone's punching bag again. If anybody else tried to knock him down he'd defend himself. And what had he been doing hanging out with Zef in the first place? The guy was insane.

No. He's not. He's just messed up.

That was an understatement. Why did he keep feeling sorry for Zef? To hell with him. If Zef liked guys, that was his business and not Jason's problem. He knew he couldn't understand it any more than he understood what it was like to be deaf or Polynesian. No, for the life of him, he couldn't imagine how anyone who had feasted all night on the banquet that was Kate Usher could find him, Jason, an acceptable dessert course.

And what about the vision, and this power? Was it real? What did it mean? How did it work? Oh, let it go for now. He'd look it up on the Internet later. He would have to start wearing gloves again too, like he did after Owen...

He reached his own driveway. The big sycamore looked like a raised club.

Three times. Right on my ass. Thank God I'm home.

He fumbled for the house key, found the one with the triangle on it, and opened the door.

One feeble light flickered in the den. Charley barked but quieted when she saw him, or smelled him. She turned a little circle and whined.

Jason stopped in the archway. Eliza lay on the sofa.

"Hello, m'dear," said Jason.

She didn't look up.

She lay flat on her back. The afghan had slipped off her. Her housecoat hid one hand. The other lay on her chest almost at her chin, the fingers curled inward.

"Eliza?" he whispered.

Her eyes were closed, her mouth open.

Charley whined again, licked Eliza's fingers, and nosed the bowl of popcorn overturned on the floor.

She's dead, thought Jason. His whole body turned cold. *Oh my God, she's dead. She's had a... heart attack or a stroke. Oh my God.*

He stood frozen in the archway. Inside, he was screaming at himself to move, to check her pulse, to call an ambulance, to act. But he couldn't make himself cross the threshold of the room. To enter would be to step into a world where this horrible thing would be real.

"Eliza?" he called, louder.

The television flickered. On the screen reared the Headless Horseman, pumpkin held high, paused in still frame.

She died watching the Disney cartoon...

He stumbled to her side and took her hand in his. Now what would he do? Eliza was the only person left to him in the world. He rubbed her knuckles with his thumb and tears began to well up. Her hand was still warm.

Not yet, he told the universe. *Not yet. I'm not ready. I need her so much. I—*

"No, Honey. You'll mess my polish," said Eliza. She pulled her hand away. Her eyes opened. "How was the dance?" she said.

Jason stood and looked away. If he couldn't control his face he could at least control his voice.

"Great," he said. "It was a great time."

"Did you dance? I hope you danced."

"Yeah."

"Did you drink?"

"Of course not."

"Jason..."

"Okay. Half a beer."

"You smell like cigarette smoke."

"It wasn't mine."

"Yep yep yep," she said, retrieving the afghan and tossing it over her legs. "Someone had a time."

"You shouldn't sleep on the sofa," he said. "Let me get you to bed."

"No, I'm snug as a bug. I couldn't get up and limp in there if John Gavin himself were waiting for me."

"Who?"

"Actor. Never mind. I'm comfy, baby. I spilled my corn, though, dang it."

"I got it," he said, sweeping the kernels back into the bowl with his palm. The salt stung his cut hand. He stood. Eliza took his arm, her grip tight.

"Don't forget these years," she said. "Dances, music, beer and girls and staggering home late. Good thing you had cousin Zef to drive you. Make sure you know that the good times are happening when they happen. It's easy to miss them."

She patted his arm, turned and thumbed the remote control, banishing the Horseman from the den. She pulled the afghan to her chin and settled in. Jason kissed her forehead. Relief flooded through him again, relief to have her here, giving advice, looking out for him, filling up his life and helping to give it shape.

As he carried the popcorn bowl to the kitchen, he realized that he should put ice on his eye or else tomorrow morning Eliza would be asking him how he got a shiner. Oh, he would remember the good times, sure he would. As soon as they started.

He reached the kitchen and both feet shot out from under him. He fell, hard, on his tailbone. Popcorn showered him like a salty blizzard. He lay there, staring up at the ceiling, unbelieving.

"Ow," he said, to no one in particular.

"Oh, Honey. Did you fall?"

"I'm all right," he said, trying to ignore the rotten odor of whatever soaked his back.

"I spilled some milk in there. You let it go bad, boy-o. Wipe it up, will you? It smells awful." Her voice became small and apologetic. "Sorry to leave a mess. I couldn't help it."

He sat up, turned over, and the stench rose to embrace him.

"It's okay," he called to her. "I don't mind. Love you."

"Likewise!"

That's four, he thought, and grabbed the paper towels.

16   RAINBOWS AND UNICORNS

On the morning of Monday, October twenty-first, James Osorio received the following e-mail:

> From: Sally.Howston@NYDS.DCS.554.gov
> Re: Crane/VanBrunt Exhumation
> To: James Osorio, Director, Sleepy Hollow Cemetery
>
> The New York Department of State, Division of Cemeteries has approved the request to perform an exhumation on the remains of <u>ABSOLOM CRANE,</u> described as <u>lot 44 of SLEEPY HOLLOW CEMETERY / Van BRUNT tomb</u>. Applicants <u>JASON CRANE and HADEWYCH Van BRUNT</u> may arrange for the performance of the exhumation at any time, as per the statute referenced below. Please confirm receipt, and return the written copy of this approval with the signatures of each of the applicants.
>
> Thank you,
> Sally Howston
> Assistant Director
> New York Department of State, Division of Cemeteries

§ 1510. Cemetery duties
(e) Removals. A body interred in a lot in a cemetery owned or operated by a corporation incorporated by or

under a general or special law may be removed therefrom, with the consent of the corporation, and the written consent of the owners of the lot, and of the surviving wife, husband, children, if of full age, parents or surviving descendants of the deceased. Notice of application for such permission must be given, at least eight days prior thereto, personally, or, at least sixteen days prior thereto, by mail, to the corporation or to the persons not consenting, and to every other person or corporation on whom service of notice may be required by the court.

James Osorio smiled, forwarded the e-mail to FlyingDutchman1@RMail.com, and made Hadewych Van Brunt a very happy man. Hadewych called Valerie, who called Eliza, who told Jason to keep Thursday afternoon free for rifling the crypt of his great-great-great-grandfather. Jason nodded, shook his head in general disbelief, and pushed his bicycle out the door.

Jason rode to school on the aqueduct trail. It was flat and easy, since Gory Brook and the high school were on the same basic elevation. That was great, but it also meant that Jason wouldn't be getting a car any time soon.

Maybe this winter. When it gets too cold to bike...

He decided he liked this new commute. The town drifted by below, blue and grey and drowsy. Despite everything, the place had grown on him.

He liked being back at school, too—going to class, meeting new kids, wasting time in the library (where he did most of his actual learning) and, especially, having a schedule to give structure to his day. After all the changes lately he craved normality again. He chained his bike in the parking lot, shouldered his red backpack, and climbed the steep stone steps in front, joining the river of kids that flowed uphill from the town.

Once inside, he avoided touching anything. He dreaded a repeat of the incident at the dance. The first time he opened his new locker he wrapped his sleeve around his fingers. He entered his first class by pushing the door open with his shoulder. He met new people, but tried not to shake hands.

Not many hands were extended in welcome, though. The entire

student body had witnessed his humiliation. The girls needed their hands free to giggle behind as he passed. The boys needed theirs for flicking paper footballs at his head or knocking his books to the ground—and afterwards for making elaborate gestures of apology as they backed away. Only Eddie Martinez didn't need his hands. He just crashed into Jason, sent him sprawling, and walked on like a human snowplow.

Jason had dealt with bullies before. It had been the same story in Augusta. He couldn't understand why the best students and the nicest people always take punishment from the worst. Maybe he'd find an answer someday. He'd keep looking for one, but he wasn't going to cry over it in the meantime. He heard Eliza's voice: *fact of life, boy-o, be tough.*

Jason spent his brightest hour of the day in Mr. Smolenski's Mythology and Folklore class. The morning sun cleared the hills and blazed through the southward windows—right behind Kate Usher, who sat three desks away. Jason couldn't help but stare at her. It bothered him that they'd never made amends after the dance. She'd never given him a chance to undo whatever he'd done.

She ignored him, eyes cast down at her paper or looking straight ahead.

The bearded teacher paced behind his desk, enthusing over Arthurian legends one minute, bewailing the tragic end of the Knights Templar the next. This was the type of history Jason loved, but he couldn't concentrate on any of it. Why hadn't Kate smiled once, at least, or said hello? Why wouldn't she even look at him? He cleared his throat several times, hoping to catch her ear. No luck. The girl to his right tossed him a cough drop. He wagged his pencil between his fingers, trying to catch Kate's eye. She put her chin in her right hand and raised two fingers to her temple, blotting him out.

"Did you have a question?" said the teacher, smiling.

Jason brought his hand down. He'd caught the teacher's attention, not Kate's. His jaw worked as he thought. He wasn't sure of the subject today.

"Uh, bathroom?" he muttered. Then frowned at himself. Kate stared at him now, with a mixture of amusement and pity.

So stupid.

Mr. Smolenski sighed, nodded, and returned to his lecture.

Jason stood in the hall, thumped his head against a random locker for five minutes, and went back to class.

After lunch, Joey showed Jason the best place to hang out if you wanted to avoid the Sleepy Hollow Boys. Outside by the dumpsters, a long steel-mesh stairwell zigzagged up the side of the school—open to the sky but hemmed in by high brick walls. Sitting at the top, you were invisible to anyone below. The only problem was the smell, not just from the dumpsters but wafting up from the grate beneath your feet. Kids dropped their trash through the mesh into the space beneath, which was idiotically designed so that no janitor could get inside to clean without unscrewing and ripping up the mesh. As a result, the stairwell had become a grain silo of refuse—soda cans, potato chip bags, half-eaten sandwiches, broken glass, a pair of soiled underwear—it all piled up like a landfill down there.

"You don't want to be up here in summer," said Joey, "but this time of the year the breeze takes care of it."

"What if somebody drops a cigarette?" said Jason.

"Not good. That happened last summer. See the black streaks?"

They sat in the shade at the top and shared a bag of beef jerky.

"I've got to tell you something," said Jason.

"Okay. I sort of do too."

"You want to go first?"

"Uh… no," said Joey.

"'Cause what I've got to tell you is weird. On Saturday night…"

Joey held up a hand.

"Let me guess," he said.

"I don't think you can, man." Jason stared at his hands. "It's freaking me out."

"I think I know what happened."

"You do?" Jason frowned. Did Joey know about his abilities?

Joey took a bite of jerky. "Zef tried to kiss you, didn't he?"

Jason's jaw dropped.

"Yeah, he did. How did you know?"

"What did you do?" Joey said.

Jason looked towards the river. He couldn't see the lighthouse from this far away.

"I—made a face and dodged him and he got pissed and punched me."

Joey sighed.

"Yep. Yep. Yep," said Joey, lifting his Coke and shaking his head. "That's our Joseph."

"Who?"

"Zef. It's short for Joseph."

"Really?"

"Dutch thing," said Joey. "Go on."

"He punched me hard. On the face, right here. The bruise is gone now but he said he'd kill me if I told anybody and he hates my guts. But—you knew already, right? So I still haven't told anyone."

"Nobody knows about him," Joey said, "except me."

"Promise," said Jason. "Don't say I talked. He threatened to open my veins."

"He's all twisted up about it. And he's got a temper," said Joey, shrugging.

"You think? Yeah. He's got a temper like the sun's got a fever. He's apeshit crazy. Have you even seen him in school this week?"

Joey shook his head.

"He's probably off axe-murdering orphans and widows," Jason spat. "I keep expecting him to jump out at me with a folding chair over his head." Jason's voice dropped to a whisper. "You think all gay guys are like that?"

"I tried to warn you," said Joey.

"When?"

"That night. Remember? I said you had a chance with Kate but I couldn't tell you why?"

Jason shook his head, protesting.

"I have no chance with Kate," he said. "It's not like I'm going to tell her. If she doesn't know she's not going to hear it from me."

"Or from him. She's a senator's daughter. Hadewych would kill Zef if he lost that connection. Zef is under orders to turn on the charm and marry well."

"Yeah, he's a charmer, all right." Jason let loose with a string of curses. He rubbed his jaw. "So, what? He tried the same shit with you?"

Joey rose to his feet.

"We better get to class," he said.

"What? What did I say?"

Joey stared at his soda. He walked a few steps, turned and came back. He sat, one step higher than before, and spoke to the back of Jason's head.

"Yeah, he tried that... shit... with me. Last Easter, *Praise* was playing at this diner over in White Plains and Zef showed up for our last set. Lousy gig. We made like twenty dollars each. Anyway, Zef was by himself and he looked miserable. I said like, 'Hi, what a coincidence' and he said he'd come to hear the band, that he'd seen our flyer and, well... okay fine he kissed me in the car."

"Wow," said Jason, "how did you handle it? I freaked out. What did you do?"

Jason turned around. Joey looked sheepish.

"Uh... I enjoyed it?"

"You did?"

"A lot."

"Oh," said Jason. "So... you're..."

"Yeah. Um... and that was what I was about to tell you. But you went first."

They sat in silence.

"It was my first kiss," Joey continued, "and last. We just sat and talked a long time. It was a Saturday night and on Monday... he didn't punch me out, but he avoided me. Okay. He hid. Then he said nothing all spring while Martinez and the others called me 'fag' in the hall. That hurt. Look, I don't hide it or anything, okay? I'm pretty out there and... see, my parents know... my friends know... the whole school knows and... so... Zef just can't be seen with me, you know?" Joey chuckled, but there wasn't any humor in the sound. "But I don't blame him. I blame his dad and... everything. The world. But the silent treatment, man, it's worse than getting punched, I think. He hasn't said two words to me since. It would have been better if he'd just punched me. So anyway that's my story. And I'm sorry too."

"Sorry? Why?"

"Because if you and I hadn't been hanging around together at the dance, Zef wouldn't have figured you were... kissable..."

"Oh."

"Are we cool? You're not my new basher now or anything, right?"

Joey waited for Jason's reply.

This is what went through Jason's head, though it only took a second. First, he wondered whether Joey was going to make a pass at him like Zef did. He took notice of the fact that they were alone on a secluded stairwell. He wondered if Joey had been flirting with him the night of the dance, and whether he'd just been too oblivious to see the signs. He wondered why he had become gay catnip this semester. He realized that if he and Joey sat here talking together the other kids might think—what? That they were a couple? What would Kate think? No. No. He didn't need any more problems. He thought he was now expected to call Joey "fag," punch him and run. But… what kind of person does that? Who's that much of a jerk? He wasn't. He wasn't so terrified of being unpopular that he would punch somebody in the teeth to keep his reputation. That's Zef's reaction. To hell with all that. People could think what they liked. A friend is a friend. What problem? Joey was the most generally decent person he'd met in this town. He was smart and talented as hell, at singing anyway. Jason liked him. It was the damn twenty-first century and his generation was going to be the first to see past all this crap.

He turned to Joey again, his face sympathetic and grave.

"I knew all along," he said.

"You did?"

"Oh, sure."

"Why? Does it… show?"

"It shows. Yeah. You've got like this rainbow and unicorn glow about you."

"Rainbow."

"Yeah. And unicorns. It's pretty obvious. I'd butch it up some."

"Okay, sure. I can do that. How's this?" Joey adopted a deep menacing voice. "I have been waiting for you, Obi-Wan…"

"Better. Have some more jerky."

"Yeah. That there's man food."

Joey took a big swaggering bite. Too big. He started choking, then laughing, then choking some more. Jason slapped him across the back.

"Come on, soldier. Cough them unicorns out."

"Stop," gasped Joey. "You're making it—worse." But the damage had been done. They were both laughing and choking now. It really hurts to snort salty jerky juice up your nose.

"Just tell me one thing," Jason said, standing and wiping his eyes.

"What?" said Joey, recovering, dropping the bag of jerky into the trash below. "What do you want to know, Sarge?"

"Just—is anybody at this damn school *straight?*"

"All of them, far as I know. It's just me and Zef. Me anyway."

"So out of the whole school the first two guys I meet… What are the odds?"

"I guess you're just lucky."

Jason thought about that one as they made their way down the stairs. Lucky? Yeah, that must have been it. He threw a friendly arm around Joey's neck and they talked about video games all the way back to class.

#

Joey's favorite game was called *Death and Carnage.* He was good at it, but Jason caught on fast. They spent Wednesday afternoon at Joey's house slaying a pack of werewolves controlled by the Witch-King of Terracore. Pat Osorio brought them snacks. Joey's mom was thirty-fiveish and she loved to dance. You could tell from the way she did things. She closed cabinet doors with a hip bump, stacked plates in rhythm, and drummed with forks. She ironed shirts like a hoofer auditioning for a Broadway show, every wrinkled shirt choreographed especially for her.

Jason had already met Joey's dad, of course. James Osorio from Sleepy Hollow Cemetery gave a little start of surprise and a nod of greeting when he came home to find Jason munching chips in his living room. He sank into a recliner, weary from a long day of fractional real estate.

Later that evening, after the last werewolf had been slain, Mr. Osorio laid his paper down, puzzled by something.

"Jason's in your class?"

"Yeah," said Joey.

The man turned to Jason.

"Aren't you too old?"

Jason remembered the fake ID. Hell. He'd told this man he was eighteen.

"I was held back," he blurted.

"You were?" said Joey.

"Yeah. I'm… uh… stupid. Hey, let's watch that zombie movie?"

"Now?" said Joey.

"Yeah, come on."

On the way to Joey's room, Jason turned and looked back. Mr. Osorio had thankfully returned to his paper.

"What was that about?" said Joey.

"Shh. One second," said Jason.

They stood in the hall, listening.

"So," said Joey's mom, "what do you think?"

"About what?" said his dad.

"Think Joey's got a boyfriend?"

Joey's dad shrugged and turned a page.

"It's about time," he sighed.

Joey put both hands over Jason's ears.

"I hate them so much," he mouthed silently, dragging Jason away.

Joey's room was a jumble of laundry, plates and extension cords—cords to his computer, to his laptop, to his keyboard, to the UV light that shone over the habitat of his ornate wood turtle. Booger the Turtle sat fat and happy on a warm rock; his head came up as they entered, but with no earthworm or strawberry forthcoming he made a little sound of disgust and went back to working on his tan.

"You got held back?" Joey said.

"No. No. It's just this thing that's happening tomorrow. After school. I've got to do this thing at the cemetery and your dad thinks I'm eighteen. It was a… white lie. No biggie, okay?"

"What thing?"

"I got roped into it."

"Wait," said Joey, "the Van Brunt exhumation?"

"You know?"

"I'm supposed to be there to help. I was mad I had to work. That's you?"

Jason dropped onto the bench by the keyboard and stabbed at a few keys, but the power was off.

"That's why we were at the cemetery that day. Hadewych and I are… working together to open that tomb."

"What the hell for?"

"Okay. Long story." Jason turned. "This summer my grandmother left for one of her genealogy trips…" He told Joey about Eliza and the house, about the body in the millpond, about the Project. Joey sat at the computer, listening. Booger became offended at not being the center of attention and dug a hole to sulk. Jason was reciting Brom's letter to his son Dylan (as best he could remember) when Joey interrupted.

"What's the Horseman's Treasure?" he said.

"We don't know."

"You're doing all this and you don't know what you'll find?"

It was a good point.

"It happened pretty fast," Jason conceded. "It could be anything."

"Something good?"

"A real treasure? Some priceless artifact?"

"Yeah."

"I don't know," Jason said. "I don't how good it'll be." He shrugged. "I'm just praying that it's not something bad."

17 EXHUMATION DAY

Exhumation day arrived, whipping in from the north.

Thursday morning was overcast, punctuated by distant thunder. Weathercocks spun in disagreement. Weathermen placed their bets. Horseman's Hollow might be canceled. Maybe not. Halloween might be washed out. Maybe not. No one could predict the outcome but all agreed that the odds favored the storm clouds. Time would tell.

In the afternoon, low-pressure and high-pressure systems bumped gloves and began the Battle for Tarrytown. The neighborhood trees applauded raucously, twisting side to side as their sympathies shifted. The winds circled, came to blows, and a rain of fat droplets battered the face of the millpond.

But at five o'clock the bell of the Old Dutch Church brought the Hollow to an obedient hush. The opposing forces of Autumn and Winter stopped struggling. They retreated to their respective corners, still combative but out of breath, and the sun broke through with authority—as if Summer had decided to referee.

Hadewych stood at the threshold of the Van Brunt tomb, leaning on a crowbar. A long shadow spilled away from his feet and into the tomb. It threw itself across the sarcophagi, embracing them.

How many times had he stood like this, rattling this gate, wondering when it would open for him? He'd tried to gain entrance so many times. Ever since he'd realized what was inside, ever since he'd become heir to the Van Brunt papers. He had inherited them from his mother—so regal, so hard— so defiantly Dutch. So proud to have married into such an ancient family.

"You are a Van Brunt," she would say. "You sailed here before any of the rest. Don't forget that. You were here first."

He'd been six when he'd first asked her about the Treasure. He and his mother had been making supper from limp carrots and canned beef gifted to them by the Christian Care Pantry. They'd always prepared their food in the ladies' bathroom of the shelter, using the lid of a toilet for their chopping block to ensure that none of the other bums saw or smelled the food. Thieves love to target a vulnerable woman and child. Hadewych had been dreaming about the Horseman's Treasure again, a tale his grandmother had spun for him when he couldn't sleep for hunger. The old woman had died in June of that year, of a series of strokes that stole her away little by little. Her legs, then her hands, then her eyesight and all the rest.

Mother didn't believe in the Treasure.

"That old tale? We just tell it to make ourselves more interesting. Brom left millions when he passed on. The Van Tassel Estate, the quarry, Gory Brook, his aqueduct interest, even a signed contract with Archbishop John Hughes of New York to supply all the stone for St. Patrick's Cathedral. *Dylan* lost our fortune. That's the hard truth. *He* ran off and let the contracts lapse, not Brom. *His* young wife squandered the money. It was *Dylan* that ruined himself in the Civil War. But they say old Brom denied him some magical Treasure and that's why we're broke? That's just stupid. Dylan was a bitter dying man and he'd say anything at that point."

"But what if?" young Hadewych had said.

She had slapped him. Not hard, just enough to get his attention. "There's no magic to make it 1850 for us, son. You have to work twice as hard as everybody else, understand?"

"Yes, ma'am."

She'd tucked her sweaty brown hair behind her ears. "What happens to shirkers?"

"They don't eat."

"And lazybones?"

"They sleep outside."

She'd held the kitchen knife towards his nose: not to threaten, just for emphasis. It worked. "Don't cut corners, and don't look for shortcuts, son. We'll get there. With work and nothing else."

He'd nodded, and they'd returned to peeling the scrawny carrots.

He'd been an obedient boy, adhering to all his mother's rules. He was never a lazybones, and he'd never slept outside. He said "please" and "thank you." He never claimed charity as his due.

"Never scream for government freebies," Mama said. "No one's *entitled.*"

No one's entitled…

He was alone on the streets at fourteen. A cab struck his mother as she crossed Second Avenue. The cabbie's fault, but no one wrote down the license plate. When she didn't come home, Hadewych went searching. She'd been buried as a "Jane Doe" before he could find her body at any of the city morgues. That would have outraged her. Not the accident, but the loss of her family name.

He had nowhere to go. He had never known his father and he didn't care to. He had his mother's cherished papers, though—old documents passed down reverently through five Van Brunt generations though no one could read them anymore. He considered selling them to a collector or scholar. Surely someone would buy papers written by a famous literary figure like Brom Bones. But Hadewych had been taught that he must "look to family" and preserve it. "Look to family" was the Van Brunt motto, emblazoned on his mind by a thousand casual repetitions. If he sold the papers he might as well change his name to Smith and be done with it.

He kept the documents safe in his otherwise empty pockets. When the other young homeless at Covenant House were asleep, he'd take them out and trace his fingers across the strange letters that looked like curling brown hair. These papers were all he had from her. They represented the only family he would ever know.

That summer he spent many nights just walking, hoping to find some kindness. He didn't find any, but the hustlers and dealers found him. They tried to catch his eye, making little "nick" sounds from the shadows, as if calling a horse.

Hook you up, man? Hook you up?

He stayed away from drugs, as his mother would expect, and he never stole. He relied on the churches and the public library. He perfected his diction by watching old movies. Everyone respected him when they heard him on the phone, but they treated him like dirt in person. He longed to have nice clothes.

He felt vulnerable living in Manhattan. He didn't want to turn out like the other boys he'd seen, selling all they possessed for cigarettes and coffee and a few dollars passed through a window. That disgusted him. It gave him a lifelong revulsion toward a certain class of men. So, finally, as fall approached, he decided to leave New York.

He knew where he belonged.

He took a bus to Tarrytown.

He found fewer places to stay, though, and nobody willing to hire a minor. So he broke his mother's rules for the first time. He took his first shortcuts and became both liar and forger. He lied about his age to become a General Motors janitor. When he forged his ID, he half-expected his mother to swoop down from heaven and cut his nose off with a kitchen knife. But he had to work, didn't he? Those innocent shortcuts meant food in his stomach.

He rose at the factory, and by the time he was twenty he had his own apartment and a good living. He told himself the streets were behind him forever. He married Jessica Bridge, a sweet girl who sold popcorn at the movie theater, and before their first anniversary Joseph Dylan Van Brunt came and completed his father's world.

Hadewych had come to identify with Dylan, by then. He sympathized with the son of Brom who'd lost everything. Sometimes he would park across the street from 417 Gory Brook and sit in the car, staring at the place. He even began to save his pay, putting cash aside for his dream of buying back the old house that Dylan had lost. He would save his pennies, he would buy the Gory Brook house, and then he would leave it to his son so that the place would never leave the Van Brunt family again.

He lived scrupulously and honestly, obeying every lesson he'd learned from his mother:

Don't lie. Don't steal. Work hard. Lazybones sleep outside.

No shortcuts.

But, just before his twenty-seventh birthday, General Motors closed the Tarrytown plant, laying off four thousand, including Hadewych, in the first wave of firings. He found no other work. Too many locals were in the labor pool at once. He broke Mother's no-freebie rule and took New York State unemployment, but the benefits ran out. So did Jessica. She fell out of love with him and in love with another man. She left, not even challenging him for custody of Zef. She and her new husband would want their own family. Early that fall, Hadewych spent the last of the Gory Brook savings to buy Zef his school clothes.

Zef didn't understand what had happened. He missed his mother. He complained that they never went fishing anymore at the Tarrytown lighthouse; *his* lighthouse. He didn't understand that the factory had closed, the gates locked forever. He became demanding and whiny. One day Hadewych slapped him, harder than his mother had ever done.

"Grow up," he said.

Zef's tears came, and the sight of them broke Hadewych's heart.

Are there no shortcuts? Other people got around the system. Why be so damned upright? What has the system ever done for you but promised you everything then taken it away?

Mother was wrong.

The time for being a sucker is past.

He'd needed cash, of course, or he'd have no seed money.

He took the damn documents to be appraised. The rare books dealer he approached was intrigued but insisted they be translated. Hadewych traveled all the way to Albany to find a professor who knew the four-hundred-year-old language of the New World Dutch.

But weeks afterward the professor had accused Hadewych of perpetrating a hoax and had ordered him to take the pages and leave. And Hadewych didn't sell any of the documents; not once he'd read them.

Two in particular fired his imagination. The first, a long letter from Dylan to his son Jesse, written from Andersonville prison in Georgia. No one but Hadewych had read that account. The second letter he'd shared with Valerie and the others. *Mostly* shared. That letter had been written by Brom himself.

"My dear Dylan," it began. "I have buried what you seek. You will not recover it."

Well, Hadewych had thought, those desperate years ago, *we'll just see about that.*

That was the Halloween he had found Valerie. He had been standing, like this, in front of the tomb. And he had heard her screams.

Hadewych spun in frustration. Where were McCaffrey, and the old woman, and the boy Jason? Where was Zef to witness this? Hadewych stomped the crowbar on the ground. Didn't they know what this moment meant to him? No. None of the others knew anything at all. A Van Brunt family secret is not to be shared lightly.

They would come.

Patience.

The Treasure drew near, now. The ultimate shortcut. It would be his, his alone. Only *he* knew what it could do. He would get everything he deserved. He would restore his ancient family, for the sake of his son and his son's descendants. That was his destiny, and he was entitled to it.

"We are the Van Brunts," he muttered, "and we were here first."

He lit a cigarette.

#

Jason discovered Hadewych sitting on the stump above the tomb.

"Where the hell have you been?" snarled Hadewych. He whirled and flipped his cigarette butt at Jason's head, but it hit Joey in the arm. "You're late."

Joey waved away sparks and stomped on the cigarette. He picked up the butt and pocketed it.

"You," Joey replied patiently, "were supposed to meet us at the administration building, sir." (The "sir" sounded suspiciously like "jackass.")

Jason pushed Eliza's wheelchair up the hill.

"We're here now," Eliza called, waving to Hadewych. "And it's not their fault, it's mine. It was too steep for my knees and we had some business to do first."

"Oh?" said Hadewych, sounding as sullen as a teenager who'd waited two hours for a pizza delivery. He picked up his crowbar and climbed down to them. Vernon McCaffrey wheezed up the hill, wiping his forehead.

"Absalom," he explained. "The lady had to find a plot."

"Someplace else to put him," said Jason.

"And did you?" asked Hadewych.

"We had one available," Joey said. "In the Palmyra section."

Jason frowned, wishing they had been able to buy a plot up in Bridgeport, some piece of land in the cemetery above Chopsey Hill Drive. He'd rather reinter Absalom there, alongside beloved wife Annabel, mother of Jesse. The plot that they'd purchased wasn't very pretty, just a chunk of grass in the newer graveyard across the river.

"It'll be just fine," Eliza said. "You'll get the commission, won't you, Honey?"

Joey shrugged. "Some of it."

"Great. I was so worried about that," muttered Hadewych, forgetting to turn on the charm. "Can we please begin?"

"Yes sir," said Joey. (This time the "sir" sounded like "jerkwad.")

"I've got a truck waitin'," McCaffrey said, "and two Mex'cans to do any liftin'. No offense, kid."

"None taken." Joey rolled his eyes.

"Who's in charge of this exhumation?" McCaffrey said.

"I am," said Hadewych.

"I am," said Joey, simultaneously.

"You're kidding." Hadewych fixed Joey with a look that was decidedly unamused.

"Is there a problem?" Joey raised a brutal-looking chain cutter to his shoulder and stared Hadewych down.

Hadewych smiled, and raised the crowbar to his own shoulder. "Not at all. Why?"

"Whoa! I'm rolling, Honey," Eliza cried.

She was, indeed, beginning to roll backwards down the hill. Jason grabbed the handles of the wheelchair.

"Where do you want to sit?" he asked.

"Find me some shade. Charley, bad girl!"

The dog had squatted above a flat marker with the name WELLS. McCaffrey clapped.

"Dog! Git off that!"

Charley's water spread down the side of the stone. Jason parked Eliza's wheelchair in the shade of a maple tree and engaged the brake. Eliza zipped her jacket and opened her crazy-quilt purse.

"Go to it," she cackled. "I'm fine here with my iPod. Let me know when it's coming so I can take my pictures."

"I'll keep an eye on her," said McCaffrey. He'd become a little fond of the old lady. He put a hand on the back of her chair. Charley growled until he removed it, then curled up between them.

"You're not coming in?" said Jason.

"He can't," Joey explained. "I need the two of you first. If you gentlemen will follow me…"

Joey descended between the outflung arms of the hill. He turned at the gate of the tomb, one foot up on the crumbling stone. When Jason and Hadewych joined him he handed each one a flashlight and ascended the step so that his head rose higher than theirs.

"This is how we do it," he said. "The exhumation order is for one body and one body only, yes?"

Jason and Hadewych nodded.

"So we don't want to be touching any box but that one."

"They're all Van Brunts," snapped Hadewych. "I can exhume one of them any time I want."

"If you've done the paperwork," said Joey. "But you haven't. I've got one order and that's for Absalom Crane. Okay? Please don't touch anybody else."

"Heaven forbid," said Hadewych, rolling his eyes.

"Seriously," said Joey. "My cutters, my rules."

Jason straightened a little. Joey sounded very adult. (Or he would have, if his voice hadn't cracked.) Jason could almost smell the hostility between Joey and Hadewych. Jason remembered Joey's story of having caught Hadewych trying to break in with his own pair of cutters. Was he making Hadewych wait just to punish him for that? No, this was more likely about Zef. If Hadewych hated Joey for standing in his way, Joey hated Hadewych for standing in his, though Hadewych had no clue about that.

"Jason," said Joey, "since it's your ancestor, you need to give the word."

"What word?"

"Just say, 'This is the box I want.'"

"I don't know which box I want."

Hadewych ascended one step so that he towered over Joey. "We're going to have to examine each box until we find the inscription. Is that acceptable, or do I need to speak with your father?"

Joey sighed.

"Just keep the disturbance to a minimum, guys."

He raised the chain cutters, clamping the links between the two blades. He pushed the handles together and the blades bit the iron, but the chain wouldn't break.

"Little help?" Joey said.

Hadewych made a noise of disgust.

The boys took one handle and Hadewych gripped the other. They leaned toward each other, bracing their feet. Jason and Hadewych were almost cheek to cheek as they strained together. Jason could smell his bad cologne. The blades snapped through. His shoulder collided with Hadewych's. The chain rattled to the ground.

They drew back. The iron gate of the Van Brunt family tomb floated inward—effortlessly, silently, without the slightest touch.

As if someone had oiled the hinges every day, thought Jason. *Oiled them with… with…*

He pushed his hair out of his eyes. What had made him imagine that? Gross!

He had thought:

…with the rendered fat of unbaptized infants…

He chuckled at his own macabre imagination. Gruesome thoughts for gruesome deeds, he supposed.

"It's all yours," said Joey.

No one budged. They each tested their flashlights. Even Hadewych looked rattled. He took a deep breath, stepped aside and extended his arm over the threshold.

"After you, Mister Crane."

18   THE VAN BRUNT TOMB

The tomb was larger than he had imagined. Two chambers lay on either side of the entrance, protruding back under the hill the way they came, just as the cellar under Jason's house extended beneath his front yard. The walls were grey stone, identical to the stone of Jason's cellar and the stone of the weirs and ventilation shafts along the Old Croton Aqueduct Trail. In fact…

"Is this the same stone as my house?" whispered Jason.

A flashlight beam blinded him.

"Van Brunt Quarry stone," Hadewych said, reverently. He ran a hand along the mortar-less seams.

Something clanked behind them and they jumped. Joey had closed the gate.

"Sorry," said Joey.

Jason felt small. He could feel the pressure from the hill above them. He lowered his flashlight. The slabs beneath his feet were each the length and width of a man lying on his back; blue striations snaked across them like veins beneath embalmed marble skin.

Stop letting your imagination run, thought Jason.

"Okay, which one?" said Joey.

Jason wished his friend would speak more quietly, try harder not to wake the tomb's occupants. Joey had no doubt been in many such places, but his nonchalance clashed with Jason's own skittery gooseflesh.

They panned with their spotlights, searching the stage for their leading man. About seventeen stone boxes filled the space. A few,

Jason noticed, were of grey stone that matched the walls: Van Brunt stone. Others were made of marble like the floor, but most were of pink or brown sandstone, softer, with eroded corners.

"Start on the left," said Hadewych. "I'll look over here."

Jason swept dust away with the back of his hand, grateful that he had remembered to wear gloves.

ANNA VAN BRUNT

He moved to the next.

JOHANNES VAN BRUNT

He sighed, moved down the row.

Hadewych brushed an inscription.

Joey sneezed. "Try not to kick so much up?" he said.

"You can wait outside if you want," said Hadewych.

Jason brushed another lid. "Here," he said.

"You found it?" said Hadewych, his beam dipping as he joined Jason.

"No, but…"

Jason's flashlight lit the inscription. Hadewych's light doubled it.

ABRAHAM VAN BRUNT

"I found Brom," whispered Jason.

The sarcophagus of Brom Bones had been carved from Van Brunt Quarry stone, but the lid had broken halfway through at some point—about where Brom's belt would be—and the lower half had been replaced with inferior brown sandstone. A corner of this slab had fallen in at the joining, revealing the Brom Bones bones: two sturdy arm bones wrapped in a grey sleeve that had once been cloth or skin.

Jason recoiled, but Hadewych became softly prayerful.

"Hello Brom, you old trickster," whispered Hadewych, his head bowed. "Guess who I am."

Jason's eyes shot to Hadewych's face. Over the man's shoulder, the bust of Agathe Van Brunt leered from its niche in the wall, looking both menacing and protective.

They went to work on the rest. After a dozen more inscriptions had been dusted away, revealing name after name, they still had not found Absalom Crane.

"You're sure of what the letter says?" said Jason.

"Of course I am," snapped Hadewych, "Look again. I'll start on the left this time."

They switched sides and checked each other's work. No boxes were without inscription, and none bore the name Crane. Hermanus Van Brunt, Brom's father, slept in the far corner. Brom slept in the middle. The others were just random Van Brunts and one empty Affannato—important to themselves, but not to their visitors. Their dates of death became more recent, ending somewhere around 1950.

"Where is he?" bellowed Hadewych. His voice rang the stone.

"Calm down," said Joey.

Hadewych let loose a stream of profanities. His flashlight had died. He hurled it into a corner and grabbed Jason's. Then he checked every stone a third time, becoming ever more agitated as he did so. He shone his light onto the face of the bust in its niche.

"Agathe!" he demanded. "Where is he?"

Hadewych picked up the crowbar.

"Mister Van Brunt!" said Joey.

"He's got to be here," Hadewych said, and put the edge of the crowbar under the lip of the first stone lid.

"Hadewych," Jason said.

"You can't do that," said Joey.

"Stop me."

Hadewych pried the lid from the first box. It flipped to the floor, exposing a skeleton wearing a blue rag of a dress, jaw open to scream. A prowler had surprised her in bed. Jason reached for his arm but Hadewych recoiled. Jason retreated into the shadows, holding Joey back with a palm on the boy's chest.

Hadewych cracked the lids and ripped the roofs from above the heads of his ancestors. The room became crowded with Van Brunts—with men, women, children, with curled infant bodies, skulls trailing wisps of white and grey, with the eggcups of eye sockets; it became a meeting hall, with a whole choir of gumless mouths singing together as tiny black bugs scattered in fear. Brom's skull clutched its teeth in outrage, tight as a man about to whip a child with a belt. He had a bird's nest tucked under his chin.

All the boxes stood lidless. Hadewych panted in the middle of the room. He sagged, exhausted, holding the crowbar limply.

Jason heard a long low whistle. McCaffrey stood at the door of the tomb.

"Well, ain't you made a pig mess," said McCaffrey.

"Time to leave," said Joey. Jason could feel the outrage pouring from his friend.

Hadewych shook his head. "Not till I—"

"Leave now or I'm calling the cops."

Hadewych grabbed Joey by the collar. "Good. Call the cops."

"Hadewych," said McCaffrey, reaching for the man.

"Call the cops—and you people can explain—"

"Let's go," McCaffrey said.

"—explain—why you've *stolen* him!"

"Out, now," McCaffrey bellowed.

Hadewych tossed Joey to the floor. He raised the crowbar. Jason leapt between them. Joey threw up an arm. Hadewych swung the crowbar like a baseball bat and brought it down across the face of Agathe Van Brunt.

The side of the bust exploded with plaster.

"Where is he?" Hadewych said.

He struck the bust again, backhanded.

"Where?" he said, losing steam.

He swung again, missed, and cut an arcing white groove in the wall.

He went limp, dropped the crowbar and ran from the tomb like a batter headed to first base.

The dust settled.

"Christ on a cracker," said McCaffrey. "That could'a gone better." He shook his head and left.

Charley barked outside. Somewhere down the hill, Eliza shushed the dog and chirped, "Was it in there? Let me get my camera. What's wrong, Hadewych? Where are you going?"

Jason extended a hand to Joey, who pulled himself to his feet.

"I guess we know where Zef gets his temper," said Joey.

"You okay?"

"Until my dad sees this," said Joey.

The place was a shambles of dust and stone. Around them the Van Brunt dead laughed at the farce.

"Come on," said Jason. "We can put it back."

They had replaced the lids on seven boxes when Eliza rolled herself to the foot of the steps outside.

"You okay, Honey?" she called.

"Dandy," Jason said. "Don't come up, though. The graves aren't, uh, decent yet."

"Don't stay in that dust too long," she said. "You'll catch asthma." After a moment they heard her say, "I'm stuck. Honey! My wheels are stuck," and begin to grumble to herself.

Jason was struggling with the half-lid of Brom's coffin, so Joey went to her aid.

"Take a break, Jase," he said as he left.

Eliza thanked Joey. The sound of their wheels and steps receded.

"Would you mind if I took some rubbings while we're here?" said Eliza.

Jason couldn't catch Joey's reply.

Jason was alone yet not alone, a tourist in the Land of the Dead, surrounded by natives chattering together in a foreign tongue. He longed to return to the Land of the Living, where he knew the language and felt at home.

He turned his back to the boxes and set to work on Agathe's bust.

She hadn't withstood Hadewych's attack very well. Her right eye was still watchful and gentle, but the left was a circle of chalk without pupil or lid. She'd been decapitated, too, and her head had popped off. A hexagonal bar thrust up from the neck where her spine would be. The head clung to the bar but her chin faced the door now.

Jason gripped Agathe's ears and tried to restore her head to its original position, but when facing forward she wouldn't lower back onto her metal spine. He turned her to the right again. Now the two halves of her neck fit snugly, the wound closed, but she still faced the door.

He frowned.

He kept her head on the rod and twisted her by the chin. She swiveled easily—too easily. She whipped all the way around to face the back of the tomb.

And clicked.

Something behind the wall made a clanking sound, metal on metal. Some piece of machinery had engaged.

Jason stepped back.

That sounded like a… combination lock?

He tried to turn Agathe to the right but she'd stuck again. He lifted her head. The spine twisted back around to its starting position, all the way to the right.

Turn the head towards the door. Lower it onto the bar. Turn it leftward. It clicks when you stop. Lift the head again, the bar yanks back. Like… like an old rotary phone. But what number would he dial?

He saw a small bronze plaque at the base of the bust.

AGATHE VAN BRUNT
1760—
"I Look to Family."

Jason felt a small thrill.

Oh, Brom, is this your doing?

Brom had built this tomb. He'd been the one to hide the Treasure. Of course he wouldn't have made it easy. It would take more than a Crane and a Van Brunt collaborating. That just got you in here and, honestly, you could have accomplished that with a well-placed bribe. Not all cemetery directors were as honest as Osorio. The few sarcophagi that had been cracked open—Brom's own, the Italian's—indicated that others had searched this place, maybe at night.

But… had any of them discovered this lock?

He thought about calling for Hadewych, but what if this was another dead end? He thought about calling for Joey, but he was messing where he didn't belong and his pride wanted him to solve this himself.

"I Look to Family…" he whispered.

Yes, the boxes were the numbers in the combination. The bust would have to turn and face particular boxes in some order. But if Brom built this tomb, the eligible boxes would be limited to the ones installed prior to Brom's death, which ruled out anyone after the year—Jason checked the lid of Brom's box—1850. So, pre-1850 boxes only.

Jason went from inscription to inscription. He found three that met the criteria.

He turned the bust to face HERMANUS VAN BRUNT, Agathe's husband, who died in 1800.

A definite click. He lifted the head and let the bar swivel back.

He turned the head to face JAMES VAN BRUNT, who died in 1810. Had this been an uncle of Brom's? It didn't matter.

Another click.

The last box would be that of Brom himself: ABRAHAM VAN BRUNT, who died in 1850. Jason turned the bust again towards the grey box at the center of the tomb. Surely Brom had designed his own resting place.

A third click.

Jason stepped back. Nothing happened. He frowned. Something had eluded him. He felt he had the order right. What would be the point of ordering the boxes in any way but chronologically? It felt right to start with Hermanus, Agathe's husband. What about James? No, without him there were only two pre-1850 boxes and that didn't seem like a proper combination. There was no point in adding a box dated later, since this was Brom's puzzle. Who would be the fourth in line, anyway? *Dylan...*

"Jase? Why don't you come out?"

Joey stood at the door. The sunlight had dimmed.

"I'm onto something," Jason said.

"The funeral director said his workers would help me do the rest of these. Go home."

Jason's mind raced. Could he use his new ability to solve this? What if he took off his gloves and touched the bust—would he see the combination? Or should he just touch Brom's skull and pull the answer out of there? That wasn't going to happen, and how would he explain it to Joey?

"Eliza's asking for her grandson," said Joey.

Grandson... yes... Agathe's grandson, Dylan. But he wasn't buried here. Jason had seen a rubbing of Dylan's angry-looking headstone the night Hadewych had proposed this crazy adventure. Dylan was buried someplace else.

But would Brom have known that? No. Brom might have made a sarcophagus here for his beloved son... It would be...

145

"Jase? What's up with you?"

"Shut up a minute."

…It would be… Van Brunt Quarry stone.…

Hermanus's box had been of that grey stone, so was Brom's, and so was… He saw it.

The lid had fallen on its side. The inscription read: **EZRA VAN BRUNT** and **BABY BOY VAN BRUNT**—a joint tomb. The occupants were a little girl and an infant. The box itself was grey but the lid was sandstone. The original must have been carved with Dylan's name.

Three Quarry stone boxes. Hermanus, Brom, and the one intended for Dylan. James Van Brunt had a box of dull sandstone. Low quality. Cheap…

She didn't like her brother-in-law…

Jason smiled. He seized Agathe's head and twisted it.

Hermanus… *Click.*

He skipped James.

Brom… *Click.*

He turned to Joey triumphantly.

"Watch this," he said with a grin, and twisted the bust to face Dylan's never-used grave.

Dylan… *Click.*

A metallic boom echoed through the space. A hole cracked open in the floor. One of the marble slabs fell in, creating a black rectangle. Right where Joey stood.

Joey screamed and fell, disappearing into the floor.

"Joey?" gasped Jason.

A sandstone box hung over the hole, too; a sarcophagus installed decades after Brom's time by someone who didn't know about the secret lock. It teetered on the edge and, before Jason could seize it, the immense stone box fell in after his friend.

"Look out!" Jason screamed.

The tomb shook with the terrifying crash below. A column of dust flew upward and broke against the ceiling.

Jason threw himself at the opening and groped into the blackness.

"Joey? *Joey?*"

No one answered.

"Joey!"

19 ABSALOM

Jason shouted for help.

He waved dust away and swung a leg over the side, ready to leap down and save his friend. How far was it anyway? A flashlight lay on the floor nearby. He hit it against his hand and the light came on. He looked down the hole again and the floating particles dissipated before his beam.

He could make the jump. The floor was about eight feet below. He could climb down the marble slab partway. It was broken in half by the shattered pieces of the sarcophagus that lay on top of it. He was about to jump when the flashlight beam found a white hand protruding from the pile, lifelessly.

"Joey?"

He threw his arm over his eyes. He had killed his friend. But, maybe…

He leapt to his feet.

"I'm going for an ambulance."

"Good," said Joey. "You're going to need one."

Jason dropped onto his belly again, looking for the source of the voice. He found his friend standing to one side of the pile, rubbing an elbow, his face white with dust. Joey called Jason several bad names that he probably deserved.

"What were you thinking?" he said.

"I wasn't."

"Thank you for warning me…"

"I'm coming down."

Jason slipped down into the hole. The stones shifted under his feet. He reached bottom and surveyed the pile.

"I thought this box had squashed you," he said.

"It almost did."

Joey kicked the marble slab.

"It landed at an angle," said Joey. "There's something underneath it back there. I rolled off before the box came down. All I got was my funny bone thunked. Hard. Which isn't funny. Stop grinning."

"I'm grinning because..." Jason said, earnestly, "...because it could have been worse." He pointed his flashlight at the white hand protruding from the pile—skeletal remains of the occupant of the box.

"Yes. And I'm going to punch you now," said Joey, raising a fist.

Jason nodded and offered a shoulder.

Joey brought his fist down in slow motion, miming the fall of a meteor, complete with a little explosion sound as it hit Jason's shoulder; his palm opened like a cloud of debris and dropped away. It had been a purely ceremonial blow—not a gesture of anger but of forgiveness.

"So, where are we?" Joey said, turning.

"I don't know."

"You're the Indiana Jones here."

The walls of the chamber were of the same grey stone, but this space was more elegant, circular, with plaster moldings. A gear system clung to one wall, just beneath Agathe's bust. Two rods connected it to the mechanism that had released the stone.

"What did the slab fall on top of?" Joey wondered, disappearing behind the rubble.

Jason didn't follow. He was staring at a painted panel with an image of Agathe. She was beautiful, her long hair auburn like his own. She wore a smart suit that might have been a man's. She stood in front of the fireplace of the Gory Brook house. Her hand caressed some object on the mantel. Someone had whitewashed that part of the image, crudely. Jason scratched at the whitewash with his gloved finger, and it came back glittering with specks of gold leaf.

"Jason... bring the light?" said Joey.

"What did you find?"

"I think... Absalom."

The marble slab had fallen in onto two pedestals that framed the door of a separate antechamber. Two porcelain vases had been smashed to the ground. Jason hoped that nobody's cremated remains had been inside them. Inside the antechamber, Joey stood next to an immense coffin that commanded the center of the room. The coffin had been fashioned of rough wood—American chestnut maybe. The long beams and steel bands suggested a pirate chest.

"The Horseman's Treasure…" Jason said.

He brushed the dust from the coffin. He recognized the craftsmanship. It was the same make as the front door of Gory Brook: the same bristling nail heads and brute metal. Across the center strap an inscription read

ABSALOM CRANE

1850

Hi, Absalom…

The walls of the antechamber bore ropes of painted roses, pulled by fat cherubs.

"Pretty girly," said Joey. "Was Absalom somebody's gay uncle?"

An inscription on the wall behind read "A.V.B."

Jason understood.

"This must have been Agathe's tomb," he said. "Or it was supposed to be. Hadewych told me she vanished and her body was never found. Brom must have had his mom's tomb built before that happened."

Worried voices filtered down from above. McCaffrey and Eliza were calling the boys' names. Charley barked.

"Do you want me to tell them?" said Joey.

"Yeah—" said Jason. This was a group effort, after all, and he didn't want to give his grandmother a heart attack.

"Give me your gloves," said Joey.

"What?"

"Your gloves. So I can climb up."

A cold spear went through Jason's chest.

"I'd like to keep them," Jason said.

"Five minutes. The stone is sharp."

"I'll climb up then."

"What's the matter?"

Jason did not want to be in this place with his hands exposed, but this wasn't the moment to tell Joey about his visions. He pulled the gloves off and handed them to his friend.

"Back in a sec," said Joey.

Jason felt naked. He glanced around, making note of the things he should not touch. The coffin, definitely. The walls, probably. He shouldn't touch that pile of wood in the corner. Pile of wood? No, a rotted rocking chair tipped on its side. Drawing nearer, he could see the delicate upholstery. Alongside stood a tea tray on rollers. The top was enamel, and ink-stained.

A book rested there.

It was about four inches square, bound in green leather and thick with flaking pages. It bore no lettering on the cover or spine.

He could hear Hadewych's voice above, shouting with delight.

Jason's curiosity overwhelmed his good sense. He reached out and took hold of the book.

The room glowed bright with gaslights. The coffin vanished—replaced by a small chaise lounge, his living room, and the fireplace at Gory Brook Road.

An old woman sat before him, rocking in her chair, white head bowed. Her hand moved laboriously across the page. Ink stained her fingers and the ruffle at her wrist. The hand moved, drawing inscrutable, alien letters across the page...

"Jason?" Hadewych called from above.

Jason couldn't answer. This vision, like all the others, held him immobile in its grasp. He couldn't break from it until it had run its course.

Agathe looked into Jason's eyes. She was an ancient thing—nothing like the beauty in the painting. Her chin almost met her nose, mark of the elderly and toothless. The lines across her sunken cheeks spread like the tributaries of dry riverbeds. Her eyes were watery and full of motion.

She raised a finger to her lips.

This, the gesture said, *will be our little secret.*

"Jason, are you there?" said Hadewych. He was scrambling down the stone. "Good God," he said, "look at this place."

Soon Hadewych would enter and discover Jason standing in the corner behind the coffin, arm raised and frozen to the leather of the book. It would be hard to explain.

Hurry up, he ordered the vision.

"Hurry up," said a man's voice.

By the fire stood a tall blond man with thick arching eyebrows and a dimple in his chin. He wore a high-collared shirt and a cream waistcoat with gold trim. He had the most intense features Jason had ever seen—vivid eyes, gaunt cheeks, and a jawbone like an animal's.

"When can I read it?" he said.

"After I'm dead," said Agathe, her voice fragile, yet full of life.

"That will be a long time," said the man, flattering the old woman. She had to be ninety. He sat on the chaise, his fingers steepled against his lips.

"Soon enough," she said. *"And you'll be strong, won't you? It's a burden."*

"I'm ready now. I'm ready to hear it all. To hell with Father."

"It will be Hell for all of us," said the old woman. *"This is... evil, Dylan."*

So this is Dylan, thought Jason, fascinated. *Son of Brom and Katrina.*

Dylan nodded, thoughtfully. But his face kept its intensity. He tucked his chin and looked at her from beneath his brows. His hair fell forward.

"I want to know everything you know."

"Then stop pestering me," she said with affection, *"and let me write."*

Someone applauded.

"Well done, boy. Well done," Hadewych said.

The vision broke. Agathe and Dylan evaporated. The gaslights went out. The rocking chair rotted to sticks.

Hadewych's flashlight beam played across the coffin. Jason grabbed the book, spun, and stuffed the slim volume down the back of his pants.

"Now," said Hadewych hungrily, "let's see what's inside."

#

Jason watched McCaffrey's men rope the coffin, bear it down the hill, and jab it into the van. They turned around and went back to help Joey, who had to restore the tomb and lay plastic over the hole in the floor in case of rain. Joey told Hadewych to expect a substantial bill, but Hadewych appeared as unconcerned as a millionaire buying a newspaper.

Jason thought of nothing except the lump under his shirt. He hadn't mentioned the book to Hadewych. He'd slipped it to Joey with a promise to explain. That had been a good idea, because as they left the tomb Hadewych gave Jason a bear hug—in celebration, supposedly, but Jason knew he was being frisked. Once outside he'd retrieved the book from Joey. He told himself he would examine it in private—just to see what it was before it fell into Hadewych's hands.

Hadewych grinned like a schoolboy pulling the wings off flies. He jumped up into the back of the van, waved, and rode away with the coffin. McCaffrey would pry off the bolts and bands back at the funeral home, where everyone would gather for the big reveal.

Jason walked down to the administration building, retrieved Eliza and Charley, and loaded them into the Mercedes. He opened the trunk, hid the book in his backpack, and drove out of the cemetery, turning left on Broadway.

Eliza lectured him on his carelessness for ten minutes, complimented him on his ingenuity for five, and speculated about the Treasure for another ten. What could it be? Wasn't this fun? At long last! Jason couldn't help but feel happy, seeing her enjoying herself so much. It almost made the whole ordeal worth it. Almost.

"And most of all," said Eliza, patting Jason's leg as he drove, "I'm so glad to see you and Hadewych getting along so well."

20   THE HORSEMAN'S TREASURE

Valerie waited for them in the parking lot. Charley snarled when she saw her, so Jason held the dog's collar as he and Eliza crossed the lawn.

"Why didn't you come?" said Eliza, taking Valerie's arm.

"I don't like—cemeteries," said Valerie. "Too physical. I'm more—spiritual."

The McCaffrey Funeral Home was also Vernon McCaffrey's house. His mother, Sylvia, a doddering Jewish woman of at least eighty, met the group at the door. Charley wet the carpet in the entry hall and had to be banished to the back yard. She scratched at the screen for five minutes but when no one came to parole her she turned a circle and lay in the weeds by the crematorium chimney.

When McCaffrey and Hadewych turned up, they warned the ladies not to be in the morgue when they opened the coffin— "Exhumations are icky," is how McCaffrey put it—but Valerie and Eliza *had* to witness the big unveiling. They were too curious to wait outside and, besides, the boys were being sexist.

Jason would be in the room too. One more skeleton wouldn't make tonight's dreams any worse. He slipped into the restroom first and splashed water on his face, washed his dirty gloves clean and put them on wet. He wasn't going in unprotected, even if it raised eyebrows.

McCaffrey's downstairs morgue was terrifying and banal at once: a dingy room, with a drop ceiling and exposed cinderblock. Jason slipped in and stood next to an industrial sink tea-stained with rust. He tried to concentrate on a bottle of hand sanitizer and a box of Brillo pads—rather than on the embalming tables, or the rows of instruments hanging on the wall: saws, hoses, clippers, and something that looked like a shoe stretcher sized up to accommodate a human rib cage.

"Do you have a cat?" he said.

McCaffrey grinned. "It's formaldehyde. You get used to it."

Jason shuddered. How horrible to end up here—in McCaffrey's little Empire of the Dead. How horrible to be nude and helpless while that balding Texas butterball puttered about with tubes and cotton—lipstick, needle and thread. No, that wasn't how life should be.

But this wasn't life, of course. This was the other thing.

McCaffrey produced a wrench and hammer and—with elaborate ceremony—circled the coffin, harvesting a berry-pile of bolts. Jason could tell that they twisted off easily. The muscles in McCaffrey's forearms barely flexed, but he grunted dramatically, Samson testing his strength at the county fair.

Ring the big bell, cowboy. Jason giggled to himself. *Win your filly a stuffed armadilly!* Or whatever they did down in Texas.

McCaffrey popped off the metal that secured the lid. The rib that read ABSALOM CRANE–1850 came up first. He pulled the second away and piled the metal to one side. He picked up a chisel, tap-tapped around the seam, and then struck the wood with the heels of both palms.

The lid jumped and the seam became a thin black stripe.

"Moment of truth," said McCaffrey, but he didn't sound happy.

Eliza squeezed Jason's hand. Valerie tucked her chin and turned towards Hadewych. He put an arm around her shoulders, but watched Jason.

The coffin exhaled as McCaffrey raised the lid—just a faint whiff of dust and droppings, of trash left out in the summer. A grey cloth covered the figure inside—a shroud, not a layer of spider-silk as Jason first thought. McCaffrey drew it back.

Absalom Crane was too tall for the coffin. His slender body had been turned on its side and his knees were drawn up. Jason's eyes shot evasively to Absalom's feet. They were enormous. The shoes had rotted away, exposing a jigsaw puzzle of bone.

He'll have to buy new shoes, Jason thought. *Big ones. Size fourteen like me, probably. He'll have to order them online…*

He pushed the hair out of his eyes.

His mind was distracting itself, he knew—distracting itself in order to process the sight a little at a time—the tilted pelvis—the painful spine—the ribs, brown and ivory like keys on an antique piano—distracting itself so it could return gradually to the worst sight, which had been obvious as soon as McCaffrey had drawn the shroud aside.

Absalom Crane had no head.

The line of his long body ended with an anti-climactic nub of neck vertebrae. A black valise with a bronze clasp sat where the head should have been.

He glanced at Valerie. She pressed fingers to the valve in her neck, getting it ready to scream, just in case.

Can you scream with a valve in your neck? Wouldn't it hurt? Jason couldn't imagine.

Hadewych's expression was peculiar, inward-focused. Jason lost sight of it as Eliza moved in to get a better look.

"What's that down there?" she said.

Absalom's arms extended away from his body as if cradling a child. Each hand grasped the opposing forearm, making a wide but empty 'O'. Something silver lay loosely in this space.

"Hello, what have we here?" said McCaffrey.

The sheath was decorated with an elaborate intaglio—with complex symbols and thatched patterns picked out in tarnish.

Eliza turned to Hadewych. "Is… is that it?" she said.

"It may be," said Hadewych.

McCaffrey laid the sword on top of the burial cloth. The adults gathered around, whispering amongst themselves. Jason made do with a mezzanine view, peering over the top of Eliza's head. The whispering grew more and more grumpy. *This* is the Treasure? It looked perfectly ordinary to Jason, like something from a flea market.

But what were they expecting? The tablets of the Ten Commandments? This isn't the Ark of the Covenant.

He felt shut out. He retreated to the metal stool by the sink and sat staring at the man in the coffin.

Am I the only one who sees a person?

The adults huddled around the sword. It—not the corpse—was their dearly beloved. Not Annabel's husband, Jesse's dad. Jason's three-times-great-grandfather. But this was *Ichabod's son*, squirreled away in the Van Brunt tomb behind puzzle locks and cemetery rules—for what? Why wasn't he shipped back to Bridgeport with a note reading, "Dear Annabel: Sorry we decapitated your husband, signed Sleepy Hollow"?

"What's in the bag?" Jason said.

The four adults turned. McCaffrey shrugged, walked to the head of the headless man's coffin and opened the valise, producing several items:

Underwear.

A striped undershirt.

A pair of glasses in a leather case.

A train schedule and other papers.

A handkerchief.

A skull.

McCaffrey hollered when the handkerchief fell away and revealed the thing. Even after gravedigging for many years, it's still startling to find a skull in a traveling bag. He fumbled the thing and it spilled out of his hands. The adults recoiled, but Jason threw himself from the stool, landed on his belly, and caught the skull before it could smash into dust.

I've got you, Absalom, he thought.

"Nice reflexes," said McCaffrey. Jason handed the skull back, grateful that he'd worn his gloves. Hadewych helped him up and slapped his back.

"Is that—*his* skull?" said Valerie.

"Looks like." McCaffrey said. He laid the valise on its side and nestled Absalom in a bird's nest of underwear and papers.

"And there's nothing else?" said Eliza.

"Nothing but the sword," McCaffrey said. "Sorry."

"I see," said Hadewych. "Was there anything else in the tomb?"

Jason felt positively riddled as they all turned to look at him. He had hidden the book, of course, in the trunk of the Mercedes. Should he tell them what he'd found? He remembered Agathe raising a finger to her lips. *This will be our secret.* She had directed the gesture to Dylan, of course, but Jason felt bound to it himself.

"Nothing important… that I remember," he said.

Someone coughed. McCaffrey's mother stood on the stairs. She whispered in her son's ear and left.

"I got a call, y'all," said McCaffrey, "so… uh… take your time and I'll be back in a couple'a ticks."

"Can you—close the coffin first?" said Valerie.

McCaffrey struck his palm against his forehead. Jason noticed a bit of Absalom's striped undershirt that had fallen out of the coffin, and almost got his fingers squashed tucking it back in. The lid groaned shut and McCaffrey bounded up the stairs.

Hadewych drew the sword from its scabbard. It rang as he raised it, glinting under the fluorescent lights.

"What do you think?" said Valerie.

"It's old," said Hadewych. "Very old."

"Eighteen-fifty at least," said Jason, needling Hadewych a little.

"I bet it was *his*," said Eliza, her voice rapturous.

"Whose?" said Jason.

"*His*, silly. *The Headless Horseman's*." She shivered with superstitious delight.

She'd throw salt over her shoulder if she had some, Jason thought.

"May I?" she said, reaching for the hilt.

"Of course," said Hadewych.

Eliza took hold of the thing. Hadewych released it and the point fell to the floor.

"It's heavy," she whooped, spinning with the thing. "Look at me, Honey. I'm swinging the Headless Horseman's sword. Look out. I'm gonna getcha!" The whole group laughed.

When I am eighty years old, Jason thought, *I will still remember this*.

He saw *beneath*, then, back to the little girl his grandmother had once been—pigtails and a striped bag of popcorn—bouncing in a theater seat—oh so restless for her *Legend* to begin. It wasn't a vision Jason was having, just love. She'd been his mother, his father, his lawgiver and his support—and yet he felt like an amused parent. *Oh, for a camera to capture this moment.*

"We don't know—that it was—the Horseman's," said Valerie.

Eliza settled the sword and flexed her knobby fingers, feeling the strain. "It's the *Horseman's* Treasure," she said.

"But why would the Treasure be a sword?" said Jason.

"Because he *treasured* it, silly," said Eliza, as if that answered everything.

Jason took the blade in one gloved hand. He didn't want to burst her bubble, but now he was stewing over her lack of logic.

"Brom did all this—to keep a sword away from his son?"

"It appears so," said Hadewych. "Let me look at it, 'Liza."

He took the hilt but Jason held the blade. He and Hadewych played tug-of-war—with Eliza at the centerline—until the edge threatened to slice Jason's glove. Hadewych's smile flashed in the silver as Jason let go.

"It could have qualities which we haven't discovered," Hadewych said.

"A magic sword?" Eliza said.

"*Eliza*," Jason said, scoffing.

She scowled, turned her back, and patted one sore shoulder. Jason brooded and massaged.

"My ancestors might have believed that," sighed Hadewych. "It was a superstitious time. Ah, well. We tried." He slipped the sword into its scabbard, went down on one knee and presented it on open palms. "Your treasure, my lady."

Jason rolled his eyes, but the gesture did have a valiant flair—even though the maiden was over eighty and the knight knelt in a morgue.

"I couldn't," said Eliza.

"I insist," said Hadewych. "You've been such a sport, moving here and indulging us. Take it. It's a gift."

Jason was seething. *It doesn't balance the scales, you jerk. You uprooted my life. And you give us a sword? The thing's probably covered in bubonic plague. This is grotesque!*

"Ow, Honey," said Eliza. "Don't rub so hard."

Jason stalked away. Something else was eating at him, but he couldn't place it.

"That can't be the—Treasure." Valerie slammed a fist on the embalming table. A scalpel fell from a shelf. "Not after all we've—been through."

"Let's go somewhere for dinner. It's been a busy day," said Hadewych.

"No, no," Jason said, as agitated as Valerie had been. "Who cut Absalom's head off?"

"The Horseman, obviously," said Eliza.

Jason pressed his hands to his eyes. "There's no Horseman."

"Yes, there is," said Valerie.

And you believe in tarot cards, Jason thought, but he took a deep breath and said, "A person killed him, not a ghost."

"You're saying my ancestors are murderers?" said Hadewych, amused.

Jason grabbed the lid and opened the coffin over their protests. He pulled the train schedule from beneath the skull.

"Okay, here's a train schedule. From New York to… Connecticut. He came down from Bridgeport, right?—that's his travel bag—but somebody in Sleepy Hollow decapitated him."

"The Horseman…" Eliza muttered.

"Maybe. Fine. But, hold on, look at this." Jason had unfolded a piece of paper. "Isn't this Brom's handwriting?" he said. "I haven't seen it in English."

Hadewych reached for it but Jason held it back.

"Brom is *my* ancestor," Hadewych said. Jason relinquished the page. Hadewych scanned the writing. "Yes, this is Brom. *June thirteenth: Dear Ichabod,*"

Eliza gasped and leaned forward.

"May I have the honor of addressing you by that name? Honorable Judge Crane does have a pleasing sound yet I hope that we are beyond titles, you and I? In Irving's tale we shall be entwined forever more, for good or ill. It is my wish that we should meet again, and embrace each other as friends at last, two old men who stumbled into a tale together. Mister Irving has planned a Halloween Feast, in honor of the thirtieth year of his Legend. *We would be delighted if you could join us. We might explain ourselves to each other, and perhaps share stories of our departed Katrina. Six in the evening on Halloween night, at Sunnyside."*

"Sunnyside?" said Eliza.

"Washington Irving's estate," said Valerie. "He lived in—Tarrytown."

Hadewych concluded. *"Your humble servant, and now-toothless rival, Abraham "Brom" Van Brunt."*

The group sat in silence. For the first time, the four actually felt as if they were part of the old tale.

"The *Sketch-Book* says eighteen-twenty on the cover," said Jason, "so the thirtieth anniversary was eighteen-fifty."

"The year on the coffin," said Hadewych, "and the year Brom died. Just weeks after this Halloween party."

"Ichabod died in eighteen-forty-nine, though," said Jason. "He was already dead when Brom sent this invitation. So—Absalom came in his father's place. And they killed him."

"They wouldn't," said Eliza, indignantly.

"Somebody did it—probably with that sword. But then, what? Brom sticks the murder weapon in the coffin?" Jason paced. "But—why not just throw it in the Hudson? Why hide it from Dylan? Why create this stupid legend about a Treasure? It doesn't make any sense."

"Calm down," said Hadewych. "It's been two hundred years. These things become jumbled up, naturally. No one in my family would have killed your ancestor, Jason. Brom loved *The Legend*. This letter is evidence enough of that. And he buried Absalom in fine fashion—that's an expensive coffin—and in his own mother's tomb. Deep breaths. We'll figure it out. What does it matter, though? You act as if this happened yesterday."

Jason pointed at the skull. "He was a person. He—"

"Jason Crane," said Eliza. "Lower your voice."

Jason folded his arms.

"Let's take a break. Tensions are high," Hadewych said. "So we didn't find the Hope Diamond. We solved the mystery we wanted to solve. And we've found a most excellent document." He squeezed Jason's bicep. "Jason, you're wonderful. Eliza brags about you all the time—how you love history—how logical you are. So here's the logical conclusion—the Van Brunt family legend is just that—a legend. Another *Legend of Sleepy Hollow* and just as fictional as Irving's."

He released Jason's arm.

"But we were sure," said Valerie, balling fists over her head. "And now we have—nothing to—fight him with." She brought her fists down on empty air—or some invisible target.

"Fight who?" said Eliza.

"It's late, sweetheart," snapped Hadewych. He patted Valerie's back.

"Let her talk," said Jason. "What did you mean?"

Valerie shook her head and engaged her valve.

"Nothing. I'm—tired," she coughed. "It can be—hard to—make the right words."

"What a day, eh?" said Hadewych, chuckling. "What can you do?"

And now Jason realized what had been eating at him. Hadewych was handling the situation far too well. In the tomb, just a whiff of failure had driven the man berserk. He'd vandalized a dozen graves and smashed Agathe's bust with a crowbar. The ladies hadn't seen the rampage, but Jason had. Now Hadewych was acting like he didn't care. Yes. Acting. As if—

"*You* took it," Jason blurted.

"Took... what?" said Hadewych.

"The Treasure. You snuck it out of the tomb. I don't know how, but—"

"Jason," said Eliza.

"He did. He's taking this too well."

"He," said Eliza, "is acting like an *adult,* which you might try yourself."

"Okay, son," said Hadewych. "When did I even have a chance? I wasn't the one down there alone. How do we know *you* didn't take something?"

"Me? I would never—"

But Jason stopped himself. He *had* taken something. And—oh no—

What if the book *is the Horseman's Treasure?* He hadn't even considered that. Dylan in the vision had been so eager to read Agathe's book... so maybe Brom had hidden the book from him? Of course. But then Jason had something to confess. *He* was the thief—not Hadewych.

"Apologize," said Eliza.

"I—I'm sorry," Jason muttered.

"I'm sorry what?" said Hadewych.

"I'm sorry... sir."

"That hurt, Jason," said Hadewych. "I thought we were becoming friends."

Jason's hands balled up. McCaffrey entered the morgue, his face solemn.

"We got to call it a night," he said. "The police need me for a pickup."

"Someone died?" said Jason. "Who?"

"Don't ask that," said Eliza.

"You wouldn't know her," said McCaffrey. "Little blond girl. Realtor."

"Debbie Flight?" said Jason, eyes wide.

"We know Debbie," said Eliza, and her hand went to her heart. "She sold us our house…"

"What happened?" said Jason.

McCaffrey leaned in conspiratorially.

"They found her floatin' in the reservoir. Blood drained out, just like that other fella."

"What 'fella'?" demanded Hadewych.

"Darley," said Jason. "His name was Darley, right? I saw Fireman Mike pull him out of the millpond—on our first day here."

"You never told me that," said Eliza.

"Sorry," said Jason in a small voice.

"And why didn't I hear about this?" said Hadewych.

"It happened while you were in Augusta. Boxing up our old house."

"You saw the body?" said Eliza, shaking her head.

"Yeah—and Debbie Flight was with me. She saw it too."

"So did I," said McCaffrey. "I hosed the mud off so his wife could identify him. Confidentially, the fella had his wedding ring in his pocket." McCaffrey winked. "I put it back on his hand 'fore she saw that. Damnedest thing, though. He was bleach white. Like he'd been floatin' in Clorox. They hushed it up, but somebody poked his eye out. You know what with? A danged car antenna."

An inhuman sound pierced Jason's ears—so unnerving that he leapt back and almost tipped the coffin. Valerie's throat valve was *not* built for screaming after all. All she could do was fall to the floor, writhe and buzz.

#

"Do you think she'll be all right?" said Jason. Charley darted between his legs and barked, happy to be home. He wished he could feel the same. The house felt sinister after his vision in the tomb. He kept seeing Agathe rocking beside the fireplace, writing in her book.

"Valerie's a little… fragile. Poor thing," said Eliza. "You can't imagine what's she's been through. You want some cocoa?" She raised her voice as she puttered into the kitchen. "She's been in therapy almost ten years to get over it."

He stopped by the davenport. It sat in the same position as the chaise in the vision. Had Dylan's ghost been present when Jason arranged the furniture? No. That was silly. Whatever dead people did on the other side it was not... feng shui.

"Where is her mother now?" he said.

"A mental institution. She committed herself. No memory of that night, supposedly—and Valerie refused to testify against her own mother."

"Why not?" Jason said, incredulous.

Eliza reappeared with a mug in one hand. "Would you testify against me? If I stabbed you?"

"Hell, yeah."

"Only 'cause I raised you to be a little shit," she said affectionately and exited again.

Their fireplace, he realized, was Van Brunt Quarry stone. He touched the hearth then stepped back, remembering the portrait in the tomb. Agathe had stood there once, her hand on the mantle, auburn hair flowing, posing with... something... something that had been whitewashed over, long ago.

"It will be Hell for all of us," ancient Agathe had said, sitting in her rocker, right over there. *"This is... evil, Dylan."*

"I want to know everything you know."

"Then stop pestering me. And let me write."

"Tada," Eliza sang.

Jason jumped.

"There you go. Hot cocoa, à la Merrick," she said, pushing a mug into his hand. "My secret recipe—two parts cocoa mix, Ensure, half an arthritis pill and a thimble full of Geritol. Oh lighten up. I'm kidding." She raised the mug. "To the Project."

"To the Project."

"May it rest in peace," she said.

"We're through then?"

She nodded. "I think we did good." She wiped cocoa from his chin.

"You're not disappointed?"

"Me? It's been the time of my life." She turned away and shuffled toward her room. "I am tired, though. Ready to go to bed. Take your gloves off, Honey. You're in the house. Who raised you? Oh, yeah. Me. Sorry about that."

"Not disappointed even a little? It was a waste of time."

She turned at the door.

"Having adventures is never a waste of time," she said. "Sitting on your butt *is*."

He followed her into the room, but she waved him off.

"Nope. About face, soldier. I'm getting nekkid. Yes, I can manage. My hands are fine tonight. Take my cup. Scoot—finish your cocoa or be scarred for life."

He gave her her privacy, chuckling as he closed the door. She was in fine form tonight, silly old woman. Yes, she'd had a very good time—and Jason felt proud of himself for seeing things through to the end.

"What should I do with the sword?" he called.

"I don't know. Hall closet I guess!"

Hope you aren't the Horseman's Treasure, he thought, hiding the thing away. *'Cause you're getting stuck between the house slippers and the shop-vac.*

"And after all," Eliza called through the door, "think what you can tell your kids. You broke into a tomb looking for treasure. That's better than Chess Club."

"I guess," Jason said, shutting the closet again.

"You guess?" she said. She came out in her nightdress, wringing her hands with lotion. "Honey, do you hate being here that much?"

"No," he said, thinking of Kate.

"I didn't think so," she said. "I think Sleepy Hollow is a good place for you to call home. You belong here. You'll see. You take those gloves off now."

He peeled the gloves off and put them in his pocket. She watched with a twinkle in her eye, biting her lip, deciding whether to say something.

"'Night, son," she whispered, finally.

"'Night, Eliza."

"*Such* a grown-up," she said, and waited with hands on hips. "Eliza" wasn't enough, not tonight. He kissed her forehead and she leaned in as he did.

"'Night, Grandma," he said, "I love you."

"Much better. Likewise I'm sure. Oh—one more thing." She

turned at the bedroom door. "Is that boy Joey gay?"

"Uh—yeah."

She nodded.

"Good. You'll get some culture."

#

After Jason felt certain that she was asleep, he crept outside and fetched his backpack from the trunk of the Mercedes. Charley heard the click of the door when he returned, and she growled from the bedroom. Jason slipped upstairs before the poodle could decide whether he was an intruder.

In his room, he drew Agathe's book from his backpack and turned on the bedside light. He had no vision from the thing, now. Could his gift be limited to one image per item? He would have to test that. Never mind.

He would finally find out what Dylan was so eager to read. He was just as eager to read it himself. He took a deep breath and opened the cover.

The pages were blank.

He held the thing up to the light. Blank?

What the hell?

No, not blank. Not entirely...

He could make out fine brown lines that had been letters, but these had faded so badly that the ink and paper bled into each other, brown on brown. Flipping pages, he did see a few sentences here and there, but the letters were inscrutable, as alien as Arabic or Thai.

That's that.

Maybe somebody would read the thing someday. Maybe some lab could fire neutrons at it or something and recover the lost letters. But Jason was done. He felt better now, actually. He hadn't stolen some precious document, after all. This was as useless as the sword.

The visions had to be his priority now. He had to get on top of those. The Agathe vision had hit him hard and fast.

He found his laptop and googled "magic psychic powers."

Six million, one hundred and thirty thousand results.

Ugh.

#

165

"Good night, my love," said Hadewych, leaving Valerie at her front door.

"I won't be—sleeping here," she said.

"You're coming up?"

She shook her head. "I mean—I can't sleep—in the Hollow. I can't—risk—"

"Being here at night. I understand. But just because one realtor drowned, that doesn't mean—"

"Not one. Two people. It killed them. You know it did."

Headlights swept past; Valerie recoiled and hid from the lights.

"I have to go," she said, reaching for the door.

"We'll find a way to stop it," said Hadewych.

"I'll be at a hotel. I'll call—when I know."

"When will you be back?"

"Maybe in the daytime."

"And at night?" he said, touching her shoulder.

"Not till after—Halloween." She pulled away, wiped her eyes, and slammed the door.

Hadewych waited for the last of her many locks to turn. Satisfied, he walked to his car and opened the trunk.

There it waited.

He'd been longing to examine it for hours. He and McCaffrey had been so rushed, opening the coffin in the back of the van. Now he had all the time in the world.

The side of the cardboard box read THIS END UP but the arrow pointed in the wrong direction. He lifted with some difficulty and waited, listening. A few kids laughed as they crossed Patriots Park. Motorists idled softly on Broadway.

He closed the trunk of the car, making just the smallest click.

As if on cue, the wind rose—invoking a dervish of leaves that danced up the dead-end road and leapt the picket fences. Hadewych turned up his collar, embraced the cardboard box, and carried the Horseman's Treasure up the stairs.

21   THE DRAGON AND THE BRIDGE

After school on Friday, Jason hiked north on the Old Croton Aqueduct Trail in search of an isolated spot. He had an experiment in mind but it required privacy. He'd stashed three objects inside his red backpack: a hairbrush of his mother's, a pair of Eliza's reading glasses and a stuffed dragon from his childhood. He would attempt to read them and see what happened.

He'd found a promising discussion of "psychometry" online, the psychic reading of objects, but from there it deteriorated into horoscopes and crystals and homeopathy and hoodoo. He'd found ads for live psychic hotlines, stories about telepathic dogs, a website extolling "deviant witchcraft" and the blog of a Himalayan yogi who lived on nothing but sunlight. He'd given up in disgust. He refused to swallow that nonsense.

After all, what would Carl Sagan say?

No, he'd find the answers on his own, scientifically.

It was warm for October, and the sun massaged the back of his neck as he hiked. He enjoyed the exercise. He hadn't yet explored the woods north of the house. Autumn colors framed the trail as it stretched ahead, two tracks of hard grey dirt converging and disappearing. The silence here was humbling and vast. His hearing grew sharper, opening to the hushed rustle of leaves and the distant splashing of the Pocantico River.

The river trickled into town from the north, marking the eastern border of Sleepy Hollow Cemetery. He couldn't see it through the trees but he knew it ran alongside the aqueduct trail. The river diverged and turned west when it reached town, passing under the Headless Horseman Bridge and into the millpond of Philipsburg

Manor. The Dutch settlers had used the rushing water to turn the millwheels. The river poured through the sluices of their mill, ground their wheat into flour and then spilled into the Hudson, exhausted.

Another river had once flowed through the forest, but it had been manmade and deep underground. The enormous tunnels of the aqueduct burrowed south from a lake near Croton, ten miles upstate. The water flowed downhill, passing under Sleepy Hollow and emptying into a receiving reservoir in New York City's Central Park. The whole operation closed in 1955 after modern pumping stations came along. The receiving reservoir had been filled in to become Central Park's Great Lawn. But the tunnels were still down there, as unused as the veins of a corpse.

The aqueduct trail ran along the top of this buried tunnel. The ground sloped away on either side. If Jason were to turn around and hike south he could walk all the way through Westchester County and down to Manhattan, but if he took a wrong step to the left he might somersault down the hill and into the river, assuming he didn't hit a tree on the way.

An occasional chimney of stone thrust up out of the ground. Jason passed one as he hiked. It occurred to him that the tunnel must pass right under Gory Brook Road. How big was it? What was still down there? He remembered how wet the cellar under the house had been. Could water still be seeping through? He hoped Eliza hadn't bought a house with a sinking foundation. Debbie Flight had seemed pretty desperate for commissions and Eliza had bought the place impulsively.

Jason pushed his hair out of his eyes, shook his head and marched on.

The trees on the left side broke open and he saw the graveyard.

He looked down into a grassy garden of headstones. This was the newer section of Sleepy Hollow Cemetery, scooped from the forest east of the river, inaccessible from the trail, protected from vandals by a high chain-link fence. Absalom would be buried there soon.

Jason lost his appetite for exploration. This creeped him out. He hated to have a field of dead people so close to the house. He hadn't realized these graves were on his side of the river. He left the trail, skirted the south side of the cemetery fence and followed the chain link downhill to the river where the fence plunged into the water. A short wooden bridge, designed to look rustic and quaint, connected this new section to the main cemetery. Otherwise the little auxiliary graveyard was unreachable, surrounded by its lidless cage.

He felt like going home now. He shouldn't leave Eliza alone anyway. Rather than trek back up to the aqueduct trail, he decided to try following the riverbank southward. It proved to be a bad idea. He fought vines and brambles, slid in mud and stepped into treacherous crevices hidden by leaves. He started to sweat. Tree limbs rotated abruptly under his sneakers, threatening to throw him down the hill. A branch broke under his grip, pitching him forward towards the water. He caught himself before he fell, breathing hard. This was pushing his luck. If he twisted his ankle in this forest, who would hear his cry for help?

A shelf of grey stones protruded into the Pocantico River. He climbed out onto it, feeling grateful for something sturdy under his weight. He sat cross-legged on a wide flat stone almost in the center of the river. He took off his muddy sneakers and washed the soles in the current. He shook off the backpack and remembered the purpose of his hike. This secluded island was the perfect place to try his experiment.

He took out his mother's hairbrush. He held it in his lap and focused on it.

Nothing.

He shut his eyes and concentrated. He sensed a cloud passing over the sun and his body prickled with goose bumps as his sweat cooled. Around him the rushing water drowned out all other sound. It splashed around the little island where he sat, eyes closed, holding a hairbrush and feeling damn ridiculous.

He felt ready to give up when the cloud passed and the sun blazed overhead. Now, somehow, he felt a river of happiness and warmth splashing around him, a feeling of peace and contentment and summer mornings. He caught the mouth-watering odor of bacon and eggs wafting up from downstairs. He saw a hand running the brush through long blonde hair.

"It's getting cold, baby. And I need to get Jason to school."

This was a voice he hadn't heard in over ten years—his father's.

"I can be on time or presentable but not both!"

This was his mom: her husky chuckle and almost undetectable Virginia accent.

Oh, he'd forgotten… How could he have forgotten their voices?

The hand lowered the brush. He tried to catch his mother's face in the mirror, but she'd already gone. The brush rocked back and forth on the dresser. It stopped and Jason opened his eyes.

It had been so real. He looked up at the sky, now bluer than he remembered. He didn't want to cry. No, he was smiling. He ran his thumb across the hairbrush. Deep between the bristles he discovered a few strands of blonde hair. He put the brush back in his backpack, slowly and a little reverently.

He squared his shoulders and brought out the reading glasses. For five minutes he turned them over and over in his hand.

Nothing.

What was missing?

Each vision so far had involved something personal, something emotionally "hot" in some way. He counted them off. He'd been boiling with emotion when he first touched Kate's bare skin. His father's boot meant a lot. So did his mother's hairbrush. He'd been pretty worked up in the tomb. Did he feel anything about this pair of broken dime-store reading glasses? Nope. Maybe that was the secret.

Maybe you have to care.

Not for the first time, he wished that he could find a teacher to explain all this to him. Surely someone else out there had a gift. He couldn't be the only one.

He tucked the glasses away and took out the dragon. This would be an emotional item. He'd adored it when he was little. It was green, with a smiling face, a forked felt tongue and multicolored fins protruding from the back. One seam had broken and a little white cotton peeked through.

He ran his fingers across the green skin in circles trying to guess what he might see. Himself playing in the backyard? Curling up under his old *Star Wars* sheets? He felt excited, giddy with anticipation.

The river became a terrible roar. People passed all around, a rush of people, a swarm of them. He saw them from waist level: men and girls and teenage boys and women with shopping bags, chattering and stomping and laughing and bickering. He turned in place, disoriented and terrified. He tried to squeeze between a grey plastic trashcan and a silver planter stuffed with artificial ferns. He bawled, clutching the dragon. He cried "Mama!", his voice high, childish, and heartbreaking.

Jason jumped up, heart pounding. He stood on the rock again. He remembered that day when he'd lost his parents in Piney Bridge Mall. They had turned up, of course, and chided him for wandering off, but, seeing his tears, they'd bought him an ice cream to calm him down. The dragon had been with him that day. Yes. That's why he carried it around for years—because it would protect him. Protect him from losing them. Oh, how he had crumpled with fear when he thought he had lost his parents forever.

Now the adult Jason did cry.

Worse than the memory was the realization that his childhood fear had come true.

He felt overheated. He leaned down and splashed water on his cheeks. It was clear, icy, and wonderful. He cupped both hands in the wash and took a deep drink.

Instantly he realized what he'd done and started heaving. How could he be so stupid? This river ran through an immense cemetery. This clear and wonderful water had been strained through a thousand graves. He choked and sputtered. He vomited and the liquid came up red and gold, reflecting the setting sun.

Jason grabbed his backpack. He shouldn't wander the forest after dark. He reached for the stuffed dragon.

It was gone.

He saw a flash of green in the water. The dragon had slipped from the rock and was floating down the river. Jason threw his backpack over his shoulder and splashed along the shore, tearing off branches, trying to snare the beloved old thing. It darkened as water seeped into the felt.

His dragon drifted too close to a boulder roiling with foam…

No no no.

…and the swift undertow dragged it to the bottom.

Don't go. Don't go.

Jason waited, but it never came back.

But I still need you, he thought, though he was too old to believe in dragons.

He stood staring at the foam. He felt unreasonably sad and vulnerable. A piece of his childhood had drowned today.

He stomped away, red-faced, lost, miserable, tramping through thick stands of locust trees trying to keep sight of the damn river. He couldn't afford to lose his bearings. Twilight fell. He felt panic rising.

Branches caught his clothes. Mud grabbed his ankles. Twigs snapped his face. A piece of bark lodged in the corner of his eye, maddening him and limiting his vision even further.

He stumbled into a rocky clearing. To his right, a massive stone foundation hung over the water, a crumbling and sinister ruin. Vines spiraled up the nearby trees and squeezed their neighbor's trunks like fingers around a throat. The brambles were thornier here, angrier, teeming with nettles and spiders. But a clear path opened ahead. A road had once run alongside the river to this spot.

The forest had grown dark. The sun had dropped away with unnatural swiftness. Night had caught him here in this place. The moon hung low in the sky, a pale eye peering at Jason from between the trees.

Where was he? The immense stone reached over the river, calling to the other shore. Jason left his backpack on the ground and climbed up onto the rock, carefully in case it collapsed beneath him. From his perch he spotted another smaller block thrusting out from the opposite bank, also reaching to clasp hands with its twin brother across the water, long separated by the rot and collapse of the timbers between.

Jason had found the foundations of a bridge.

He could see the roof of the Old Dutch Church, beyond the trees on the far side. The moonlight rippled on the water below. Jason felt an inexplicable urge to reach down and touch the broken stone. He felt his touch would fulfill some other long-sought reunion. His fingers spread and he kneeled—but then stopped himself. He straightened and scrambled back down, careful not to brush anything as he did. He had lost his taste for visions, thank you very much, and this stone no doubt had unpleasant tales to tell.

Something caught his eye. In the crook between the old road and the bridge, the ground sloped down to a stagnant lagoon shielded by the stone and protected from the southward current. A dark shape protruded from the mud there. Jason took hold of it, pulled, and a rotted leather purse lurched out of the mud with an unpleasant slurping sound. Its broken strap came up last. Jason felt like a bird pulling a worm from its hole.

He set the thing down on the stone. He found a handful of soggy papers inside plus a twenty-dollar bill and a few singles, but they tore through when he tried to remove them. At the bottom lay a washed-out lipstick and some spare change. The pennies were green but the quarters were bright. He put these things back in the purse and rubbed the mud off its side.

A woman crashed through the brambles and into the clearing. She looked about forty and was dragging a dead body. No, not dead. And not a body. A young girl with dark hair who screamed and clutched the vines.

"What are you doing? Let her go!" Jason shouted, but the woman ignored him. She turned around and grabbed the girl under the arms. The woman's eyes were the emptiest Jason had ever seen, two black voids without reflection. She heaved the girl down the slope and into the water, as indifferently as a peasant woman might throw her laundry into a stream to beat it with a stone.

Jason noticed a black purse hanging by its strap across the woman's back, the twin of the one he held in his hands. The girl choked and sputtered in the stagnant water, her black hair a suffocating mask across her face. Jason couldn't move and couldn't help. The older woman forced her under.

"You're drowning her! Stop!" Jason cried.

Bubbles rose and broke on the surface. The girl clutched at the woman's clothes and beat her assailant's shoulder with a fist.

I'm seeing… a murder. This woman is a murderer. Oh, God stop this. Stop.

Then the girl's hand found the strap of the purse and she pulled it. The older woman's head snapped forward, but the strap broke. The purse flew and flopped against the side of the broken bridge. Something tumbled out and glittered in the mud.

A set of car keys.

The girl broke away, gasping for air. Her attacker seized the keys with her right hand, turned and grabbed the hair at the back of the girl's head. She pulled hard, exposing the white throat. She raised her right arm and Jason saw the jagged outline of a key there. The arm came down fast and speared the girl through the neck. Blood burst from the wound, spattering the woman's fist, dark and colorless in the moonlight. The key thrust down over and over.

Valerie. It's Valerie. Her mother did it. That's what Eliza said. This is her damned mother.

"STOP!" Jason screamed.

His body broke free of its paralysis and he stumbled forward, losing his balance. The woman disappeared. Valerie disappeared. He fell down the slope towards the spot where they had been. His hand shot out unthinkingly and he grabbed the corner of the black stone bridge.

Hoofbeats. Pounding hoofbeats. Coming closer. Coming up the road. Someone or something galloped towards him. The head of an emaciated horse burst from the gloom of the road. The rider was fumbling, out of control without saddle or bridle, clutching at the white mane, kicking the beast across the hindquarters with his thin legs, his face a frozen mask of terror. He whipped around to look back over his shoulder. Something chased him. Something terrible.

Jason spun away as the horse ran over him, spearing him through the chest with its iron-shod hooves. He was unhurt. The horse galloped upward and across the bridge, across strong timbers rough-hewn and knot-holed. The rider wheeled the horse about, looking back from the far shore. He was wheezing. A sloppy white ruffle bobbed under his chin. His face was hopeful now—a familiar face, much like the one Jason saw every morning in the mirror.

Something thundered up behind Jason, not with a clatter of hoofbeats but with the teeth-rattling thunder of stone on stone. Ichabod (yes, of course the man was Ichabod) wailed, and the sound of his terror echoed across the valley. The hot breath of a horse burned the back of Jason's neck. He stood frozen, unable to turn his head to see the thing behind him. He didn't want to. This was no ordinary vision. He felt with certainty that the rider behind him—no, the *horseman* behind him—knew he was there.

Ichabod kicked his horse. It reared, brayed and would have thrown him but for the fistfuls of its mane he clutched. Horse and rider spun in place on the far side of the bridge, disoriented.

The horseman behind Jason laughed, a terrible deep cracking sound from all directions like a thousand axes chopping down the woods. Jason felt searing heat as a ball of flame whipped over his shoulder. A burning jack-o'-lantern arced across the bridge. Its maniacal face spun end over end. It grinned back at Jason for an instant, spun round, and crashed into Ichabod's temple, knocking him from his horse and into the dust. The pumpkin careened upwards, exploding against the trees, shooting tendrils of flame up their trunks, igniting branches and showering the world with sparks and flaming leaves.

Jason recoiled, fell to his knees and threw his arms over his face.

His lungs and heart pumped wildly. They slowed. He brought his arms down.

The bridge was broken again.

It was over.

This is the true bridge, he thought. *The true Headless Horseman Bridge— the bridge that the spirit could never cross, the bridge where his power ends. It's here, forgotten and crumbling, while the bridge by the millpond impersonates it for the tourists.*

And there is *a Headless horseman. There* is *a Headless Horseman.*

This was too much. He had to escape. He kept his eyes fixed firmly forward as he reached for the backpack and stood. Then, summoning all his courage, he turned and looked behind him.

Nothing loomed there except the vines, brambles and dark secretive woods of Sleepy Hollow.

22 A PERFECT PLACE FOR A MURDER

"So… you have superpowers."

"That's not what I meant," Jason said. He lifted a box from the truck and passed it to Joey.

"You see things with your hands?"

"Right."

"That sounds like a superpower."

"No it doesn't."

"Does to me. Unless we're talking braille, Helen Keller."

Two men pushed past, carrying electrical cords and fixtures.

"Lower your voice," Jason said.

"Oh, right," Joey whispered. "Your secret identity."

Jason grabbed a box and stalked away. Joey lifted his own, catching up halfway across the Philipsburg Manor parking lot.

"Thanks for being so supportive," Jason muttered. "I thought you would listen."

"I *am* listening," said Joey.

"No you're not. You're making jokes."

"Aw. Come on. Don't be that way, Spidey."

Jason spun around and scowled. "Stuff it," he said, backing through plastic sheeting and into the staging area of the Horseman's Hollow event. They trudged down a path of muddy plywood.

"I didn't say I don't believe you," said Joey.

"And you didn't say you did."

"I'm working on it."

A girl in a tight sweater passed, carrying wigs; a burly construction worker ducked by, carrying lumber. Jason and Joey both stopped to

176

gape.

A man approached with a bloody hatchet. "Do you kids belong here?" he said.

"Yes sir! We're volunteers, sir. I'm Joey and that's—"

"No time for biographies. What you got?"

"CostumedonationsfromtheSleepyHollowtheaterdepartment!" Joey said breathlessly.

"That's sweet. But you're on the wrong side of the millpond. That way—past the corn maze and behind Ichabod's schoolhouse. Got it?"

"Yessirthankyousiritsanhonorsir!"

The man shouldered his hatchet and walked away. He had splashes of blood on his back.

"You're insane," said Jason.

"Insane? Look at this. This is live theater."

An enormous crew crawled over the manor grounds. The preparations must have been going on for months. The handful of mill buildings had been dressed with assorted horrors and surprises. Corpses were swung from hangman's ropes, jail doors were hung with stumps, torsos were slung on bloody spikes and heads peered from pikes. Tables groaned beneath gore and candles and smoking censers. A spattered priest sharpened his sword on a seventeenth-century grinding wheel.

Lanterns on hooks and lengths of sailing rope traced the path for visitors—leading them around the millpond and through the buildings, into the mill house and newer structures, out again, and into a fluttering white circus tent. A pumpkin-headed scarecrow menaced the boys, gleeful for a second chance at a child of Ichabod Crane.

Joey sighed. "Live theater is where I belong."

When they entered the big tent, a half-dozen monsters turned to look at them—monsters with horns and fangs and saucer eyes—with melting, rotted flesh. The monsters wore makeup bibs, T-shirts and sweatpants. A woman in a nun's habit bared jagged teeth. Joey and Jason carried their boxes past rows of severed heads, masks and prosthetics pinned or taped to wig dummies, powdered wigs, witches' brooms, angel wings, fake fingernails, false fangs, hollow-eyed mannequins of children, widows' weeds, Redcoat uniforms, shawls, tricorn hats, a cannon on rollers, four racks of colonial dresses, a shelf of candles, and a rotted corpse in polystyrene. They ogled the collection with wonder. They were on the inside. The scare-ers, not the scare-ees.

A figure stood waiting in the center of the dressing room, admiring itself in the reflection of three makeup mirrors. As they entered, it whipped about and snarled. Jason and Joey screamed and fell backwards onto the floor. Satan himself—a massive beast with two curling ram's horns, withered red skin, and eyes blazing from beneath a thick ridge of brow—loomed over them with claws raised.

"Boo, you pussies," said Satan.

"Eddie?" said Joey.

"King o' Darkness himself," said Eddie Martinez, posing. "Good to see you girls. I was afraid you broke up."

"You're *the Devil*?" said Joey. *"How?"*

"How you think? I got hired," said Eddie. "I was working construction. And this costume lady took a liking to me. She's nice."

Eddie made a number of obscene gestures.

"But—but—that's the biggest role," Joey said. "Except for the Horseman. I'm only a Redcoat. After two callbacks. And you're… you're *non-Equity*."

"That's 'cause you couldn't scare shit," said Eddie. He took a step forward and they cringed. Even in a dressing gown and boxer shorts he was a scary Devil. "Can you do *this*?" he said. He locked eyes with Joey, fixing him with an imperious glare. Joey couldn't hold eye contact and looked away. "Can *you*?" Eddie said, and he turned the same withering spotlight on Jason. Jason held his own as long as possible but he too gave in and blinked.

"I didn't think so," said Eddie, and the boys had to admit that if intimidation was an acting talent, Eddie Martinez was the Sir Laurence Olivier of Horseman's Hollow.

"Just wait until I got my goat leggings on. Wait till I'm on that throne. You're gonna think you're in Hell, losers."

They were in Hell already.

"Can I help you boys?"

A middle-aged woman peered at them through bifocal glasses.

"CostumedonationsfromtheSleepyHollowtheaterdepartment!" Joey said.

The woman sighed. "Let's have a look."

"Where you been, gorgeous?" Martinez said to her, tossing the goat leggings onto the dressing table. "I was getting horny." He pointed to his horns.

"What have I told you, kid?" said the woman. "That is *not* appropriate."

"You know you love me," said Eddie.

She opened Joey's cardboard box first.

"Hmph," the woman said, brushing her hands. She turned to Jason's box and opened it. "Hmph," she said again.

"What's wrong?" said Jason.

"Get these out of here," she said, closing the boxes. "They're full of lice."

"Lice?" said Joey. "But they were fine when we did *The Crucible.*"

"They've got lice now. Get them out before they get into any of my pieces."

"Can we help you with anything el—"

"Just get them out. I've got enough trouble. We open in six hours." She gestured to Eddie. "Come on Satan, let's see how you look with the contacts in." Eddie slapped the woman's rear as they left. "Stop that," she thundered, and Eddie gave an evil laugh.

Jason and Joey collected the boxes.

"Lice? Gross," said Joey. "I can't do anything right."

"Me neither," said Jason. "I just made an awful mistake."

"What?" said Joey.

"It's terrible. I emptied my box of costumes right on top of Eddie's furry pants."

"You did?" Joey said, smiling.

"I'm about to."

"Oh, no," Joey lamented, putting his hand to his forehead. "The lice shall surely get into them."

"Yeah," said Jason, "and won't that be hellish?"

#

After they'd made certain that Eddie Martinez would have company in his costume, they were done until Joey's six o'clock call time. Joey's car was rust-red with four patches of exposed steel on the roof. Joey said it was a Beetle and Jason said it looked more like a

Ladybug. Joey had protested and fumed but the name stuck. Joey steered Ladybug toward Gory Brook Road, but a crowd of people blocked the intersection at Broadway.

"Oh, damn," said Joey. "Was that today?"

"What?"

"The Halloween 8K."

The joggers carried a banner with a logo of the Horseman galloping and the words: YOU BETTER RUN! They were old, young, fat, skinny—and each one wore a Halloween costume. Batmen, Spider-Men, witches, vampires, fairies, skeletons and Little Orphan Annie trotted past. A fat werewolf sweated silver bullets. A middle-aged Dorothy wiped her brow with a terry-cloth Toto. A little girl in a green tyrannosaur costume stopped to growl at the onlookers.

Now this *is Halloween,* thought Jason Crane. *Grab a costume and hit the streets.*

He felt gripped by the Halloween spirit. It rose from the coffin where it slept and bit him hard. This happened every October—a week before Halloween. When pumpkins lit the porches, when homeowners strung cobwebs, when the wind turned cold and worried the leaves, something would catch him: the sight of a fright mask in the drugstore's "seasonal" aisle—$9.95 clearance, hanging on prongs through its eyeholes—or black and orange crepe, party plates, door decorations, bags of bite-size Snickers or Peanut Butter Cups or mini boxes of Milk Duds. Sometimes the trigger would be the first playing of "The Monster Mash" on local radio, or *Night on Bald Mountain,* or *Totentanz.* Sometimes it would be the sight of a TV schedule packed with *The Night of the Living Dead* and *Scream* and *My Bloody Valentine* and *Friday the 13th*—or even *Abbott and Costello Meet the Wolfman.*

This year it was the little tyrannosaur sitting on the balustrade of the Headless Horseman Bridge, kicking her feet while her mother adjusted a sports bra. This was childhood—like the green felt dragon he had lost to the river. *It's Halloween,* Jason realized, as if the idea were utterly new. Not a Halloween of gore and dangling eyeballs, either—not for jaded adults. This was a Halloween for that little girl: brewed from fear of the dark and bumps in the night.

"We'll have to drive around," Joey said as the 8K grew denser.

"Good," said Jason. "I'm not ready to go home yet."

The little girl skipped away. Jason smiled for no good reason except he was sixteen and it was time to have fun. They looped through Tarrytown and onto Neperan Road, driving into the hills above Sleepy Hollow.

"God, look at that," said Joey.

They drifted past the Tarrytown Reservoir. A stripe of police tape stretched between two red outbuildings.

"Debbie Flight," Jason whispered.

Joey turned the car into the parking lot.

"What are you doing?"

"Just for a second," said Joey.

The sign on the first shed read "PARKING LOT FOR RECREATIONAL USE OF THE TARRYTOWN LAKE AREA ONLY—No Parking After Sunset Except for Village Sponsored Events." An incompetent painter had tried to retouch the shed without taking the sign down first. The sign dripped with red paint.

Joey slipped under the police tape. Jason followed.

Reeds loomed on either side of the concrete stairs. Circling the second shed, the boys climbed to a patio overlooking the water, then walked down a pier that sloped into the murk. At water's edge the reeds and buildings hid them from the street.

"A perfect place for a murder," said Joey.

Jason had to agree. Even the wet crawlspace beneath the patio just begged for someone to hide a corpse there. Something jumped in the water. Jason's sneaker slipped in algae. He caught a handful of Joey's jacket and didn't fall in.

"Time to go," he said, recovering.

"Wait. What about those… powers of yours?"

"What about them?"

"If you're not lying or deluded, couldn't you do some good with them?" Joey gestured to the pier below. "Couldn't you see the murderer?"

Jason didn't want read those boards, but he did want Joey to believe him. He nodded, took his gloves off, knelt and pressed his palms to the wood.

"Well?" Joey said.

"God. Give a man two seconds," said Jason.

"Hey. I'm new to this, Endora."

"Just wait over there. It's hard to do it with somebody watching."

"I understand," said Joey. "You're E.S.P.-shy."

"Shut up."

Joey's giggles took a full minute to subside. When the lake fell silent again Jason tried touching the pier. Nothing. He climbed onto the patio and touched the walls of the shed. He pulled back a plywood shutter and touched the broken glass. He went back to the stairs, felt the railing, and saw nothing except a dead 'possum curled in the reeds a few feet away.

"I tried," he said.

"All right. If you were faking, you put on a good show," said Joey.

"You wouldn't have seen it anyway."

"True. Let's go."

Jason's palms were filthy. He knelt and wrung his hands in the water.

He thought he'd fallen in—that his foot had found the algae patch and pitched him into the water. But there'd been no splash. He still breathed. No. He wasn't in the water—though the world had turned midnight and hunter and jet. He saw a lantern's glare at the end of a tunnel and heard the brakes of an oncoming train. But the sound lessened and resolved itself into the scratched-metal cry of cicadas. His eyes adjusted, and he realized that he crouched on the pier at night, his hands in the water. The light at the end of the tunnel was the moon's reflection in the reservoir.

And he was not alone.

The screech of a soprano soloist rose over the orchestra of cicadas. Debbie Flight clung to the top railing even as her body lurched down the concrete steps. A man dragged her by one arm and by the back of her leather coat. She lost her grip and seized a handful of reeds, uprooting them and swinging water through the air. She kicked, she scratched. She spewed a stream of profanity without constraints or commas.

The man was blond and muscular. He wore a dark long-sleeved work shirt. He heaved Debbie onto the patio and pulled her down to the edge of the water. He stared into the distance—a sleepwalker. His eyes were blank, his face slightly puzzled.

Like Valerie's mother…

The man pulled back the sleeve of Debbie's coat and held her left arm in the water. She beat at him and kicked ineffectually. He produced a disk of metal from a pocket. Jason couldn't tell what it was. The edges glinted, red and silver. When Debbie realized what he was about to do, she stopped moving.

Jason crouched about six inches from Debbie. He could smell her perfume and hear her breath and see the tiny tag of Sleepy Hollow Realty on her chest.

She looked startled. She hadn't realized she would die until this moment. The man raised the sharp disk: a soda can flattened by someone's tire.

"I really liked you," she said.

The man hesitated—struggling with something inside.

But he sliced her wrist anyway.

She made a tiny gasp. Jason hoped that the cold water numbed the pain. He couldn't see any blood. The water was so black that her arm ended in a stump. Her breathing slowed. With a last surge of strength she clawed at her attacker. The man held her by the throat and she couldn't reach his face, but she tore something metal from his collar. It flew up to the patio and dropped between the boards.

The man brought her head down. She was headless now, decapitated by the water. Her torso disappeared next. Her leather coat billowed around her. Then nothing was visible above the waist. She stopped struggling.

The man stood and swayed. He walked back up the pier and vanished at the top of the steps.

White squares appeared in the water, drifting from Debbie's coat pockets and sailing away. They were business cards.

Debbie Flight, Realtor

Haunting the Hollow since 2008

Her cell phone rang.

Jason jumped.

It rang again and again: *We are the Champions... We are the Champions... We are the Champions...*

Uncharacteristically, Debbie let the call go to voice mail.

"Hello? *Hello?*"

Someone shook him. The sun was sudden and blinding.

"JASON!" Joey said. "Hello?"

"I saw it," Jason said. "I saw it."

"You saw her get killed?"

Jason nodded. "He cut her wrist with a soda can."

"Who did?"

Jason jumped off the pier and onto the mud by the water's edge. He dropped onto his hands and knees and wriggled into the crawlspace beneath the patio. Above him Joey groaned with disgust. Jason searched the slime, breathing through his mouth when dead minnows swam past. He found what he was looking for and backed out into the sunshine.

"Oh, won't you smell wonderful," Joey said.

"Will you believe me now? Look. He did it."

Jason held out the pin that Debbie Flight had torn from her attacker's collar. It bore a logo that Jason recognized—as he'd recognized the blond man in the vision—a logo of the Horseman throwing a pumpkin at Ichabod, beneath the letters SHFD.

"Who was it?" said Joey.

Jason shook his head.

"Fireman Mike."

23   A SHUFFLING OF CARDS

"Possession?" said Joey, "I know it's Halloween and all but— come on!"

"He could have been drugged or drunk," said Jason, "But— Valerie's mom looked the same way."

Joey bounced his forehead against Ladybug's steering wheel.

"Right," he said, "in the vision in the woods at the magic bridge with the leprechauns and Santa Claus—"

"The light's green."

"Okay," Joey said, shifting into park and turning in his seat. "Let's say I believe you."

"Okay, you believe me. Now will you drive? This guy's honking."

"What do we do about it? Go to the police?"

"They wouldn't believe us."

Joey nodded. "Padded cells."

"Padded cells. So no police, definitely."

"Definitely no police."

A policeman tapped on Joey's window. Several cars were honking now. Joey rolled down the glass.

"You know that green means go, right?" said the patrolman.

"Yes, sir. Sorry, sir." Joey shifted and the gears ground metal. Ladybug coughed and died. "Uh—"

"One foot at a time, son."

Joey turned the key in the ignition with no success. The horns grew louder.

"Sorry, officer," said Jason, patting Joey on the head. "Student driver."

The policeman nodded. He turned away and yelled "Student driver!" The horns stopped.

"You'll get the hang of it," he said to Joey, making a gung-ho gesture with one fist. He sounded like he was addressing a four-year-old.

Ladybug roared to life.

"Good job!" said the patrolman.

"Gold star!" said Jason, earning a dirty look.

"You smell like minnows," Joey said under his breath. He saluted the patrolman, found the correct gear and they drove on.

"You see? You see?" said Joey. "We just came *this close* to the loony bin."

"We did not."

"This close. 'Why did you stop at the light, son?' 'Oh, I don't know. I was talking with my friend the psychic about the possessed fireman he saw in a vision by the reservoir...'"

"Hey. You just ran that red light."

"This close," Joey shook his head. "Listen to us. Possession? Possession? We watch too many movies."

Jason nodded. "We watch too many movies."

"Way way *way* too many."

#

Credits rolled on *The Exorcist.*

Joey sat on his bedroom floor hugging a stuffed koala. Jason sat at the computer (in sweatpants and a borrowed shirt) chewing his fingers off. The movie had been more terrifying then either had remembered. Even Booger had fouled his water.

"Could the Devil be possessing Fireman Mike?" Joey said.

"I don't believe in the Devil."

"And six weeks ago you didn't believe in magic hand visions."

"True."

"But it can't be like *that*—" Joey pointed at the TV. "He won't spin his head around and puke pea soup." Joey hugged the koala again adding, "Will he?"

"The Devil's just to scare you into going to church. Which I don't and I'm not gonna."

After all, what would Carl Sagan say?

"I go to church sometimes," said Joey.

"You do?"

Joey nodded. "To sing," he said.

"That's reasonable."

"But if it wasn't the Devil, what do we think is possessing these people?"

Jason shrugged. "I want to say the Headless Horseman—"

Joey moaned and threw the koala. Jason ducked. It hit the computer screen and landed on the keyboard.

"It *is* Sleepy Hollow," said Jason, seating the koala on top of Joey's Playbill collection.

"I've lived here sixteen years," said Joey.

"And you've never seen him?"

"Not once. And I work *in the graveyard*. He's supposed to be buried there, you know."

"Yeah?"

Joey nodded. He rose to his knees and adopted his spookiest voice.

"*Among the graves of the Old Dutch Church, they say, near the northern wall, you may notice a curious depression. There, my friends, is the site—the common grave in which the Headless Hessian lies...*"

Jason remembered walking through the cemetery with Hadewych, and the little pumpkin rolling into an indentation in the earth.

"What are you reciting?" Jason said.

"The script from my lantern tour. Shh. *The body of the trooper having been buried in the churchyard, the ghost rides forth to the scene of battle in nightly quest of his head, and the rushing speed with which he sometimes passes along the Hollow, like a midnight blast, is owing to his being belated, and in a hurry to get back to the churchyard before daybreak.*"

"What's a lantern tour?"

"People tour the cemetery at night carrying lanterns. I've led a dozen of them. I think of it as an acting exercise. And I *wish* the Horseman were real 'cause it would be *so* great to see him jump over the headstones and decapitate my whole group." Joey pointed at invisible tourists. "You there. You ask too many questions. Off with your head! And the Horseman rides in and rolls their noggins back to Nebraska."

"That's harsh."

"*You* do the tours and miss Halloween. It gets old."

"So has *anyone* seen the Horseman?"

"Eh. *Most Haunted* and *Ghost Hunters* have filmed in the cemetery and they always find *something*." He rolled his eyes. "But people lie."

"Right."

"*You've* seen the Horseman, though."

"I don't know that."

"You said he threw a pumpkin at Ichabod right in front of you."

"So now you believe me?"

"Of course. You didn't plant that pin in advance."

Jason took the pin out of his pocket and ran his thumb over the logo. He got no visions from it.

"I didn't see *what* threw the pumpkin," he said. "It could have been Brom like in the story. Hell, maybe some acting troupe recreated *The Legend* on that spot and I thought it was the real thing."

Someone knocked.

"Yeah?" Joey called. Jason shoved the pin in his pocket.

"Are you two decent?" Pat Osorio said from the other side.

"Mom. He's *not* my boyfriend."

She stuck her head in and frowned.

"Excuse me for being open-minded," she said.

"What—do—you—want?" said Joey.

"Jason's clothes are dry. And don't you need to run to your little thing?"

"Crap. The Hollow!" Joey said, leaping to his feet. "I've got to get into makeup. It's almost six!"

"Honestly," said Joey's mom, "you'd lose your head if it wasn't attached."

The boys looked at each other and began laughing.

"What's so funny?" She frowned at them. "What did I say?"

\#

Eliza lay on the sofa with her feet up, munching on crackers and cheese, flipping through a stack of folders.

"I'm home to dress and then I'll be out," Jason said. "Will you be okay tonight?"

"Have fun, Honey," she said, nodding. "I'm just catching up on my paperwork." She lifted a file. "Real estate office dropped these off. I called them. That Debbie Flight was supposed to send my papers a week ago, bless her lazy soul."

Jason stopped on the stair. He didn't want to think of Debbie right now.

"Have a dull time, I guess."

"I've had plenty of fun. Loads of it. Go forth. Dance and be merry."

Jason climbed the stairs.

"Look nice," she called from below.

#

He did look nice, he decided. He'd had a haircut just yesterday and, once showered and shaved and spritzed, he'd become an almost passable human being. He turned in the mirror, pulled a spot of shaving cream off his earlobe. He had just pulled on his black jeans when he heard a terrible cry from downstairs.

"Oh, my God," Eliza bellowed. "Oh. Oh, no!"

Jason bolted through the bedroom door barefoot and shirtless and stumbled down the steps.

"What? What? Did you fall?"

Eliza paced the center of the living room, papers in her hand. Charley turned circles and jumped at her.

"That son of a bitch," Eliza growled. "That shady son of a bitch."

"Who?" said Jason, reaching for the papers.

She kept her distance.

"I'll handle it," she said.

"No. Who's the son of a bitch?"

Eliza's jaw worked as if she were cracking nuts with her teeth or grinding iron rails into ball bearings.

"I am going to kill him," she said. "I will."

She let loose a stream of foul language that chilled Jason worse than her shouts had. Eliza only swore like that when someone had a brutal beat-down coming.

"What's happening?" he said.

"We're moving back to Maine, that's what's happening."

"Why?"

"I am sorry I brought you here. And I am going to beg your

forgiveness when this is over. But I'll make it right, I promise."

"Did Hadewych do something?"

She raised a palm, forbidding Jason to ask any more questions.

"This is my own stupidity. I'll handle it. Go. Have a good time and leave it be."

"Are you sure?"

Eliza nodded. "I'm sure, just—"

"What?"

Her voice grew steely. "Don't get too attached."

#

Valerie thanked the clerk, and carried her luggage and groceries up the stairs and into room 208. The White Plains Motor Lodge was no luxury hotel, but it would do until after Halloween. This would be home for the next week. The room was clean, with two beds, a table and generic Hudson River paintings. And it was safe.

She sat, opened her purse and checked the map again. Yes, she was safe—just beyond the distance a horse could travel and return between dusk and dawn. She had drawn a circle around Sleepy Hollow, marking off about ten miles in diameter. In this direction the Horseman's reach only extended as far as the Kensico Dam. She unpacked, put her groceries away and showered.

She put on her dressing gown, arranged the small blue kidney-shaped tray upon the left side of the dressing table, and the two porcelain bowls upon the right.

She turned on her humidifier.

I will play the Vivaldi, tonight, she thought. *The Seasons, yes: "Fall."*

She filled one bowl with a solution of hydrogen peroxide and water.

Mother played that one, in Vienna, when she was young and Janigro conducted his last concert.

She filled the second bowl with saline solution.

Yes, "Fall." That's the mood I'm in tonight.

She opened a package of pipe cleaners, set four to one side.

Don't think about it.

Next to these, she placed a small handful of Q-tips and a small tube of lubricating jelly.

She dragged me by my hair, she thought.

Valerie stood, pushing the memory away. Tiny bottles of complimentary shampoo bounced and quivered.

Vivaldi.

She fetched her music player, synced the Bluetooth speakers, and selected a track.

Yes, this is exactly what I wanted tonight.

The piece began jauntily. The melody bounced and cavorted, and Valerie swung the tassels on her dressing gown in time to the music. She smiled, enjoying it, even though the violins did seem shrill on the old recording. Too much hiss and scratch.

It was *1957, after all.*

Had her mother ever recorded this piece? No. Mother Maule didn't care for the older composers. Nothing earlier than Mozart for her. *Good.* Valerie let it play as she washed her hands, applied talcum, and rolled on the dull yellow gloves. They were surgical gloves, bought in bulk from a Broadway pharmacy.

Get it done.

She returned to the dressing table, sat, and looked at herself in the mirror. Her dark hair was soft and attractive, short, with a stylish curl at the tips.

Janice did a marvelous job, with all the wind this week.

Her cheeks were rosy, the tiny lines that reminded her of dried apple hidden behind powder and base.

I will look like her someday, she thought, *but not yet.*

She pursed her lips. Yes, these were acceptable. Her eyes passed a shade too quickly from her chin down to her cleavage, of which she was quite proud. Then they slipped too far, down to the sickening yellow surgical gloves, and she sighed.

Accept, she told herself. *Get this done and, for once, don't think about it.*

She looked at the valve on the front of her neck, a letter 'X' inside a letter 'O'.

A kiss and a hug, she thought. *A kiss and a hug from Mama.*

She detached the valve, removed it. The inner tubing came out with it, trailing grey-green mucus. She picked up a pipe cleaner.

Accept.

Accept.

I can't. I can't.

Her mother had done it with the car keys, since no knife had been at hand. If she hadn't had the keys, what might Mama have used? What would she have found, there in the forest? A branch? Would she have stripped a branch from one of the old poplar trees and used that? She imagined the thing, whittled to a point, piercing her throat. *That would have been better, perhaps. That way I might have died. The keys were far too dull to complete the job, and now look at me.*

Don't do this to yourself. Listen to the music. Hurry up.

She swabbed the hole in her throat, dipping the cotton tip, expanding her lungs, and rotating it against the inside of her trachea.

She could see her mother's blank, befuddled face as she pushed her daughter's head into the river. She saw the keys raised high in her mother's hand, felt them stab downwards again and again, twisting, digging a hole to spill her blood. She saw herself kicking but unable to scream, pushed down into the cold water of the Pocantico River, dragged there by her hair and arms and leather belt, dragged, seized and plunged into the icy water.

Mother is murdering me, she had thought. *Mother murdering mother murdering murdering me. Smothering. Murdering. Mother mother no!*

Stop this.

The peroxide frothed, just as the river had.

Stop this!

Her blood had gushed. Her body higher than her head so that gravity pulled her life out through the hole in her neck, out through her mouth, through her nose. And as the blood had left her, she had felt Him.

This is how He *died.* She knew that somehow, though she could not imagine who He might be. *He died here, on this spot, and lost his blood to this river.* She felt Him. She felt his hands on her, holding her down, sacrificing her. She felt some spirit inhabiting her mother, possessing her, using her. Commanding her to be its instrument.

Genesis, she thought: *Take now thy son, thine only son Isaac, whom thou lovest, and get thee into the land of Moriah; and offer him there for a burnt offering.*

Mother, no...

As she weakened, as the blood left her, she felt Him growing strong. Her strength, her power, giving substance to his veins, his hands, his muscle. It was a transfusion of her soul. The water was drinking *her*, and He, the Horseman, grew thick and sated on it.

Then the hands were gone. Where the thing went, what He may have done in his awful vitality, she didn't know.

And out of that darkness, new hope. Think of that. Think of Hadewych.

She had drifted out of consciousness, as her mother had regained it. Mother Maule had awakened on the shore of the Pocantico, clothes torn, arms scratched, her beloved daughter gasping and dying at her feet. She screamed to a man passing on the opposite side of the river. A man with blond hair. He had splashed across.

Valerie remembered, vaguely, his arm slipping beneath her knees, his other cradling her wet shoulders. She remembered the branches of trees overhead, scratching out the eyes of the constellations. She remembered falling into the back seat of a car. The man had torn off his necktie, and Mother Maule held it pressed against Valerie's throat with bloody fingers, so gentle, her face so concerned, so frightened, tears running down her neck as they drove.

Valerie put the valve into the saline solution. She leaned over the humidifier and inhaled.

Hadewych saved my life.

She saw his face first, when it was over. Her mother wasn't beside her when she woke. Mother Maule had been taken into custody.

Hadewych sat with her through that long difficult night, refusing to leave, holding her hand, answering the questions she had no voice to ask, answering as many as he could, answering as best anyone could when discussing something inexplicable. The ventilator punctuated his words every few seconds, pumping her with air, her chest rising and falling against her will. She felt like a bicycle tire being filled at a gas station air machine; it was too much. She would burst, from too much air, too much sadness, too much terror, from too much confusion; yes, she would burst from it all. But Hadewych held her hand, held her together. He explained that an emergency tracheostomy had been performed, a cuff inserted, and she would live.

She would live, he promised.

He promised, too, that he would not leave her.

Mother Maule claimed not to remember a thing, when interrogated, only that she and Valerie had hiked up Witch's Spring Trail in the Rockefeller Preserve and had picnicked at Spook Rock. There, she had fallen faint, and that was the last she remembered of the incident. There was more to tell, of course. The women had not been sightseeing, or hiking. They were not two bird-watchers on an afternoon jaunt. No. There had been more to it. But neither Valerie nor her mother spoke of that to anyone.

Valerie reinserted the valve, tightened it, twisting the little 'X' inside the 'O'.

I miss my mother. When did I visit her last?

She stripped off the gloves, toweled her face, frowned, reached for her makeup kit.

I miss her. But it's for the best. She can't hurt me again.

That had been October twenty-ninth, almost ten years ago. The anniversary was fast approaching. Her fingers still shook whenever she thought of that night. She thought of it three times a day, every time she cleaned her valve as per her doctor's instructions.

The Vivaldi ended. She put away the medical supplies, gave herself one last appraisal.

How lucky am I, to have a man who wants me, despite everything.

She pressed her fingers to the valve, testing it, forcing the air upward to her vocal cords. "Hadewych," she said, in her deep crumbling voice. The sound frightened her, still.

She turned off the lights.

Mother can't hurt me again.

Was that true? She had hoped to feel safe in this hotel room, but she found that she missed her many padlocks and metal shutters. She missed the guns, too.

Mother can't hurt you again. But you know better, don't you, than to relax your guard. It was never your mother, that night at the river. It was something else, something that was using her.

And if it could use her, it could use anyone.

She took off the dressing gown and slipped into a pair of jeans and a sweater. She poured herself a glass of cold milk and sat cross-legged on the bed. She took the few things she needed out of her purse—the incense burner, the candle, and the tarot cards.

She lit the candle and the incense. She shuffled the cards.

Once.

Twice.

Three times.

She cleared her mind of the past, and focused on the future.

24 HORSES AT THE STARTING GATE

A crowd had formed in the parking lot of Philipsburg Manor, waiting to be let in. Security patrolled the entrance to the event, keeping the crowd at bay until darkness fell. The *Horseman's Hollow* banner hung above the gates: a vampire and witch gargling blood for the camera. The line stretched from the gates all the way to the concession stand at the other end of the parking lot.

Jason slipped behind the concession stand, into an area about twenty-foot square and hidden on all sides by black tarp on poles. He stuck his head through the inside curtain and watched the actors mill about in the distance. He had texted Joey earlier and his friend was already waiting. Joey wasn't quite made up. He didn't have his coat on yet, only his ruffled shirt and blue pants with buttons up the side. His face was covered in greasepaint with dark circles under his eyes.

"What?" he said. "I'm already late."

"There's no ticket," said Jason.

"I told them to comp you. Can you… just buy one?"

"I guess."

"Argh. Straight people," said Joey. He turned to go.

"Hold on," said Jason. "At least until we know I can get in."

"Be fast," said Joey. "They've got my teeth waiting."

Jason sprinted away.

The woman at the ticket booth sat happily counting twenties. Her teased hair filled half the booth.

"One, please?" said Jason.

"Oh, sorry, baby. Sold out."

"No, no, no."

"These tickets go on sale weeks in advance. We only have a few the night of. Look—wait over there and I'll let you know if we get anything."

Jason nodded and turned. The crowd began to applaud. The Headless Horseman had arrived, riding Gunsmoke. Zef had come to woo the crowd. The Horseman turned a circle and posed for pictures. Jason looked for Kate. She stood in line. By herself.

"Don't get too attached," Eliza had said. But he *was* attached.

And if we do move back to Maine... I might never see her again.

"Oh please, please," he said to the ticket lady. "You've got to get me in."

#

Redcoat zombie Joey didn't go back into makeup right away. He peeked from behind the tarp and watched Zef work the crowd. Person after person stroked the horse, made crazy faces for the cameras, pretended to be petrified or menaced by the rider.

What did Zef do, hidden inside there? Laugh at people? Stick his tongue out at them? Call them names under his breath? Listen to a song on his iPod? What was Zef thinking inside that costume?

And—Joey thought—*when he takes that costume off is he just wearing a different disguise?*

Joey thought so. He hoped so. He didn't quite know which was the true Zef—the one who sided with the bullies at school? The popular kid on the horse? The honor student? The one dating Kate? Paul Usher's protégé? Or was the real Zef... the one who had come to watch Joey sing in White Plains, the Zef who'd sat with him in the parking lot until two a.m., talking about nothing in particular, the Zef who'd kissed him and jumped out the passenger side as if chased by the Horseman himself?

Who knew?

Probably not even Zef knows.

Gunsmoke galloped toward Joey and he jumped back. Horseman Zef rode right through the slit in the tarp and turned the horse around inside the hidden area. Joey took Gunsmoke's bridle.

"Hey, beautiful," Joey said. "Gunsmoke," he clarified. He patted the horse's cheek while the Horseman fiddled with his gloves.

"You know," said Joey, "some of us are going out after. I thought you could come? Kate too. Just—" Joey gave up pretending. He hadn't been alone with Zef for almost a year. "Can we talk? We never—we never talked? You know? After that night?" Gunsmoke sidestepped and Joey held the reins tighter. He lowered his voice to a whisper. "After you kissed me?" The Horseman shifted in the saddle. "If it was one time, that's fine. I don't expect anything. Punch me if you want, but—but—I think about it. A lot. And if you want to talk—anytime?" Joey raised his voice. "Hello? Can you talk to me?"

"Talk about what?" said Zef, entering from the parking lot.

Joey spun round. Oh... he—

Zef tugged at the Horseman's cape. "You okay in there, Puleo? Hey, Puleo?"

The Horseman heaved the heavy costume up. Jimmy Puleo was inside. He wore his usual black knit cap. His face was red and dripping.

"HOLY CRAP, ZEF!" Puleo gasped. "How do you breathe in this thing?"

"I just do," said Zef.

"I can't. I'm not doing this again."

"One night. I've got to have one night to see the show."

Joey tried to slip away.

"Osorio," said Zef. "You needed to talk to Jimmy?"

"To me?" said Jimmy. "Sorry, I can't hear anything under here."

Joey shook his head.

"It's fine," said Joey.

"You sure?" said Zef.

"I just wanted to say... have a good show."

"Oh, yeah?" said Puleo, laughing. "You too, fag!"

Joey's eyes shot to Zef's face, not Puleo's. Zef's lips were pressed tight in—Anger? Suffering? Joey could have sworn that Zef shook his head, just a little. What signal was he sending? Was he saying he couldn't defend Joey? That he wouldn't? That he supported Puleo? That he was sorry? Was he begging Joey not to say anything? Pleading for him to understand? Was he saying, "I know you wanted to talk to me but you can't because I can't be seen with you"? All of the above?

Joey couldn't guess.

So he nodded, just a little, himself—not knowing what he wanted to say either.

Puleo pulled the tunic and empty collar of the Horseman costume back over his head.

"I need to go," Joey said.

Zef took a step forward.

"No," Joey repeated. "I've got to go." He cocked a thumb towards the backstage area. "I'm... scaring people tonight."

#

Jason tossed a rumpled ten onto the counter, accepted his change, and took his pie and cider. He had cursed his luck when Zef joined Kate and kissed her. The line had started moving a little. Joey had gone too. Jason had no ticket and no options.

Kate's head rested on Zef's shoulder. Jason harrumphed and walked to the picnic area.

Another blond caught his attention.

Fireman Mike.

Mike wore a security uniform—black pants and T-shirt. He stood beneath the *Horseman's Hollow* sign holding a scanner.

Jason sat at the picnic table, took off his gloves and scarfed his food.

Maybe if I shook Mike's hand—

"Can I help you?" Mike said as Jason approached.

"Jason Crane, sir? We met?" He held out a hand.

Mike didn't shake. He pressed a finger to his earpiece.

"We can start letting them in," he said to the other ticket-taker.

The bar-code readers beeped like a heart monitor with each ticket. Kids began to file past, full of mirth and excitement.

"We met?" Jason repeated, his hand still extended. "You showed me the fire truck?"

Mike lit up.

"Ichabod!"

Ugh. Adults.

"What can I do for you, buddy?"

He still didn't shake. Jason dropped his hand.

"I just wanted to say how sorry I was to hear about Debbie."

Mike's face darkened. "I know. Isn't it disgusting?"

"You seemed friendly."

He nodded. "We flirted a lot. I… I really liked her."

Jason felt the truth of this. He didn't sense evasion or fear or deception or… anything. He remembered Eliza telling him that Valerie's mother claimed not to remember attacking her daughter. Jason was certain that Mike didn't know what he'd done either. He had one more test, though. He reached in his pocket.

"Here," he said. "I think this is yours?"

"Hey, my pin? Thanks!"

Mike didn't look like a murderer confronted with incriminating evidence. He just grinned and took it.

"I wondered. Where'd you find it?"

Jason shrugged. "Sidewalk."

Kate and Zef approached as the line moved up.

"I should go," Jason said.

"Thanks," said Mike, attaching the SHFD logo to his shirt. "These pins are pretty cool, huh? Come by and I'll show you the other truck. It's bad-ass."

Jason nodded.

"Mike," he added, "I—I think she really liked you too."

Mike smiled. He shook his head.

"I wish I had taken her out," he said.

Jason was walking back to the picnic tables when he heard the woman with the epic hairdo calling.

"Hey, kid. I've got a ticket for you, if you want."

"How much?"

She shrugged. "Here. Just take it." She put a page with a bar code in his hand.

"Free?"

"It was a comp to begin with. But these girls don't want theirs."

Jason noticed three little girls, barely eleven, giggling with each other.

"We're too scared," one of them said.

"It's scary," the next one said.

"Really scary," agreed number three.

They each nodded and giggled again.

"Thanks," Jason said. Maybe his luck had turned around. Too bad this hadn't happened earlier, though. Kate and Zef were almost inside, and Jason would be at the back of an endless line.

"It's a VIP ticket, too," said the woman.

"Our daddy is the mayor!" one little girl shouted as if she expected free ice cream every time she said it.

"What does the VIP ticket do?" Jason said.

"Lets you skip the line, of course."

25   THE HORSEMAN'S HOLLOW

Valerie turned the first card.

It was **The Fool.**

She stared at it.

Her mother had taught her to give each card its due, to absorb the meaning over time.

She hugged the pillow to her chest.

The Fool wears motley clothes and carries all his possessions in a bundle over his shoulder. A small dog tries to warn him of coming danger, but The Fool is so absorbed in his visions that he cannot see the perilous cliff opening at his feet.

She touched the card.

This is the boy.

#

Jason's pupils gorged themselves on the sights across the water. Blue light splashed across the Manor's windows and etched lines in its façade so that Jason imagined an icy campfire beneath the chin of a storyteller. A blurry duplicate floated in the mirror of the millpond.

The wind stirred a cauldron of sound; phantoms warbled through the fog; witches at Sabbath cawed and bubbled; a skeleton played the harpsichord. The first clots of visitors began to circulate, adding a new ingredient to the brew—yelps of surprise that skipped over the millpond, raising ripples of nervous laughter from the kids still in line. Somewhere in the night the Devil perched on a tombstone and fiddled for the dead.

Fireman Mike scanned Jason's ticket and passed him through.

#

Valerie laid a second card across the first. This was The Fool's challenge.

The Lovers.

A male and a female figure, both nudes, stand before two trees and two paths. The Fool reaches a crossroads. The One stands before him and he no longer knows which path to follow.

Valerie stared at it, considering.

Is the boy in love?

#

Zef slipped a hand around Kate's waist as they walked. Jason hung back until a handful of others had entered and ambled into the darkness himself. He kept his eyes on Kate, but he trailed behind as much as he could. He felt like a stalker and he didn't want to be obvious.

An embankment and fence rose on the right, hiding the road above. Poplar trees blocked the view to the left and made a canopy over their heads. A row of lanterns on hooks hung at waist level, drawing them along.

A figure lurched from the shadows. Several girls squealed and spun. A human lobster raised claws toward Zef.

"Nice costume," Zef said, circling Kate to avoid the thing. Claws snapped at him. He flinched and laughed nervously.

Zef is scared.

Jason split his face grinning. A terrified Zef might be fun to watch.

Jason's grin died as they filed over the walkway that ran adjacent to the Horseman Bridge. Jason had been standing just there, on the other side of the balustrade, when Fireman Mike drew Darley from the water. The ground dropped away and they crossed over the Pocantico. He could see the other bridge on the far side of the water—an aisle of rickety boards that ran along the top edge of the millpond's dam. A row of dwarfish shadows had assembled there. Children? Mannequins? How had he missed them before? The figures opened glowing eyes and began to sing a playground tune—*la la la la la la laaaa…*

Jason's flesh crept. Why are children so terrifying?

I wasn't that creepy when I was little… was I?

Jason glanced down at his own hand on the railing. His glove was gone. Both gloves were. Where—?

Oh.

He had left them on the picnic table.

#

Valerie turned the third card—the past of The Fool.

The Queen of Pentacles, reversed.

She put the pillow to one side. She sipped her milk.

The Fool will lose his connection to the simple things of his past—sunsets, laughter, his safe and happy home—and to the woman who provides them.

Valerie frowned. Was this Eliza?

#

Eliza stared up at the many steps that led to Hadewych's apartment. She had never climbed them before. Her friends had always met her downstairs at Valerie's, to save her the trouble. Now she had no choice. She had called Hadewych's number all afternoon, leaving progressively angrier messages. So she'd had to drive the Mercedes herself, squinting against the setting sun. He hadn't answered his phone, but here his lights were on. She spat curses and began to climb.

#

Valerie turned over the fourth card—to see The Fool's future.

The Magician.

The figure on the card raised his rod, proclaiming his dominion over the pentacle, the cup, the sword and the wand.

Valerie covered her mouth. *Hadewych?*

She leaned back against the headboard.

No. There must be another interpretation. The Magician represents a master of secret and arcane forces…

That can't mean Hadewych… can it?

#

Eliza reached the top of the stairs at last.

A television played inside Hadewych's apartment. Eliza's knock was too feeble to be heard over it. She leaned on the doorbell and heard it ring. Moths swept the exposed bulb of the porch light, kicking up tiny particles of dust.

"Hadewych," she said. "Get your ass out here!"

The TV clicked off.

"Hadewych?" Eliza said. "Zef?"

The inside light went off.

With a surge of strength born of fury, Eliza seized a terra cotta pot from the landing, got her thumb around the dead root inside, and hurled pot and plant both against Hadewych's front door. It shattered and fell—leaving a blotch of dirt on the wood. The moths fled, terrified.

"I can keep knocking all night," said Eliza.

#

A moth struck Jason's temple and fluttered down the line of lanterns. The lanterns ended at The Graveyard, a field of false headstones lit with green and pink. A man checked their tickets again and passed them through.

Some of the kids probably try to jump the fence back at the bridge, Jason thought.

Kate's hair shimmered green as she strolled among the graves. Zef hesitated.

"Let's go," said a boy in an orange jacket. Zef turned, ready for a fight, but the boy backed down. Zef muttered something, turned, and stomped after Kate.

The path led into a false tomb. Inside, a coffin containing a corpse drew Zef's attention and he failed to notice an actor disguised as a statue. The statue shrieked. Zef jumped comically, struck the doorframe and stumbled through.

Jason gave a thumbs-up to the statue as he exited the tomb. He pushed the velvet aside and thought that Kate had caught sight of him and waved—but maybe not. She was grinning, having fun, and was much amused by Zef's skittishness.

A gravedigger sprang from the shadows. Zef cried out. A skeleton popped out of a carriage. Zef cried out. A branch poked his sleeve. Zef cried out. A girl in line said "Boo." Zef cried out—earning laughter and catcalls.

Jason didn't join in. He felt that the crowd was winding a toy that might explode at any minute. He'd seen the Van Brunt temper. But it *was* funny. He found himself fumbling for his phone.

Joey should see this.

A figure appeared at his side at once: a security guard dressed in black from tricorn hat to leather gloves, his face shrouded by black cloth.

"No video," muttered the faceless thing.

Jason tucked his phone away and nodded in apology. He found himself remembering the photo of Darley. The security-ghost left. Jason turned and cursed. He had lost Kate and Zef. He hurried past a row of skeletons on pikes. The first raised its hands to its ears and crushed its own skull. The second blinded itself with bony fingers. The third offered Jason its own jawbone.

Hear No Evil, See No Evil, Speak No…

\#

Evil… evil…

Something was evil. Valerie could sense it. She lifted a palm and considered sweeping the cards from the bed. But…

Give the cards their due.

She took another drink. The milk had warmed and it coated her throat. That felt good.

Valerie turned another card…

The Nine of Swords.

…and began choking.

\#

Hadewych coughed elaborately as he cracked the door. He did not unlatch the security chain.

"Eliza. What a nice surprise," he said. "I was… asleep on the couch."

Eliza pulled the folder from her purse.

"Explain this," she said.

"What is it?" said Hadewych. His fingers slipped through the crack, reaching.

She pulled the folder away.

"The title to my house. I want an explanation. You open this door and let me in."

"I'm not decent."

"I don't care if you're buck naked," Eliza said, beginning to burn hot. "I promise I've seen worse than your spotty ass."

Five layers of charm evaporated from Hadewych's face, leaving an irritable onion core.

"Fine," he said, dropping the chain. He tried to come out but Eliza brushed past and crossed the threshold. What she found inside shook her—to her core.

She was surrounded by trash on all sides.

#

Now that Jason was in the midst of The Hollow, he felt surrounded.

A three-quarter moon hung above. Fences stood at right and left. Kids milled and giggled in front, parents consoled weeping children in back. From all directions came the cries of actors, the squeals of girls, the drone of ghosts, the children's choir, the crunching of feet on pebbles. Pumpkins flickered, candles danced. Crimson, orange, and blinding white burned in every tree. Floodlights turned the plaster of the manor into cracked blue skin.

He pushed the hair out of his eyes. What was happening to him? He felt the place triggering his imagination—the way flickering light might trigger another kid's epilepsy. He shook his head and pushed on.

He found Kate and Zef in the Lair of the Redcoat Zombies.

Joey tried in vain to menace Zef. His makeup was terrifying, but a ridiculous purple wig spoiled the effect.

"Nice hair," Zef giggled.

Apparently Joey was the only thing Zef *wasn't* scared of.

Joey rose to the challenge, though—hissing, clawing the air and chewing the scenery *(literally; he grabbed a severed arm and gnawed on it)*, but the damn wig was just too silly. He gave up, disappointed, and Kate and Zef walked on.

"Run!" Jason whispered in mock terror as Joey approached. "It's the flesh-eating corpse of the Queen Mother!"

Joey stayed in character. He seized Jason by the neck and clacked teeth to bite through his skull, but then stopped, released Jason and shambled away wheezing, "No brains… No brains…"

Zef cried out ahead. People laughed. Someone had gotten him. Jason pushed through and saw Zef cursing at one of the actors, a Redcoat buried in dirt to the waist, disguised as a severed torso leaning against a fence. Zef was kicking dirt in the man's face and screaming at him. Kate was turning circles with one hand raised to her temple. A black-shrouded security-ghost appeared and ordered Zef to leave.

"They're all targeting me," Zef snapped.

"Rip out 'is spine and chew on it," hissed one zombie.

"Stick 'is head on a pike for the crows," gibbered another.

"Oy! 'e's not such a bad bloke!" said Zombie Joey, defending Zef as usual.

Zef climbed over the rope.

"Let's go," he said to Kate.

She shook her head. "I'm going through," she said. "This cost money."

"Fine. I'll be outside when you're done having fun," said Zef. He stalked away with the security guard. Kate walked backwards up the trail, half-expecting Zef to return. He didn't. She disappeared around a corner.

"Oh my…" said Zombie Joey, wheezing into Jason's ear. "It's wandered off, ain't it? Ought to be careful, tasty little thing like that, eh? Someone might—" He clacked his teeth. "—eat her up." He pushed Jason forward and limped off to dine on a tourist from Florida.

#

Valerie cleared her throat. She was wheezing but at least she could breathe.

The new card had fallen to the floor. She picked it up and put it into place again.

This signifies the near-term outcome.

The Nine of Swords.

On the card, a figure sat in bed, just as she did.

The sleeper awakes from a nightmare, or cannot sleep for terror or despair. He (she?) covers their face with their hands. On the wall behind the bed hang nine

alternating swords.
The Long Dark Night of the Soul.

#

Eliza turned and faced Hadewych.

"I don't know you, do I?" she said, indicating the room.

Hadewych lived in a hovel—a trash-filled hovel of stained newspapers and reeking dishes. One room off the hallway looked neat and tidy. Through the door she saw a military-tight bedspread, fresh paint and a boy's letter jacket over a chair. Zef's room defiantly rebuked his father's squalor.

Hadewych wore boxer shorts and a greying V-neck T-shirt. "I'd like you to leave," he said, holding the door open.

"Valerie lets you live like this?" she gasped.

"She's... out of town."

"For two days. You didn't do this in—"

"I don't see how my house is your concern."

Eliza's amazement turned toward anger again.

"Fine. It's not. But *my* house is. Why—" she said, holding up the paper, "—is your name on my title?"

"On your title?" said Hadewych, feigning surprise. "That can't be right." He looked at the paper, shaking his head. "There has to be some explanation."

"Let's hear it."

Hadewych gave the papers back and turned away.

"Look what you've done," he harrumphed. He brushed the dirt from the door and tsked over the broken terra cotta, sweeping the pieces onto a newspaper with one hand. "You've been very unreasonable."

"And you're just buying time to make up some lie."

Hadewych kicked the door shut and carried the mess to a trashcan. The can was already full, so he left the broken pot on the counter among dishes and spoiled food.

"I can't say that I care for your attitude, 'Liza. This is just as much of a surprise to me."

"I bet."

Hadewych snapped his fingers.

"That realtor," he said. "She must have made a mistake. She

probably assumed that because I handled the transaction I was one of the buyers. That's all. Simple enough. And the girl was in a bad state. Do you think she killed herself?"

"No. I think you killed her."

"Good God, no."

"To keep her from talking?"

"I had nothing to do with that," said Hadewych. His voice sounded sincere now—but that made Eliza madder because she realized that she had never heard his sincere voice before.

"That was not me," Hadewych said. "I swear."

"I don't believe anything you say." She drew another paper from her purse. "I called my broker. He says you're on my stock accounts too."

Hadewych opened his mouth. He failed to find any words, so he opened the front door instead.

"Goodbye, dear," he said.

"Don't you 'dear' me, mister. If I were twenty years younger I'd snap my foot off in your ass."

"Try it," he said.

Eliza felt the precariousness of her position. She was alone with him. He could push her down the stairs.... She glanced at the broken terra cotta on the counter. She shoved the papers back into her purse.

"I've had plenty of men come sniffing for my money," she said, "but..." her voice broke, "...you were like a son to me."

Hadewych had dropped all masks. She saw ruthlessness in his face. And contempt.

"I'm not your son," he said. "I'm a Van Brunt. My family *built* that house. It was always mine. And it will stay that way."

She nodded and backed towards the door, feeling old and feeble.

"I'll call the cops," she said as she left. She felt more confident outside. Hadewych followed her, watching from the landing as she hobbled down the steps.

"I had full power of attorney, remember? You couldn't be bothered with paperwork. You were too caught up in The Project. So everything I did was legal, and..." She looked up. "...I think old lady Merrick is a little senile, don't you?"

She hurried down the steps.

"Be careful not to fall, 'Liza." Hadewych called casually.

"Someone might have heard you shouting and we can't afford a scandal."

She turned at the bottom and raised an uncertain finger.

"I'll get you, you son of a bitch. Even if I have to hire somebody."

"You're beautiful when you're angry, dear."

"I'll get you."

"Not if I get you first," he whispered. He waved goodbye and slipped inside.

#

As soon as he crossed the threshold of the mill, Jason knew that he'd lost control. His fingers brushed the wood of the gristmill and his gift began to run away with itself. Just inside the door, a bloody Marie Antoinette leapt at him. He fell back, startled, and grabbed a wooden beam.

A fake corpse lay on the grindstone but it faded before Jason's eyes. The gears of the mill were turning now. The disks of stone began to rotate. Cracked wheat spilled from between them. Figures blurred past. Jason saw a black man in a purple tunic collecting the wheat. The man's sleeve caught in the machinery. *"Pull the nut! Pull the nut!"* he screamed. The gears bit away his fingers. He wailed and wrested the stump of his hand away. Blood spattered Jason's legs. The man clutched the stump and watched helplessly as his severed fingers were ground into meal and the wheat went red.

Jason wrestled his own his hand away from the beam. He had screamed in terror. Marie Antoinette took credit for the scream. She bowed and the onlookers applauded her epic scare.

Jason glanced down. There was no blood on his clothes.

Kate stood at a second door looking back, her face full of concern.

#

Zef wandered up Broadway. He turned and saw the manor glowing in the distance. He had ridden to the Hollow with Kate and Carlos, with Gunsmoke behind in the trailer. He should have waited for Kate like he told her he would; at least he wouldn't have to walk home. But he felt no regret. He needed to be alone. He needed to get away from her.

He didn't want to hurt Kate's feelings and—he did love her, didn't he? He enjoyed kissing her and touching her. He *wanted* to feel some profound connection with her. He hated not feeling it. Sometimes he could almost force himself to feel the passion he wanted to feel. But half the time all he felt was the satisfaction of an actor who'd given a good performance.

Zef hated himself.

He took the flask from his pocket and drained it. He knew the burning sensation in his chest was only whiskey, but it helped him imagine another life, a better life in which he felt a burning desire for Kate—just like everyone expected him to.

Just like he wanted to.

Thank God for the firewater, he thought. *Without it I'd be nothing but ash.*

#

The smell of incense became overpowering, but Valerie couldn't stop to put it out. She flipped more cards, gasping.

Such a powerful reading. So many major Arcana.

The Moon.

A time of transformation.

The Hanged Man...

#

Jason felt he was being targeted. Every specter, every monster, every green-faced hag caught him unawares. Creatures jumped from the shadows, barked in his ear and cackled behind, making him stumble and lose his way.

He stepped to one side, trying to collect his wits. Across the field he thought he could make out one of the security-ghosts standing motionless. The figure blended into the background: a man-shaped hole in a charcoal backdrop.

Jason blinked and the ghost vanished

"Long live King George," shouted a voice to his left.

Jason turned but no one was there.

He felt sick and dizzy. He had to get out. He stepped into the stream of kids and they carried him along—down a chute of muslin and wood and into the presence of Satan.

#

Eliza sat in the Mercedes, shaking. She had been *such* a silly old woman. So gullible. So taken in.

She started the car.

Go home. Lock the door. Call the police. Find Jason and leave this town.

Why didn't she listen when the boy nagged her to get a portable phone?

She slipped the Mercedes into gear and backed down the driveway. An oncoming car blew its horn. It almost clipped her. Her cataracts stole her night vision, and she was crying.

What was she going to do? Calm down. She would calm down. Drive home. First things first. She turned on her lights and eased onto the road. She drove past the park and up to the intersection at Broadway. Cars whizzed in both directions. The headlights and taillights were haloed by her cataracts—just red and white circles bearing down on her from either side. She waited for the light to change.

My will…

She gasped.

I have to change my will…

#

Hadewych lifted the cardboard box from the closet where he'd hidden it. The bundles of soiled sheets and pornography fell aside. It had not been a good idea, he decided, to stack the magazines on top. Zef was seventeen now. He might have searched out his father's stash. But the *Playboys* and *Hustlers* sat untouched.

It might be fun to check Zef's browser history sometime.

Hadewych smiled. He had been young once.

He was avoiding admitting what he intended to do. Ever since he'd met Eliza and had decided that she would be the means to his end of restoring the Van Brunt fortune, he had known it would come to this. But he hadn't expected it so quickly.

Thank God Valerie is out of town. Eliza would be downstairs telling her everything.

He hadn't told Valerie a quarter of what he knew. He'd shared half of Brom's letter to Dylan—but not the other half—and had hidden the letter Dylan had written to his own son, the letter that explained the Treasure and what it could do.

But—had he ever believed the family legends?

"There's no magic to make it 1850 for us, son," his mother had said.

He found himself shivering. An unpleasant pit opened in his stomach.

Yes, I believe. Now that I've seen the thing…

He had hoped that the Eliza situation would… resolve itself. Without… intervention. She was so old and so careless with her papers. But he had underestimated her.

He sighed. He did admire the old woman just a little.

Stop this now, came the atrophied voice of his conscience. *You still can!*

He entered the bathroom and lowered the box onto the dingy sink.

Stop. No. Don't do this to the boy!

To which boy? To Jason? Or to my own son?

He didn't care about Jason. Jason would have to go, eventually. Would Hadewych's actions hurt Zef? He didn't plan to get caught. The whole point of using the Treasure was that he would never be caught. Zef would never find out, either. Hadewych thought of the Legacy, of Eliza's will. That greedy passion awoke in him again as it had months ago—that passion for the easy score, the big win. The shortcut.

I can't stop now. This will help Zef. This will assure his future.

Hadewych opened the box.

#

Valerie swallowed the last of the milk. It was sour now.

The next card represents those with whom the boy—The Fool—interacts.

She turned the card of influence.

The Devil.

#

Eddie Martinez perched on his throne a dozen feet in the air. His bat wings blotted away the moon and the stars. Flames of Hell lit him from below. His chest was bare and painted crimson. He wore a necklace of finger bones. The ram's horns made Jason feel that this

Devil could rear and crack a man's skull open with one head butt.

Yellow eyes blazed with reflected flame.

If Eddie's body crawled with lice, he didn't show it.

I will not blink—those yellow eyes snarled. *I will not scratch. Lice can gnaw at me until I am only bone but I am Satan and I will not lose to* you.

Jason could feel the hatred and contempt there. He tried to hold the gaze but his eyes began to water.

Crying already? You know you got no chance—said the yellow eyes. *Evil wins in the end. Evil always wins. You know why? 'Cause Evil lifts at four in the morning. Evil eats raw egg and whey protein and bloody hearts. Evil shoots itself full of anabolic steroids and benches three times its body weight while Good wastes the day in some library. Satan is coming for you, Jason Crane—with an army of jocks at my command. You pathetic nerd. You loser. You nothing. You better run when the bell rings, kid, 'cause we are going to kick your ass after school.*

Jason blinked.

Satan broke into a triumphant sneer.

Jason staggered away from the throne, looking for an exit, and fell into Ichabod's schoolhouse.

Ichabod stood before his chalkboard. He held a birch rod in one hand and a lantern in the other. The birch was bloody. A row of dead children sat at the desks, skin cut to ribbons by Ichabod's whip. The jump rope song played over and over. *La la la la la la la—when will school be over—la la la la la la la—we'd rather be out in the sun—la la la la la laaaa—but we would rot much quicker then—every one—every one. La la la la la la la—*

Ichabod raised the lantern to confirm Jason's identity.

"THE HESSIAN IS COMING," he said.

26 RISE HEADLESS AND RIDE

It might have been a lantern once, but was encrusted with gold now. Layer upon layer of gold, fresh from the forge—each layer building upon the layers of metal and blood beneath it. It had been hammered and shaped, this secret thing. Agathe had made it herself. She had built for her Treasure a reliquary modeled after the gilt cases she had seen in the Catholic churches. She was Dutch herself, and therefore Protestant, but this thing would be a home for evil—so a papist reliquary had seemed appropriate to her.

A reliquary is a sacred vessel, an earthly container for the remains of a saint—for a finger-bone of St. Francis, perhaps, or a chip of St. Adolphus's skull, or a knot of viscera from the belly of the Madonna. Such remains are supposed to possess healing powers and to bestow blessings upon the church that obtains them. Reliquaries are made to drive away evil spirits.

But not *this* one.

This was the Devil's *own* reliquary, built not to dispel evil but to gather it.

Hadewych peered through the smoky glass. He felt an urge to smash the container against the tile of his bathroom, to pry the gold away, to see for himself the source of the Van Brunt power and glory.

He longed to rip the thing open and gaze…

…upon the head of Agathe's Horseman.

The head of the Horseman waited within, its flesh rotted away to bare bone. That smudge—was that the eye socket? Did the eye still sit in it? Was it open—? Or closed, waiting to awaken?

In the medicine cabinet he found razor blades. Small vents pierced the top of the reliquary at the bottom of a shallow depression in the gold, just as Dylan had described. Something thick and black encrusted the edges of the tiny holes.

Hadewych held his hand over the thing and pulled the razor blade across his palm. Blood ran fast from his closed fist as if he were squeezing a heart. It gathered in the reservoir and dripped into the Devil's lantern.

#

Ichabod struck the slate with his whip.

"THE HESSIAN IS COMING," he said.

The Hessian? What the hell is the—

But Jason remembered his history, and understood.

Hessians were murderous servants of King George. Fearful German horsemen—mercenaries who killed for fun. Women, children, babies in their cradles…

And one of them had lost his head.

The rotting children rose and reached for Jason. *La la la laaa…*

He turned and ran.

"HE IS COMING SOON," said Ichabod.

Jason pushed through the crowd, deeper into the bowels of the mill. His hand brushed wood and he heard a whip crack. Had this been the slave quarters? No—he saw spectral girls in the lofts around him, brushing hair, talking to each other. Was this the… dormitory?

To Jason's right, an actor in an executioner's mask drew an electrical device across a wall, throwing sparks. The present and past overlapped. He saw the ghost of a girl pass through the executioner. A group of kids tried to pass through Jason and knocked him over. He grabbed a wooden crossbeam with both hands.

Agathe lay there screaming and struggling.

Agathe? How?

She was young in this vision, with porcelain features and auburn hair that tangled in the straw. A toothless figure lay on top of her, covering her mouth. She cried for help.

Someone. Anyone.

Her attacker drew a hand-scythe from his pocket. Agathe saw the curving blade and fell silent. The claw fell from her mouth and unlaced her blouse impatiently. Her tears ran from eyes that glowed with hate. Her lips moved soundlessly as she fell back, staring at the ceiling.

"THE HESSIAN IS COMING," whispered Ichabod from somewhere behind.

Firelight played over Agathe's face. Something was burning.

Jason followed her gaze. The executioner and his sparking whip had vanished. So had the ghostly girl. An enormous jack-o'-lantern sat on a table—a sagging thing four feet around. Flames leapt upward from its eyes and nose and mouth and caught the ceiling afire.

"I said MOVE, kid!"

Someone shoved Jason. His hands tore from the wood. He saw burn marks where his fingers had been. His head throbbed. He staggered deeper into darkness, bewildered by skulls and corpses and severed heads, not knowing which were real and which were not; he hit his knee and battered an elbow as he fell; voices assaulted him from the stone floor. Kids passed, laughing. *Coward.* He crawled through spider webbing and into the corn maze. There he hid—sobbing beneath a bower of dead stalks.

#

It was not enough. Not enough!

Dylan had described the awakening of the thing. Dylan had explained what to expect. It had not happened.

What had he missed?

The timing was right. Halloween approached—the anniversary of the Horseman's death. Two people were dead, killed by whatever haunted the waters of Sleepy Hollow. *The water-haunting.* Similar occurrences had been reported for over a hundred and fifty years, yet no one had noticed the pattern. Hadewych and Valerie had discovered the files at the Historical Society. She called the killings "shark-baiting" since each one bloodied water. They were a mystery that Dylan had never addressed. Had such occurred in Dylan's day?

As a survivor, Valerie had a unique perspective and a likely explanation. Something existed that wanted to strengthen the Horseman. It possessed people like her mother and used them against their will. Valerie had felt the Horseman drawing her blood. She had *felt* him absorbing her energy. She had *felt* him grow stronger.

Valerie had been so invaluable that Hadewych regretted deceiving her—but why end evil when you can harness it? Oh, well. Soon he wouldn't need her either. Soon he could wash away the stink of her.

Hadewych tightened his fist and let another rivulet fall.

An incantation in Old Dutch appeared, shimmering from within the gold.

Hadewych's first experience of magic.

So the legends are true.

He couldn't read the letters but Dylan had left a translation.

"Rise..." Hadewych whispered.

"Rise..."

Nothing.

"What more do you want from me?" he groaned, panicking.

A spike rose from the top of the reliquary. A rusty nail—sharp as Satan's horn.

Hadewych knew what he had to do. No *small* sacrifice would be enough. He glanced at himself in the bathroom mirror and saw tears on his cheek. His breathing grew quick. He raised his palm above the spike.

For Zef.

"Dad? I'm home." The front door slammed.

Hadewych froze.

"I'm in the bathroom, son," he called. "I—I ordered a pizza for us!"

"Great. I'm starving."

Yes. I have to be quick because the pizza man is coming. I have to sign for the pizza. I have to put my signature on the credit card slip. I have to sign for the large pepperoni with extra sauce and a double side order of alibis...

He looked at the spike again.

Oh... thought Hadewych, in that moment just before he did it. *Now that Zef is home I won't even be able to scream.*

He raised his palm—a man swearing an oath, if not on a Bible.

He picked up a toothbrush. It would be something to bite, at least.

"Rise headless and ride..." he whispered.

He slipped his bit into his mouth.

One. Two—

His arm came down and the spike shot through the back of his hand.

#

"Goddamn it," Eliza said. She was crawling. She squinted at the road. The car behind her blew its horn like Gabriel's own trumpet.

"Go to hell," she muttered. She shot the finger at her rearview mirror.

#

Across town, James Osorio dreamt that all the bodies in Sleepy Hollow Cemetery yawned, stretched, and turned on their sides. He would discuss this with his wife Pat in the morning and he would discover that she had dreamt the same thing.

#

Somewhere in the hills above Sleepy Hollow a pack of wolves looked up and howled at the moon. Down below, Charley the poodle heard them and answered.

#

In Joey's room, Booger dug a hole and hid.

#

Something in the attic of 417 Gory Brook Road stirred and began to laugh triumphantly.

#

The blood called to the Hessian, as it always did.

He pushed through the sod, climbing towards the night. He clawed through the bodies of six Colonial soldiers. These had tried for centuries to hold him down but they had failed time and again. *He* was the dominant spirit of the Old Dutch Burial Ground, and commander-in-chief of all the powers of the air. *He* could not be contained, not when blood was in the water, not when he was at full power, not when he was summoned—

—not when a Crane was in the Hollow and the Hallows drew nigh.

#

Valerie turned the next-to-last card of the Celtic Cross. This was the card that signified all The Fool's hopes... and fears.

Judgment.

An angel blows its trumpet and the ground cracks. The dead rise at The Fool's feet. The tombs are opened and The Resurrection is at hand.

Rejoice, the dead proclaim, *for He is Risen.*

Her shaking hand went to her valve. The valve that was her trumpet.

She did *not* rejoice.

Because Valerie Maule knew who *He* was.

#

"Jason..." said Kate, "it's okay."

Jason wiped his face. Kate knelt over him. She reached into the dark place where he had hidden and offered her hand.

"It's your Gift, isn't it?" she said, her voice low. "You can't control your Gift?"

He didn't care how she knew it. He nodded.

"I'll get you out of here," said Kate.

She reached for him, but he pulled his hand away. She nodded, understanding, and took him by both elbows. She brought him to his feet and led him into the maze.

#

Eliza had lost her way on side streets. She couldn't see the signs. She hit the curb and her purse fell to the floor, spilling papers and pills and nail polish bottles. She rolled down the window.

Gory Brook Road.

There. She had found it.

But the way steepened unnaturally. She pumped the gas pedal. The car inched forward. Was she riding the parking brake? No. She could smell the gas. She'd have flooded the engine of a lesser car. The house was in view now but it grew no closer. She floored the Mercedes. It flew forward, overshot the driveway and careened across the lawn toward the sycamore. She twisted the wheel and the car spun, clipping the tree with the back fender and spraying the bay window with mud.

She turned off the ignition and almost fell out of the car, shaken but unhurt.

Thank you, German engineering.

Thunder rolled. A storm approached. A tree branch fell, mortally wounded.

Pain shot through Eliza's hand. Was she hurt? Was it her arthritis? She held her palm up to moonlight. She watched as a wound opened there and bled something fierce. Oh, she had cut herself.

The wind grew stronger, louder. Someone's shutters started banging. The noise sounded like a fist pounding on a door—the storm seeking shelter from itself.

The Hollow fell silent.

The wind, the shutters, the branches above, the barking of the dog inside. Nothing.

Had she gone deaf? Was this a stroke?

Oh, Lord no—I have to change the will first. For Jason's sake.

She heard a single sound: distant but unmistakable.

Hoofbeats.

#

The maze stretched endlessly. Kate batted away stalk after stalk. Jason kept close to her back, making himself as small as possible. Hands reached for him from the corn; actors in masks leapt from corners.

"Not now," Kate said.

His face pulled into a grimace of fear; muscles in the back of his skull began cramping. A leaf hit him in the eye. He couldn't take it— the lights, the shouts, the screams! He pushed past Kate and ran ahead.

He threw kids aside, shook the walls of the maze, found the end of it, stumbled into a womb-like chute of inflated fabric—clawed through claustrophobic blackness— stumbled through a doorway and into moonlight. And there, something rose up out of the shadows before him: the Horseman, dressed in red velvet—raising a double-bladed axe—

Jason punched the actor in the bloody stump of his prosthetic neck.

#

Valerie swept the cards from the bed. She had seen enough. She threw her clothes in her bag, leaving the Tarot reshuffled on the floor.

One card remained on the bedspread—the card predicting the Outcome. She had laid it down, completing the cross, and had known immediately that she had to rush home.

The card was **The Ten of Swords**.

A corpse lies face down in mud, one hand twisted unnaturally. Ten swords protrude from its back like needles in a pincushion.

She had to get home. Because Hadewych had *lied* somehow. He had *lied* to her. And to Eliza. And to the boy. He had lied to everyone.

Jason was never The Fool.

They *all* were.

And The Fools had been stabbed in the back—by someone with a silver sword.

It began to rain. She slammed the door behind her. The last card trembled and fell among the others.

#

Rain poured on the roof, gathering in gutters to sluice into her front lawn.

Almost there. Almost there.

The hoofbeats grew louder, thundering up the aqueduct trail. Eliza fumbled for the house key, the one with the triangle on it. But her hand bled so heavily that the ring grew slick and she dropped it.

The keys lay on the welcome mat. She reached for them but her body would not bend.

She heard something laughing at her. From upstairs?

The back door...

The back door might be open. She stepped back down into the mud. Thunder galloped. Hooves boomed.

She stepped in puddles. Her hair melted down her face. She pushed water from her eyes with a bloody hand. She tasted copper.

Oh, no.

The staircase at the rear of the house might have been Everest, or the stair to St. Peter's gates. She couldn't imagine climbing that far. Not as sore as she already was.

But she tried.

One step.

Two.

Three.

She heard the thing galloping across her front lawn.

Four.

Five.

Six.

She pushed her legs down with her hands.

Seven.

Eight.

She pulled herself along by the rail. She couldn't breathe.

Nine.

Something popped in her hip.

Ten.

He's here.

She knew what the thing was as soon as it thundered into the yard below. She knew without looking. The hooves, the cracking laugh, the jack-o'-lantern that careened off the wall next to her. She knew.

The bastard will just have to come up and get me.

Eleven.

Twelve.

The greatest achievement of her life, she felt, was reaching that thirteenth stair. She felt immensely proud of herself for climbing so far and grasping the doorknob.

Even though it was locked.

She saw Charley at the window.

"Be good to Jason," she told the poodle.

The rider had dismounted. She felt a step on the wood below.

She turned slowly. From where she stood she could see the Old Dutch Church. She could see the manor, lit for the Horseman's Hollow. She could even see the cemetery from here.

As she faced Him *(Can you face something that has no face?)* she heard Bing Crosby whispering in her ear, reciting the last few words from Disney's 1948 classic *The Adventures of Ichabod and Mister Toad.*

"Rumors persisted," said Bing, "that Ichabod was still alive, married to a wealthy widow in a distant county. But of course the good Dutch settlers refused to believe such nonsense, for they knew the schoolmaster had been spirited away…"

"…by the Headless Horseman," Eliza whispered.

Oh, how she'd loved that film.

Silly old woman.

#

Jason sat shivering in the rain. A security-ghost shouted at him. The crowd around them squealed and ran for shelter. He couldn't hear, though. He was shell-shocked.

"Jason!" Kate came down the path, trying to shield herself from the rain. "I thought I'd lost you."

"Is he with you?" said the security-ghost. "'Cause he's in trouble."

Rain had collected in the ghost's tricorn hat. When it leaned forward, the water hit Jason in the face, waking him up.

"Eliza!" he yelled and shot to his feet.

He pushed past the guard and ran. He ran out of the event, across the parking lot, pushed through a line of kids, knocking umbrellas from their hands. He heard Kate calling his name but he couldn't stop. He had no thought but to get home. He ran out of the parking lot.

The rain weighed him down. He stripped off his jacket and threw it in the middle of Broadway. He ran uphill, pushing against a terrible weight—in slow motion, dreamlike.

Yes, let this be an intense and terrible dream. I can forget dreams.

But he couldn't wake up from this.

He pumped his legs, wiped a cup of water from his face, leapt a fence, stumbled through a backyard koi pond, fought wind and lightning and thunder and his own burning lungs.

Hail fell on Gory Brook Road.

He saw the sycamore peeking over the roof of his house. He would be home soon and Eliza would scold him for being so foolish and she would make cocoa and—

He saw the Mercedes on the lawn, back fender crumpled against the sycamore. The driver's door hung open, no one inside. He bounded onto the porch and fumbled for his house key.

"Eliza? Eliza!" he yelled.

Where were his keys? His pockets were empty and—

The jacket. My keys were in the jacket—

He'd made a fist to break the window when he saw something glittering on the mat:

Eliza's keys lay there, covered in blood.

He seized the keys and twisted them in the knob.

He slammed his palm across light switches, blinking against the sudden sting of light. He ran from room to room, leaping over furniture. Charley circled and jumped and barked. He brushed her aside and leapt the stairs three at a time.

"Jason?" came a voice from downstairs.

"Eliza?" he said. "Thank God."

Lightning flashed in his bedroom window, and by the time the thunder answered he was downstairs again.

Kate had called his name. She shivered on the front porch.

He groaned in disappointment and whirled around.

"Eliza?"

Charley yowled. Jason ran to the kitchen and found the dog leaping at the back door.

Oh, God… the stairs…

"The stairs."

This is a dangerous stair, he had thought on his first day at Gory Brook.

He turned the knob.

The rain battered his cheek as he stood on the landing. Kate's hand fell on his shoulder. The storm had passed. The muddy yard sparkled with hailstones. At the bottom of the stairs, floating among those stars, lay the unnaturally twisted figure of Eliza Merrick.

#

Zef brushed a scattering of garbage out of the armchair and onto the floor—a beer can, a wet newspaper, crumbs of chips and sandwich crust. He turned on the television. His father stood behind him serving the pizza. Zef could see Hadewych reflected in the TV screen, superimposed over the black and white images of Dr. Frankenstein. The Halloween programming had begun.

His father came up behind, passed a plate of pizza into Zef's hands and leaned down. He kissed Zef's head and the boy jerked away.

I hate when he does that.

"You came home early," said Hadewych.

"The Hollow was rained out."

"How is Kate?"

"She didn't go. She wasn't feeling good."

Zef reached for a slice of his pizza but Hadewych wrapped an arm around his chest, hugging him painfully.

"Have I told you how much you mean to me?"

"Let me go," said Zef. He didn't want Hadewych to smell the whiskey on his breath.

"Listen to me. Family is everything. You'll understand when you have children. Nothing is more important in life. Everything I've done has been for your future. For you and your kids."

"Hell. What did you do to your hand?"

"Oh, this?"

Zef pushed Hadewych away. The wound in his father's palm wasn't bleeding, but it was as livid as something you'd see on a statue of Christ.

"Minor accident," said Hadewych. "It's healing fast."

"You need stitches."

"Nah," said Hadewych, plopping on the sofa with his pizza. "It's loads better already." He giggled, and Zef thought he sounded hysterical.

Wow. He's as drunk as I am.

Zef ate his pizza and watched Frankenstein. Hadewych held his hand under the lamp, staring at his wound as if it were something miraculous. He turned to Zef and grinned.

"You know," he said, "I hardly feel anything at all."

27 MORE THAN A LITTLE BIT

Kate didn't know what to do.

She sat with Jason, keeping his hopes up, rubbing his back in circles. He barely registered her presence or touch. He sat cross-legged in a plastic chair, staring into space, tearing a travel magazine to confetti.

After they had discovered Eliza, Kate had called the ambulance. Jason had run to the yard to kneel at Eliza's side. He'd checked her pulse, he'd held her hand, he'd shielded her from the rain with his body—while wetting her body with his tears. Kate found a blanket and joined him. They knelt in the mud together and made a tent over the old woman. They shivered. Jason kissed the white forehead and wailed until the sirens came.

He rode in the back of the ambulance with Eliza. Kate followed behind in the Mercedes. The car started easily enough, but it stuck in the mud of the front yard. She found a branch that had fallen and shoved it under one of the back tires. That got it going, though the car slid dangerously before it gained the driveway.

Once she'd reached Phelps Memorial Hospital she'd found Jason easily enough, ranting at an admitting clerk who'd grilled him about insurance paperwork. Fortunately, Kate had rescued Eliza's crazy-quilt purse from the passenger-side floorboards. They found a Blue Cross card inside and blows were averted. Jason fell silent like guns after battle. He sank into the orange chair and stared at the hospital logo on the wall.

They heard no news for over two hours. Their clothes had dried except for chilly seams. The waiting room was warm but that just made it more difficult to stay awake. She and Jason sat bolt upright when anyone approached. The nurses would loom over them, wring their hands, but walk away without a word. This happened twice before Kate realized that a dispenser for hand sanitizer hung on the wall behind their heads.

Zef answered his phone at around three a.m. He was pissed off at being awakened. Kate didn't respond in kind, though, thinking that he had a right to be angry with her for not meeting him after the Hollow as they had agreed. His voice sounded slurred and she guessed he'd been drinking. She hated that about him. He had a great future, but would screw up their life together if he didn't stop hitting the bottle.

Jason didn't talk. He hugged the purse. He looked as though he were watching a sad foreign film—staring straight ahead, glancing down occasionally to read subtitles. Kate made conversation with a fat man on her right awaiting the birth of his sixth child. He didn't seem too excited about it. She guessed that by number six the novelty wears away in tandem with the bank account.

When Zef and Hadewych walked in around four a.m., her relief overwhelmed her. The situation required an adult. The expectant father slid aside to make room for Zef, who slipped an arm around Kate's shoulders. Hadewych spoke with the doctors and reported back.

"It's quite bad," he said. "She may not last the night."

Kate glanced at Jason but he didn't react.

"Did she—break her back? Or her neck?" she whispered, reaching for Jason's limp hand.

"She didn't break anything, amazingly enough," said Hadewych. "She has excellent bones for her age. She's very bruised. She has no internal bleeding or—"

"So what's killing her?" Jason snapped, breaking his trance.

Hadewych knelt. He put hands on Jason's knees, brushing Kate away.

"'Liza's heart is racing. Adrenaline's pouring through her. She's fighting... something."

"Fighting what?" said Jason, attempting to brush Hadewych away in turn. Hadewych remained crouched, looking prepared to leap on Jason if he were to bolt.

"Easy, son," Hadewych said.

"We suspect a stroke," said a man in scrubs. He wiped his forehead and raised one surgical glove. "Doctor Tamper. I'm the attending. We can't find the cause but it's ramping up her nervous system. It might be a blood clot in the amygdala, that's—"

"The fear center," said Zef, earning a nod from Hadewych.

"Right," said the doctor.

"And—what's that doing to her?" said Jason.

"All her fight-or-flight responses are off the charts. The simplest way to put it is that… she's being frightened to death."

The doctor paused to let that sink in.

Kate noticed that Hadewych was staring downwards—at Eliza's purse, which lay by Jason's leg.

"I want to see her," said Jason.

"You should," said Hadewych, his head snapping up.

The doctor considered, shrugged. "Maybe you can calm her down."

"Is she violent?" said Zef.

"Oh, no," said Tamper. "Whatever she's fighting, it's in here." He tapped his temple.

Jason shot to his feet and turned back to the group.

"She needs me," he said. He looked at Kate, and silently mouthed "Thank you."

She nodded. Jason and Doctor Tamper hurried away. Hadewych pivoted and took Jason's chair. He patted Kate's left knee. "You can go now," he said. "Zef will take you home." Her boyfriend stood near the door, trying to get the candy machine to accept a wadded bill. The machine refused and stuck his dollar out like a taunting tongue. Zef punched it in the glass.

"You've been a good friend to Jason," said Hadewych. "You *are* just friends?" He leaned in, raising eyebrows.

"Of course," she said.

"Of course. You're a good girl," Hadewych said. "I tell Zef all the time 'Kate is a keeper.' If he's smart, I hope to have a daughter-in-law just like you."

"That's not Zef's call," she said. But she smiled.

"I know. But it is *my* most fervent wish," said Hadewych. He kissed her cheek. "Give your father my best?" Hadewych said.

Kate nodded.

Zef returned with a handful of kisses. He took Kate's arm. She glanced back at the door. Hadewych was perusing a green folder that he had slipped from Eliza's purse.

Poor Jason, Kate thought on their way out. *He does seem like a nice boy.*

#

Jason badgered Doctor Tamper into letting him sit with Eliza through the night. The doctor agreed, noting that Jason's presence did seem to calm her. Eliza's breathing became regular. Jason brushed her hair with his fingers, bringing it into some semblance of order. He talked to her, about nothing much except his love. Her lips moved endlessly, silently. Around dawn, her mouth opened in surprise, and that is how she remained through the morning. The nurse warned that Eliza's throat might dry out. Jason was given a sponge on a plastic stick. He wet her tongue and the insides of her cheeks every ten minutes. Her eyes opened, staring fixedly. They were drying out, too, but he could not force her to blink. They brought saline at his request. Hadewych came in around ten a.m., bringing Jason caffeine pills and an Egg McMuffin. Jason dozed sporadically throughout Sunday, his head on the bed by her knee. He woke in the late afternoon to find her gripping his hand painfully. Her eyes were bright with triumph.

"I beat him," she croaked.

"Who?" Jason said.

She nodded and grinned.

"I kicked his sorry—" But her head fell back on the pillow, exhausted. "Oh. I beat him." She sighed and smiled. "I didn't go— easy. I beat him."

"Who did you beat?"

She whispered something he couldn't make out. A name? It sounded like "Head" something.

Hadewych?

She stared at the ceiling.

"Did someone attack you?"

She raised her other hand and patted Jason's head.

"Good boy," she said.

"Can you hear me?" Jason said.

The heart monitor skipped a beat. He stabbed the button to call the nurse.

"Eliza? *Eliza?*"

He laid both his hands on hers.

Jason stood in the attic of the old house in Augusta, Maine. Late afternoon sunlight shone through the dormer windows, and dust motes leapt through shafts of light like children playing in a lawn sprinkler. He glanced down and saw little legs and feet and red shoes badly tied. They stepped from beam to beam, over air conditioner ducts and cotton-candy tufts of insulation.

Careful, kid. Don't fall through the sheetrock.

At the end of the attic, under the beautiful rose window that so many visitors admired from the lawn, Grandpa John had laid sheets of particleboard to make storage space. Jason watched his stubby fingers opening boxes, discovering old flower arrangements and Christmas tree ornaments and warped LP records that had been foolishly stored. One box contained a trove of titillating paperbacks from the sixties: *Passion Carnival... Hospital of Sin... The Flesh Peddlers.* He remembered sneaking some of these downstairs when he was older, but in this vision he tossed them aside, not yet old enough to know that a boob was a boob.

He fought the vision.

Stop this. I'm in the hospital room. Eliza needs me!

The afternoon sun and skipping dust overpowered everything else.

He moved on to a trunk of clothes—an army uniform (*Whose had that been?*)—a box of porcelain cups. Picture albums.

What is this vision? What object am I reading? How am I seeing this?

"Oh, we've got a little prowler," said Eliza.

She had been watching him the whole time, from the top of the pull-down attic stairs.

This is a memory of hers. A memory of me. I'm reading her—*she's struggling for life and I'm reading her memories. Is her life flashing before her eyes? Why this, why this day?*

"I's just lookin'," said Jason.

Eliza gasped dramatically. "At what?"

She climbed up. She wore jeans (which Jason hadn't seen her wear in ages), red sneakers, and a bandanna around her neck. She was suntanned from gardening. Her hands were bare, he noticed. She was either between husbands or had taken the ring off to keep it clean.

"Who's that?" said Jason, pointing at a picture. A grey woman in grey dungarees stood by a grey Packard. She held her grey head proudly against a grey sky and blew a kiss with black lips.

"My aunt Tab," she said.

"And him?"

A bald man grinned from a scalloped photo, his colorized cheeks strangely peach and rouged.

"Uncle Joe."

In the next one a pretty blonde raised arms in triumph. The scoreboard above registered a strike.

"Is this Mama?"

"No. That's your cousin Regina."

"I want a picture of my mama and daddy. Where are they?"

"On my dresser, of course."

He found loose sheaves of photos in a shoebox. He scattered the pictures across the particleboard. Some fell face down, just scribbled names and dates. Others were obscured, a raised hand or an eye peering from behind the others. Yet a hundred faces looked up at the little boy and the old woman—a dozen Bicycle decks of kings and queens and one-eyed jacks and jokers. And, even now, Jason couldn't recognize one quarter of them.

"These are my people," said Eliza. "They won't matter to you, Honey. And when I'm gone…" She gazed off, patted her knees to get his attention. "You know what? I'm going to write it all down. So you'll know. See—here's your daddy's box. Your daddy and his daddy and his daddy too."

Andrew Crane smiled from the deck of a fishing boat.

Adam Crane posed with his young bride.

Jack Crane posed stiffly in a hard-backed chair.

And all three wore gloves.

Jason stopped breathing. No—he was breathing fine. Wasn't he? Something felt wrong. What did it mean? Did his father and grandfather and even great-grandfather all possess the same ability he did? And, if so, why did she never tell him? Was she trying to tell him now?

"All these people," said Eliza, putting a palm to his chest, "are *in you*, Honey. Your daddy and his daddy and his daddy and your mama and my Arthur. All of them are in you. And a little of me, too. At least a little bit? Huh?" She put the other hand around his back and pushed her palm tight against his heart. He looked down. She tweaked his nose. "Gotcha!" She laughed.

Eliza swept the photos into the box and lifted it.

"Let's look at these downstairs! It's time I did something with them. Maybe I'll start a new hobby."

Little Jason sneezed.

"God bless you," she said, laughing. "Get out of this dust or you'll catch asthma, Honey. And tie those shoes. You'll break your neck."

He fumbled with his laces. She kissed his head with an enormous "mwah" sound and walked away. She turned back and stepped onto the ladder, grabbing the rail with one strong hand and cradling a box of memories under her arm.

He watched as she backed down into the square of light.

#

"I said *move*," said Dr. Tamper, pushing Jason aside. Jason's hands were ripped from Eliza's. A nurse pulled him over to the bathroom door. Someone dropped a plastic cup over Eliza's face, squeezing a bulb. Machinery rolled about like bumper cars.

Jason staggered into the hall and cried.

His hand went to his chest, where her palm had lain on his heart.

He slipped to the floor.

There would be no miracles. He knew that.

He had felt her last kiss; heard her last "God bless you."

And he had watched her go.

28 THE LEGACY

Bad memories flooded over Valerie. This was the hospital where they had installed her valve, ten years ago. Oh, how they came back, those bad, rotten, no-good, ugly memories. All those feelings. Shame at being attacked by her own mother. Pain, of course, and also fear—fear that she would never be loved again, that no man would want to hear pillow talk from a woman who sounded as she did. The endless hours of rehab and counseling. Hadewych had stood by her through all of that. She had come to depend on him. What if she couldn't depend on him any longer? Impossible. They were a team.

She roamed the corridors, searching. She could still hear the sound of that ventilator—filling her up until she would burst.

She dreaded seeing Hadewych. The tarot reading had made her feel that Hadewych had been deceiving them all somehow. And her mother had taught her that the cards must be given their due.

"There you are." Hadewych waved from the end of a corridor. They walked to each other and met in the middle.

"Zef—told me," Valerie said. "How—is Eliza?"

"Dead," said Hadewych.

Valerie backed away, clattering into a gurney. Her hand found a pillow there and clutched it for support.

Hadewych had announced it with a smile.

"What... what did you do?" she said.

She saw no shock in Hadewych's face, only a flash of annoyance.

"Do?"

"You're smiling."

Hadewych pulled his face into an unconvincing semblance of

grief. "She's out of pain," he sighed. "How can we not be grateful for that?"

"Grateful? This is our—friend!" She hit him with the pillow. His eyes darkened.

"Acquaintance. And collaborator," he corrected.

Valerie gaped at him.

"And a very sweet old woman," he concluded. He sniffed a bit and held up a hand. He turned away and collected himself. But when he turned back the smile had returned. He couldn't help himself.

Valerie dropped the pillow. She threw herself at him and beat at his shoulders with her fists. He grabbed her arms and cursed.

"What is this?" he spat. He pushed her back into an alcove next to an ice machine. She stumbled against a mop bucket and grey water splashed her stocking.

He waited, holding her by the wrists, until she quit struggling. She couldn't speak. She couldn't engage her valve.

"I will not be struck for no good reason," he said coldly. "I've done nothing. Nothing but indulge you. I brought Eliza here because *you* wanted me to. *You* wanted the tomb opened more than I did. I knew we wouldn't find anything. I knew it was a waste of time. But we did it, and now this woman is dead."

He loosened his grip, brought her hands down and held them at her side.

"I don't blame you," he added. "It was an accident. No one is to blame. But it's your fault she came here. Don't put this on me."

Valerie's mouth opened and she made a feeble attempt at words.

"Don't say anything. I don't want to hear it."

He let her hands go. Her fingers went to her valve and he slapped them away.

"Please," he said. "Spare me the noise."

"Noise?"

"Yes, noise." He imitated her, brutally. "Hadewych. Hadewych. Hadewych. It's like thumbtacks in my ears."

"Hade—"

"Shut up," he said. "Shut up shut up shut up! I can't listen to that right now. I'm too upset."

She hesitated, but engaged her valve. He winced before she even spoke. "She—adored you."

"I don't need adoration," he said, rolling his eyes. "I'm tired of all you adoring women. You strangle me. Do you know that?" He wrapped hands around an invisible neck. "You strangle me. You're paranoid and superstitious and you have these ridiculous fantasies that I try to—I'm the one that should have the locks on my door. To protect me from the crazy woman who imagines I'm her boyfriend."

"You're—not?"

He shook his head, like a pet owner who has discovered yet another mess on the rug. "Valerie. It's time we were frank with each other. Our supposed 'relationship'—it's just another fantasy rolling around in your head."

She pulled to the right, batting the handle of the mop away as she tried to escape him. She got around him. She held her hands up, warding off emotional blows. He followed as she stumbled into the hall.

"What, then—" she said, bleakly, "were the past ten years?"

Hadewych looked at her with infinite regret and kindness.

"Pity," he said.

Valerie ran down the hall, through two sets of double doors. She ran through Radiation, through Emergency, and didn't stop until she staggered into a rainy twilight parking lot.

#

Jason stared out the window of the Mercedes. Night had fallen again. He had been awake for over twenty-four hours. His energy ebbed away with the fall of rain, disappearing into the gutters—into the little river, into the Hudson and out to sea.

"I'm so sorry," said Hadewych, turning out of the hospital drive and right onto Broadway.

"What do I do now?" said Jason, after a minute of silence.

"Nothing. Let me handle things. The… arrangements."

Jason turned to look at him. Beyond Hadewych's shoulder, Sleepy Hollow Cemetery drifted past.

Her funeral. He's talking about her funeral.

"Don't *I* have to?"

"No," Hadewych said. "That's the executor's job."

"You?"

"She asked it of me. She didn't know anyone in Sleepy Hollow."

Hadewych sighed and shook his head. "I never dreamed this would happen."

The Old Dutch Church looked solemn and sad as they drove past.

"I'll want to confirm that," Jason said.

"Of course," said Hadewych. "I have the will. We'll see the lawyer in the morning."

"I can't even think about it," said Jason.

Philipsburg Manor looked like a haunted dollhouse. They crossed the Headless Horseman Bridge and stopped at the light.

"I called McCaffrey…"

"No," Jason cut him off. "Not him."

"He's a friend. He adored Eliza."

Jason rose in his seat and slapped the dashboard. "No. No. No. Anyone but." He could not permit Eliza to be taken to *that room*.

"It's done, I'm afraid. And it *is* my decision."

Jason wanted to jump out of the car and run, to find anyone—a policeman, Fireman Mike—anyone who could stop this abomination.

"But—" Hadewych said, seeing his expression, "—I don't want you to be upset. Don't worry. I'll find someone else."

Jason went limp with gratitude. He fell back into the passenger seat, more exhausted than ever. The light changed and they rolled forward.

"When?" Jason said.

"The twenty-ninth?"

"No. Not that day." The twenty-ninth of October? The tenth anniversary of his parents' death?

Hadewych frowned. "I already called the cemetery."

"Not that day."

"The thirtieth, then."

Jason nodded. They turned towards Gory Brook Road.

"I'm surprised you're being this difficult," said Hadewych.

#

Justin Piebald, attorney-at-law, smiled benevolently from across the wide cherry-wood desk of his conference room.

"Shall I begin?" he said, putting on his glasses.

Jason nodded. Hadewych straightened his coat jacket and took a drink of water.

"I, Elizabeth Jane Merrick," read the lawyer, "being of sound mind and desiring to make my last wishes known in the event of my demise, do make this my Last Will and Testament.

"I currently reside at 417 Gory Brook Road, Sleepy Hollow, NY, 10591. I am a widow and divorcée; I have been married seven times, to Gerald Logan, William Ferrer, John Dawes, August Beringer, David Puck, Roger Fellowes, and Arthur Pyncheon. Arthur Pyncheon was my first husband, the love of my life, and father to my only child Dianne Elizabeth Pyncheon.

"Arthur Pyncheon died after twelve years of marriage. My other marriages ended in divorce. None of my former husbands have any claim upon this estate. If any of the aforementioned assert such rights they are to be given one dollar and sent on their merry way."

Piebald looked up, amused, and wiped his forehead.

"I had one beautiful daughter by my first husband: Dianne Elizabeth Pyncheon. Dianne married Andrew Crane, and that marriage produced one extraordinary child—my grandson Jason Crane."

Jason swallowed and looked at his hands.

"Both Andrew and Dianne Crane are now deceased. Jason Crane, as my sole family and heir, is to inherit everything I own. My house at 417 Gory Brook will go to Jason Crane. My stock accounts, 401(k), checking and all other accounts shall go to Jason Crane. In short, all real property and financial accounts shall go to Jason Crane.

"In addition, I give Jason Crane all my interest in the Legacy."

"The what?" Jason said.

Hadewych leaned forward. Piebald held up a finger. He turned a page and continued.

"I hope I have had the opportunity to explain this to you, Jason, before I go. I have delayed doing so to this point in order to assure that you grew up with a mind for thrift and an appreciation for the value of a dollar. The Legacy is a series of financial accounts left to me by your grandfather Arthur Pyncheon. As of the date affixed hereto, the Legacy is valued at approximately one hundred and twelve million dollars."

"What?" Jason blurted. "Repeat that?"

The lawyer nodded, amused. He was the lottery commissioner

personally presenting Jason with an oversized check.

"The Legacy," he repeated, "is valued at approximately one hundred and twelve million dollars."

"How is that possible?" Jason said.

"Let the man finish," said Hadewych.

"This Legacy is over one hundred years old, and has been passed down through generations of the Pyncheon family. In all that time the principal has never been touched. Never. Not one dime is to be spent, my love. The interest alone will be enough to support you as lavishly or as frugally (I hope frugally) as you desire for the rest of your life. This Legacy is to be passed intact from eldest child to eldest child with no expenditure of the core funds. If you should die without children, it shall be delivered to the nearest Pyncheon relative. And, most importantly, the Legacy may be added to, but must never be diminished under any circumstances."

Hadewych's right hand, Jason noticed, had meandered to his left palm and was busy scratching it.

"Oh, my love," read the lawyer, awkwardly, "my Jason, my little adventurer. I have always been so proud of you and of the man you are becoming. I hope that you will miss me, but keep marching forward. I hope I have set you on a glorious path."

Jason leaned back in his chair, overwhelmed and moved.

Piebald turned another page.

"Regarding the executorship. The executor of my will shall be my dear friend Mr. Hadewych Van Brunt. If he should be unable or unwilling to act as executor, I nominate Ms. Valerie Maule. The executor shall serve without bond and shall see that all transactions herein described are faithfully executed. In gratitude for his friendship, I leave him the sum of thirty-five thousand dollars."

Hadewych adopted an air of gratitude and bowed his head to Jason.

"In gratitude for her friendship, I also leave to Valerie Maule thirty-five thousand dollars in the hope that it helps her to overcome her challenges."

Piebald looked up.

"Where is Ms. Maule, today?" he said.

"She claims to be sick," said Hadewych, with a shrug.

"No matter."

"Is that all?" said Jason, placing his palm down on the conference table.

"One more paragraph," said Piebald. "Guardianship. As of this writing, my grandson is not yet a legal adult. Should he be eighteen years old at the time of my death I hereby revoke my assignment of executorship and name Jason Crane sole executor without bond. However, if Jason has not achieved the age of eighteen years he shall require a guardian of his person and a guardian of the estate, to see that he is taken care of physically, and to oversee the management of his inheritance until he is of legal age. For both roles I declare and appoint Mr. Hadewych Van Brunt to be his caregiver."

"*What?!*" Jason screamed, bolting to his feet.

"Sit down, son," said the lawyer.

"Jason," Hadewych said. "Come now. Sit."

"You?" Jason said, pointing at Hadewych. "My *guardian?*"

Hadewych tried to reach for Jason's arm. Jason snatched it away.

"How?" Jason said. "Why?"

"I told you. After she moved here she didn't know a soul in town except Valerie and I. And I never dreamed—"

"Don't give me that again. You knew this all along." Jason gripped the back of the chair. He turned to the lawyer. "Is there anything else?"

"A little," Piebald said. He wiped his brow and held the paper up to the light. "Hadewych, please take care of my boy just as you have your own. Jason deserves the finest possible care and love. Signed by my hand, the fourteenth of September: Eliza Pyncheon Fellowes Puck Beringer Dawes Ferrer Logan Merrick."

Piebald laid the paper on the desk and folded his hands. Jason looked at the white rectangle as if it were the guilty decision of a jury sentencing him to hang by the neck until dead.

"I will never be your…"

"Ward," said Hadewych.

"Never." Jason shook his head.

"You don't have much say in this, young man," said Piebald.

"You talked her into this," Jason said to Hadewych.

Hadewych rolled his eyes for the lawyer. "Do you see what I have to deal with?"

Jason walked to the window. He saw Zef's face reflected in the glass, not his own—Zef on the night of the lighthouse, screaming "I hate him. You don't know what he's like."

Jason buried his face in his hands. Did they actually expect him to submit to this? Did they think for a second that he'd allow Hadewych to take control of—

"Her money," Jason said, and his voice had the implacability of a man stating absolute truth. "You killed her for her money."

"How dare you," Hadewych said, standing. "I adored your grandmother."

"Oh, you bastard," Jason hissed. He knocked his chair over, clearing the space between them. He could grab that chair, he thought, grab it and raise it—as Zef had raised the folding chair that night—yes, he could grab it, bring it down legs first and open Hadewych's veins.

"Mister Crane," said the lawyer. "Collect yourself or I will call the police."

"Call them." Jason said. "He's a murderer. I don't know how, but he is."

"A murderer. Really," said Hadewych. "What possible evidence would you have for that?"

Jason had no evidence, he had to admit. Just a deep, gnawing gut certainty that Eliza's death was connected to this will. He *knew* that Hadewych had desired this vast Legacy as soon as he'd heard of it—he would think nothing of using Jason and his grandmother in order to seize it. Had the entire Project been designed to bring them to this day? Had he and Eliza been manipulated from day one?

"Jason," said Hadewych. "I'm on your side."

Jason batted away Hadewych's offered hand.

"These are serious charges, Mister Crane," said Piebald, "and let me tell you this. We have these little things called slander laws in this country."

Hadewych righted Jason's chair. Jason did not sit. Hadewych did, though, legs crossed and arms folded.

"I've known Hadewych here for twenty years," said the lawyer. "He's one of the finest men I know."

"Right," spat Jason. "He's a saint."

"You could do a lot worse for a guardian. Look at his son. Zef's one of the brightest boys in town. He's good-looking and athletic—"

"He's a mascot," Jason said.

"He is going places. He was raised right. He's well-adjusted—valedictorian—dating that pretty Kate Usher."

He's a closeted homosexual who's drinking himself to death for fear of disappointing his father, Jason thought, but he could never have said that aloud, for Zef's sake.

"Your point?" Jason said.

Piebald sighed.

"It was Ms. Merrick's appointment to make, and she made it. You two are going to have to work it out. At least for the next year."

"The next year?" Jason said.

"You won't need a guardian when you're an adult. So just suck it up for now. You'll be eighteen soon enough."

Hope leapt in Jason's chest. He reached into his pocket and drew out his wallet.

"I am so relieved, sir—" Jason said. He threw the fake ID on the table. "—because I *am* eighteen."

He knew he couldn't hope to get away with it, but he had to try something. He waited for the response. Hadewych shook his head, a chess grandmaster amused by the move of a four-year-old. He opened a briefcase. He laid a state-certified copy of Jason's birth certificate on top of the ID.

Piebald looked at the document. "I see what you mean," the lawyer said with a sympathetic headshake.

Hadewych sighed and threw up his hands.

"The boy is *such* a liar!"

29 RED SNEAKS AND WILDFLOWERS

The hinges of Eliza's bedroom door cried when Jason entered: a lonely kittenish whimper. He tried the switch and discovered that the overhead bulb had burned out.

He would have to change it. He would have to find a ladder or fetch a chair from the kitchen. He would have to climb up, wobble precariously, and loosen the fixture. Yes, he could see the dead bulb in his mind: the frosted glass would be smoked from the inside, the filament would be broken and trembling. He let the imaginary thing fall and crash against an imaginary floor. He would never have to change that bulb. Never again.

Jason was escaping.

He faced the corner as he turned the bedside lamp on. He was glad that he did. Even the sight of Eliza's robe hanging behind the door was painful to see. He turned and faced the room, struggling to stay detached and calm. It tore at him to see the indentation in the mattress, the hint of makeup on the pillowcase, the plastic wrapper from a packet of saltine crackers on the bedside table—held down by a few crumbs left inside.

Her room.

He couldn't sit on the bed. He didn't have the heart to replace her indentation with his own. He pulled the little tasseled stool from beneath her makeup table and sat on that instead.

The stool had once been the bench of the old pump organ—the battered old instrument that had been his favorite thing in Eliza's house. It stood about four feet high and bristled with spindles and carvings and shelves that were meant to hold knick-knacks or plaster saints. Eliza always left her reading glasses there. On its top, a stained glass sailboat drifted past. The two pedals at bottom were embroidered with a girl carrying a parasol (on the left) and a leering young man (on the right). Jason would stomp their faces with his sneakers and work the pedals like those of his tricycle. He didn't have much leverage at that age, so he would hold the stool on either side—just as he was doing now—with no hands free to actually play. But the keys stuck and would stay pressed while he pedaled. Dissonant clumps of notes rose and fell as he pumped air through the organ with his feet. He worked his legs and giggled and filled the house with mad music. A row of organ stops had protruded above the keyboard, but the only label he still remembered was "Vox Humana."

What had happened to the organ? When had it stopped breathing? He wanted to play it now—play some song for Eliza, some song that she had loved. "All the Things You Are," maybe, or Irving Berlin's "Always." But the organ was long gone—hauled away after some yard sale. The buyers had put it onto the back of a truck. He'd bid the sailboat Godspeed and it had drifted down the block.

The tasseled stool remained behind, though. The buyers had forgotten it and never came back. Eliza saved it and this mirrored tray, too. She'd almost shrieked when she saw the tray tagged with a price of five dollars. She had it from her grandmother and it wasn't for sale. Here it still sat on her makeup table, bearing regimented rows of red fingernail polish—marshaled in order from virginal pink to dissolute scarlet.

Everything in this room evoked associations and memories. How could he leave any of it behind? But he would have to. He'd have to stay for Eliza's funeral, of course, but afterward he'd take the MasterCard, climb into the RV, and escape. He hated the thought of leaving Kate and Joey but he would not live under the thumb of Hadewych Van Brunt. Not now, not ever. Even if Hadewych hadn't killed Eliza. Jason doubted that now. He couldn't conceive of anyone being that evil, not even Hadewych.

The RV would be an okay place to live. He couldn't plan the future beyond that. Would he drive to Colorado and live in some national park campground? Charley would enjoy that. He might get a job in some rural town under an alias and support himself until he turned eighteen. Who knew? He couldn't predict what lay ahead—any more than he could predict the future after his parents' death when he'd thrown a box of Cheez-Its in a pillowcase and run away from home. Was he repeating that? Was he running away from home again? If so, he would get farther than the playground up the hill this time. He'd run as far as he could.

This time Eliza was not going to find him and rescue him. Eliza would never wrap him in her winter coat and take him back home. Never again.

"We all die, baby," she'd said to him—that morning by the seesaws. "In all the long, long, history of the world, there's not been one of us who didn't."

"I'll die," he had responded, and she had squeezed him tight.

"Yes. And I'll die. A lot sooner. It's just *there*. It just *is*."

It just is…

He looked around the room.

"But we're here now," sixteen-year-old Jason whispered, "and it has to be enough."

He wiped his face and went to work.

He couldn't leave Eliza's treasures behind. He couldn't leave them for Hadewych. He grabbed packing boxes—boxes that had come down from Augusta only a month before. He opened one marked "JASON'S ROOM."

First he added her jewelry box. Costume pieces, mostly, but also her many wedding rings, a heart-shaped diamond necklace on a white gold chain, and a string of black pearls she'd received as an anniversary present—from which husband, Jason didn't know. This had been a long double necklace but Eliza had broken it so many times—losing so many pearls under furniture or down subway grates—that the thing was just a choker.

He found her personal papers in the closet—a landfill of bills, tax statements, deeds, titles, account balances and old checkbooks. He had no idea what to take and what to leave—it was all so… adult. And he had no time to go through any of it, so he just dropped the whole stack on top of the jewelry box and moved on.

Jason lifted the boxes and stacked them in the kitchen.

He filled a box marked "SEWING" with shoeboxes and envelopes of family photographs. He glanced at these. Yes, the men on his father's side wore gloves. He shook his head. He couldn't stop to puzzle out the implications. Why had no one told him anything?

He wore no gloves himself but saw no visions as he packed. Maybe he was too shut down inside, too guarded, too business-like. Maybe his ability had burned out at the Hollow. He didn't know. He didn't allow himself to linger on any objects, just in case.

He filled a box marked "DISHES" with Eliza's scrapbook and her pilot's license and a wire-mesh chicken that she'd bought on vacation in Naples.

He filled a box marked "KITCHEN" with her slippers and home movies (on VHS tapes), an Easter basket and a rabbit-fur coat. The coat looked too tiny for such an epic woman. He stuffed it in a box.

How could he leave *any* of it? How could he take a fraction with him? He pulled things from closets, from the dresser, from under the bed. The volume overwhelmed him; he dropped to the floor and lay there staring at a Chinese fan and a box of Bing Crosby LPs.

I'm not ready for this. I'm not ready to be alone.

He noticed that one wood panel had a handle protruding from it. He rose to his knees and drew the panel aside. A safe. When did Eliza install a safe? Did it come with the house or had she bought it? It looked new. Had workmen been to Gory Brook to bolt the thing down? On some afternoon when Jason was at school or at Joey's house?

And... and here was the most important question... What was the combination?

Anything Eliza had to put in a safe would be too important to leave behind. But how would he get it out? He considered grabbing the tire iron from under the carpet of the RV. But he knew that wouldn't work. This was a strong safe. Could he call a locksmith? He doubted he'd be able to get one out here before the funeral.

Beyond the window a flash of lightning broke the sky above the Hudson. Thunder hit the house like an avalanche.

And he knew. Of course he knew...

He turned the dial.

10-1-19-15-14

The safe clicked. The numbers of the combination were letters in the alphabet. They spelled his name.

He turned the handle.

A row of pictures in gilt frames stood on the shelf inside the safe. Pictures of him. Most had been taken digitally but she'd had prints made and framed. Here he was at birth, in the arms of his father (yes, Daddy wore gloves); here Jason was coming home from the hospital; here taking his first step—fists clutching his mother's two thumbs. Here was his awkward, long-legged childhood: summertime pictures (taken at Camp Wallahoo) that made him look like a praying mantis in swimming trunks; studio pictures of him looking pimply and pensive. Here he stood with Eliza in a field. He stared at this picture for a long time. He was so little in this one, a real squirt. Eliza wore a loose floral print. He wore a buckskin jacket with fringed sleeves. They wore matching shoes—four red sneakers in the grass. The squirt carried an armful of wildflowers he'd picked for her. She wore a daisy in her hair.

Jason's cries came like the notes of the old organ, wheezing and hollow and dissonant, louder and softer as he pushed the air through the bellows, dwindling only many minutes later as he exhausted himself. He looked away and wiped his face again. The back porch light illuminated the raindrops on the bedroom window. The drops looked like falling black pearls.

He set the photo aside and drew out the last picture—a horrible middle-school graduation photo. His hair stuck out and he wore a plum purple robe.

At the back of the safe sat two bars of gold.

He lifted one. He didn't expect it to be so heavy, like something Eddie Martinez might curl in the gym. The words "Pamp Suisse— One Kilo Fine Gold 99%" had been punched into the surface.

The mystery of Eliza's money exasperated Jason. He couldn't wrap his mind around the size of the Legacy. How had she kept such a fortune secret? They'd never lived like multimillionaires. Eliza clipped coupons for fabric softener and had yard sales and bought her Diet Dr. Pepper in cases to save fractions of a cent. She'd never been extravagant—the opposite, actually.

The whole question of the money wounded Jason's heart and muddled his head. Yes, he was a very rich young man. But also broke, everything tied up in accounts that he couldn't access without Hadewych's signature. Eliza had left him this wonderful gift of a fortune, but why had she hidden it from him? Was she ashamed of it?

He knew almost nothing about his grandfather, Arthur "Artie" Pyncheon. His mother hadn't even known the man. Dianne had been born six months after her father's funeral. Eliza called Artie her one true love. He'd been her high school sweetheart and she'd never been satisfied with any man afterwards—though not for lack of trying.

Jason imagined Grandpa Pyncheon as a tall, dark-haired man with a lantern jaw and a deep voice, like the cartoon Brom.

So he'd been fantastically rich, huh? And Eliza had kept the money hidden for all these decades, keeping it safe from her fortune-hunting husbands? This is what exasperated Jason. Had he ever even known his grandmother? And now he couldn't ask her.

In one hand he held the picture of the two of them standing in the field. In the other hand he held the bar of gold. He didn't have to check the spot price to know which of the two was more precious. He put the bar down and collected the pictures into a stack.

He was glad of the gold, of course. It meant that he would have more than enough to live on until he turned eighteen. But—he would trade it all to have Eliza back.

Just for one more game of Scrabble.

Lightning struck again. Thunder boomed. And something upstairs laughed.

It was a woman's laughter, a snide and echoing sound—sniggering from the bottom of a well.

Jason stood.

"Hello?" he called.

He heard it again.

"Hello?"

Someone else was in the house.

30   THE HOUSE THAT LAUGHED

"Hello?"

Jason walked into the kitchen.

The kitchen window hung open. Rain had dappled the sill. He closed it.

Another giggle...

"Who's there?" he said.

The sound came from... from...

He and Eliza had never done anything with the downstairs guest bedroom. The laughter came from there—down the hall in that spare room.

Laughter, and something else—a knocking sound?

"Hello?" he said again. He stepped gingerly around the davenport, past the stairs and into the hall. Portraits of long-dead ancestors drifted past, faces captured in sepia and amber: women leaning on old cars—men saddling horses—an unpleasant couple sitting stiffly, she in her Sunday black bonnet and he strangled by a high starched collar. These dead frowned at Jason as he passed by. *How dare you not know our names.*

The light was off. He reached inside and found the switch. The guest room appeared normal—stuffed with boxed books and lamps and a mattress turned on its side.

But something didn't feel right.

Was someone hiding behind those boxes? Jason stepped inside the room, fading to his left, craning his neck, but he didn't see a thing. He'd found the source of the knocking, though. A twiggy branch of the persimmon tree that grew in the side yard beat its soft fruit against the glass. The battered fruit refused to fall, clinging stubbornly to its twig. It left pulpy marks on the glass as the storm tried to beat it to death.

Something black pounced from a crevice and ran toward Jason, streaking between his legs. He jumped, caught his breath again and cursed.

"Charley, bad dog!"

As Jason turned to go, he thought he saw a woman's hand and shoulder swimming in the shadow behind the door.

"Hello?" he whispered.

He turned sideways, extended his right foot and snagged the knob with his fingertips, jerking back. He'd seen a mop loitering against the wall—its ragged hair knotted like dreadlocks.

See? Nothing.

Light blazed behind the persimmon branches—a close lightning strike—and thunder cracked his ears. He shut his eyes at the sound. A moment later he opened them—or had he?

He had. But the lights had gone out.

The wind dashed the persimmon fruit against the glass, over and over. Charley barked from somewhere in the house. Jason's eyes adjusted and he felt his way down the hall. He tried a few switches but the electricity was as dead as the people in the photos. He stepped into the dining room and peered out the bay window. The houses down the hill were still lighted. The grid wasn't down.

So his fuses had blown. And he didn't know what to do about it. Where was the fuse box?

He felt like a silly starlet in a horror movie, about to be murdered by the guy in the scare mask, or bitten by a vampire bat swinging from a fishing line.

Crap crap crap. Get a grip.

Jason cursed his damn imagination—his photographic recall of every slasher and horror flick he'd ever seen. Which one was he in tonight? *Friday the 13th? The Haunting of Hill House? The Blair Witch Project?* Were hordes of zombies out of *Night of the Living Dead* about to crash through his bay window? Should he grab a hammer and start building barricades? He imagined Redcoat zombie Joey reaching in through boarded windows—all gnashing teeth and vacant eyes and that ridiculous purple wig.

Headlights splashed in the rainy window, fell away as the car turned.

Where is the fuse box?

He walked through the kitchen. The back porch light had gone dark too, and no moon broke through the storm clouds. He stumbled into the utility room. He ran his hands along the wall and swung his arm at darkness. He knocked over something cardboard and caught it as it fell. Powdered detergent poured through his fingers. He wiped the grit away on a dimly perceived pair of boxer shorts. His hand stank like an over-chlorinated swimming pool.

The persimmon beat on the window of the guest bedroom. Thump thump thump thump. Endlessly in the distance.

Could the fuse box be in the entry hall closet?

No. It isn't there. You know where the fuses are.

Still, it couldn't hurt to check. Jason sleepwalked through the kitchen and into the living room. He barked his knee on the davenport. Charley barked from beneath it, startling him again. He should spray-paint the poodle white, he thought—for moments like this.

He felt behind the coats in the hall closet. No, the fuse box was *not* here. The sword from the Van Brunt tomb fell across his shoes.

Jason kicked the sword aside. He hated being right.

The fuse box was in the cellar.

It would be, of course. He was in a horror movie. The cellar was the most terrifying place in the house. It was only natural that the fuse box would be there, and he'd been an idiot to consider any other possibility—it was a dark and stormy night, after all.

Brom... Brom... Brom...

He looked up and backed away from the stairs.

Brom... Brom... Brom...

The House that Shouted was shouting again.

This wasn't a vision. He wasn't touching anything. This wasn't a memory or a vivid daydream either. Something was in the house. Something was in the house *with him.*

Brom... Brom... Brom...

He'd heard this same creepy shout on the day he'd met Hadewych and Valerie.

Brom...

Tiny scorpions of fear skittered up the back of his neck.

"Hello?" he said, whispering up the stairs.

Brom... Brom... Brom...

It was a woman's voice. The shout wasn't angry, exactly. It was insistent, harsh—an old woman calling for her servants. Calling for help? Yes—calling for her son. Her son Brom.

Agathe. This is Agathe's voice.

He recognized the texture of it now. Ancient Agathe from the vision in the tomb. Yep. That was her. His own grandmother had gone, but Dylan's grandmother was throwing a tea party upstairs.

Oh, right. Her body was never found...

Jason hit the wall with one fist. What was next? Was the house built on a sacred Indian burial ground too? Ever since he came to Sleepy Hollow it had been one ghost thing after another...

Brom... Brom... Brom...

His hand drifted to the staircase rail. No. He would not go up there. Not with the lights still off.

Call me a chicken-shit, but no way.

Brom... Brom...

"Shut up!" he yelled.

He didn't want to go down to the cellar either—not without light.

Something moved in the vicinity of the fireplace. The little scorpions of fear bit him now.

"Charley?"

The dog was in the kitchen.

His steps made a cross-rhythm against the endless persimmon massacre still unfolding in the back bedroom. He rummaged through the kitchen drawers. He found batteries, but no flashlight. He found spoons, forks, a lemon squeezer and a broken egg timer. He found a cheese grater and brought his fingertip to his mouth, tasting blood. He was more careful exploring the next drawer and did not slice himself on the butcher knife there.

He lit the gas stove. The pilot light clicked and a wreath of blue tipped with orange spun into existence. Now he could see. Yes. There was the sink, the cabinet, and the refrigerator. The light inside the refrigerator wouldn't come on of course. It was as dead as the people in the pictures and his grandmother and the old lady haunting his attic.

Why don't you just stop now and eat all the ice cream before it melts? Wouldn't that be sensible, Jase? Much more pleasant than facing the cellar or the thing upstairs. I think we have rocky road…

In the last drawer he found a small paper bag with candles inside. Birthday candles. Eliza had bought them in preparation for his seventeenth birthday—November first, a few days away. Had she ordered a cake too? Was some bakery frosting a birthday cake that no one would ever pick up? There would be no birthday for Jason this year. He would be spending his birthday in the RV, escaping from Hadewych.

He found a card inside the bag. One of those cards with a music chip inside. It played "Raindrops Keep Fallin' on My Head." He held it up to the stove. The front read "Showers of Kisses on your Special Day." Eliza hadn't had time to write anything inside.

Brom… Brom…

"Leave me alone," he muttered. "I'm having a moment here…"

He killed the music and set the card down. He lit a birthday candle on the burner, but blew it out again. He should wish for brains, he thought, since he wouldn't be able to carry a lit candle through the storm. He found safety matches on top of the stove. Yes. Good. This was progress. He turned the stove off, stuck the candles and matches in his pocket, and opened the back door.

He ran down the thirteen steps as quickly as he could, rain pelting the back of his neck. He had his keys out before he reached the bottom. He concentrated on getting the door open and avoided looking at the spot where he'd found Eliza. Helpless to quiet his own brain, he remembered the blood on the key ring when he'd found it on the welcome mat. He twisted the key and the door swung outward. The cellar was black and wet. He put a shoe on the stair and lit a candle.

He found the fuse box right away, just behind the water heater below the utility room. He cycled the switches and ran outside to see if the lights had come on, but the kitchen windows remained dark. He cursed Tom Edison and went to find the fuse box again. His candle had blown out. He fished for the safety matches.

The cellar door slammed shut, plunging him into darkness.

Just the wind. Just the wind. But he'd seen too many movies to believe that.

The door wouldn't open again, of course. He pushed hard,

bracing his feet on the stairs. He beat on the door with his fists, making his hands ache. It didn't budge.

A light grew and flickered behind him, and now he could make out the red flakes on the rusty door. But the overhead bulb still wasn't working—this was a soft light, like the light of tallow candles.

Made from the fat of unbaptized infants… No, stop it. Stop it!

The light seeped from around the edges of a second door at the opposite end of the cellar. Had he seen that door before? No. He had never ventured that deeply into the dungeon that extended under his yard. And he didn't want to do so now.

But it might be the way out. Maybe it leads to…

Oh.

Oh, crap.

The door leads to the aqueduct tunnel beneath Gory Brook Road.

Brom had built the aqueduct too. The Van Brunt Quarry broke the stone for those weirs and shafts along the trail. So Brom built his mother's house above the aqueduct—why? So she'd have access to fresh water? Jason didn't like it. The thought of endless tunnels under the house freaked him out.

He stepped around the boxes and beams, drawing near to the light. He heard a distant rushing sound beyond the door. Yeah, the aqueduct was in there.

He reached for the knob.

"Jason…" someone whispered.

He snatched his hand back, stumbling backwards.

The door in front of him flew open and the light went out. He saw the dim shape of a woman standing overhead, a faint blue outline made from his memory of the gaslight. He twisted away and kicked a path through the boxes. The spirit—whatever she was—strode past him, blasted open the cellar door and turned in the direction of the stairs. The dog yipped above.

"Charley?" Jason said.

He ran from the cellar and up the thirteen steps.

The back door was locked now. He hadn't locked it.

He wiped rain from the window. Inside, the stove was burning though he hadn't left it on. The corner of the birthday card had caught fire and the drapes would be next. Jason knocked the glass out of the window with his elbow and opened the door. The flames roared a foot high. The room was hot. He twisted the knobs of the stove but they came off in his hands. He threw the burning card in the sink and turned the water on. The card gargled its little song. He threw handfuls of water at the curtains, stuck the knobs back on the stove, and twisted the gas off.

The ghost of Agathe laughed at him hysterically from upstairs.

"Bring it, bitch," Jason said, burning the last of his testosterone, trying to mask the terror he felt. He tripped over his moving boxes and recovered in the living room, where he spread his arms and shouted up the stairs. "You just come down here and bring it!"

A crack of thunder scared the dog and she ran into Eliza's room.

Jason panted and seethed. He stumbled across something as he neared the stairs: the sword. He grabbed it and drew the blade.

"Don't make me come up there."

Brom... Brom... Brom...

"Brom's dead and so are you," he said. "Get out!"

The persimmon fruit beat itself frantically on the guest room window, louder and louder. He heard an explosion of broken glass and the rhythm stopped. Agathe giggled again.

"I'm coming up..." he said again, but with less confidence.

One step.

Two steps.

The birthday card began playing in the kitchen: distorted, dirge-like notes. *Raindrops keep fallin' on my head on my head on my head head head head head heeeeaaaaaddddd...*

It was a decapitation song.

The ghost giggled again.

Three steps.

Four.

"I want you gone," Jason said.

Five.

Six.

"The power of Christ compels you!" he called, quoting *The Exorcist* and feeling stupid.

Seven.

Eight.

He heard the sound of a faucet left on. He bounded up the remaining steps.

The floor of his bedroom ran with water. He felt it through his shoes. He knelt and splashed the floor. Lightning lit his bedroom window. He looked up and saw that the stain on his ceiling drooled like an open mouth. He threw down his bedspread and some dirty clothes to absorb the water and ran up the second flight to the attic. He stopped himself halfway, remembering the sword in his hand.

Do not run with sharp objects, kid.

He continued at a more deliberate pace, until the black square of the open attic door engulfed him. A flash of lightning lit the octagonal window at the far end. Thunder followed, rolling through the darkness.

He heard the water rushing in before he saw it. He found the leak with his hands. It poured in through the crack in the eaves where Debbie Flight said the sycamore had broken through. He pressed his hand across the hole. It was like trying to block the nozzle of a fire hose.

Brom! Brom Brom Brom! Agathe shouted. *The water's bleeding in...*

Jason saw her figure at the attic window. Hair in a tight bun, black dress, pearl buttons. Her form brightened and dimmed—drawn in the air and erased again, over and over.

Brom? she sang, raising bloody hands. *Brom... the water's bleeding in...*

Jason crossed the space and swung his sword at the dead woman, but hit empty air. Her face reappeared in the rain on the other side of the window. Was she on the roof? He wrestled the window open.

No. Nothing there but the rain.

Agathe laughed from downstairs now. From his bedroom?

"Go away," Jason said. He splashed down to the second story. Agathe stood on the roof above the kitchen, just outside Jason's bedroom windows.

Bleeding in the waters... she giggled.

Cold droplets hit his neck from the leak in the ceiling. He tore open the window and swung the sword. The figure vanished again. Charley barked. Jason whirled. Agathe stood on the stairs! Rage filled him. The thing was baiting him, toying with him, making him crazy. He wiped his face, got detergent in his eye, gritted his teeth and raced after her. He bounded down the stairs two at a time.

Brom! Brom Brom Brom!

The knocking sound had moved. Something beat on the front

door now. Beyond the wet windows he saw Agathe's figure standing on the porch. He threw the door open and swung the sword blindly…

…at Kate.

31 KATE

Kate dove backwards onto the porch. Jason's swing went wide and missed her. The edge of the sword bit into the front door and lodged in the wood. Kate stumbled away, backing onto the lawn.

"I'm sorry," Jason said. "God, I'm sorry."

Jason pulled the sword from the wood and threw it down, raising his hands to show he was unarmed.

"You could have killed me," she said.

"I—I didn't know it was you."

"Who, then?" She was soaked now. She spat her hair out of her mouth. "Well?" she said, climbing back onto the shelter of the porch. She picked up her closed umbrella, ready to defend herself if necessary, and put one shoe on the sword.

"I had an intruder," he said.

"A burglar?"

"No," Jason said. He hesitated, scratched the back of his head and broke into a grin. "A squirrel," he blurted.

"A squirrel."

"Yeah. I chased it all over the house and… what can I say? They make me crazy."

"You were chasing a squirrel with a sword," she said, her voice dripping with mockery. Better than anger, he decided—and much better than explaining his urgent need for Ghostbusters.

"It was a pretty big squirrel," he said. "A super-squirrel."

She shook the umbrella. "A super-squirrel."

"A Jurassic monster squirrel with—fangs—and… it could have fought Godzilla."

"So. You had a… Mothra-level squirrel," she said.

Jason nodded.

"Mecha-squirrel," he said, raising claws.

She leaned on the umbrella handle.

"Really?" she said.

Jason nodded. "Bite your head off, lady."

She bent and picked up the sword. "Let's just put this away," she said.

"Good idea."

She watched Jason as they entered the house. Maybe half-expecting him to pull a chainsaw next? He found the scabbard on the floor and gave it to her. She slid the sword into it, and closed the front door behind them.

"Do you have any… lights?" Kate said.

"Actually, no. No lights." He took the sword and put it in the closet.

"So we'll just hang out in the dark?"

Jason hoped that Kate couldn't see his expression. Hanging out with her in the dark didn't sound half bad. "The fuses," he muttered. "They're blown."

Kate nodded. She touched a switch and the lights came on.

"Oh," said Jason.

"Oh."

Stupid stupid stupid.

"Towel," she said.

"What?"

"Towel? I'm dripping."

"Oh, um… one second."

He bounded through the kitchen and into the utility room. He dove into the laundry and came up with an orange beach towel. He brought it to her.

"They just want shelter from the rain, you know," Kate said.

"Who?" said Jason.

"Squirrels."

She dried herself in the kitchen, looking around. Rain stippled in through the shattered back window. Muddy footprints soiled the tile and hardwood. The charred remains of the birthday card lay in the sink, and the water still ran.

"Looks like Godzilla lost," said Kate.

"It was nuts." Jason immediately regretted the pun. He turned off the water and grabbed the burnt birthday card. It croaked out one final "Raindrops Keep Fallin' on My Head" on the way to the trashcan.

"Are you going somewhere?" said Kate.

"No," he said. "Why?"

"Okay, then are you building a fort?"

"Oh, those. The boxes. Yeah. I wanted to put away my grandmother's, you know—things."

"Right," she said. "I had thought I'd better check up on you."

"Thanks. That's great," he said. And he meant it.

Kate put the towel over her head, drying her hair. He risked a glance. Her clothes were soaked through, all right. He could see her...

"Eyes up here, mister," she said, tossing the towel at him. She'd caught him looking again. He remembered the first time he'd seen Kate, slipping into Zef's car the night of the dance. She'd caught him looking then, too. Did she set these traps on purpose? And had he failed the test or passed it?

But the towel reminded him of something else—

"Oh, hey," he said. "I have to—uh—"

"What?"

"Take a leak," he said.

She frowned.

"Take care of a leak." *Stupid stupid stupid.* He held up the towel. "I have a leak. Just—stay here?"

He ran through the living room and up the stairs. Kate followed him. But his room was dry. The water wasn't bleeding in anymore. The stain above was almost too faint to be seen.

"Where's the leak?" said Kate.

Jason ran up to the attic. It was dry and dusty as ever.

"It was pouring in bad," Jason said, returning to the bedroom, "I swear."

"I believe you," said Kate.

She noticed the cut on Jason's finger. It still bled, just a little. "What happened?" she said.

Jason couldn't honestly remember.

She rolled her eyes. "Don't tell me. Squirrel."

He nodded.

"I'll get you a Band-Aid," she said. She walked to his bathroom and he hoped desperately that everything was, well, flushed.

He saw his backpack on the floor. He tore it open. Agathe's book was okay. He tucked it in the nightstand. *The Sketch-Book of Geoffrey Crayon* was okay too.

"What's that?" said Kate, returning.

"It's a first edition of *The Legend*. Eliza gave it to me."

"Nice gift," Kate said.

She joined him on the bed.

"Hey. Did I thank you?" Jason said.

"For?"

"For staying with me? At the hospital?"

"You did, sir." She made him hold his finger out and wrapped the Band-Aid around it.

"Thank you again. That was nice of you."

"All done," she said. She leaned down and kissed his fingertip.

They sat in silence. She'd been kissing the boo-boo to make it better, that's all. But the room became… fraught…. Jason felt that they had both become aware of the room, that it was his bedroom, that they were horny teenagers on his bed, and that there were no adults in the house. He could hardly think of anything else.

Kate slipped from the bed and onto the floor. She leaned back on her hands and he immediately thought that the floor might be nice too. He joined her. She backed off as he sat—a little farther away than he'd hoped—stopping, framed in Jason's windows.

"Thank you for rescuing me," said Jason.

"It's only a Band-Aid," said Kate.

"No. In the maze. At the Hollow. I was in bad shape."

"I saw you freaking out."

"And—how did you know?" he said.

"Know what?"

"You said—" Jason hesitated. "You said, 'Is it your Gift? You can't control your Gift?' How did you know?"

The window had fogged. Kate wrote "Jason's Room" on the center pane. She added a smiley. She glanced at him and wiped the smiley out, absent-mindedly.

"Your Gift is in your hands, right?" she said.

He nodded.

"So why aren't you wearing your gloves?"

"I—"

"Where are they?"

"On the dresser."

She fetched the gloves. "You should wear them," she said. "All the time. At least at first. Not now. Not over your Band-Aid but—tie them to your sleeves or something so you don't forget them again."

He nodded.

"And if you lose them, use your fingers to touch things," she said. "That's usually okay. Just not your palm." She returned to the window and sat again. The back porch light made the rain on the window look like fireworks behind her. "What have you been seeing?" she said.

"The past. Things that happened."

"Visions? Off objects?"

He nodded. "And people sometimes."

"That's called psychometry," she said.

"I read that. On the internet."

"It's not common. It's pretty rare, actually."

"And how do you know that?" Jason said.

She held up her own hands. "I see too."

"You see? What?"

She rolled her eyes, embarrassed. "The future," she said.

"You're kidding."

"I wish," she said. "It can be a pain. I see flashes. Potentials. No lottery numbers."

Lightning lit behind her. "But, yeah, I have a Gift too."

"So—we're alike," said Jason.

A soft rumbling thunder answered.

She shrugged. "Opposites, I guess. You see back, I see ahead. But yeah."

Jason grinned. "So where're *your* gloves?"

"Me? I can handle *my* gift."

"Oh, you can?"

"Yeah. I'm not a clueless newbie."

Jason threw a pillow at her for that. She dodged it and scowled in mock outrage.

"It's true," she said. "You don't know anything, do you?"

"No."

"Your parents never told you?"

Jason hugged his knees. "They died when I was seven," he said.

"Oh." Kate smoothed the pillow in her lap. "I didn't know. See, it runs in families."

"Why?"

"It just does. I got mine from my mother. She saw. Pretty accurately. At least short-term. She saw her cancer coming. Two years before the diagnosis. She stopped going out, stopped having fun. She decided—'What's the point?,' I guess." Kate looked out the window. "You should know—these Gifts can be awful."

"I think my father had this thing," Jason said. "And my grandfather. I saw them wearing gloves in old pictures."

"That makes sense."

"It does? I think it's crazy."

"No. Every generation inherits the Gift—at least the potential for it—all the way back to your Founder."

"You lost me."

"Your Founder is the person who developed the gift first. Someone somewhere in your family line. For you, I'm guessing Ichabod."

Jason looked at his hands.

"How would I inherit this from Ichabod?"

She came closer, and Jason felt his heart speed a little. She sat her elbow on the pillow in her lap, challenging Jason to arm wrestle.

"Afraid I'll beat you?" she said.

He reached for her hand but she drew it back.

"Put your glove on first."

"Why?"

"I'm—a little worried about us touching," she said.

Jason wasn't worried about them touching, not at all, but he put the glove on as ordered and took her hand in an arm-wrestling position.

"Okay. You're Ichabod," she said, "and I'm the spirit world."

"The what?"

Kate slammed his arm down.

"You lose," she said. "You got targeted by a ghost and it killed you. Try again."

Jason frowned. This time she pressed and he pressed back. He still wavered though. Kate was strong.

"Feel that?" she said.

"What?"

"The struggle?"

Jason nodded. They both trembled. She smelled good.

"That's your soul fighting the ghost," she said.

"Okay. I'm fighting the ghost."

"—and it gets stronger. And if you win…" She relaxed. Jason swung her arm down onto the pillow. Their forearms pressed together for one maddening second. "…If you win, or survive, you still keep the… strength that you built up. Like a spiritual muscle."

She squeezed his bicep. He flexed so it would seem more impressive.

"And that's how a Founder gets his gift," she said.

"Because Ichabod was targeted and survived—"

"He came out of it seeing visions. And he passed that Gift along."

"To me."

"Yeah. To his kids if they were born after. Then to all his direct descendants. And it makes sense, doesn't it?"

"What?"

"That your gift would be… a scholar's gift? A schoolmaster's? A gift for…"

"History," Jason said.

She nodded. And there it was, the underlying pattern of Jason's life. The explanation for his curiosity, his love of the past, his ability to see *beneath*. He'd inherited the soul of a schoolmaster. He'd inherited his ancestor's Gift for… for knowledge.

"You in there?" Kate said. "I feel like I've lost you."

"If there are ghosts—spirits—how do they target people? Can they think?"

"Most can't. Only the really really strong ones. Most are just… needles on a record, doing the same things over and over. Like most people, I guess."

"Wait—could a ghost… possess someone?"

"If it's strong enough. But the host wouldn't be Gifted after. Not unless they drove it out."

Jason nodded. He felt joy rising in him for the first time in days. He had not been mistaken about Kate. They *had* to be together. They were *alike*. He could talk to her. She understood—much more than he did. And damn she was beautiful sitting on his bedroom floor with fireworks behind her. He removed his glove, held out a hand to her.

"Show me."

"Show you my Gift?"

"I'll show you mine," Jason said and bit his lip.

"Oh, you will?"

"Just show me," he said. "What's my future?"

She reached for him, but stopped.

"What's the matter?" he said. He reached for her hand but she pulled it away.

"What happened to us on the dance floor?" she said.

"I don't know. It was—intense. And I wanted to apologize. I don't know what I did, if it was me."

She nodded. "I never felt anything like it. Whatever you did it scared me. Bad." She took a deep breath, deciding. "Okay." She took his hand and closed her eyes. Jason closed his too. They sat holding hands as the rain fell. She pulled away, frowning and shook her head.

"What?" Jason said, "Was it bad?"

"No, no. I didn't see anything. You're dark to me," she said, "but I haven't had one single vision since the dance. Not one. You know, I'm starting to get worried. It's like I'm burned out."

Jason thought of the light bulb in Eliza's room. He remembered his own vision. Of Kate walking up the aisle to him.

"Did you see anything, the night of the dance?" he said.

She chewed her index finger.

"I think—I saw you," she said. "As a little boy. Random images. I don't know. Did you see anything?"

"I might have," Jason said. "Future things."

"What things?"

He shrugged. He didn't want to say. He felt her withholding something too.

She leaned back on her hands again. "If you saw the future and I saw the past—could we have swapped Gifts for a second?"

"Can you do that?"

"I don't know," she said. "I don't know everything."

Jason had to ask. "If you can see the future," he said, "does that mean you know, say, who you're going to marry?"

"I think so," she said. Her smile grew wider. She took her shoes off and rubbed her feet.

"Who?"

"Zef, of course. Why else do you think I put up with him?"

"Zef? But he's—"

"He's what?"

"He's Zef."

"I saw it. I had a vision. The first time I kissed him."

"Do I want to hear this?"

"It was third quarter at a Horsemen game, the first night he rented Gunsmoke from us. He and I brushed him, after, in the parking lot, waiting for Carlos to bring the trailer around. Zef still wore half his Horseman getup. The breeches and the boots. He was cute, so I kissed him."

She looked away, a little embarrassed.

"It was a good kiss," she said. "Eddie Martinez must have thrown a touchdown 'cause the crowd went wild and—"

"Oh, I hate this story," said Jason.

"Anyway, we kissed and I saw the future. I saw him in a suit, a blue suit with a grey tie. Waiting for me at the altar of the Old Dutch Church. How about that?"

That sucks. That's how about that.

"Did you tell him?" Jason said, hoping she'd scare Zef off.

"Of course not. That might change the whole future. The future's much trickier than the past. Besides—Zef doesn't know what I can do."

"You haven't... come out to him?"

"Why do you look so weird? No. And you can't tell him." Her face darkened. She took hold of Jason by his sleeves. "Listen, have you told anyone about your Gift?"

He nodded. She gasped.

"Did you tell your grandmother?"

"No."

"Good. I was afraid that—"

"What?"

"*Never* tell anyone about your Gift if they don't have a Gift themselves."

"Why not?"

"It's the first rule. The first thing your parents should have taught you. Maybe it's a superstition, but I was taught that if you tell any outsider, bad things happen to them."

"What things?"

"They die," she said. "Everybody we tell dies."

Jason withdrew and sat up on his haunches. This worried him. "How?" he said.

"I had a friend growing up," said Kate. "Jill. She came from a supernatural family too—"

"A what? Never mind," said Jason. His ability to absorb and accept this stuff was maxing out.

"Jill could hear sounds from far away—that was her Gift. She told a girl at school what she could do. She wanted to show off. Well, the girl wanted proof, so Jill had the girl walk farther and farther down this hill—and the girl whispered and Jill shouted back whatever the girl said. And, finally, the girl was convinced that Jill had the Gift. That's the point of no return. When they believe it."

"So. What happened to the girl?"

"She backed into the road. Right there."

"Oh."

"The driver who ran her over said something held his arms so he couldn't turn. And years later, Jill swore to me that she could still hear that little girl whispering every time she used her Gift. I've heard a hundred stories like that. Do *not* tell anyone who's an outsider. It never ends well. Sometimes they do get attacked and survive—and become one of us. But mostly they die."

"Wait," he said, holding up a hand. "Were you thinking I killed my grandmother?"

"Maybe…" she said.

"I didn't tell her about my Gift, okay?"

"Fine."

"I didn't kill her."

"You said you told somebody—I just assumed—"

"No. *Joey*. I told Joey."

Kate rose to her feet and sat on the bed.

"That's bad," she said.

"So you're saying, 'Don't kill Joey too?'"

"I'm saying—watch out for Joey. Because everyone we tell dies."

"That's just great," said Jason. "Great." His frustration and pain felt like a fist squeezing his heart. "Hey, Universe, just take everybody. Why not? You should go, Kate."

"Go?"

"Yeah. Go. Do. Go. Really. I can't talk to you. Not anymore. Not tonight."

"Jason," she said, "you're being childish."

"I'm allowed," he bellowed. "Tonight I am *allowed* to be childish."

"Fine," she said, pulling her shoes on. "I'll go."

"Yes. Please. Just go," he said. "I can't take this shit right now."

"Shit? Shit? Really?"

"Yeah. It's horseshit. Supernatural families? Like who? The Munsters?"

Kate made a face of revulsion and marched out of the room. He followed her down the stairs.

"Yeah. Bye, Kate. Say hi to the Frankensteins for me."

"You're an asshole," she said.

"And the Draculas, of course."

"*Never* talk to me again."

"Just go," he snapped.

"Fine!"

"Fine!"

Kate slammed the door.

Charley barked from Eliza's room.

Jason opened the door and said: "Give my best to Casper!" He slammed it again.

As he stood alone in the center of the living room, everything he'd experienced in the past month spread out on the floor like so many tarot cards. His Gift, his visions, the ghost upstairs. How could he make fun of what Kate believed, when he'd seen so much with his own eyes? Her explanations had made a crazy sort of sense. Did he have any better theory? And—was he still the complete skeptic he'd been a month ago?

He was. He believed only in those things he could see and feel and touch.

But I have seen and felt and touched the supernatural.

It was something definite, something finite, an understandable part of the universe. It was something he would have to study and break down and understand in his own way. But—he didn't want to face it alone. He needed help. He needed Kate.

And, of course, he was in love with the girl.

He ran out the front door and into the rain. He saw that vision of her—walking up the aisle. He wanted that vision to be true. He wanted the supernatural to be real. Yes, he wanted all the magic he could find.

He found Kate down the road. She'd left her umbrella inside. She fumbled with the keys to her car. He took her by the shoulders, spun her around—and kissed her.

The cold rain and her warmth fought each other. The warmth won. She accepted the kiss, returned it for one lingering moment—then stuck her leg between his, flipped him to the ground, and jerked his wrist up from behind. The wet grass scoured the side of his face. Her knee jabbed into his back.

"Not cool," she said. "You know I'm with Zef."

"I know," said Jason. "I don't care."

"I do."

She released him and he rolled over onto his back, looking up at her from the mud.

"Say you're sorry," she said.

Rain fell into his eyes.

"I'm not sorry I kissed you," he said. "But I'm sorry for how I acted inside. I'm done being childish. Come back in?"

She walked away, standing in the street.

"I don't want to be alone," he said. He sat up, wiping his nose, and held a hand out to her.

She stared at his hand. Maybe she was afraid to touch him, still, afraid of what might happen if past and future came together, palm to palm.

"As a friend?" she said.

"As a friend."

She walked to him. She took his hand and helped him up.

They ran for shelter together.

Kate slept over that night. She wouldn't get into trouble. Her father wouldn't find out. He'd started some senate campaign in Massachusetts. They searched the cupboard for food but didn't find very much. It was Eliza, ultimately, who made dinner for Jason and Kate—they discovered one of her famous lasagnas in the freezer. And, happily, the rocky road ice cream hadn't melted.

After dinner they watched *Seabiscuit* on cable. Kate swung her legs over Jason's and threw popcorn at him when he tickled her feet. Charley ate the kernels that fell to the floor.

Not once did they discuss their Gifts, or the spirit world, or supernatural families. Jason forgot about Hadewych, about the Legacy, about the funeral, and about his grief.

They slept on Jason's bed, in their clothes. He slept under the covers. She slept above. He woke in the middle of the night to find her arm draped across his body. Something unknotted inside him. Denial and anger became acceptance and gratitude. He would be leaving town soon, he knew. But at least he and Kate had spent this one night together.

Even as friends it was pretty damn good.

32 STAINED GLASS

The Sleepy Hollow Chamber of Commerce canceled the Annual Haunted Hayride and Block Party due to the inclement weather. They offered no refunds and promised instead to reschedule the event for early November. This outraged the village children. Rescheduling was *not* acceptable, in their opinion. A hayride in November wouldn't be a *haunted* hayride at all, just an—an early Thanksgiving float. How dare they? Was nothing sacred?

Moods soured. Worries deepened. Surely Halloween would go forward as planned? The children nagged their parents to *do something*. They checked the weather reports. They stared out the windows of schoolrooms.

Rain, rain, go away.
Come again another day.
Little goblins want to play.

#

On the evening of the twenty-ninth, Jason sat in the living room of 417 Gory Brook and watched *It's the Great Pumpkin, Charlie Brown*. He clutched Eliza's afghan. On screen, Linus Van Pelt threw arms wide and proclaimed his pumpkin patch to be the most sincere pumpkin patch in the world.

Jason thumbed the TV off, threw the afghan aside, and paced. He couldn't leave town yet but he couldn't bear to remain in Sleepy Hollow another minute. He'd tired of the rain and the constant rumble of thunder. He'd narrowed Eliza's possessions down to a half-dozen crucial boxes and carried them out to the detached garage.

He'd wadded most of his own clothes into trash bags. He'd hidden one bar of gold in the glove compartment of the RV and buried the other in the muddy side lawn—between the roots of the persimmon tree.

He picked up a stick of firewood and hit the stone of the fireplace with it. That felt good, so he kept swinging until he'd covered the hearth with bark. He dropped the wood and told himself to chill out.

He went upstairs to his room. His good suit hung from the back of his bedroom door, waiting for Eliza's funeral. He took a legal-sized envelope from his dresser. Inside, he'd folded the only records of Eliza's genealogical research that he would be taking away with him.

The grave-rubbings.

He sat on the bed and unfolded the fragile sheets. He made note of the rubbings he had made himself—Jim Crane, Bethel Crane. Eliza had made notes in the corners of these ("taken by Jason on September 21st, Calvary").

He found **William Crane. Soldier. Died 1792.**

He found William's son: *Sacred to the memory of* **Hon. Ichabod Crane, 1775 to 1849.**

No Absalom, of course.

He flipped through Jesse, Jack, and Adam Crane. He found the rubbings he had been searching for.

Andrew Crane. Dianne Crane.

His parents.

Today was the day, the terrible day—the twenty-ninth of October, the anniversary of their deaths. The *tenth* anniversary, and it came around at a moment when he had suffered yet another awful loss. He thought of the vision of his mom and dad, the hairbrush vision.

"It's getting cold, baby. And I need to get Jason to school," said Andrew.

"I can be on time or presentable but not both!" Dianne had said.

And once again, though it has been barely—what?—eleven days since that vision? I can remember the words… but not their voices.

Jason's phone rang.

"Hello?"

"Ah—good. You picked up this time," said Hadewych. "Change of plans, I'm afraid. Too wet for a funeral tomorrow. They say we'll have to put it off and hope for a clear patch."

"Fine," Jason said. He hung up and threw the phone to the floor. He smoothed the paper against the bedspread, careful not to smudge the charcoal.

The rain continued through the night.

Joey came over. They played Scrabble.

"You're really leaving?" said Joey.

"I have to."

"I guess so."

Joey won the game. He received sixty-two points by playing all his letters on the word "DESOLATE."

#

On the thirtieth of October the village children grew apoplectic. Their worst nightmares had come true. Weather forecasters proclaimed that the showers would continue through Halloween and into the first week of November. Despair filled every heart. What a trick fate had played! Candy-hungry monsters stomped feet and demanded restitution. Hunger strikes were declared—"Let it be Proclaimed to All and Sundry that We Shall Eat No Vegetables Until Halloween is Restored to Us!" A few tykes were even rumored to have lost their faith in the Lord and converted to Satanism out of spite.

Homeowners began to take down decorations. Diabetics sighed with relief.

But on the morning of the crucial day—just when the ruination of every witch, superhero and tin-foiled robot seemed inevitable—just as the weather stood poised to thrust a rusty razor blade into the great candy-apple core of the holiday—the heavens above Sleepy Hollow opened and the sun grinned above like a plastic pumpkin. A cheer rose. Goodness had triumphed. Hope was rekindled, faith in God restored. (Except, perhaps, in the hearts of those few impish ragamuffins who took the good weather as evidence that their midnight goat sacrificing had paid off.)

Relief. Blessed relief. Sleepy Hollow's children would have their Halloween fun.

And Eliza would have a Halloween funeral.

#

The sun shone into the chapel through the stained glass images of St. Matthew, St. Mark, St. Luke and St. John. The Gospel authors knelt and faced inward towards Jesus, who loomed magnificently at center—arms outstretched.

Jason raised a gloved hand and smoothed the hair at Eliza's temple.

Hadewych, to his credit, had done everything asked of him. Not a detail had gone awry. The gladiolas and roses made the chapel smell like a flower shop. Eliza's cherry-wood coffin gleamed; her blue dress fit perfectly; her hair was immaculate; her knobby hands rested demurely across her midsection; her fingernails were, as Jason had requested, Jungle Red. Even the tiny whiskers had vanished from her chin, though Jason sort of missed those. She looked as though she had drifted to sleep on the sofa. She neither grinned nor scowled. Her expression held a wisp of a smile, contemplating a job completed and completed well. Beams through the stained glass cast patches of soft blue and pink across her cheeks and eyelids.

Jason took a daisy from his dime-store bouquet and tucked it behind her ear.

"I'll miss you forever," he whispered.

He kissed her forehead. She wasn't cold—or warm either—she was exactly the temperature of the room.

He didn't cry. He felt strangely numb. Empty. A desert. Even his lips seemed cracked and parched.

"That's a beautiful touch," said Hadewych, straightening the daisy. "I hope you're pleased?"

"I am," Jason said. "Everything's perfect."

"Some of my best work," said McCaffrey.

The funeral director stood behind Hadewych. He wore a bolo tie.

"*Your* work?" Jason said.

"She deserved the best," McCaffrey said. "Nothing too harsh. And Hadewych give me lots of pictures."

Jason turned to Hadewych and struck him in the chest with the bouquet.

"I told you I didn't want him. I said 'anyone but him' and you promised."

"Don't embarrass me," said Hadewych, taking the flowers and brushing a leaf from his lapel.

"Embarrass you? I said no."

"I get it," said McCaffrey, his voice low. "Hadewych said I wasn't your first pick. That's okay. I figure you didn't like what you saw—behind the curtain? But everybody's morgue's like that. It ain't a pretty business. And... nobody would've given your granny more respect. No sir." McCaffrey's voice caught. He sniffed and twisted a length of paper towel. "Fine lady."

Jason balled his fists, thinking of that dingy little room.

I couldn't even spare her that...

"You said everything looked perfect," Hadewych said. "Not one minute ago. What's changed?"

"I just wish I didn't know..." Jason said.

Hadewych put a hand on Jason's shoulder and whispered in the boy's ear. "You should thank him."

"Thank him?"

"Vernon did the funeral for free," Hadewych said.

Jason frowned but thought, *I'll be sneaking away tonight. It's better if Hadewych thinks I'm resigned and beaten.* He nodded. He touched McCaffrey's arm but couldn't manage an actual thank you.

"She looks very pretty," he said.

McCaffrey gave a little bow and shuffled off.

"Do you approve of the location at least?" said Hadewych.

Jason nodded.

They weren't going to fill the Chapel of the Sleepy Hollow Cemetery. They would be lucky to fill a pew. He and Eliza hadn't made too many friends in town yet. But Eliza would have adored the stained glass—not the images of Jesus and the Gospel authors, but the immense windows on either side of the double entranceway.

The leftmost window depicted scenes from *The Legend.*

The life-sized Ichabod at center wore his hat cocked at a jaunty angle. His features were drowsy and a little secretive. He held the hands of two children—a girl and a boy. They made a merry trio dancing off to school together.

Smaller panels depicted scenes from the story: the schoolmaster at the blackboard (Ichabod apparently taught basic addition the way another man might proclaim the Book of Mormon), Ichabod wooing Katrina by the millpond, Katrina spurning Ichabod's love (the schoolmaster clutched his brow like a foiled super-villain) and finally—Ichabod clinging to his horse as he fled a shadowy pursuer.

"How're you folks doing?" James Osorio emerged from an interior hall.

"We were just admiring the glass," said Jason. "It's great."

"I do notice," muttered Hadewych, "that there's no depiction of Brom."

"Sure there is," said Osorio. He pointed to the horseman pursuing Ichabod. "Right there. That's Brom, right?"

Hadewych did not look pleased. He tossed the bouquet in the trash.

"Indeed."

The rightmost window depicted scenes from the life of author Washington Irving.

The full-size Irving raised a quill pen in greeting. He carried *The Legend* stuck under his arm. He stood framed in a wreath of leaves and clover, among rabbits, ships, banners, branches and berries. Panels showed him receiving his degree, writing at his desk, presenting papers to some king, and—

"What's he doing here?" said Jason.

"Building Sunnyside," said Osorio.

"His estate—down in Tarrytown," said Hadewych.

"Right. I remember."

"He named our cemetery. His grave is on the tour."

Osorio stepped aside to wait by the doors. Jason and Hadewych stood looking at Irving's window. The last Crane shoulder to shoulder with the next-to-last Van Brunt.

How odd to see a literary figure enshrined in stained glass—a mere human being with a career and bills—but, come to think of it, were the stained glass depictions of Matthew, Mark, Luke and John so different? Weren't the Gospel authors, in a sense, also literary figures? Jason wondered for one blasphemous moment whether Jesus was their Ichabod.

"What's this?" said Hadewych, glancing down. The sword from Absalom's coffin leaned in the corner.

"Oh. I'm giving that back to you," said Jason.

"No. It's yours."

"I don't want it."

"She adored the thing," said Hadewych. "How about we bury her with—"

"No," Jason said, horrified. He would not bury his grandmother with that sword in her coffin like Absalom. "Are you high?"

"Bad idea," Hadewych nodded. "I agree. Bad idea. Eliza wasn't a Viking, was she? Keep the sword though. I think you'll come to treasure it. In time." Hadewych patted Jason's shoulder and walked away, leaving the sword in the corner.

Would he? Jason thought of Eliza... *gonna getcha!* Maybe he would.

He wandered back to her side. His hand touched the rail of the coffin. He smiled sadly. Actually, in another place and time Eliza could have been a Viking. Yes. He could imagine that. He had a brief image of his grandmother in a horned hat with a spear. Yeah, she would have made a good Viking. A fighter. Ready to sail away on a burning ship to...

His breath caught.

... *Valhalla.*

That was the name of his parents' cemetery.

Valhalla. The majestic hall of Asgard, built for heroes who died in combat.

Eliza hadn't believed in any afterlife, no, but no one more deserved one more. She deserved to be led to heaven by Valkyries— and not because she had been some holy roller, either. She deserved another life because she'd never been bored by living. She deserved to go on, like... he glanced at the stained glass... like the best stories go on. Never forgotten, always returned to, reimagined by every generation afterward. His grandmother deserved to be an immortal or, at the very least, to be a time-honored tale passed along to Jason's kids, just before bed. The epic grandmother. A figure of myth.

No... a figure of Legend.

The entrance door cracked open.

"Can I—come in?" said Valerie, her head silhouetted against the afternoon sun.

"No," said Hadewych. "You are not invited. I told you that."

Hadewych took hold of the door, ready to shut it, but she had already put one foot in the chapel.

"Eliza was my—friend," she said.

"Please leave."

Valerie shook her head, sadly. Her eyes appealed to Jason.

He couldn't decide whether he wanted her at the funeral or not.

He'd have thrown Hadewych out if he could, but the executor paid the bill. Jason wasn't really sure if he hated Valerie too. Why were she and Hadewych suddenly enemies? Wasn't she still his mistress or something?

Hadewych acted the part of the man in charge. He lorded over Osorio.

"I insist that she be asked to leave the viewing."

Osorio looked to Jason. "Mister Crane is the family member?"

Jason stepped around the pews and offered a hand to Valerie. "She can stay," he said. "She's never done anything to us, that I know of."

Valerie closed her eyes and bowed her head. She took his hand and entered without a glance at Hadewych, who looked as disgusted as a five-star bellhop permitting entrance to a leper.

Valerie wore a becoming black dress with four tiny white buttons. She'd color-coordinated her throat apparatus again. It looked like a glossy black plastic necklace with her breathing valve for an ornament. The first time he had seen Valerie, she'd worn a white valve with a white dress. How many of those did she have?

Jason led her by the elbow to Eliza's side. He stood at the head of the coffin, stock-still, military, one hand on the wood protectively. Valerie held a cloth to her mouth. Do flowers irritate her throat? *How sad*, Jason thought. Valerie gazed down at Eliza and raised the cloth to catch tears.

I still haven't cried.

Soft music began to play. Osorio must have decided that the official viewing period had begun. Hadewych glanced at his watch. They were on the clock now.

"I'm so sorry," said Valerie. "The Project was a mistake."

He started to agree, but shook his head. Recriminations were useless today.

"Eliza thought it was a… grand adventure," Jason said. "It made her happy."

"I'm—glad we didn't—find anything."

This surprised him.

"You were pretty angry about that before."

"Now I'm glad. It would have been—terrible." She looked at Eliza's body. "Even more terrible—than this."

"Why?"

She looked at him and her eyes were so gentle.

"I know more now. I know—everything."

"What everything?"

"What we were—looking for. How it got there. Everything."

"Okay. Tell me."

She raised her purse and opened it, reconsidered. "No. Not today. It's not the—time. Or place." She glanced at Eliza again. "No more dark things. Not today."

"Yeah," said Jason, gripping the wood. "You're right."

"Come to dinner—tomorrow? I'll tell you. What I know."

Jason nodded.

She had been about to close her purse again, but she reached into it and drew a small card.

"May I?" she said.

She wanted to tuck a tarot card in the coffin.

"No," Jason said.

"It's the Sun. Her significator."

"No," said Jason. "I don't believe that stuff and I don't want it."

"Of course," she said. She put the card back in her purse. "Of course."

Valerie kissed her fingertips, pressed them to Eliza's sleeve, and slipped away.

"Jason," someone stage-whispered. Joey waved from around the corner of an inside hallway. Jason stepped from the chapel and joined his friend by the men's room.

"How are you holding up?" Joey said.

"I'm okay."

"I'd come in but—" Joey indicated his blue and green workman's clothes. They were splashed with dirt.

"I don't care about that."

"My dad would. I'll be at graveside, though. Let me know if you need anything done."

"Like what?"

"Like digging an extra hole for that Hadewych son of a—"

Joey broke off and stared over Jason's shoulder. Zef and Kate had entered the chapel, walking toward the coffin. Zef looked sharp in an expensive dark blue suit and matching tie. Kate wore the black blouse she had worn to the Spirit Dance, with a black jacket and skirt. She'd put her hair up again.

"Damn," the boys muttered simultaneously. Kate and Zef made a gorgeous couple.

"I'm going now," said Joey.

"You have to?"

"Before Zef sees me. I look like somebody's yardman. Oh, by the way…" Joey produced a small gift-wrapped package. "Happy birthday," he said.

"It's tomorrow," Jason said.

"I know. But… you'll be gone, right?"

"Yeah. And that's between us, okay?"

Jason opened the gift. Spare gloves. Just for the palms—no fingers.

"They're lifting gloves," said Joey. "They're… butch-er."

"Thanks."

Joey clapped Jason on the shoulder, glanced once more at Zef, and left.

Jason greeted the newcomers. Zef and Kate made all the necessary and proper inquiries into Jason's state of mind and voiced all the appropriate expressions of dismay at the tragedy of Eliza's death. But there were no tears from either. They hadn't known Jason's grandmother. When Zef had come to Gory Brook Road the night of the dance he'd barely even looked up when Eliza opened the door. Kate had first seen Eliza on the night she died—the night of the Horseman's Hollow. Slim acquaintance.

But Jason didn't mind Kate's kiss on his cheek, not one bit.

"Babe," Zef said, "can I have a second with Jason?"

Kate nodded. "How about some water?" she said.

Jason and Zef watched Kate go. Zef began to speak but, uncomfortable within Eliza's earshot, he led Jason to the corner to stand beneath the stained glass feet of Washington Irving.

"This guardianship thing," said Zef. "Dad just told me."

"I'm not going along with it."

"He makes it sound like you don't have much choice. He's saying…" Zef sighed, scratched his head. "He's saying you and I are going to be…"

"What?"

"Brothers."

"No. No no no."

"That's what I said. Like we're all going to be one happy family? No way."

"No way. You're not my brother," Jason said. "I don't even want you for a third cousin."

"Anyway…" Zef looked stricken.

"What?"

Zef looked at his shoes, at the window, at the room—he looked at his father, who had slipped an arm around Kate's waist.

"I need you to promise not to… not… you can't… tell him."

"About?" Jason knew, but he wanted Zef to say it.

"The lighthouse," said Zef.

"You're just lucky I'm not pressing charges."

Zef's eyes shot to his. Anger flared there but dimmed and he gave a bitter nod.

"I was drunk," said Zef.

From the way he clutched the doorframe, Jason suspected that Zef wasn't too sober even now.

"I remember," Jason said.

"I was being stupid."

"You succeeded."

"Let me explain."

"No. I'm not involved in your drama, guy." Jason stepped back. "I wash my hands of it."

Zef mumbled profanities. "Sorry for trying to make it right," he said.

"I get it. You were drunk. It wasn't what it looked like. Blah blah. I don't care. I don't. I'm not the guy you owe an explanation to—" Jason cut himself off.

"Who?"

Jason didn't spell it out. He waited. Zef's face drained of color.

"What's Joey saying?" he said. "Shit about me?"

"Nothing. Joey stands up for you. All the time. 'Zef's a good guy'—that's what he says. So, if you're—" he put a palm on Zef's chest and looked him directly in the eye "—*not*—" Zef glanced away. "Then you should tell *him*. Not me."

"Of course I'm not. I'm with Kate," Zef said.

"Fine. Great. Tell him that. Once and for all. So he can get over you. He's too good for you anyway."

Zef straightened defiantly but shrugged, perhaps even agreeing. He looked sad. He glanced down and frowned.

"What gives?" Zef said.

"What?"

"What's my dad's sword doing here?"

They stood near the corner where Jason had left the sword. Zef picked it up.

"Your dad's?" said Jason, "No. It's mine. He gave it to us."

"He would never do that," Zef whispered, shaking his head. "It's a family heirloom. Damn it, Jason. Did you *steal* this?"

33 SWORDPLAY

"No, I didn't steal it. What do you mean it's your dad's?" said Jason.

"My dad's. What's it doing here?" Zef demanded softly.

"What's it to you? It's my sword."

"No. It's not. It a Van Brunt family heirloom. You've seen me with it, remember?"

"I did? When?" Jason thought. The sword had come from Absalom's coffin. Hadewych had given it to Eliza. It had been in the hall closet...

Kate strode towards them with bottles of water in her hand.

"Kate," Jason whispered. "You saw me with this sword the other night. Remember? Squirrel?"

"No, no. Baby—this is mine, right?" said Zef.

She looked at the thing. "It was dark."

"But you know it's mine," said Jason.

"No," Kate said. "I recognize it now. It's Zef's. Remember the dance? Zef was the Horseman?"

And now Jason did remember—Zef had a sword in his duffel bag on the night of the dance. Jason had seen a sword in the bag—under the table—when Zef had retrieved his flask and his maroon hoodie.

"I pulled the sword on you, remember?" said Zef.

Jason remembered the ringing sound as Zef had drawn his sword. He remembered stumbling back and falling off the stage.

"That was *this* sword?"

"I snuck it out of my dad's closet. To complete the costume."

Jason took the sword from Zef.

"Wait. Wait. Valerie knows," Jason said.

Valerie sat in a pew, flipping through a hymnal. He slipped in beside her. Zef came round to her other side, leaving Kate to stand at the end of the row.

"Hi," whispered Jason. "Zef sort of thinks this sword is a piece of his Horseman costume."

"No. It's an heirloom of my family."

"Tell him where we found it," Jason said.

"We did—an exhumation—of Jason's ancestor—and found this sword—in the coffin," said Valerie.

"No no no," said Zef. "I snuck it out of dad's closet. Not two weeks ago. It belonged to Dylan."

"To Dylan?" said Jason.

"It's his civil war sword. See the 'D' on the hilt?"

Jason hadn't noticed the 'D'. But he did now. A tiny angry letter. He and Valerie glanced at each other.

"Just tell me," Zef said. "Did you swipe it out of my car or something?"

"Zef," said Kate. "Don't say that. It's his grandmother's funeral."

"Right," said Zef. "I'm sorry. And, actually I do remember putting it back in the closet."

"In the closet? Figures," Jason muttered. Zef shot daggers down the pew. Valerie squeezed Jason's hand. Jason stood. He kept his voice firm and reasonable. "Guys. We took this sword from a coffin buried in eighteen-fifty."

"How would you have done that?" said Kate.

"It's impossible," said Jason. He turned towards the back of the chapel. The other three turned to stare behind as well. Hadewych chatted with McCaffrey there, through a mouthful of chicken salad.

Jason cut across the pews and down the aisle. He threw the sword at Hadewych's feet.

"Explain," he said.

"Explain? What?" said Hadewych, matching his volume.

"Zef says this is Dylan's sword."

"Ah," said Hadewych, frowning at his son.

"I thought he'd swiped it," said Zef. He retrieved the sword from the floor.

"You put it in the coffin, didn't you?" said Jason. He turned to

McCaffrey. "You helped, right? You two opened the coffin. When? Before we came down to the morgue? No? In the van?" McCaffrey looked away. "In the van," said Jason, nodding. "So I was right—you stole the real treasure. And you put this in. Why?"

Zef had slipped between Jason and Hadewych. If Jason wanted to strike the father, he would have to go through the son. Kate and Valerie came up behind.

"What was in—Absalom's coffin?" said Valerie.

"Nothing," said Hadewych. "Can we discuss this privately? I don't want Kate to get a bad impression. It's just a misunderstanding, dear. Zef—take her outside?"

Kate stood firm. "I'm fine," she said.

"What was in the coffin?" Jason repeated.

"Nothing," said Hadewych. "That's why I put the sword in. All right. I admit it."

"You admit you tricked us?" said Jason.

"I couldn't resist peeking on the way over. So we opened the coffin early. Sue me. I couldn't wait. But there was nothing inside. So—yes, I put the sword in."

"You just happened to have it with you," Jason said.

Hadewych glanced from face to face, a mountain climber looking for purchase.

"Imagine if we opened the coffin and found nothing," he said. "Nothing—after all that work. Eliza did so much to make the Project a success—she put in so much time and money. I didn't want to see her disappointed. I brought my ancestor's sword so she'd have something to find in case there was no treasure."

"You gave away a family heirloom? Right."

"I didn't want to, I admit. I didn't want to give it up, but I was glad to make the sacrifice. It made her happy, didn't it? Forgive me for not wanting to disappoint a dear old friend. It was a small deception and I do apologize." Hadewych bowed his head. "Now," he said, tapping his watch, "If you'll go to your cars, it's time for the service."

Jason held up a hand. "Is that what happened?" Jason said, turning to McCaffrey.

"I'm not getting involved in this," said McCaffrey.

"Is that what happened?" Jason said.

"I've got work to do—I'll bring up the hearse."

"McCaffrey?"

But the funeral director had hurried away.

"I didn't mean to cause a mess," said Zef.

"It's a misunderstanding," said Hadewych.

"Why didn't you—tell *me* about—the sword then?" said Valerie.

"I was going to," said Hadewych, "but you got yourself so worked up, and you ran off that same night."

"No," Jason said. "No. You took something. Absalom's arms were like *this*—" He made a wide 'O'. "His arms were wrapped around something for a very long time. What?"

"Lower your voice, son," said Hadewych, frowning at Jason and gesturing. Osorio had come up the aisle, about to intervene.

"I'm not your son," Jason said through his teeth. He stabbed a finger at Zef. "*He's* your son. Make *him* miserable. Not me. You are *never* going to be my guardian."

"It's not like you have any other options." Hadewych sighed. "We have to make allowances for Jason today, everyone, all right? He's under a lot of strain."

"Excuse me, folks?"

The group turned to discover a sloop-shouldered man standing at the door.

"Excuse me?" the man repeated.

"Can we help you?" said Kate.

"Is this the Merrick service?" the man said.

Jason shaded his eyes. The sun shone behind the man. As Jason neared, the face began to swim into view. The man was around eighty or so, and wore thick glasses.

"Jason?" the man said. "Look at you. Jason Crane. All grown up. Bet you don't recognize me."

Jason did recognize… something—something to do with Halloween. The man reminded Jason of Halloween on the year his parents died. Jason had worn a vampire costume and this man had—had hammered some wood together and staked him through the heart. He was much smaller than he'd been, or Jason was much larger, but this was definitely—

"Grandpa John?"

The old man nodded and opened his arms.

Jason laughed. He paused on the way to the door and said, "Hey, Hadewych, maybe I do have other options, after all."

John Dawes gave Jason a bear hug. Jason didn't want him to let go.

Kate and Zef argued under their breath. Zef had a hard time tamping his anger and he'd turned his irritation on her. She told him to cool off in the car and he stalked away, carrying the sword out of the chapel. She followed.

Jason finally broke the hug.

"How did you know about the funeral?" said Jason.

"A nice fellow called me," said Grandpa John.

"What fellow?"

"Dunno. Funny voice. Real deep."

"That would be—me," said Valerie, joining them. "I thought Jason—should have some—*family* here."

Hadewych scowled. Jason smiled and took Dawes's left arm. Valerie took the right. They helped Dawes up the aisle, leaving Hadewych to grumble along behind.

"Grandpa John—" said Jason.

"Just John. I haven't been married to Eliza for a decade. Oh, there she is, poor sweetness."

"Okay. Here's the thing. I'm seventeen now, and so I'm almost an adult, you know?"

"You're tall. Like your daddy."

"They say I need a guardian, just for the next year."

"Oh?" The old man stopped briefly. He saw the next question coming and wanted to be braced for it. "That's what they say?"

"So—would you be my guardian?" said Jason.

"You already have a guardian," said Hadewych, stepping in front of them.

"This is Mister Van Brunt," Jason said. He didn't release Dawes's arm when Hadewych extended a hand.

"Eliza's choice for guardian," Hadewych added.

"We don't exactly see eye to eye," said Jason. "I'd much rather have you."

"I'm not blood."

"Neither's Hadewych. And you're more family than he is."

"Hell," said Dawes. "You're a grown man. Why do you even need a guardian? I was on my own at your age."

"Exactly," said Jason. "You wouldn't need to do anything. It's only paperwork."

"You wouldn't even—need to—live together," said Valerie.

Dawes shrugged.

"I'll think about it," he said. "If it's the right thing to do, okay. But—" He gestured towards the coffin. "—let me say my goodbyes first?"

"Of course."

Dawes continued up the aisle. Jason left him with Valerie. He whispered to Osorio.

"I want Mister Van Brunt to leave."

"I will not," said Hadewych. "I'm the executor. I'm coming to the service."

"Fine," said Jason. "This isn't the service. Get out. I'll see you graveside. I'd like to say goodbye in a room that doesn't stink of you."

Hadewych began to bluster, but Osorio patted his arm.

"Family's decision," Osorio said, and led Hadewych from the room.

Jason joined Valerie and Dawes at the side of Eliza's coffin. A cloud must have moved aside, because the windows flared magnificently and bathed the coffin in color.

"Oh, look at her go," said Dawes, happily. "She always did love the sun."

"She did," Jason said, thinking. He glanced at Valerie. "Okay. Let me see the card?" he whispered.

Valerie slipped the tarot card out of her purse and gave it to Jason. The card displayed a baby riding a white horse, giggling happily, arms and legs thrown out with abandon. The baby wore a crown of sunflowers, picked from the field of sunflowers in the background. A dazzling sun filled the sky above the child's head. A happy card.

Jason nodded. "I'll put it in," he said.

Valerie nodded. She and Grandpa John shuffled away.

Jason said his final, private goodbyes. One of Eliza's buttons had slipped loose, and he fixed it for her. He tucked the card into her hand. The tears came now, finally, a river that felt wider and deeper and older than the Hudson.

He was grateful for the little card, grateful that she would always have the sun.

He exhausted his inexhaustible tears. McCaffrey stepped forward and closed the lid.

34 GRAVESIDE

McCaffrey and his men carried the coffin to the hearse. Jason went to Osorio's office to retrieve his backpack. Crossing the darkened chapel, he heard angry whispers coming from the hall. Hadewych had Zef backed against the men's room door. He wagged a finger in the boy's face. Zef made some self-justification and Hadewych slapped him. The sound was like a ruler on a chalkboard.

Jason gasped. They turned in his direction, embarrassed. Zef stumbled away, grateful to escape. Hadewych and Jason scowled at each other across the length of the hall. Jason walked on.

He stiff-armed the rear doors and found the shady driveway on the eastern side. Wind bit his cheeks. Zef joined Kate in Hadewych's car. Valerie led Dawes to her own vehicle. Hadewych and Jason both reached for the passenger-side handle of the hearse.

"It's my place to ride with Eliza," said Jason. "You can ride in the back. Next time it's available."

Hadewych slunk away. He joined Kate and Zef.

McCaffrey slid into the driver's seat and the caravan rolled out. McCaffrey inched along so that nothing in the back would shift. The sprays of gladiola and roses that lay with the coffin filled the cab with perfume. Beyond the window, the rows of flowers along the driveway became manicured hedges and ranks of headstones. Tombs passed. Jason felt as empty as the branches above the road.

"How much did he pay you?" he said.

McCaffrey looked in his rear window, side window, anywhere but Jason's eyes.

"Two hundred."

"I should have known you'd already opened it," said Jason. "The bolts were loose. You made a big show—so we wouldn't guess, right?"

"They were tough the first time," McCaffrey said. They crested the hill and rolled downward. "The bands too. The ol' van was dark. Bumpy. Almost put my eye out."

"And what was inside?"

"Something big. Gold."

"Gold?"

"Worth more'n two hundred, easy." McCaffrey shook his head.

They drove past the Van Brunt tomb. Jason remembered the painting of Agathe, down in the secret chamber, the painting of her as a young woman standing at the Gory Brook fireplace, her hand on the mantel near… something… that had been whitewashed over. He had scratched at the whitewash and his glove had come back with flecks of gold leaf.

"And he just took it," Jason said.

"Popped it in a cardboard box lickety-split. Stuck it in his trunk. That's all I know."

They drove in silence.

"I liked your grandma a lot," said McCaffrey.

"I believe you," said Jason.

They passed a stone cenotaph honoring soldiers of the American Revolution. Tiny flags bustled at its foot. Ancient maple trees, older than the country, maybe, spilled blood-red branches overhead. The hearse found a straight road along the river. The waters of the Pocantico were angry, gorged with rain. Jason recognized the faux-rustic bridge that led to—

"Where are we burying her?" Jason rolled down the window. The flowers had become overpowering.

"The Palmyra section."

McCaffrey turned onto the bridge. The hearse's wheels sounded like hoofbeats on the wood. Water thrashed below. A chain link fence appeared on the right. Jason remembered skirting it from the outside the day he'd lost the dragon. The hearse drifted uphill, entering the cage of the auxiliary cemetery.

"Here?" Jason said.

"You'd already bought the plot," said McCaffrey.

"For Absalom."

"We put Absalom back yesterday," said McCaffrey.

"Back? Back under the Van Brunt tomb?"

"Nah, that woulda been a pain. Above. In one of the boxes."

McCaffrey turned the hearse. Headstones dotted the slope. More hoofbeats clattered behind them as the other cars followed. Jason watched the graves go by. This was the plainest part of the cemetery.

"When this is over," said Jason, "I'm going to want Absalom out of there."

"No problem. You and Hadewych will need to sign another exhumation order, though."

That vindictive son of a bitch.

They stopped. On the slope, a mound of green Astroturf sat beside an open hole, the bare dirt hidden by fake grass and standing wreaths. Joey stood at the curb with three other workers. McCaffrey parked the hearse.

Joey and the workers joined McCaffrey and Jason to act as pallbearers. Hadewych reached for the coffin rail, but Jason's hatred could have set the man on fire. Hadewych stepped back and joined the others. Kate, Zef, Valerie, Dawes, and Hadewych stood in a semicircle around the grave. The earth was too soft for chairs. The bearers laid the coffin upon the sling of straps that would lower it into the ground. A minister from the Reformed Church of the Tarrytowns stepped forward and began a canned speech, a tribute to Eliza from someone who had never met her. Jason's thoughts drifted.

Eliza's grave lay in the farthest corner of the cemetery, within sight of the river and close to the forest. A tidy birch tree stood a little down the slope, providing shade. Beyond the chain link, a few joggers loped past: the aqueduct trail—the path back home.

Not a bad spot, actually.

The minister worked hard to get in his entire repertoire of platitudes. Finally, like a man out of toothpaste no matter how hard he squeezed, he ran out of words and had to put the cap back on. He blessed the grave. Jason was thinking of the Eliza he knew, the one the minister had never met. The one who made cocoa and swore like a sailor when she stubbed her toe. The one who didn't suffer fools, who ate crackers in bed and liked dirty jokes and yelled at the television and loved her grandson and her puppy dog. The minister asked if anyone present would like to speak. The group looked to Jason but he didn't trust his voice. He shook his head. He didn't have the words. The too-brief service ended. Joey reached for the crank that would lower the coffin.

"May I say something, please?"

Had Hadewych asked it? Jason might have lunged if he had. But Grandpa John stepped forward and the minister ceded the stage.

"I was Eliza's husband for four years," said Dawes, "and those were the happiest four years of my life. I had a fine young man to raise. I can't believe you got so tall. And I had a real lady to come home to. But I couldn't keep up with this crazy woman, though I tried. She danced, she gardened, she traveled, she painted—before her fingers started hurting—she did pottery and leaded glass and flower arranging and jet skied. She used to fly airplanes, too, little Cessnas. She missed that when she couldn't do it anymore. She always looked up. Shook her head. She hated being stuck on the ground. She had a poem that she liked, something about touching the face of God. I wish I'd brung it. And—she started a business, did you know that? Her own pizza place. Got bored in two months and sold the joint at a profit. You know she closed the Holland Tunnel once? Ran out of gas halfway in and they thought she was a terrorist. She was a dang nut, your grandmother. And she was *never* old. She was still breaking hearts at seventy. She was always going someplace new, always saying goodbye. I was proud she stayed with me as long as she did. What can I say?" The old man sighed and shrugged. "They broke the mold."

He raised his palm and touched the wood of the coffin.

"Kick ass in heaven, lady," he said.

Joey turned the little crank and the coffin sank into the grave.

The service was over.

Hadewych thanked the minister and stood talking to the man at graveside. Kate and Zef held hands nearby, waiting for Hadewych to say his goodbyes.

"She was such a good friend," Hadewych said. "I'm heartbroken."

The minister embraced Hadewych, comforting him. Jason wheeled in disgust and walked away. He saw Joey down the hill, waiting by a truck full of shovels. Joey raised a hand and Jason returned the gesture. He found Grandpa John standing under the birch tree. The old man offered Jason half a stick of Juicy Fruit but

Jason declined.

"That was a nice speech," said Jason.

"I just wanted you to know. She had a good life."

Jason nodded.

"About this guardianship," Dawes said. "I'm hesitant."

"I get that."

"I'm an old man, you know."

"Oh, you could still beat me up if you want."

Dawes nodded and grinned. "Maybe. Maybe not."

"Think about it, though?" Jason said, lowering his voice to a whisper. "Hadewych is... a creep. He hits his son and I don't trust him with the estate. Please help me."

"If it's like that, then... let me mull it over and I'll let you know. I got Valerie's number."

"Thank you."

Jason hugged the man. Another bear hug, but the bear felt very frail in his arms.

Valerie stood at graveside, looking down at the coffin and weeping, so Dawes flagged down McCaffrey.

"Can I get a lift back?" Dawes said.

"Sure. Hop in the hearse." McCaffrey shook Jason's hand. "Fine lady, Ms. Merrick. Real shame. My boys will do the rest. Sorry for your loss. Sorry for—" he glanced at Hadewych. The minister was patting him on the back as he wept. "—for everything."

McCaffrey and Dawes climbed into the hearse and rode away.

Kate left Zef with Hadewych and found Jason wandering among the graves.

"You shouldn't be alone," she said.

"I am alone," Jason said. "More than I've ever been. What am I going to do? Eliza wanted to set me up, you know? After she was gone? Now—what a mess."

"It will be okay," Kate said. She put her head on his shoulder for a moment. He did feel better. She squeezed his arm. "I need to tell you something," she said, "but don't get mad?"

"What?"

She brought her lips to his ear.

"Your fly's undone," she said. She drew back, biting her lip. "Sorry. I thought you would want to know."

His fly was undone. But Jason didn't feel stupid. Not with her. Not anymore. He nodded, zipped, and gestured to his face. "Hey," he said, "Eyes up here, lady."

She blushed and covered her mouth. Jason smiled. They laughed. She hugged him. It was good. It had felt so good to laugh. She joined Zef at graveside with Hadewych, who was wiping his eyes with a handkerchief. She slipped her arm around her boyfriend's waist. She glanced back once.

"Pretty girl," said Valerie, stepping up behind Jason. "You like her?"

"Yeah."

"More than—like her?"

Valerie gave Jason a knowing smile.

"Is it that obvious?" Jason said.

"No. But the cards—never lie. Come to—dinner tomorrow? Yes? I have so much to—tell you."

She started to walk away, but Jason reached for her. He had remembered his plan to leave that night, to climb into the RV and escape. If she had anything to say—this was his last chance to hear. Jason's hand caught the strap of her black purse. Valerie turned around. She looked at his hand on the strap. He felt certain that they both were thinking of the night at the bridge, of a black purse strap breaking, and keys falling out into the mud. But the strap didn't break, and Jason let go.

"Tell me," he said. "Please?"

"Now?"

He nodded. "I have to know now. Tell me."

"I can do—better. I can show you." She glanced over to Hadewych, who had walked up the slope to light a cigarette, hands shaking, putting on an immense show of grief. Kate and Zef and the minister were all consoling him now. Valerie reached into her purse and produced a document in plastic. "Read it," she said. "The translation's on the back."

Jason read the thing aloud, his voice low.

"My dear Dylan, I have buried what you seek. You will not recover it. She is gone, our Agathe, and her prize rests in my hands at last. Looking upon this thing, I know I shall not keep it or use it myself. I cannot, though this be, ay, the foundation stone upon which our fortunes rest. I leave you with ample stone, my

son, stone enough. You have no need of the Horseman's treasure."

"It's the same letter," Jason said. "I've seen this."

"Keep reading," said Valerie.

"*I have built within the new graveyard a tomb where I shall lie with my sire, when God calls and when it shall be his mercy and pleasure to accept this poor sinner. I would take the boon into my own grave, were it not for your demanding want of the thing, which I would not satisfy. Therefore in our tomb I have buried, in service to his widow whom we [cannot] find, the body of the unfortunate Absolom [sic] Crane. I think it meet that this son of old Ichabod and I shall lie side to side for eternity. As I share Irving's Legend with the father, I shall share a tomb with the son. It is with Absalom that the thing is buried. You shall not look upon it again, for without consent of the man's widow he may not be raised.*

"*Do not long for that of which I have deprived you. My quarry you shall have, and my gold, and whatever you—*"

Jason turned the page…and there *was* another page.

"*—you provide yourself by ingenuity and industry.*"

Jason looked up. "This is the whole thing. The whole letter."

Valerie nodded.

"You had this from the start?"

"No. I'll explain. Just read."

"*I know that you have used the thing, my son. As soon as Crane came up dead at the skirt of Wiley Swamp, I knew. Pray that none other witnessed your quarrel at Sunnyside on Halloween night, else suspicion may fall upon you.*

"*I had grown tired and had laid myself to rest at back of Mr. Irving's writing room, drawing the curtain as not to embarrass myself before the other guests. I heard your words together. Though you raved at the man, the son of Ichabod spoke truly. Our wealth was indeed 'amassed by trickery from the first'. We* are '*the wretched villains of the tale'.*

"*I have read our Agathe's diary. I have heard the full truth as you have not.*"

Jason hesitated. Was Agathe's diary the book he'd found in the tomb? He had no doubt, and he wished desperately that the faded thing could be read somehow. He returned to the letter.

"*Luc Fontaine died so that your grandsire might purchase the Quarry land. Uncle James died for challenging Agathe in her widowhood. My rival, poor Ichabod, was driven away in terror so that I might marry well. Katrina's father, our own merry Baltus, fell beheaded so that your mother might inherit early. And fear of her own husband's kin drove my Katrina to her early grave.*

"*My life is not as I believed. ALL has come by my mother's evil design. How many lives were sacrificed to strengthen Agathe's phantom lover? How much midnight blood has blackened the waters beneath my mother's home?"*

This chilled Jason. He had to pause a moment before continuing. Agathe had sacrificed people down in the aqueduct tunnels beneath Gory Brook? She'd spilled blood in service to the Horseman? But— *she was still in the house.* He had *seen* the ghost of Agathe, and—

Valerie rubbed Jason's back.

"Why did you stop?" she said.

—and he knew. He knew, with certainty, the answer to one mystery, at least.

Agathe had possessed Fireman Mike. And Valerie's mother. And whoever killed Darley. Because Agathe is still spilling her midnight blood…

Brom Brom… there's bleeding in the waters…

Jason stood silently, looking at Eliza's grave. His grandmother had been such a wise woman, in so many ways. But she'd been mistaken, so mistaken, when she'd made her pronouncement at the Bridgeport cemetery. Jason's field of vision expanded beyond Eliza's grave, to include the rows of headstones that marched up the hill in every direction…

"The dead do *not* stay put," Jason whispered.

"What?"

His head shot up. "And you let Eliza *buy* that house?"

"I didn't know," said Valerie.

"Did Hadewych?"

"Yes. He had this letter—from the start. Probably before I—even met him."

Jason shook his head.

"How much midnight blood has blackened the waters beneath my mother's home?" Jason read, *"And you, my son, you would claim these swevens and nightmares for yourself? You would summon the Horseman, yoke yourself to his service that your enemies may fall and your name be raised high? You would feed his spirit and see your hands burn?*

"Hist! Admit your action [against] Crane. You claim innocence, but what motive other than your vengeance would drive our servant-ghost to target Ichabod's son? I know my Dylan and his flaring anger. You answered Crane's insult with murder. You did this thing. The man was our guest. And so I deny you the Treasure forever.

RICHARD GLEAVES

"I choose to finish the tale. I choose to entomb the truth behind marble. I reject my inheritance. Let the Horseman be confined to Legend. Let him dwindle and weaken. Let the waters of Tarrytown run clear again.

"Raise a family ignorant of evil, my Dylan, if defense of kin is your true desire. Safeguard the Van Brunt name by saving the Van Brunt soul. Look to Family, my Son, and to your God.

"Obey me in this as in all things, else forfeit my favor and fortune.

"Signed, Abraham Van Brunt"

Valerie took the paper back.

"And now he has it," Jason said. "McCaffrey told me. He said it was big and gold. Hadewych took the damn Treasure."

"No. That would mean that—Hadewych could— summon the Horseman. Like Brom thought— Absalom did."

Jason felt another realization growing within him, coming up in waves, like something being born. Something breech and bloody and too painful to endure.

"That's how he did it," he said.

"What?" Valerie said. Jason pointed to the grave. Her eyes grew wide and he knew that the thought had been born in her as well. She put a hand to her heart. "Oh, Jason. I am so sorry... I'm so, so—"

Jason didn't hear the rest. He tore away, marching up the slope. He pushed past Kate and Zef. He pushed the minister aside. He made a fist, drew it back, and popped Hadewych in the mouth.

298

35 JASON'S CHOICE

It was a good punch. The satisfying, gratifying punch of the nerd bullied too long. The punch of the underdog who snaps after a long string of abuses and bloodies the lip of his tormentor. Jason felt his body behind it, his soul behind it. His knuckles found the man's teeth. Hadewych's head snapped and twisted and his hands came up in fear. He stepped backward, his foot caught a headstone, and he fell right on his slick, lying, murderous ass.

Zef cursed. He tackled Jason and threw him to the ground. The minister screamed like a woman. Kate shouted something that Jason didn't hear. Zef punched Jason in the ribs, twice.

"That's my father!" Zef shouted. He lost control. He kept hitting Jason. Jason scrambled backwards, up the pile of dirt alongside the grave. The Astroturf slipped under his feet as he climbed. Zef grabbed his leg.

Someone stepped between them and struck Zef's shoulder with the heel of one hand, knocking the boy back and away from Jason. Zef snarled and raised a fist.

It was Joey. He stood between Jason and Zef and raised a shovel.

"Go ahead," said Joey softly. "Hit me. Come on. Hit me while defending your father."

Zef's red face went blank. He blinked. His jaw dropped slowly. His raised fist sagged. His hand opened. He backed off and turned away, his face full of torment. Kate went to him.

"You okay, Jase?" said Joey. Jason nodded. Joey offered a hand. Jason stood and sat on the dirt pile, holding his side.

"Leave him alone, everyone," said Hadewych. "Everything's fine."

He dabbed a bit of blood from his split lip. "The boy's upset. It's been a painful—"

"Shut up," Jason said.

"It's been a painful day and he's projecting his grief on me."

"You killed my grandmother."

Hadewych shook his head. "We'll get through this, Jason. Together."

"You did," said Valerie. "You killed her."

Zef pointed a finger. "Shut up, you witch," he said. "I was with him that whole night."

"He used—" Jason said, trying to find oxygen. His side really hurt. "The Horseman. He summoned the Headless Horseman. That's how he did it."

A high laugh pierced the air of the cemetery. The group turned toward the sound. The minister covered his mouth and pulled his face back together into a mask of grave concern.

"Now, now," said Hadewych. "I'm sorry you had to witness this, Reverend." He took the minister by the elbow.

"He used the Horseman!" Jason said. But even Valerie looked a little embarrassed now that it had been said out loud.

"Well, aren't we in the Halloween Spirit," said Hadewych.

"This isn't helping, Jase," Joey whispered.

Kate looked at Jason with puzzlement and more than a little disappointment.

"You believe me, though, Kate?" said Jason. Kate couldn't meet his eye. She turned away.

Zef lit a cigarette, muttering something about crazy genes.

"Zef," said Hadewych. "Why don't you take Kate to the car."

"I'm not leaving," said Zef.

"I don't think Jason will be punching me again, will you Jason?"

"No," said Jason. He would be dreaming about that one punch for years. It had been quite satisfying.

"There," said Hadewych, "it's fine. See the reverend to his car. Apologies again, sir."

The minister muttered something about family counseling and gave Hadewych his card. Hadewych offered his hand and Jason spied a square of folded bills in his palm. It wasn't there when the handshake ended. The minister hurried down the hill, trying not to giggle again. Zef scowled and followed. Kate did not look back. Valerie came to Jason's side and took his hand.

"You. Osorio boy," said Hadewych.

"You know my name," said Joey.

"You can leave, too."

"No way." Joey shook his head.

"It's okay," Jason said.

"Leave," said Hadewych. "Unless you want me to tell your father that you threatened my son with a shovel?"

Joey turned to Jason. "I'll be down by the truck," he said. He handed Jason the shovel. "Just in case."

He left, joining the workers who still waited below. Waited to do the dirt work.

Hadewych, Valerie and Jason stared at each other across Eliza's grave. The wind bent the cemetery grass.

Valerie's hand came up to her valve. "Oh, Hadewych," she said, softly. She sounded scared and, oddly, a little sorry for the man.

"McCaffrey told me you took it," Jason said. "Come on. No one but us can hear. Don't you want to brag?"

Hadewych folded his arms.

"And it summons the Horseman, right?" said Jason. "Brom thought Dylan used it on Halloween to kill Absalom. That's why he locked it up."

"Who told you that?" Hadewych looked startled and angry. "That's a preposterous slander."

Valerie produced the letter. She held it up by two fingers, like a woman with a dead rat.

"Where did you get that?" said Hadewych, his voice measured and deadly.

"I'm still your—landlady. With my own—keys."

Hadewych nodded. "When?"

"When you were—with the lawyer."

"You had no right."

"I had every right. By the way—you're evicted."

"Is that so?" Hadewych reached for her, but Jason stepped between, raising the shovel. Hadewych stepped back. Jason glanced down the hill, hoping Zef didn't see and intervene, but Zef was bickering with Kate in the car. Joey had seen, though. He looked worried. Jason raised a palm.

"And, dearest Hadewych," Valerie said. "Don't expect—your cleaning deposit back."

"Give me that paper," said Hadewych. He held out a hand. It was shaking. Shaking with—what? With fury?

"I'll help you, Jason," Valerie said. "I'll help you—fight him. In any way I can. Lawyers, investigators. I'm rich, you know. He will never—be your guardian."

"Thank you."

"You're wrong about me, Jason," said Hadewych. "Did Valerie mention that I dumped her only four days ago? Hell hath no fury. I wouldn't put too much stock in anything she says. She's unstable. Everyone knows that. Unstable and vindictive."

Valerie faced Hadewych and raised her chin.

"You'll see how vindictive I can be," she said.

"I look forward to it."

She turned and walked away.

"Give me the letter, Valerie," said Hadewych.

Valerie stopped.

"Give me the letter," he said. His voice became husky and pleading. "Please. If I ever meant anything to you."

Valerie stared at Hadewych. She looked astonished.

"Please," said Hadewych, his voice rising. "My papers are all I have from my mother."

Valerie's hand went to her valve. She touched the little 'X' and 'O'. Her eyes narrowed defiantly. "*This*—is all I have from *my* mother. Thanks to your ghost."

She raised the Brom letter and tore it to bits.

Hadewych's cry was small and childish. He clutched at the pieces as they fell among the graves. Valerie shook her head, looking down at the pathetic man she had once loved.

"You can't control the Treasure," she said. "It's an evil thing. Nothing good can—come of it. You've doomed yourself."

Jason noticed that her voice had softened as she'd spoken. She'd exercised her vocal cords today. Her voice had smoothed and had become lighter, more feminine—a husky but graceful voice. Hadewych tried to snatch the ripped pieces from the grass. The wind had begun to take them. He slipped to his knees.

"I pity you," said Valerie.

Hadewych's face darkened, a vein stood out on his neck and Jason felt sure he was about to leap on Valerie. He stepped between them again.

A horn blew.

"Dad," Zef yelled from the car. "What's the holdup?"

Hadewych collected himself.

Valerie shook her head sadly. "Leave something better to Zef," she said. "Jason, do you need a ride?" Jason shook his head. She walked down the slope, turning back once again as she reached the road. Her voice could be heard clearly across the distance.

"By the way, you didn't dump me, Hadewych," she said smoothly and without break. "You stopped deserving me. There's a difference."

Valerie climbed into her car and drove off.

"Help me," said Hadewych, down on all fours, snatching at bits of paper.

Jason considered killing this evil man, right there in the cemetery. Here was Hadewych kneeling at his feet. He could raise the shovel, swing it down, and kill him. He could see the scene clearly. The satisfying whomp of the metal on Hadewych's skull, the brains on the grass, blood splattering the headstones. In his mind he brought that shovel down a dozen times. But, no. He would spend the rest of his life in jail. Zef would grieve. Kate would hate him. And it wouldn't bring Eliza back.

It would feel good, though…

But, even now, he couldn't believe that anyone could be so evil as to murder his sweet trusting grandmother. Like all young men who have a conscience, Jason expected others to have a conscience too. He shrank from the sight of evil, denied it, because he had to live in the world—and how can you live here if monsters are real? How can you stand to live on Earth if men like Hadewych can exist and thrive? No. Better to give people the slightest benefit of the doubt, rather than accept the existence of such mad, unnecessary horror.

He made his choice and tossed the shovel into the grass. No matter what happened now, at least he would be able to live with himself.

Hadewych had snatched up most of the fragments, holding them to his heart. A few, however, caught in the wind, slipped through the chain link, and vanished into the forest. He calmed and tucked what pieces he had into his jacket pocket. He wiped his cheeks and returned to the graveside.

"No," Jason said. "Stay the hell away from us."

Hadewych smiled. "So you and Valerie are an 'us,' now?"

"Not me and Valerie. Stay away from me and my grandmother."

Jason and Hadewych looked down at the coffin. Jason wondered what she'd say now, and her voice spoke clearly in his imagination: *"Honey, I would have swung the shovel…"*

He and Hadewych glared at each other across the hole. Hadewych shook his head. "If you really loved her," he said, "you wouldn't have ruined her funeral."

Jason stood dumbly, shocked and horrified and unable to speak.

Hadewych reached beneath the Astroturf. He took a fistful of dirt and held it over Eliza's coffin.

"Don't you dare," said Jason.

"If one tenth of what you think of me were true," Hadewych said, "and if I really can summon the Horseman and kill whomever I like, whenever I like—" Hadewych tightened his fist, squeezing the dirt into a ball. "—would you really want me for an enemy?" He dropped the ball of dirt, contemptuously. It hit the coffin with a thump. "Goodbye Eliza," said Hadewych, brushing his hands. "Thanks for all your help."

Jason felt immobilized by fury.

"The guardianship hearing is on Monday," Hadewych said. He had regained his swagger. "Be there."

Hadewych walked down the hill and slipped casually into his car, the picture of nonchalance. But he slammed the door. Kate raised a hand and pressed her palm to the rear window. The car disappeared and the sound of hoofbeats clattered up from the bridge.

The ball of mud with Hadewych's finger-grooves sat on the lid of the coffin. Jason fell to his knees, wetting his slacks in the grass, and reached for the clump.

"Careful, Jase," said Joey, appearing at his side. He took Jason's arm so he wouldn't fall in.

"Get it—get it off please," Jason said.

Joey produced a second shovel. Together he and Jason fished the clump from the coffin lid. Jason dropped it on the grass and stomped on it. He brought his knee high and stomped on it over and over, until not a spot remained to dirty the grass. His breathing came sharp, his face reddened, his knee hurt with the violence of the act. But he won, at least, that one small victory. The terrible thing was gone. Forever.

He stood staring grimly at the place where it had lain.

I could have borne anything, anything, *but that clump of dirt.*

36 MONSTERS

Wind poured through the broken windows of Gory Brook Road, pushing aside the plastic that Jason had taped over the holes on Tuesday morning. The wind rustled the curtains and curtseyed up the stairs. In Jason's room, it found a dancing partner. A grave-rubbing slipped from his dresser and into the air, accepting the wind's invitation to waltz.

Charley saw the paper spiraling, rising, doing somersaults. The rubbing whirled with abandon and tore through the air like an escaping ghost. Charley barked at the thing and the rubbing clutched at the railing of the second flight as if startled. It trembled there a moment and fled upwards. Charley whined. Those stairs led to the attic. The poodle ran and hid beneath the davenport.

At the threshold of the attic, the grave-rubbing paused, exhausted. It slipped to the floor. The dipping sun cast a shadow through the octagonal window. The shadow of a telephone wire fell across the beams like a thread of black spider-web that dipped across the room.

The spirit of Agathe Van Brunt stood shimmering at that window, looking down upon the village of Sleepy Hollow. She'd loved this view in life—the Hollow spread beneath her feet. Her dominion. Her realm. They had ruled here once, she and the Van Brunt family.

She concentrated herself, drew herself together by an act of will. She felt her mind clearing. It was difficult. Sometimes she would lose herself in her memories.

Brom... Brom... Brom... she called, though he never answered. *The Van Brunts are coming home. I have seen. His name is Hadewych. Yet he is weak. He needs his Agathe. You weak men have always needed Agathe. Agathe and her Horseman.*

Children wandered the streets below, dressed as witches and skeletons and beings with magical powers. Yes. All Hallow's Eve. So innocent, so trusting: a night when evil is just a game and children roam the night with certainty—or hope—that nothing monstrous exists.

Let some poor child be fortunate enough to find a real Monster tonight, she thought. *Let some exile find a Monster to work their retribution. Let some orphan or abused castaway find a Monster—as Agathe had found her Horseman.*

She drew herself together, solidified. Now she remembered clearly: the morning after that fateful Halloween night in seventeen-ninety. She had stood at the side of the Philipse millpond, looking towards the church, and she had felt the Monster's eyes upon her back. She remembered turning, seeing the severed head floating in the murk, caught in the roots of a poplar tree, watching her with veiled grey-blue eyes. She had lifted it, gazed at it, and she had found that face handsome.

Afterwards, how the little burghers and shop-keeps and petty deacons had bowed when she passed. They had bowed to *her*, to little Agathe Van Ripper, once their inferior. They had bowed to the mill worker orphaned by the war. They had bowed to the flour-splashed waif they'd abused and despised. They had bowed to the Lady Van Brunt, the wife of Hermanus and true architect of his fortune. They would bow again.

She sought the Horseman with her thoughts, her Monster, her servant. She felt his spirit there in the burying ground of the Old Dutch Church. She bade him to rise, be strong.

I have made my sacrifices.

On the night when the boy had opened the cellar and released her, she had gone into the blonde girl—the one named Flight—even as the slut had fondled her lover by the millpond. The girl had been weak, but Agathe had been strong enough, once within her host, to tear the stiff wire from the hood of the vehicle and pierce the man's eye with it. That had been her first sacrifice.

The blonde herself had been next to die. The fireman had been a more powerful host, though less compliant. He had fought Agathe from within, threatening to drive her from his body. Moral strength. Difficult to overpower. Yet that second deed had been accomplished and the girl's blood had washed into the water. To feed Agathe's

Horseman, to make him strong.

She raised her arms.

Rise… she called. *The boy is the last of your enemies. The last Crane. Take him…*

She felt her Monster answer. She felt him gathering together.

The grave-rubbing danced across the attic, whipped in the air, turning, twisting, capering, loving this dance macabre—this rollicking Witch's Sabbath. Its lover wind thrust it backward—through Agathe's form—and flattened it against the glass of the window. The rubbing trembled there with joy, or fear, or anticipation.

The setting sun shone through the letters.

William Crane. Soldier. Died 1792.

Yes, take the boy. The last descendant of the man who killed you.

Take the head of the last Crane child and throw it into the Pocantico River…

…just as they did to yours…

#

The door of storage unit 327 rattled in its tracks. Hadewych slipped inside and pulled the door shut. He crept in, edging around boxes of cracked dishes and stolen library books.

Let Valerie evict me. I've been moving out for weeks. I have somewhere better to go.

417 Gory Brook.

Dylan's home, once; mine soon.

Long ago, he had made a daily pilgrimage to stare longingly at the place. He'd attempted to scrape together the money to buy it. On a factory worker's salary. He had gone without clothes and movies and vacations. He'd denied his son. He'd denied his wife. He'd made foolish little trips to the bank to deposit his weekly pittance. He'd prostrated himself before officious pricks and begged them for a mortgage. He'd done everything right. What a good little boy he had been. What a fool. And now, with a few shortcuts… the house would be his, outright. He was half-owner already.

"There's no magic to make it eighteen-fifty for us, son."

You were wrong, Mother.

I will recover all the Van Brunt possessions. I will have the house, and the reliquary, and everything else. And I will have the Pyncheon Legacy, too, in time.

The Legacy would require one more unthinkable act… two, if you count the boy himself. But Hadewych looked forward to the end of the boy. He could think of that act with great satisfaction. It was just too bad that Jason would have to live, for now, until the rest was ready.

Hadewych was still angry from the funeral. Zef had asked to drive—Hadewych had been so lead-footed and erratic on the way home.

How dare Valerie steal from me? How dare she? I trusted her, or at least trusted in her foolishness.

He would have to be more careful.

How fortunate that he had rented this unit before the bitch broke into his papers. She might have found the Treasure. She alone, of all people, would have known what it was. And what might she have done? Break it open? Take the skull to be blessed and buried? Yes, she would have thrown the power away, and for what? To assuage her own fear of the dark? Stupid, paranoid, selfish cow.

He found the storage chest he'd bought from Navy surplus, with money nicked from Valerie's purse.

Still locked.

He relaxed. He twisted his key and opened it. He pulled away the blood-spattered pillowcase. The reliquary sat inside, untouched.

Good.

Oh, Brom had been a fool to lock it away.

He couldn't blame Dylan for murdering his father in the end, after Brom had denied him this wonderful thing. Brom had no right. Dylan had *not* raised the Horseman on Halloween. He had *not* killed Absalom. He had *not* been responsible. Dylan? Commit such an obvious act? Don't insult the man's intelligence. *Someone else* had called the ghost. Or it had risen and destroyed Crane for its own reasons…

Dylan's letter—his last letter from Confederate prison—lay safe inside the chest.

I should have kept all the letters here. One foolish mistake. But no real harm done, except…

He slipped the pieces of the Brom letter into the chest.

Valerie will pay for that.

He was about to close the chest again when he noticed a faint light coming from the reliquary. He stood, frowning. He found the light switch, and plunged the space into darkness. Yes. The reliquary glowed with cold white light. The letters had returned. The letters burning from within the metal.

But those should only glow when the Horseman is about to rise.

He lifted the reliquary. He'd forgotten how heavy it was. He sat on a box of books and held the Treasure in his lap. He cradled it, as he had once cradled Zef at feeding time.

"No, no," Hadewych said. "Shh. Sleep. I haven't summoned you."

The glass cleared, as Dylan had promised that it would.

"No. No. Go back to sleep."

Hadewych stared at the back of the skull within, at the spidery river-map of the sagittal suture. He rotated the reliquary. The back teeth came into view. The gold corner tore a stripe from the cold light. Hadewych turned the thing fully around and stared into the Horseman's eye sockets—

He heard words in his mind, words he could not understand—yet did. Not the language, only the meaning. The meaning of the words and the emotion behind them, which was Hate.

"Kill… who?" said Hadewych in a tiny whisper.

The name hissed between the grinning teeth.

"No," said Hadewych. "I need him."

The name came again.

"It's not time. Not yet."

Again.

"I forbid it."

The reliquary shone in his hands.

I don't—I don't—I don't control it.

Hadewych Van Brunt became terrified by the thing, all at once— terrified of what he cradled in his arms, terrified that he'd brought it into the world, terrified that he was responsible for it. Terrified that *he* would be to blame for anything it chose to do. He regretted everything, suddenly. The deceptions, the thefts, the forgeries, the false kisses, the phony charm, the murder of Eliza, the murders to come. He regretted every shortcut he'd ever taken, every action that had led him to this moment. The truth struck him blind. He had birthed and raised this evil thing. His life would now be yoked to its will. He was the steed and this ghost would ride him wherever it wished.

He saw himself. He saw himself—for once—with perfect clarity, as if the glass had cleared and this harsh light had burned away his own flesh to reveal the soul within. He was *not* the victim of an unjust system, striving to regain his rightful due. He was *not* the scion of a great family reclaiming his place in the world. No. He was a cheap, frightened gigolo crouching in the darkness of a steel cage, absolutely alone and holding pure evil in his hands.

He felt immense loathing. Loathing for what he had become. And pity, too. He remembered Valerie's pity for him. He felt pity for his son. Pity that Zef should have such a father, and fear that his boy should ever see him as he now saw himself. He shoved the reliquary back inside the pillowcase. The light glowed through the bloodstains. He threw the thing into the chest. He locked the lid, blindly, by touch.

His hands seemed to glow now, to burn just as Brom had written. St. Elmo's fire. No. Nothing saintly about it. Flames of Hell. The red glow of hot metal, as if—

—as if the rider had branded him.

He sank to the floor and lay on the cold, cold, metal. The ghostly flames spindled away from his fingertips and vanished. The little cube was dark again. Only a faint spear of light fell from the keyhole of the trunk. It fell across a cardboard box marked "Baby Clothes and Mementos."

What's done is done, he thought. *If I am evil, damned, cursed, it's for Zef's sake that I am. Oh, I have failed him so often. So, so often. Let me win, this once. Let me be successful in this, at least. Let me win a future for my boy. Let me gain the whole world… even if I… even if I loseth my soul…*

Hadewych brought his knees to his chest. His right thumb circled the ring finger of his left hand, over and over.

But he had to cover his ears, finally. He couldn't bear the sound any longer. Even over the frantic pumping of his heart and lungs and tear ducts he could still hear the thing hissing inside the chest…

…Jason Crane…

…Jason Crane…

…Jason Crane…

…Jason Crane…

#

Jason closed his eyes as the dirt fell into the grave. He imagined himself down there, alongside Eliza. The dirt was a tornado battering the door of their storm cellar. He held her and kept her safe until it had passed over.

The backhoe finished its work and fell silent. The sky stopped falling in. Jason opened his eyes and inhaled life again.

That had been the worst of it.

The workers took up their shovels and cleared the rest of the dirt from the graveside pile. They took the boards away and fluffed the grass beneath. They covered the grave with Eliza's flowers and carried their tools to the truck.

And she was buried.

"Do you want to ride with us?" Joey said.

"No. I can't leave her yet. I need a few minutes alone." Jason pointed to the top of the slope, to the aqueduct trail above the cemetery. "I can get home that way, right?"

"You can't get through the fence," Joey said. He knelt and drew a map in the mud. "Go back over the bridge, okay? Hang a left. That's south. There's a gate next to the Old Dutch Church, but it'll be locked by now. You'll have to climb up the embankment, cut through the graves at the old burying ground, then you'll be on Broadway."

"Got it."

"But you'll still have a long walk home, Jase. If you need a ride, come look for the lanterns. I'll give you a lift if you can wait until after the tour."

"Oh, right. Your lantern tour. Happy Halloween," Jason said, his voice morose.

Joey answered in kind. "Happy Halloween. You're leaving tonight?"

"Yup. Post haste."

Joey nodded. They stood in silence.

"But I'll e-mail you," said Jason. "I'll e-mail when I know where I am."

"You gonna be okay?"

Jason shrugged. "I'll try to be."

One of the workmen honked the horn of the truck.

"Go. Go," said Jason, offering his hand.

Joey took it. "I'm going to miss you, Spidey," he said.

They broke the handshake and stood, side-by-side, looking in different directions.

"Zef's an idiot," Jason said, finally.

"So's Kate," said Joey.

Each punched the other in the shoulder. Joey gave a final wave and climbed in the truck.

The engine started, the truck clopped over the bridge and Jason was alone.

He slipped to the cold ground. It was wet but he didn't care. He drew his backpack into his lap and hugged it. A small sign stuck up from the earth nearby, like a seed package on a stick to mark what had been planted.

Eliza Merrick, it read.

He unzipped the backpack. He'd meant to put the *Sketch-Book* in the coffin. But he was glad he hadn't. Eliza would have been pissed off considering what she'd paid for it. He saw poor Absalom's writing inside the front cover. What did Annabel think, when her husband never came home? Did she guess that he had died by the hand of the Horseman?

His gloves were muddy. He stripped them off. But he saw no vision when he touched the book.

He leaned against the birch tree and opened the pages. He remembered the night Eliza had given it to him. In the RV, on their first night at Gory Brook, when they'd been locked out and had camped in the driveway. *"Read it close,"* she had said, whispering from the bunk below. *"Read it close. Pay attention."*

He found the page, and he began to read to Eliza, in the tone of a bedtime story:

"The Legend of Sleepy Hollow; Found among the papers of the late Diedrich Knickerbocker.

"A pleasing land of drowsy head it was,
   Of dreams that wave before the half-shut eye;
And of gay castles in the clouds that pass,
   Forever flushing round a summer sky.
—CASTLE OF INDOLENCE.

"In the bosom of one of those spacious coves which indent the eastern shore of the Hudson, at that broad expansion of the river denominated by the ancient Dutch navigators the Tappan Zee, and where they always prudently shortened sail and implored the protection of St. Nicholas when they crossed, there lies a small market town or rural port, which by some is called Greensburgh, but which is more generally and properly known by the name of Tarry Town. This name was given, we are told, in former days, by the good housewives of the adjacent country, from the inveterate propensity of their husbands to linger about the village tavern on market days. Be that as it may, I do not vouch for the fact, but merely advert to it, for the sake of being precise and authentic.

"Not far from this village, perhaps about two miles, there is a little valley or rather lap of land among high hills, which is one of the quietest places in the whole world. A small brook glides through it, with just murmur enough to lull one to repose—"

Jason stopped to listen to the Pocantico. It did murmur. And it did make him feel a little drowsy. He looked back to the page.

"—and the occasional whistle of a quail or tapping of a woodpecker is almost the only sound that ever breaks in upon the uniform tranquillity."

Yes, he heard the birds.

"I recollect that, when a stripling, my first exploit in squirrel-shooting was in a grove of tall walnut-trees that shades one side of the valley. I had wandered into it at noontime, when all nature is peculiarly quiet, and was startled by the roar of my own gun, as it broke the Sabbath stillness around and was prolonged and reverberated by the angry echoes. If ever I should wish for a retreat whither I might steal from the world and its distractions, and dream quietly away the remnant of a troubled life, I know of none more promising than this little valley."

Jason's hand brushed over Eliza's flowers.

"From the listless repose of the place, and the peculiar character of its inhabitants, who are descendants from the original Dutch settlers, this sequestered glen has long been known by the name of SLEEPY HOLLOW, and its rustic lads are called the Sleepy Hollow Boys throughout all the neighboring country. A drowsy, dreamy influence seems to hang over the land, and to pervade the very atmosphere."

Jason's head slipped to rest against the birch.

"Some say that the place was bewitched by a High German

doctor, during the early days of the settlement; others, that an old Indian chief, the prophet or wizard of his tribe, held his powwows there before the country was discovered by Master Hendrick Hudson. Certain it is, the place still continues under the sway of some witching power, that holds a spell over the minds of the good people, causing them to walk in a continual reverie. They are given to all kinds of marvellous beliefs, are subject to trances and visions, and frequently see strange sights, and hear music and voices in the air. The whole neighborhood abounds with local tales, haunted spots, and twilight superstitions; stars shoot and meteors glare oftener across the valley than in any other part of the country, and the nightmare, with her whole ninefold, seems to make it the favorite scene of her gambols...

"The dominant spirit, however, that haunts this enchanted region, and seems to be commander-in-chief of all the powers of the air, is the apparition of a figure on horseback, without a head. It is said by some to be the ghost of a Hessian trooper, whose head had been carried away by a cannon-ball, in some nameless battle during the Revolutionary War, and who is ever and anon seen by the country folk hurrying along in the gloom of night, as if on the wings of the wind. His haunts are not confined to the valley, but extend at times to the adjacent roads, and especially to the vicinity of a church at no great distance..."

37 THE GOBLIN CHASE

Jason woke to the sound of hooves.

The cemetery had grown dim and blue. The shadow of every headstone had lengthened, flattened, and reached up the hillside.

The book still lay open in his lap.

I should have read "Rip Van Winkle," he thought. He closed it.

Something stirred. Two eyes watched him from a few feet away. Gradually he made out the form of a red deer, male, with fuzzy antlers and powerful hindquarters. The hooves of the deer had awakened him. It nibbled on a flowering bush. Jason sat still, careful not to scare the thing. He watched the animal eat. He imagined the life of this deer, trying to survive in the forest, slipping in here to nibble on grave bushes. Where did it sleep, where were its babies, what would happen to it?

What will happen to me?

But Jason's ass was cold and wet. He shifted. The deer's white tail shot up. It leapt backwards, spun, and bounded across the headstones. Jason watched it run. It clattered over the road. It found some bolthole in the chain link and disappeared.

Wish I could leave that way. I have to take the long way 'round.

He found the crude map Joey had drawn in the mud. He squinted at it. Jason had never worn glasses but his night vision was poor—especially now, at twilight, when the sky was bright as midday but everything on earth disappeared behind a widow's veil.

Okay. Go down the road and go back over the bridge. Hang a left and walk to the Old Dutch Church. Cross over the old burial ground and you're on Broadway. Got it.

He put the *Sketch-Book* back in his bag. He was about to stand when a tiny green-yellow light streaked past the corner of his eye.

A firefly? In October?

He'd only seen fireflies in the heart of summer, drifting in the tall grass. It lit again near the ribbon of Eliza's coffin spray. Other fireflies appeared. Each lighted near the base of a headstone, drizzled upwards, and vanished. The effect was eerie yet somehow relaxing. Jason felt himself leaning forward as if to list and topple down the grass and into the river. He righted himself and shook his head to clear it. What was wrong with him?

He stood, shouldering his backpack and wiping his pants.

"I have to go, Eliza," he said. "I'll… be good."

He glanced back when he reached the road. He kissed his fingertips, raised them, then walked on. He had to hurry or else he would be caught in the cemetery when night fell. It was already becoming difficult to see. He could hear the river to his right, though, which assured him of the direction. He mounted a small rise. Branches thickened overhead. He felt the road dipping down again, bending towards the woody dell where the bridge passed over the river.

The fireflies followed him as he walked, making him blink with surprise. He didn't bat them away, though. Weren't they endangered or something? Or was that just the bees?

He stopped in the road, not knowing why he did it except that instinct had stilled his feet. Two red eyes stared at him from the slope ahead. They hung near the ground, crouched among the graves, surveilling him with anxious interest. He shrunk to the far side of the road as he neared the spot. The strange watcher followed him with its gaze. But the eyes were only vigil lights—electronic candles staked into the ground to signify eternal remembrance; for convenience they lit automatically at dusk (which kind of defeated the purpose).

Jason sighed. He was beginning to spook himself as usual.

The sky shone ice blue but the trees above had closed in. He viewed the sky as if through a caterpillar-eaten leaf. He hurried his steps.

Just get home.

Just get home.

Headstones drifted past on his left.

Reynolds. Abramowitz. Stephens. Vadas. Xie. Crane.

Crane?

Jason stopped to look. A firefly lit as he approached the stone.

Crane?

It was a double headstone. The names read:

Andrew Crane.

Dianne Crane.

His parents? His parents weren't buried here. They were buried in Valhalla Cemetery. Weren't they? A firefly blazed across his vision again. He swatted it away violently. His eyes had to adjust afterwards.

Now the stone read **Ichabod Crane.**

"No," Jason said. This was—

Another firefly blinded him.

Absalom Crane.

"But—"

Another light. He blinked.

He lurched away as the next name appeared.

Jason Crane.

And the date beneath the name is… today.

He started to shiver. What in the name of Carl Sagan was he doing in the cemetery on Halloween? What was he thinking? He—he hadn't been thinking of danger, only of Eliza. He whirled, expecting the Headless Horseman himself to be waiting on the road ahead. Or was he lurking behind?

He saw only desolate road in each direction.

And if he attacked Ichabod and Absalom, does this mean he attacked my parents too? They died only a few miles from here. And, oh, has Hadewych decided to summon the thing and kill me too? Tonight?

He pushed the hair out of his eyes. The headstone read **Isadore Plochman** now. A few little stones sat on the top edge.

Maybe he had imagined the names?

The hell I did.

He wanted to run, but now the bridge ahead worried him. Doesn't the Horseman haunt bridges? He trotted downward and to the right. He stopped at the foot of the bridge. Could he avoid crossing it somehow? It terrified him. Why? It was just a stupid bridge. A phony modern thing made to look old. Probably a steel frame underneath. Not a scary bridge at all.

Keep telling yourself that, kid.

The gloom beneath could have been the lair of a troll.

Billy Goats Gruff. Mama used to read that. The troll waits beneath for the fattest, sweetest goat…

Stop it.

Jason thought he saw something on the far end of the bridge. A shape of some sort. He faded left, trying to make the thing out.

Stop being stupid.

He stepped onto the bridge and gripped the knotty railing. He felt the ground drop away beneath as he edged forward. His eyes remained on the shape.

It's nothing.

It's nothing.

Is it nothing?

A branch broke behind him; he whirled, half expecting to see the Horseman.

The red eyes were there again. The vigil lights. But hadn't he left them far behind? As he watched, the lights drifted rightward. They passed through the fence and disappeared into the woods.

Jason let out a string of curses at the top of his lungs. A bird answered from the branches of the forest. Jason spun and stomped over the bridge. No troll attacked him and he reached the other shore. The looming shape was only a stupid stairwell opposite the bridge that climbed up the hill and into the main cemetery. He glanced back. The lights had been some animal. And the headstone had been an illusion.

Like hell they were.

He turned left and ran, admitting defeat and letting the fear take him over. He ran southward down the long dark road. His initial burst of adrenaline ran its course and he slowed, then walked again, limping a little. His damn dress shoes were already biting his feet and he was sweating. He pulled off his tie and stuffed it in the backpack. He didn't like the way it reminded him of his neck.

Headstones slipped past on the right. He still had enough light that he caught his reflection occasionally in the polished stone. He looked very young and very thin. He could feel his vulnerability as he walked along. To his left, the river dropped away into the ravine. He missed its rushing energy. The road felt very quiet and gloomy, with only his own steps to keep him company. The leaves made a faint oceanic rustle all around. The insects sang their three-note songs.

jason*CRANE*… jason*CRANE*… jason*CRANE*…

He grew aware of his own body: his cold wet backside and his biting shoes, the touch of his starchy dress shirt and his jacket and the soft weight of his backpack. He saw himself reflected in the headstones—just a container of warm fluids, flimsy work for a blade or a hoof or a sword. He felt shatter-able and transient and his next breath was not guaranteed, oh no.

Jason sang a wretched pop song as he walked—something about having no self-control and no bitches and not enough money. He sang it softly, absent-mindedly, as if reciting a psalm.

He passed **Reese, Finarton, Bane, Ekdahl, Forrest, Black, Small**…

There.

He saw the gate at the end of the road. It had an actual traffic light hanging beyond. He felt safe now that he was within sight of the modern world. But the gate would be locked, he remembered. He would have to climb the embankment and cross over the churchyard. He could see the spire of the church above and the weathervane spinning against the sky.

He would rather climb this gate than face that churchyard, but the spikes on top made leaping the fence impossible.

Okay, just be quick.

Something caught his ear—a brittle, clipping sound. He scanned the crest above and saw a horse silhouetted among the graves. It looked to be tied to a branch of the locust tree. He had heard its hooves as it shifted from foot to foot. It… rustled, somehow.

His breath caught. He forced himself to be calm and rational.

Some Halloween thing… maybe? For some event?

He found the stairs and ascended, sideways, ready to bolt if necessary. He watched the horse, but when he neared the top he saw The Rider, standing upon the shallow depression of the Horseman's grave. The figure was motionless, a dim shape that absorbed light and gave nothing back. He could make out the shape of the boots and the legs and two arms held away from the body, palms down. Just a man? But the cape of the thing was not normal. It contorted painfully, twisting in the air even though the wind wasn't blowing. It wrung itself and billowed and whipped, slowly, as if the figure wore a wave torn from a black ocean. And above its shoulders…

Is he headless? Is he headless?

Jason peered over the retaining wall. The black figure looked to have a head but… as Jason shifted his position the head drifted away from the body. No. The head was merely the stub of a headstone on the knoll beyond.

Jason dove behind the wall, trying not to breathe. His nerve endings were jangled as if someone had begun to scream silently in his ear. He felt the *energy* of a scream, making him shut his eyes tightly. His own scream? Or were all the spirits in the burying ground screaming because the thing had awakened? The soundless noise made him stiffen painfully. He covered his ears, though the night was silent except for the distant breathing of the horse and the faint tearing sound of cloth whipping in wind.

It's— It's—

No. Could it be—Zef? Someone in a costume?

Something in the back of his brain knew better. Alarm bells rang through him. A snake. A spider. Death itself.

No. This is happening. Go. Go.

Jason scrabbled down the stairs as silently as he could. He had seen the Headless Horseman. *The actual Headless Horseman.* Had the Horseman seen him? Had it? Could it see with no eyes? Could it hear? Could it feel his quickening breath? His heartbeat? Jason slipped over the road and into the bushes.

He crouched painfully still, wishing himself into the shadows.

He couldn't see the rider now. He watched the horse. He thought he could hear its moth-wing breathing.

Okay, the gate blocks the way to the south. The river is behind me. Only thing I can do is go back the way I came.

Not on the road, though, you're too exposed on the road.

Something touched his back and he jumped. He'd retreated into a tree. He stepped around it, his eye never leaving the horse. But a branch rotated beneath his foot. His weight came down and it cracked like a starting pistol. Jason looked down and steadied himself.

After he'd recovered he looked up again.

The horse was gone.

Where is it where is it where is it…

Just go. Go.

He moved as silently as he could. The forest engulfed him. He found a path parallel to the road. He hurried along, looking back occasionally to the swath of light that fell through the gap in the canopy where he had entered. The path descended as he walked, diverging from the road. The trees above him swayed, creaking like a roomful of rocking chairs.

He was terrified. Sweat trickled down his spine. He thought he heard the sound of snarling dogs somewhere in the night. A gnat buzzed in his ear and he slapped his own cheek, regretting the sound and glancing back again. The path slipped down into the ravine and he heard the river. The branches ripped apart above the water. He dimly perceived a massive shape ahead. He drew near. It was a pier of stone alongside the path. He stepped onto it.

The other half of the broken bridge.

He shivered. He was standing on the spot where Ichabod had been struck by the pumpkin. He felt as if he'd been drawn there, as Valerie had been dragged to the pier on the opposite shore, to be the midnight blood that fed the Horseman. He pulled back from the edge, and a piece of the bridge broke under his step and fell into the water. A bird leapt from the bushes with a startled cry.

Jason hurried back to the path. A log blocked the way. He had thrown his left leg over it when he saw—far down the path, at the place where he had left the road—

—a shape had ridden into the light.

The Horseman sat high in his stirrups, searching.

Terror overcame Jason. He swung his leg over the log and ran. His backpack caught in the clutching branches and he left it dangling there. He kicked through the twiggy mass and ran upward. He heard the thing laugh far behind—crazy laughter that sounded like hysteria and chopping wood. Jason pushed through a thicket that smelled of juniper and black walnut and rotted leaf. He tumbled onto the road again.

At the far end, back at the cemetery gate, the figure of the Horseman rode out of the forest. He drew his hatchet.

They regarded each other across the vast distance.

The Horseman kicked the horse and it whinnied like the slaughter of animals. It reared and kicked the air. Its front hooves slammed against the road and sparks flew. Jason cried out, turned and ran.

The chase was on.

He felt the Horseman gaining immediately. He couldn't outrun a horse on foot. He flew blindly down the road. He saw nowhere to escape: the hill to his left was too steep and the woods to his right thinned with every step. Jason zigzagged in desperation. The thing was playing with him. He was going to die. He could already see his own head rolling up the asphalt. But he'd reached the glade where the bridge crossed. He could go back over, climb the chain link and reach the aqueduct trail and—

The black shape of the Horseman thundered up, blocking the bridge. The Horseman's hatchet whipped through the air an inch from Jason's face.

Jason spun away and fell—on the stairs.

The stairs.

He leapt them three at a time, hoping the horse couldn't follow.

He gained a landing and it veered left but he jumped the low wall and fell up the grass and over a curb. This road ran parallel to the road below, overlooking it. He heard no hooves following on the stairs. He saw a memorial bench with a circular balustrade to his right. It hung from the hill like a balcony. He threw himself behind the bench and froze there.

He heard the shuffle of hooves below, a faint heave of horse breath. The sounds drifted away to the left...

Is it over? Is it over?

His own breathing came labored; his ribs ached; his capillaries flushed and prickled his scalp and cheeks. He wiped his tears and a thread of snot. His breathing slowed. He shed his suit jacket and threw it under the bench, loosened his collar and rolled his sleeves. He would be cold, but agile.

He rose a little and peered over the balustrade. The road below was empty. He drew back and looked behind... to his side, the name on the memorial bench read **Baby Boy Crane.** A lump rose in his throat. He crouched and circled the bench. The hillside road was empty too but it drifted downward—maybe joining the road below.

If the Horseman follows, he'll come from that direction.

Jason scuttled over the road and onto an incline thick with grave markers. He kept low and began climbing the rock wall of headstones, heaving himself upward and catching their granite edges as his feet caught in mud. His fingers slipped and he almost fell backwards but he dug his fingers into a mound of turned earth.

"You're running out of time..." something whispered. He whirled.

"Hello?" he croaked.

Was that a woman's voice? A child's?

A firefly swept the air.

He fought through a thorny hedge.

He stood at a crossroads now. Sinewy paths curled away in every direction, each leading into a void. He had lost all sense of direction. He couldn't hear the river... only the branches rocking above... and the three-note cricket song... sawing through a fizzle of cicadas...

jason*CRANE*... jason*CRANE*... jason*CRANE*...

Another rhythm answered from the darkness.

clippety*CLOP*... clippety*CLOP*... clippety*CLOP*...

The Horseman galloped onto the road below, stopping near the place where Jason had hidden.

He'll know I was there... my jacket... my footprints...

Jason couldn't force his legs to move. He gripped the thorny hedge and watched.

The Horseman rode to the side of a black oak. He raised his hatchet and thrust it into the wood. He let it hang there and waited among the graves, his black cape whipping in the air. Fireflies rose at the horse's feet. Around each yellow light shadows gathered together to form human figures. Jason felt waves of inexplicable melancholy and grief.

He's raised— He's raised—

The Horseman had raised the spirits of the dead. Jason remembered a passage from *The Legend* that he had read earlier: *"The dominant spirit, however, that haunts this enchanted region, and seems to be commander-in-chief of all the powers of the air, is the apparition of a figure on horseback, without a head."*

The dead stood at attention, awaiting orders from their general. He must have given some silent command because the ghosts turned and pointed upward—toward the place where Jason was hiding.

The Horseman seized the hatchet.

Jason bolted, choosing a path at random. He knew that if the Horseman found him again...

I don't want to die young.

But where? Where? Where to hide?

jason*CRANE*... jason*CRANE*... jason*CRANE,* sang the crickets.

Where?

He slipped between two tombs, sideways, holding his breath. The Horseman rode up to the crossroads, searching. Jason wriggled through to the other side and found two ruts of gravel that snaked uphill like a trail of dim blue breadcrumbs leading him into a forest of marble.

His first step on the gravel was deafening. He avoided the ruts as he ran. He wished desperately that he knew the direction. Two moths circled each other and vanished.

jason*CRANE*... jason*CRANE*... jason*CRANE*...

He slowed as the tombs pressed in. The shroud of melancholy still wrapped him. Everything warm and wholesome and human felt unreachably distant.

I might as well be on the moon.

No. Even the moon gets sunlight...

...and there are no dead things there.

He tried to calm down, but he felt an empty dreadful sense of panicked helplessness. The doors of the tombs yearned for him. Through the barred gates he could sense forsaken things. They whispered: *A visitor... a visitor... stay awhile... we'll tell you our stories...*

He sidestepped a broken column—symbol of a life cut short. He wished desperately that Eliza hadn't taught him to read such symbols. His mind raced. A fallen tree means mortality. The winged skull announces ascension. Thistles mean earthly sorrow. Dogwood means eternal life. Harvested wheat laments the elderly dead. Empty shoes grieve lost children.

He smelled something putrid here: a mixture of allspice and mold and sympathy flowers and candy-sweet formaldehyde—of powder and clay and his own ripening underarms. And bone dust.

He passed statues with worn away faces, an angel with skeleton ribs, urns that trailed marble drapery. A nude male statue twisted in spiritual ecstasy, head thrown back and reaching for Paradise; a daddy longlegs crept across the man's face. Jason's skin crawled. Stone eyes followed him as he passed by.

He was so tired.

Why not just stop here and become a statue? Stand here till

morning. Stand here till winter. He imagined snow collecting on his body. His fear felt like frost on his shoulders.

No.

He pushed the hair from his eyes. His forehead was wet, though the wind was cold.

No. Something's trying to hold me here, to drain me so I can't get away. Keep going.

jason*CRANE*... jason*CRANE*... jason*CRANE*...

The bugs were calling.

clippety*CLOP*... clippety*CLOP*... clippety*CLOP*...

The Horseman was coming.

Jason quickened his step.

If only I knew which way to run.

A mournful note sounded, behind and to the left.

The train. The train runs along the Hudson. I know where I am.

But as he turned south he heard music rising ahead—the voices of children, singing a jump-rope song. He stopped short.

What? What?

Fireflies began to flicker in the tombs. He heard stone scraping within, the clank of chains and the squeak of gates. Something groaned behind the bars to his left. A skeletal hand reached through and found the knob...

He hid behind a headstone. In all directions, fireflies rose. The Horseman had called his army. A whole army of the dead. Dead adults and children and old men and women... all their spirits had risen from sleep to search for a terrified boy. Jason sprinted across the grass. He heard the clopping... the gallop... louder, ever louder, echoing across the hills of the Sleepy Hollow Cemetery.

clippety*CLOP*clippety*CLOP*clippety*CLOP*

He ran, losing himself in his terror, weeping.

His knees struck metal and he spilled over the top of a wheelbarrow. A shovel broke beneath his body; his shoulder struck the ground and he rolled. A board flipped beneath him and he fell hard in muddy water.

At first he thought he'd gone blind. Something prickly wrapped his head and upper body. It smelled of bug repellent. He struggled, pulled it free and threw it aside. It was a length of Astroturf. He pulled his throbbing, pinched arm from beneath his body. It came up wet and black. He reached out and felt cold earth in every direction. Above, he saw a rectangle of sky torn by branches. A single star hung there, distant and dim.

He'd fallen into an empty grave.

Involuntarily, he made a strangled, whimpering sound. He stood up slowly, water trickling from his hair and down his spine. His body felt battered and unsteady. He slipped, fell forward and muddied his nose and lips on the edge of the grave.

Beyond the hole, the gathered shadows that had once been alive stood sentinel at their various graves. He could feel them keening, moaning silently, sending out their webs of melancholy to snare him. If the Horseman came now, he would be defenseless, trapped. He listened for the hoofbeats; strangely, they had gone silent.

Jason wasn't sure if that was good or bad.

He leapt and clutched at the earth but fell back holding double handfuls of mud. He stretched and reached for the wheelbarrow handle, for the board he had flipped, but he couldn't snag them. He knelt and tried rolling the Astroturf into a bundle to stand on, scraping dirt from the wall to make a step, but both just sank down into the water and mud.

Desperation fueled him. He began hopping, turning circles, panicking, looking for any way out.

The narrow end of the hole seemed slightly lower. He gathered his strength, crouched, and jumped as high as he could. His chest hit the dirt, he stumbled backwards, teeth clacking. He flailed his arms. His ankle twisted and he fell over hard into the water, clutching his foot, trying not to scream.

Something sharp stabbed him in the shoulder blade and drew blood. He winced. He had almost impaled himself on the broken shovel handle. It must have rolled in with him. He threw it aside and cradled his injured ankle, shivering, gasping, sobbing. He rolled over onto his side.

Trembling, he drew the Astroturf back over himself like a shroud.

The sky above disappeared as he covered his head. Waves of desolate emotion poured in from above like falling dirt, burying him. He fell into thoughts of death, of pain, of loss. Wood covered his heart. Nothing seemed worth the effort of action.

Maybe it wouldn't be so bad to die. To... *end*, to *go*, to... *evaporate*. Would it be like falling asleep? Like falling asleep, maybe to dream?

Now who's Hamlet, Joey?

Joey would find him here in the morning. White and dead and waterlogged and silent. Silent forever. Decapitated like Absalom, probably.

Had Absalom known he was going to die? Did he feel like this, in the end? Did he give up and give in to some beckoning grave? Yes, Jason decided. He'd probably welcomed it. Why not? It wasn't so bad to die, really.

This will be my own grave. I won't be getting out again. I'm done. I tried. It's over. I'm sorry. I'm sorry, Eliza.

Eliza had always been his strength. She was the one who'd rescued him when he'd given up on life. She was the strong one. She would never give up, oh no, not her.

But she was gone. Gone forever. And that was that. He had nothing anymore.

Jason's breathing came in short bursts. Then it slowed. He went numb inside.

He stopped caring.

Let the Horseman come. Let me die. Let me be with them. With her. With my parents. I'm not strong enough to go on alone… not strong enough…

He hugged himself tightly, closed his eyes.

Let the Horseman come… I'm ready.

"What kind of talk is that?"

He heard Eliza's voice in his mind, as he had at graveside. He heard her as clearly as if he were late for school and she were standing at the foot of his bed, shaking his leg.

"Get your be-hind moving, Honey."

"I can't," he whispered.

"Of course you can. What do you think I raised? A quitter? Just shoot me now if my boy's going to give up and lie in the mud. You've got to live."

"Why? Why bother? I'll end up dead someday, in the end."

"Well, boo-hoo. Aren't you pitiful. And what will you have in your grave but your memories? What will you have to keep you warm through eternity if you've got no memories of sun and wind and dances and drinking and laughing? No achievements or failures or love? Didn't I teach you anything about life? You've got to be tough, boy-o."

"I'm not tough. I'm a nerd and a geek and a loser and I'm going to die."

"Bullshit. You're my *grandson. If you've got anything of me in you, you'll climb out of this goddamned hole and pop that Horseman a good one."*

"How?"

"How? That's what your brain's for. Figure it out. Find a way to live, honey. Get through the night. Pop the spook like you popped Hadewych. Make me proud. Just get up."

Jason sniffed.

"And if I don't? Will you be ashamed of me? If I fail?"

Ashamed if you fail? Of course not. I'll only be ashamed if you don't try.

He nodded. He threw the Astroturf aside and sat up against the wall of the grave.

"Good. Get up. Climb out of this ditch and quit wallowing. My boy's a hero. That's what I tell all my friends. Don't make me a liar."

Jason felt steel rising in him. He rose to his feet. He could do this. He could get up and get out and survive. He was smart. He was strong. He was Eliza Merrick's grandson. He would survive this night.

"'Cause if I die, who would feed Charley?" he whispered.

He cared again. He cared very much. He wanted all of it, his own eighty years of adventures and memories. He wanted his own heroic story, his own Legend to leave behind.

He wanted to live.

He jumped, scrambled for purchase, slipped down again. He tried again, digging his fingers into the ground. No good. It was no good! He needed something to pull, he—

He seized the broken shovel handle.

He leapt a third time and thrust the shovel handle into the ground beyond the hole. It held his weight, just enough. He pushed his legs against the dirt behind and managed to brace himself. He pulled the handle up and thrust it farther into the ground beyond. He pulled himself upward, legs flailing. He used the stake to claw his way back to the world. He gripped grass and heaved himself over, rolling onto his back, gasping for air, his breath ragged and labored. His ankle throbbed. He'd left a dress shoe in the water below.

But he had done it.

"I'm proud of you, Honey. Never, never be less than you can be. 'Cause I'll know. And I'll tan your little hide."

clippetyCLOPclippetyCLOPclippetyCLOP

A legion of the dead loomed over him and all around, their fingers pointing at him accusingly. He leapt to his feet, spinning, trying to find direction. He caught the sound of the distant jump-rope song again. He followed it. He recognized the music now. The music came from the Horseman's Hollow. Halloween was going on—somewhere ahead. The good Halloween—the fun Halloween—

He dashed across the field. His arm brushed the vaporous spirit of a little girl and went cold. He shook it as he ran up the hill. Pins and needles bit his palm and fingers as if they had fallen asleep. He caught his leg on a hanging chain. He hopped, ran on.

Keep moving. Keep moving. Go go go.

He'd reached the highest point in the cemetery—a crest surmounted by an enormous pillar flanked by statuary. And—there. Through a gap in the trees he saw the Tappan Zee Bridge twinkling on the horizon. And... something else glowed softly just ahead. Firelight?

CLOPCLOP*CLOP!* CLOPCLOP*CLOP!*

No!

The Horseman's anger was more terrifying than his laugh had been. His cape whipped and crashed and splashed the air. He holstered the hatchet and raised a hand. A face seemed to fly out of the darkness. A burning pumpkin, someone's jack-o'-lantern spirited from a porch. It came into his hand and he lifted it high. Jason wheeled about and slammed his skull into the extended arm of a marble Jesus. He grabbed his forehead and ran with one eye shut in the direction of the Tappan Zee—tipping forward, lurching between the graves.

Just survive. Just survive.

The ground became perilously steep. He spun and tumbled facing backwards, barely on his feet—and glimpsed the Horseman bounding after. A headstone knocked him around again and he saw a soft glow beyond the—beyond the what?

Beyond the edge.

The ground ended ahead.

But Jason had lost control.

His arms pinwheeled.

He lurched forward—

—and went over into space.

38 THE FLIGHT OF JASON CRANE

"And here is the highlight of our tour," said Joey, raising his lantern.

The small group gathered in front of a row of tombs, raising their lanterns as well. "This is the Irving family plot. That white stone in the middle there is the grave of Washington Irving himself. Can anyone tell me what he's famous for?"

A few of the tourists chuckled.

"Yes," Joey said, "Irving is most famous for *The Legend of Sleepy Hollow*. But he also gave us other stories. *Rip Van Winkle*, for one. He gave us the idea that Columbus was trying to prove the world was round. That's not true. That's an invention of..."

He waited.

"Washington Irving..." a woman said helpfully.

"Washington Irving. Yes. And you—" Joey crouched and pointed to a boy in a skeleton costume. "What does Santa fly in?"

The kid rolled his eyes. "A sleigh."

"A magic sleigh. And we get that from..."

He waited.

"Washington Irving..." said a few voices.

"And the New York Knicks—and 'Gotham,' for you Batman fans, and—"

"Hey," said the kid, immensely annoyed. "It's Halloween. Is this thing going to get scary or not?"

A wailing figure hurtled from the sky. It came down head over heels, flopped onto the grass and rolled to a stop. It was a muddy young man with blood on his head and one dress shoe.

"Jason?"

Joey ran to his friend's side and set the lantern in the grass.

"Are you okay?" he said.

"AHHHHHH!" The skeleton kid screamed and pointed.

The Headless Horseman leapt from the roof of the tombs above, landing like an earthquake upon the grave of Washington Irving. The rider hurled a pumpkin that burst and caught the trees afire. The tourists ran screaming into the night, dropping their lanterns behind.

The skeleton boy ran fastest of all.

Joey threw himself behind a tree, his mouth moving like a trout thrown onto shore. He watched, wide eyed, as the rider and steed stepped into the circle of lantern light to stand above Jason's fallen body and straddle him from above.

#

Jason opened his eyes and saw the Headless Horseman clearly at last.

The head of the horse came into the light first.

Its nostrils were two eye sockets broken from the face of someone's skull. Jason could see the pinprick holes where the tear ducts had been. The champing teeth were finger bones, animal bones, and chips of broken wood. The bit and bridle were an iron spike and a length of rotted rope. The eyes of the horse were wide and rabid—the eyes of a terrified thing that had been whipped and beaten. It took Jason a moment to realize that the eyes were snail shells. The horse's pupils were their round, hollow entrances. The head and body were made of autumn leaves, brown and black and spoiled yellow, layer upon layer that shivered in the wind. A line of red and gold ran up the center of the snout, meeting a mane of cemetery grass that rustled down the thing's back.

The Horseman sat upon a saddle of human leather and braided hair. He was a thing of smoke and ash and cremated remains—a human form of complete darkness, cold as dry ice or the heart of a mountain. His cape was a black burial shroud, spider-silk and moth-eaten.

The Horseman and his steed had gathered themselves together, Jason realized, from the land and stone and graves and hearths of Sleepy Hollow. They were the spirit of the town and the town itself.

Even the sparkling eyes that Jason thought he saw for an instant, looking down at him, floating in the air above the neck—were the two brightest stars that hung over the Hudson.

The Horseman raised his hand, summoning a pumpkin. The jack-o'-lantern's face was a crude death's head, a child's nightmare. The horse-thing raised a leg and brought a hoof down on Jason's chest, painfully, pinning him to the ground. The hoof was a shard of broken stone. The rider climbed down and stood over the boy, gloating over his victim. Jason felt waves of satisfaction and eagerness and triumph coming from the Horseman. His moment had come and he was savoring Jason's death. He took the pumpkin in both hands and raised it high.

Jason fumbled in the grass, desperately scrabbling for a rock, a stick, anything he could use to defend himself. His hand closed on something metal—the handle of the lantern—and with a shoulder-wrenching heave he swung it 'round backhanded. It struck the head of the horse and flung fire down its body. The leaves caught, and the horse burst into flames. It screamed and reared. Its hoof left Jason's chest. He rolled away. The hoof came down again, hard, in the same spot. The Horseman seized the reins of the steed, but his whipping cape caught in the burning twigs and bones. Bright fire ran along it, wrapping the Horseman in its embrace. His form shivered, cracked, and with a scream that echoed over the hills he broke into dust and ash that whipped into the sky, falling as a rain of cinders and burning leaves. The jack-o'-lantern arced through the air, went dark, fell, and broke on the grass.

The Horseman was gone.

Jason swatted at sparks that caught in his hair and eyebrows and bit his arms like angry gnats.

"That was—" whispered Joey. His voice was full of shock and wonder. "That was—"

"It was," said Jason.

"That—was—was—?"

"Let me just sit for a minute," Jason said.

"I've seen the Headless Horseman," said Joey, talking to the graves. "The Headless Horseman of Sleepy Hollow. I've seen him." He jumped and shouted. "I've seen him!"

"Great," said Jason. His foot throbbed and he was muddy and cold.

"I must be asleep," Joey said, giggling, turning circles and slapping himself.

"You're not."

Joey collapsed in the grass, leaning against the headstone of Washington Irving. He threw an arm around it and pressed his forehead to the stone. "The goddamn Headless Horseman…" he sighed.

At the foot of the hill, the bones of the Horseman's steed rolled along the path, bumping each other, clinging together. The wind kicked leaves up the hill.

"We need to go," Jason said, getting to his feet.

"I can't believe I—"

"You did. And if you want to see tomorrow let's get the hell out of this cemetery. Look!"

Jason pointed. The Horseman was re-forming.

Joey saw the cinders gathering in the air. "I—I—I—don't need to see him twice," he said.

"Go."

The boys scrambled away together, up the slope. They turned at the top. The Horseman's shape was already complete, standing alongside a new steed. They felt rage tumbling up the hill to burn them.

"We can't outrun him."

"Uh—uh—here," Joey said.

"Where?"

Joey fumbled a key ring from his belt. He ran to a door set in the hillside.

"Oh no," Jason said. "No way."

"It's empty. It's empty. Come on."

The metal swung open with a piercing groan. They backed inside and slammed the door—plunging themselves into absolute darkness.

"Where are we?" said Jason, panting.

Joey stuck out an arm and accidentally poked Jason in the eye.

"Ow!"

"Sorry. It's the receiving vault."

"The what?"

"The receiving vault. Before we had backhoes the ground would freeze and they'd keep the bodies in here—you know, until spring."

"Joey."

"Relax. We never use it—

"Good."

"—unless some movie crew needs a scary location."

"That's just great," Jason said.

"At least we're safe." Joey said. Something crashed against the door. "I hope," he added.

"Why didn't you grab a lantern?"

"Why didn't *you*?"

Jason turned and fumbled about, finding cold walls and metal rings. He felt like a bat. The floor sloped down. He felt a drain under his sock. He was becoming claustrophobic. They were both starting to panic.

"Here—" said Joey.

"Here what?"

A rectangle of light blossomed so intensely that Jason had to whip his head around to look away.

"My phone," said Joey. "We can call my dad."

Joey turned in circles, trying to get reception. Jason shook his head.

Something crashed against the door again. A pumpkin? Or was the Horseman hacking through?

No, the door's metal. It's metal it's metal it's metal.

"I've got no bars," Joey said.

"We're behind stone, nitwit."

"As long as we're safe."

Something groaned behind the marble.

"What was that?" Joey said.

"Oh, um—" Jason said, "Here's the thing, um—the Horseman can kind of… raise the dead."

Joey's phone went dark.

"I wish you hadn't told me that," he said.

They felt the ghosts, the wave of melancholy. They were not alone in the tomb. Joey lit the room again. Spectral shapes slipped in through the marble, reaching.

Joey squeaked and killed the light again. "This was stupid this was stupid this was stupid…" He was freaking. Jason felt his arm go cold as something brushed him. His cheek began to prickle.

"Shut up," said Jason. "Let's just run. Where do we go?"

"Uh—"

"Uh—"

"The Horseman Bridge," said Joey.

"It won't work. That's not the real bridge."

"Then—holy ground."

"Holy ground?"

"Holy ground. Definitely."

"I don't believe in holy ground," said Jason.

The door thumped again.

"It doesn't matter," Joey said. "As long as *he* does."

"Fine. Where?"

"The chapel."

"Can we make it?"

"Yeah. I know the way."

Behind them a piece of marble dropped away and broke. Another piece struck Jason's shoulder. He covered his head and pushed Joey towards the door, protecting his friend.

"Fine. Just go. Go."

They pushed the door open and blinked against the starlight.

"I don't see him…" Joey whispered.

"Joey… go," Jason said. The ghost of an old man, not unlike Grandpa John, stood in the vault behind them. He threw more stone at the boys. A bit struck Jason in the temple. His ears rang.

"This way," said Joey.

They left the vault, slamming the door, and turned in the direction of the chapel, but the Horseman rode from the shadows and onto the road. They stopped short and backed away.

"I guess the chapel's out," Jason said.

They found a long ramp of brick heading back towards the Irving grave. Jason fled to the bottom. But Joey stopped at the top.

"Wait," Joey said. He pointed to his phone. "I can get a picture."

"No."

"We'll be famous. One second."

Joey raised the camera. Jason ran back up the ramp, to grab his friend, to stop him. In the endless time before he reached the top, Kate's voice came back to him…

"Watch out for Joey," she had said. *"Because everyone we tell dies."*

NO!

With the phone to his eye, Joey didn't see the pumpkin coming. But Jason did. He threw out an arm to grab Joey's shirt, but his hand closed on air. The pumpkin cracked against Joey's head, lifting him off his feet and tossing him like a rag doll onto the grass.

"NO NO NO NO NO!" Jason screamed. He whirled to face the Horseman. "I'll kill you!"

The Horseman drew the hatchet and kicked his horse.

Oh shit.

You have to run. You have to run. Lead it away from Joey. Joey might be okay. Please be okay, Joey. Please!

He turned and sprinted down the brick lane, gathering momentum and speed. When he reached the road he leapt it. The ground threw him forward and he ran. He ran for his life. He ran to keep his heart beating.

Hooves clattered behind. Headstones flew by on either side.

Every strike jarred his legs and splinted his shins. He pumped his arms; his hands came up quick and high; he skidded, sprawled and leapt between the graves. He lost the other shoe and ran in stocking feet. The Horseman's hatchet carved downward and nicked Jason's shoulder. Jason felt the blood.

He saw the Old Dutch Church, far down the hill.

Holy ground.

I have to make the church.

I have to make the church.

He ran diagonally across the rows of headstones. He ducked a branch—the hooves thundered behind and shot bullets of dirt that struck his shoulder and cheek. He found a rut between the stones and brought his legs together—*precise*—*toe first*—and leapt like a gazelle with hunters after.

The way ahead was clear now—an endless aisle between two rows of headstones—downhill all the way to the church.

He fell forward—he was falling forward—gravity had taken him. Every step left a muddy footprint across a different grave. Fear pushed him on; the church grew larger.

The demon spurred his steed and swung again and Jason/Ichabod dodged the blade. It breathed against his cheek—*so close so close*—he flinched and leapt a root. Something in his ankle tore and oh it hurt but—no, he could not—would not—dared not stop because the Horseman gained upon his left and whipped his horse and hurried ahead—to head Jason off—to lop off Jason's head before he could reach *the church the church.*

Jason's pelvis struck a stone edge-on and oh, how he suffered but Jason Crane would make *the church the church the church.* The church became his only thought: *the church the church the church.* The rhythm thundered in his head beside *the hooves the hooves the hooves the hooves.* He still could reach *the church the church the church*—but would he make the door?

Where'd they put the door?

He had run straight for the church, straight *at* the church—*not at the door*—just at the church.

But he would get inside the church.

The church the church the church...

He would get inside the church.

The hooves the hooves the hooves...

The Horseman wrenched his reins. The black steed reared and twisted 'round upon the shallow place where the Horseman was buried. The ghost swung his hatchet a final time. Jason saw his only chance and took it. His foot found the top of a weathered headstone and he pushed off from it, feeling it crack beneath his weight. He leapt and his arms flew outward, breaking an invisible tape with his chest. The Horseman's hatchet came round and sliced the air beneath the boy's feet.

The demon rider cried in anger. He and his steed hurtled onward and broke against the stones of the church with a blast of heat and light and scattering leaf. Jason fell through the whipping cloud. He saw his own terrified reflection for an instant. His elbows struck the silver window, something slashed his scalp, and with an explosion of glass and wood, with a spray of blood and plaster, he fell unconscious onto the floor of the Old Dutch Church.

EPILOGUE

From the *Tarrytown Leader*, November 2nd
OLD DUTCH CHURCH ATTACKED BY HALLOWEEN VANDAL

The Old Dutch Church of Sleepy Hollow, a New York State historical landmark, suffered possibly irreparable damage on Halloween night at the hands of a mindless teenage vandal. The boy, whose name has been withheld pending charges, showed no concern for the three-hundred-year history of the church when he carried out what village historian and SHHS teacher Daniel Smolenski described as a "unforgivable attack."

Jennifer Paulding, part-owner of the Horseman Restaurant, described the scene. She and her husband Samuel Paulding had just left the Historical Society's annual "Horseman's Hollow" event when they heard "a crash like a china cabinet [that had fallen] over." They rushed to the vicinity of the noise. They found the church doors open and a tumult occurring within.

Witnesses say that the vandal threw himself bodily through the window of the church, using a fragile tombstone outside to assist his jump (this tombstone, which has stood in the Old Dutch Burying Ground for three hundred years, was also broken and will need extensive repair). Wood and glass showered down on the people inside who had gathered for a candlelight reading of Washington Irving's *Legend of Sleepy Hollow*.

"It was just crazy," said Marcus Fractowicz, 42, who had attended the event with his family. "The reader had just come to the most exciting part. Ichabod crossed the bridge and the Horseman threw his pumpkin and, at that moment, the window cracked to bits and the kid fell through."

Fireman Mike Parson, who investigated the case for the Tarrytown Police Department, said that the damage might cost the town many thousands of dollars to repair. "It's not just the glass," said Parson. "The windows have to match, the wood has to match. And, of course, we'll never get that tombstone back to what it was."

Local teen and celebrated SHHS trombonist Sally Blatt declared herself shocked by the wanton damage. "It's bad enough to see our local landmarks crumbling away as a consequence of nature but when someone damages property in this way, deliberately, it is soul-destroying."

Once in police custody and conscious, the vandal claimed to be "fleeing the Headless Horseman." Police investigated the site to determine whether the boy had been subject to a practical joke. Although several days of rain had preceded the holiday, investigators found only one pair of footprints in the mud.

"No hoofprints, sorry," laughed Thomas Stafford, Tarrytown Police Chief. "This is a simple case of criminal mischief. The boy cut himself up pretty bad, though, so we haven't ruled out the possibility that someone tossed him through."

No other injuries were reported.

#

From the *Tarrytown Leader*, November 3rd

CEMETERY WORKER NEAR DEATH

Joey Osorio, 17, son of Sleepy Hollow Cemetery director James Osorio, was discovered unconscious in the cemetery on the morning of November 1, sources say. The boy was rushed to Phelps Memorial Hospital and is reported stable but comatose. It is not yet known what caused the incident and no connection has been found to the concurrent vandalism of the Old Dutch Church of Sleepy Hollow, which occurred on Halloween night a short distance away.

Osorio is reported to have been conducting a lantern tour after cemetery hours. Several spilled lanterns were discovered in his vicinity. No attendees of Osorio's tour have come forward with information as of press time.

Police are investigating.

#

From the *White Plains Daily Voice*, November 4th
STATE SENATOR USHER CONDEMNS CHURCH VANDALISM

In answer to a question asked at Sunday's AARP meeting in Boston, State Senator and United States Senate candidate Paul Usher decried the recent vandalism of the Old Dutch Church of Sleepy Hollow, declaring it a "clarion call that announces a nation in decline."

The senator pledged to make youth issues part of his campaign.

"For too long," Usher declared, "the good people of our communities have been told to step back and let the parents handle these matters. But where are the parents? Where are they?"

Usher, who seeks the seat vacated by the death of Massachusetts Democrat Frank Slezinski, is a long-time Sleepy Hollow resident.

#

Jason pushed the hair out of his eyes.

He tried not to pick at the stitches on his scalp. They made him feel like a baseball. He was grateful that his hair was thick and tangly and would cover up the scar.

He folded his hands on the table in front of him and sat up straight. He hoped he looked presentable. He'd ruined his best suit in the cemetery and he was bruised and battered. On the way into family court he'd stopped in the men's room to check his face. It wasn't too bad. The shiner that the marble Jesus had given him had almost faded. The stitches on his shoulder itched. He reminded himself not to scratch when the guardianship hearing began. The hatchet-nick on his neck had closed. The Horseman had barely missed his artery. That was lucky. And his ankle had been twisted, not torn. It would heal. He limped for now, but the swelling would be controllable with ice and elevation.

The worst wound was that Joey was still in the hospital. Jason blamed himself. He had invoked some curse and raised a ghost to strike down his friend. He'd visited Joey in the hospital, mostly at night. Joey's parents had lost their fondness for Jason now. They saw him as a dangerous influence and suspected him of being responsible for Joey's condition. After Mr. Osorio discovered Jason's true age he considered him to be a liar and a fraud as well.

Joey lay in a room not far from where Jason's grandmother had died only two weeks before. Joey reminded Jason of her. He wasn't wrinkled and his hair hadn't gone white, but he had the same look of a person fighting a bad dream, speaking to something unseen. Sometimes his mouth would open with shock and surprise and he would stay like that for hours.

Late one night, Jason had come to the hospital and had seen Zef Van Brunt standing just outside Joey's room. Zef stood in the empty corridor, clenching his fists. He didn't see Jason. He wiped his face, hit the wall and left. Jason discovered a new bouquet on Joey's bedside table that night. There was no card.

The adjudicator would be deciding the guardianship question today. Jason tried to stay hopeful but the adjudicator looked like a vindictive elf. The man was huddling with the two lawyers at the moment—and berating Anna Franklin, the woman Valerie had hired to represent Jason. That wasn't good.

Grandpa John had sent Jason an e-mail via Valerie. It read: "Jason—I'm so sorry but I'm not in any condition to take on the responsibility of being your guardian. Due to a heart condition, I am advised to avoid stress. I do hope that you sort out your troubles."

That had hurt, but Jason understood it. He didn't blame the man for not wanting to get involved with a mess like his. Jason Crane had become a well-known Troubled Kid and Public Enemy since the Halloween incident. He'd spent his seventeenth birthday in a juvenile holding cell.

"Jason."

Kate appeared to his right. He felt himself light up. He hadn't seen her for days. She looked happy too. She heaved a bright red backpack onto the chair next to him.

"You found it?" Jason said.

"Right where you told me."

"Thanks." He had lost the backpack near the broken bridge and he'd hated to think of Absalom's *Sketch-Book* being lost or ruined. It was still inside though, with no damage.

"Guess what else?" Kate said.

"What?"

She took a deep breath, leaned down and touched her forehead to

Jason's temple. She whispered the news in his ear.

"Joey woke up," she said.

Jason's throat swelled and strangled him. He let out a moan that was both happiness and relief—the sound that a pack animal might make when relieved of a burden too great for it to carry.

"How is he?" Jason said.

"He's fine. His memory's fuzzy but he's out of bed. They say he'll be home in a few days."

"That's fantastic. How did you hear?"

She shrugged. "Zef told me. You know what that means, don't you?" She slipped an arm around Jason's neck.

"Yeah—I have my best friend back."

"And," she said with a conspiratorial smile, "Joey just might be one of us now."

"What?"

"He was attacked and survived. Just watch. He'll have a Gift too."

"Which Gift?" said Jason.

She shrugged.

"It could be anything. Anything at all."

The adjudicator strode toward the bench, stopping to gather his papers and accept a cup of coffee from the clerk.

"Gotta go. Good luck," Kate said.

"Wait." Jason took her sleeve. "Which side are you on? Mine or Hadewych's?"

She spread her hands. The answer was obvious.

"Whichever side makes you happy," she said.

She kissed him on his tangled head and slipped away.

Jason had wanted to ask her that for days. Her father, State Senator Paul Usher, had been a key character witness for Hadewych. Why not? They were practically in-laws.

Usher strode into the hearing room, pausing at the door for the convenience of any photographers who might be waiting inside. None were. Once again, Jason was impressed by the presence of the man. He obviously lifted weights. He had size and solidity. But he was also movie-star handsome, with wavy gold-brown hair that seemed to twist like braids of Medusa. He smoothed his temples and joined Hadewych at his table, putting an arm around his friend's shoulders and slapping his back.

Paul Usher's eyes met Jason's.

They held each other's gaze.

Neither blinked. Jason felt he had been turned to stone.

"Eyes forward," said Valerie. She had slipped in alongside Jason. He broke eyes with Usher. Valerie sat drumming her fingers on the table nervously.

"Hear ye, hear ye," the bailiff cried.

The adjudicator climbed up and took his place. Jason imagined the little man to have a telephone book in his chair so he could see over.

Just before the adjudicator spoke, something caught Jason's eye. As Valerie drummed her fingers, Jason noticed that a paper clip sat on the table underneath her palm. She wasn't touching it, but the paper clip spun like a pinwheel. She noticed him looking and pressed her palm flat. He didn't have time to wonder.

"Mister Crane," said the adjudicator.

Jason shot to his feet. The elf shook his head. A derisive chuckle perked through the room.

"No need to stand," he said.

Jason sank back into his chair.

"You have petitioned this court to be emancipated from the guardianship stipulated in your grandmother's will. Your argument has been that you do not need a guardian and that you are near enough to the age of majority that the court should allow you to live as an adult. I have one word for you, young man—and that word is… baloney. You have repeatedly falsified your age. You have demonstrated an arrogant compulsion to aggrandize yourself through your supposed descent from Ichabod Crane. And worst of all—and this hangs heaviest on my heart—you have desecrated a sacred monument, a national treasure. Therefore it is the decision of this court that your request for emancipation be denied."

"Your honor," Anna Franklin stood.

"Counselor?" the little man scowled.

"We would like to re-assert our petition for Ms. Valerie Maule to be Jason's guardian."

"That petition has been heard and denied. She isn't a relation and the will doesn't nominate her—while Mister Van Brunt is already executor."

"Still—"

"Denied. I don't like repeating myself."

Anna Franklin sat. Jason saw Paul Usher nodding and patting Hadewych's back again. Hadewych was looking at Jason with a grin of triumph.

"The will stands," said the adjudicator. "Mister Van Brunt shall be guardian of Jason Crane's person and estate. Mister Crane, I am told that you are a flight risk and that you had made preparations to escape the judgment of this court. You are therefore ordered not to leave the town limits of Sleepy Hollow or Tarrytown for any reason without the express permission of your guardian. This order shall stand until you reach your eighteenth birthday. Case dismissed."

The gavel came down like a horse's hoof.

#

Hadewych waited by the Mercedes afterwards.

"I'll drive," he said brightly.

Jason climbed into the passenger seat and slammed the door. Hadewych turned the key. He closed his eyes with pleasure as the engine roared to life.

"Put on your seat belt, son," he said.

Jason winced, but he obeyed. The car pulled away from the courthouse. They chased autumn leaves down the Albany post road. Jason leaned his cheek on the cold glass and watched the town go by.

What a mess I'm in.

He glanced at Hadewych, who was strumming his fingers on the steering wheel. It killed Jason to see the man so happy. He could guess why. He didn't know how Hadewych planned to get his hands on the Legacy, but he knew Hadewych had a plan, and that, so far, everything was proceeding to schedule.

He would lose everything. He *had* lost everything. He was alone in the world. Alone. And now he'd been given into the custody and care of this evil man.

The trees grew thicker beyond the windows.

The Horseman still roamed those woods, too. Eventually he would find Jason again, when he couldn't run anymore.

Sleepy Hollow owns me… Jason thought. *It does.*

They passed Sleepy Hollow Cemetery. The spikes atop the fence seemed ready for severed heads.

The cemetery owns me.

They passed the Old Dutch Church; workmen were boarding up Jason's window.

The church owns me.

They passed the millpond, wide and sinister and choked with leaves.

Philipsburg Manor owns me.

They turned uphill.

And Hadewych—

Something rolled under Jason's feet as the car climbed. He reached down and picked it up. It was a bottle of nail polish. Jungle Red.

He stared at the thing.

What am I thinking?

No one owns me.

Never.

And he wasn't alone. He could hear Eliza whenever he chose to listen for her. He didn't need to use his Gift. He didn't need visions. He knew her so well, and loved her so much, that he could write her lines for her. She was like a character in a beloved story, read so often that he knew every word by heart:

"Your daddy and his daddy and his daddy and your mama and my Arthur. All of them are in you. And a little of me too? At least a little bit? Huh?"

That's what she'd said in the vision of the attic, right before she died. Was that her final message, her final question? Little Jason hadn't answered then. But his heart answered her now.

More than a little bit, you silly old woman. You know that. I am you. I'm what you made me.

His held the bottle against his heart. Another fragment drifted to mind. The night of the dance, when he'd slipped in the sour milk…

"Sorry to leave a mess. I couldn't help it," she had said.

"It's okay," he'd called to her. *"I don't mind. Love you."*

"Likewise!"

She had left a mess then. She had left a mess now. But he could clean it up. He didn't blame her. She tried so hard. Pain shot through him, a bright angry needle of pain. All she had wanted to do was to set him up in life, to set him on the right path! And now look at things!

Yes. Look, Jason Crane. Really look. Really look at things.

Look at the people you've met here. Look at Zef or Kate or Joey. Look at Valerie. Look at Hadewych, even, or Brom or Dylan. Our parents never set us up perfectly in life. Never. Every generation leaves problems behind. And we all get different things. Unrealistic expectations, or unconditional love, a handful of documents or a terrible injury, a stone quarry or a dark legacy. We might be left with a bar of gold or just a photo of red sneakers and wildflowers. It doesn't matter. It's still up to us in the end.

When you lose the head of your family, you don't just give up because no one's there to do things for you. You have to do things for yourself. You have to rise to the occasion, and ride out to meet your challenges. That's what every generation does. That's what we always will do, no matter what problems we inherit.

And Eliza had made him strong. Not muscles. That wasn't her kind of strength. She'd passed along her love of life and her will to make things happen. *That* was her bequest. *That* was Jason's inheritance. She'd left him *himself,* his *own character.* She'd made him a man. And a good man. She'd left a far better legacy than any supernatural Gift or psychic power.

He closed his hand around the little bottle of nail polish.

Thank you for that, my dear. My dear grandmother. You did fine. Wait and see. I have everything I need. I have myself, and a lot of you.

They turned onto Gory Brook Road. Jason looked at Hadewych, who was smiling.

"You don't even know, do you?" Jason said.

"Know what?" asked Hadewych indulgently.

"That you've already lost."

Hadewych chuckled. "It would appear not."

"Not yet," Jason said. "Round one to you, maybe. But you're going down in the end."

"And why is that?"

Jason closed his fist on the bottle and looked out the window. "Because I'm Eliza Merrick's grandson," he said.

Hadewych didn't reply. He frowned and looked away, worried. The house drifted slowly into view.

Jason heard Eliza at his shoulder once more, his good angel, saying: "My Jason is better. He's a hero, this one. I want you to have a heroic life. Like me."

And I will, the boy thought. *I will.*

The Mercedes slowed and came to a stop in the driveway of 417 Gory Brook Road.

A shadowy figure moved in the attic window...

...and a little black poodle leapt with joy at Jason Crane's return.

THE END

Coming Next:
Jason Crane: Book Two
"Make for the Bridge"

APPENDIX

FOUND AMONG THE PAPERS OF
THE LATE DIEDRICH KNICKERBOCKER

[First page missing]

..and your absence is keenly felt by the trees and grounds of Sunnyside, which are in need of your ministrations. As to myself, while pleasures of town, table and the gaming board may enforce a certain literary abstinence, copious servings of praise from visitors (upon which an old man may hope to grow fat), the contemplative peace of my home (broken only by the damnable clatter of the tracks), and the consoling draught of a bottle at hearthside (but only one) are far preferable to any solitary fagging of the pen in pursuit of the almighty dollar.

I write to you now, imposing upon myself a painful separation from these delights, in fulfillment of my long-delayed promise to supply you with some account of the *Legend of Sleepy Hollow*, how it came to be, and what truths if any may be found within it. I confess that this *Legend*, upon which some small part of my reputation is based, was not wholly fashioned from the flax of imagination. Though no man other than myself could have told it in so pleasing a fashion, I confess my ability to conceive of such a one as the Headless Horseman would have been incommensurate to the task had the specter not been described to me by one Hans Van Ripper of Tarrytown.

This incomparable fellow was a benefactor of my youth, in the days of my long wanderings. The offer of his hay barn, on one occasion, made all the difference twixt a warm night among the milk goats and a frostbitten bed in some field. This generosity, he explained to me, was given as Christian recompense for the blessings of that Providence which had raised him from past indigence to his then-current station of mere penury. Long hours did I spend at the Van Ripper table, fed with ham and Indian pudding by a gentle goodwife who, having no children of her own, looked upon me as their surrogate, the tow-headed substitute for her own wistfully imagined but ne'er-born brood. For my part, I assisted with the light labors of the farm as, in the *Legend*, I assign to Ichabod, as recompense for his own board. In my tale the pedagogue *"helped to make hay, mended the fences, took the horses to water, drove the cows from pasture, and cut wood for the winter fire"*, and so did I.

In the early weeks of October, 1798, fear of the pestilential fever that was then engulfing Manhattan forced my removal to the Tarrytown home of my friend James Paulding, a writer of merit (if not fame). This same Paulding was, of late, the Secretary of our Navy. Ah! In those days he and I brimmed with such rising sap as must find release in either literature or the fair sex, in frolicsome words or in ribald deeds (the former may be found in *Salmagundi*, the latter I shall not recount lest I offend your sensibility, or the postmaster's.)

One day I took advantage of my proximity to renew my acquaintance with Van Ripper. Arriving at his farm, I discovered him loading a wagon with his household goods. He explained that his harvest had been poor and, having no children or wife (the distaff Ripper having gone to her rest), he had sold his farm with the intent of seeking his fortune in Kentucky, a state which, judging from the great Exodus of our citizenry, must surely be another Eden. It is this spectacle of Van Ripper, astride his laden wagon, that prompted my portrayal of Ichabod's similar ambitions.

A shot rang through the valley, the rifle of some hunter laying up game for the winter. The sound was piercing and clear and the horses took fright or were "spooked". The luggage on Van Ripper's wagon, high as a Tower of Babel, became shaken and all the goods confused, which may be counted a singular piece of luck or a great calamity, for a book fell directly at my feet and thus was the *Legend* born.

I picked up the book and observed the title to be Cotton Mather's "History of Witchcraft". This was extraordinary, and I expressed my surprise to the old farmer, who in my experience was neither a man of letters, nor even of literacy. The pleasant, shabby fellow confided that the book had been left behind by one Ichabod Crane, an itinerant schoolteacher much prone to superstition, who had domiciled at the Van Ripper farm for a time, until his disappearance under most mysterious circumstances.

And so that day Providence, plague, gunshot, witchcraft, and the state of Kentucky all conspired to bring the *Legend* to my attention. My curiosity whetted, I invited Van Ripper to a local tavern, in which we tarried that long October afternoon.

The regret of my life is that I doubted the truth of Van Ripper's account. I found the story of Ichabod to be a delightful episode on which to hang a tale, but I was not so credulous as to believe that these strange events had transpired in actuality. My reasoning mind (unreasonably) credited Van Ripper with possession of an imagination; thus when in time I came to pen my own telling of the *Legend*, I retained the names that had been given me: Van Brunt, Van Tassel, Van Ripper, and Crane; yet had I known that the man Brom Bones existed in the person of wealthy and powerful Abraham Van Brunt, owner of the Tarrytown Quarry, builder of the Croton Aqueduct and confederate of Archbishops, I may well have reconsidered the use of his cognomen.

Similarly, had I foreseen the injury that would be done to the person of Ichabod Crane, who saw his political ambitions in New York dashed by the association of his name with my *Legend*, I would have forgone my ridicule of his physiognomy. I met him briefly once, in New York. The judge, in truth, was in all particulars the ludicrous scarecrow I describe, but such truths and such estimates are seldom published to the entire world.

Most importantly, if I had known the Horseman himself existed, if I had known that I would invoke a spirit of great fury and power, if I had then seen him with my own eyes as I now have, never would I have turned my talent to giving him shape.

Yes, nephew, the Horseman exists.

Do not imagine this to be the fantasy of a feeble old man. You would be repeating the same mistake I made with Van Ripper. This I tell you in all earnestness:

The Horseman rises, headless, and rides.

I do not know from whence the Horseman sprang, aside from Van Ripper's contention that he was a Hessian soldier killed in war. I believe Van Ripper withheld the truth, which I suspect involved his sister Agathe, wife of Hermanus Van Brunt and mother to the aforementioned Abraham. Yes, the old farmer was uncle to Brom Bones, and his sister Agathe was long rumored to be the consort of the Horseman in some fashion. I have often wondered whether Van Ripper, in journeying to Kentucky, was fleeing some other kind of bad harvest. Some family legacy that he feared, even he did not wholly understand it. I can believe no evil of that generous man. Agathe is dead now, as are Van Ripper, Van Brunt, the fair Katrina, and the unfortunate Crane. I do not know from what source we will ever know the truth of these matters, unless their souls also rise from their several graves to inform us.

I am thankfully discharged of my duty, now, and the history of my *Legend* is told you. As you love me, dispose of these pages and not keepsake them; do <u>not</u> entrust them to old Knickerbocker.

Further, as you value your own hide, heed this: when next you visit, <u>do</u> <u>not</u> <u>travel</u> <u>alone.</u>

I have oft seen the Horseman riding in the Hollow. I will not speak of these sights here. My pen has given far too much substance to the fiend already.

Your Uncle,
Washington Irving

ABOUT THE AUTHOR

RICHARD GLEAVES is the composer, lyricist and playwright of **Dorian, World and Time Enough, The Golden Days, Oswald on Ice, Omniscience** and **Adrenaline Junkie.** He is winner of BMI's 2004 Harrington Award for Outstanding Creative Achievement, and is composer-in-residence for New Music New York.

In collaboration with author Dianne Durante and software designer Adam Reed, Richard is editor and composer of **Monuments of Manhattan,** a videoguide for Android devices.

Jason Crane: Rise Headless and Ride is his first novel.

FOR DISCUSSIONS AND EXTRAS
VISIT JASON ON FACEBOOK

FACEBOOK.COM/THEJASONCRANESERIES

**ALL THE LOCATIONS IN THIS BOOK EXIST
FIND THEM IN SLEEPY HOLLOW, NY**

If you enjoyed JASON CRANE: BOOK 1 "RISE HEADLESS AND RIDE", please consider posting a review on Amazon. In the brave new world of publishing, your comments will probably reach more people than a review in the New York Times would.

Made in the USA
Lexington, KY
07 October 2013